ALSO BY JOHN BURDETT

Bangkok Tattoo

Bangkok 8

The Last Six Million Seconds

A Personal History of Thirst

BANGKOK HAUNTS

BANGKOK HAUNTS

JOHN BURDETT

Alfred A. Knopf New York 2007

THIS IS A BORZOI BOOK
PUBLISHED BY ALFRED A. KNOPF

Knopf, Borzoi Books, and the colophon are registered trademarks
of Random House, Inc.

Grateful acknowledgment is made to The New York Times Agency for permission
to reprint "Erotica Inc.—A Special Report; Technology Sent Wall Street into
Market for Pornography" by Timothy Egan (*The New York Times*, October 23, 2000).
Copyright © 2000 by The New York Times Co. Reprinted by
permission of The New York Times Agency.

Library of Congress Cataloging-in-Publication Data
Burdett, John.
Bangkok haunts / John Burdett.—1st ed.
p. cm.—(Borzoi book)
ISBN 978-0-307-26318-6 (alk. paper)
1. Police—Thailand—Bangkok—Fiction. 2. Snuff films—Fiction. 3. Sex
oriented businesses—Fiction. 4. Bangkok (Thailand)—Fiction. I. Title.
PR6052.U617B3626 2007
823'.914—dc22   2007061472

Manufactured in the United States of America
First Edition

For Nit

You cast your spell and I went under
I find it so difficult to leave

Bob Dylan, "Tonight I'll Be Staying Here with You"

The Eternal passed by in the form of a pimp. The prattle ceased.

Jean Genet, *Our Lady of the Flowers*

The clinging consciousness is very deep and subtle;
All potentials are like a torrential flow.
I do not explain this to the ignorant,
For fear they will get the idea it is self.

The Gautama Buddha, *The Sandhinirmochana Sutra*

A PERFECT PRODUCT

1

Few crimes make us fear for the evolution of our species. I am watching one right now.

In a darkened room in the District 8 Police Station with my good friend FBI agent Kimberley Jones, a forty-two-inch Toshiba LCD monitor hangs high up on a wall, out of the reach of villains.

The video I'm sharing with the FBI uses two industrial-quality cameras that between them seamlessly provide all the tricks of zoom, angle, pan, et cetera, and I am told that at least two technicians must have been involved in its production. The color is excellent, thanks to however many millions of pixels that contribute to their subtle shading; we are looking at a product of high civilization unknown to our forefathers. At the end of the movie, though, tough-guy Kimberley bursts into tears, as I'd rather hoped she would. I did. She turns her head to stare at me wild-eyed.

"Tell me it isn't real."

"We have the body," I say.

"Oh, god," Kimberley says. "Oh, sweet Jesus, I've seen things bloodier, but never anything this demonic. I thought I'd seen everything." She stands up. "I need air."

I think, *In Bangkok?* But I lead her through a couple of corridors, then out into the public area, where brown men and women not much more than half her size wait to tell a cop of their homely grievances. It's not exactly a festive atmosphere, but it's human. An American extrovert, Kimberley doesn't mind dabbing her red eyes with a tissue in front of an audience, who naturally assume I've just busted this female *farang* on some minor drug charge—cannabis, perhaps. Like my own, her eyes naturally seek out any attractive young women sitting in the plastic seats. There are three, all of them prostitutes. (No respectable Thai woman dresses like that.) They resent the attention and glare back. I think Kimberley would like to hug them in gratitude that they're still alive. I take her out into the street: not quite what the words *fresh air* normally evoke, but she fills her lungs anyway. "My god, Sonchai. The world. What monsters are we creating?"

We have achieved that rare thing, Kimberley and I: a sexless but intimate rapport between a man and a woman of the same age who are mutually attracted to each other but, for reasons beyond analysis, have decided to do nothing about it. Even so, I was surprised when she simply got on a plane in response to a frantic telephone call from me. I had no idea she was specializing in snuff movies these days; nor did I realize they were flavor of the month in international law enforcement. Anyway, it's great to have a top-notch pro familiar with the latest technology on my side. She's not intuitive, as I am, but owns a mind like a steel trap. So do I treat her like a woman or a man? Are there any rules about that where she comes from? I give her a comradely embrace and squeeze her hand, which seems to cover most points. "It's great to have you here, Kimberley," I say. "Thanks again for coming."

She smiles with that innocence that can follow an emotional catastrophe. "Sorry to be a girl."

"I was a girl too, the first time I saw it."

She nods, unsurprised. "Where did you get it, in a raid?"

I shake my head. "No, it was sent to me anonymously, to my home." She gives me a knowing look: a personal angle here.

"And the body, where was it found? At the crime scene?"

"No. It had been returned to her apartment, laid neatly on the bed. Forensics says she must have been killed somewhere else."

Now the American Hero emerges. "We're gonna get them, Sonchai. Tell me what you need, and I'll find a way of getting it to you."

"Don't make promises," I say. "This isn't Iraq."

She frowns. I guess a lot of Americans are tired of hearing those kinds of jibes. "No, but that movie had a certain style, a certain professionalism about it, and if that alpha male isn't North American, I'll turn in my badge."

"A Hollywood production?"

"For something like that, frankly the U.S. is the first place I would start looking. Specifically California, but not Hollywood. San Fernando Valley, maybe, with international connections. This could tie in with what I'm doing stateside."

"What would you look for? He was wearing a gimp mask."

"The eyeholes are quite large—light had to get in. You have isometric surveillance at all points of entry to this country. Give me a copy of the DVD—I'll get our nerds on the case. If they can make a good still of his eyes and enlarge it, it's as good as a fingerprint. Better. Are you going to let me see the body?"

"If you want. But how deeply involved do you want to get?"

"Look, I don't know much, but Chanya told me you're very upset. That touches me too. If I can help, then that's what I want to do."

"Chanya spilled her guts?"

"She loves you. She hinted that you need a little moral support from a fellow professional. I said okay, I'll do what I can, so long as he lets me in."

The FBI has no idea how many points she's accumulated with me for treating a pregnant third-world ex-prostitute as a friend and equal. That kind of heroism leaves us slack-jawed in these parts. Chanya loves her too, of course, and when a Thai girl loves, she tells all.

A *tuk-tuk* passes, spilling black pollution from its two-stroke engine. They used to be a symbol of Thailand: three wheels, a steel roof on vertical struts, and a happy smiling driver. Now they're a tourist gimmick catering to a diminishing number of tourists. So far the new millennium has not delivered much in the way of new; instead we have a certain foreboding that a return to old-fashioned grinding poverty might be our share of globalism. Kimberley hasn't noticed this yet—she's been here only two days, and already the work ethic has gripped her. She's not seeing the *tuk-tuk* or even its pollution.

"I'm not going to use our guys to copy the DVD," I say. She looks at me. "That kind of thing is produced in very limited numbers, sold to a specialized international market." She is still looking at me. I feel blood rising up my neck, into facial blood vessels. "This is a poor country." Still the look: I have to come clean. "They would sell it."

She turns away to save me from her contempt. A couple of beats pass, then briskly: "I'm okay now. How are you going to copy it?"

"I'm not. I'll put it in my pocket. You can use the business center at the Grand Britannia to e-mail it straight from the disk."

She waits in the public area while I go back to retrieve the disk: five point seven megabytes of distilled evil. Out on the street she pauses to stare at a young monk in his early to mid-twenties. He is tall, and there is an exotic elegance about him incongruous with the Internet café he is about to enter.

"Using the Net is frowned on by the Sangha, especially in public areas, but it's not a serious offense. Often monks use it to check Buddhist websites," I explain, glad to talk about something lighter than a snuff movie.

"Is he a regular around here? Somehow this doesn't seem like the kind of place a monk would want to hang out." Kimberley feels the need for small talk too.

"I saw him for the first time yesterday. I don't know which *wat* he's attached to."

2

In Dr. Supatra's underground kingdom rotary saws and twenty different varieties of knife hang on the walls, from meat cleavers to the finest stilettos. I haven't told her about the DVD yet; actually, I haven't told anyone except the FBI and Chanya, which doesn't say much for Thai integrity, does it? Not that I don't trust Supatra. In times when honor is hard to come by, those who possess it tend to do so in great measure. Supatra is as incorruptible as I am. The reason I didn't tell her about the video is that I didn't want to prejudice her mind.

I introduce her to Kimberley. Dr. Supatra looks at her a little suspiciously; we're all somewhat weary and wary these days of the Western superiority complex; but Kimberley is not quite like that anymore. We met on a case here in Bangkok about five years ago when she was a hormone-haunted manhunter. She's a lot sadder and wiser these days. She's even learned enough about Thai customs to press her hands together and raise them to her lips in a not-bad *wai* that acknowledges Supatra's superior status in terms of age: she's over fifty, no taller than five feet, slim and stern in her white laboratory coat. Now that Kimberley has shown humility, Supatra is prepared to open her heart, and she's leading us out of the lab to the vault. As she walks with her head held contemplatively to one side, a technique that somehow compensates for her lack of height and makes it seem as if she is the tallest person around, she asks, "So, Sonchai, do you know who the victim is?"

A wince crosses my features so fast, Supatra doesn't catch it. Kimberley does, though, with those merciless blue eyes.

"I checked her prints on the national database. A girl called Damrong, from Isakit."

"A prostitute?"

"Of course."

"Hm."

We have come to death's filing cabinet, about one hundred man-size drawers set into a wall. Without needing to check the number, Supatra goes to one at about knee height and beckons to me to pull. It's heavy but pleasingly mobile; a medium-to-hefty tug starts the drawer rolling, and Damrong comes out headfirst. Another wince on my part. Supatra assumes it's my sensitive nature; the FBI has other ideas.

Even bloated in the face by the effects of asphyxiation, she still impresses. You can see the perfect line of her jaw, her high cheekbones, the Egyptian slant to her eyes, the infinite range of smiles available to those thin but sensual lips, the perfect white teeth, even that extraordinary something . . .

Who am I kidding? Of course the strangling has hideously altered the perfect balance of her features, bloating them almost beyond recognition; the others see only an ugly corpse—their minds are not prejudiced by prior knowledge. When the drawer is fully extended, though, there is no doubting the perfection of her limbs, the fullness of her breasts, the firm but yielding thighs. Her pubic hair has been shaved, and there is a silver ring set in one of her labia. The tattoo in the area of her navel is an unremarkable serpent coiling around a sword. Despite myself, I cannot help reaching out to her limp left wrist and turning it: a thin whitish scar no more than an inch long from a longitudinal cut into a minor vein. Dr. Supatra nods. "I saw it. An old wound. If it was an attempt at suicide, it was not a very serious one."

"Yes," I say.

Supatra has done a not-bad job with her stitching, which is famously neat. My eyes want to gloss over the great Y cut across the top of her chest, all the way down to her pelvis. All the organs have been removed, something I'm finding hard to assimilate, especially with the FBI now concentrating on my face rather than on the corpse.

"So," I say, swallowing, "what can you tell us?"

"About the cause of death? In this case what you see is what you get. She died of strangulation by a nylon rope about one centimeter thick. The orange rope your men found around her neck is the rope the perpetrator used: the fibers correspond. There is no competition for cause of death—all her organs were in perfect condition, and there were no signs of other wounding or any viral or bacterial agents that might have contributed in any way to her demise."

"No signs of forced penetration?"

"None at all. It seems as if a lubricant was used. Of course, that does not necessarily mean intercourse was consensual, merely relatively painless."

"Sperm?"

A shake of the head. "Both vagina and anus had recently been penetrated, one assumes by a penis, in which case a condom must have been used. There is no evidence of sperm or male seminal fluid."

I let a beat pass, because Supatra is holding out, playing the high priestess, saying nothing until asked, so I say, "And?"

"No recreational drugs. Whatever her state of mind when she died, it was not influenced by narcotics."

"Signs of struggle?" the FBI asks hopefully.

Supatra shakes her head. "That's what's strange. You would at least expect some bruising somewhere on her body from attempted resistance, a few strained muscles at least. It's almost as if she were strangled while tied up—except there are no indications of forced restraint either."

"Damn," Kimberley says. Supatra cocks an eyebrow. "I just don't want to be convinced by the ending, I guess."

"Ending?" Supatra wants to know. "What ending?"

Kimberley covers her mouth, but it's too late. I come clean and tell Supatra about the DVD. Supatra nods; the total pro, she understands perfectly why I didn't tell her about it before. She even gives a matriarchal smile.

"Indolence is a national weakness," she explains to the FBI.

"Sonchai was afraid that if I saw the movie, I would get lazy and not do a thorough job."

"I decided to keep back the disk before I knew you would be the pathologist on the case," I explain.

"I think you decided to keep the disk a secret for other reasons too, no? A snuff movie fetches a lot on the international market, they say. You are holding a very valuable product." Turning to Kimberley: "But what is it about the ending that you find so hard to cope with?"

Kimberley doesn't want to answer, so I promise to show the whole video to Supatra, as soon as I've got time. The FBI has another question, though. "Dr. Supatra, have you ever before come across a case of strangulation where there were no signs of struggle at all?"

Supatra looks at her curiously, as if she has realized what this case might mean to a *farang*. "Not that I can recall, but you have to bear in mind this is a different culture, producing a different kind of consciousness."

Kimberley frowns. "Different kind of consciousness?"

"Death," the pathologist says, "the way a culture views death defines its attitude to life. Forgive me, but sometimes the West gives the impression of being in denial. The Thai attitude is a little different."

"What's so different about Thailand?"

"Oh, it's not Thailand in particular. The whole of Southeast Asia has the ghost bug—the Malaysians are even worse than us. There are no statistics, of course, but to listen to Thais, you would likely conclude that the undead outnumber the living by a hundred to one."

"But you don't think that, Dr. Supatra. You're a scientist."

Dr. Supatra smiles and casts a glance at me with eyebrows raised. I nod. "I'm a scientist—but I'm not a Western scientist. With Sonchai's permission I would like to show you something." I nod again on Kimberley's behalf, and we follow Supatra into her office, which forms part of the morgue. Still maintaining an ambiguous smile, she takes her laptop out from a drawer, along with a Sony Handycam video camera. "This is what I do most nights," Supatra says. She demonstrates how she points the camera at her office window, which gives onto the morgue, facing the rows of cadavers in their steel tombs, and records onto her hard disk. "Would you like to see last night's collection?" She checks my eyes once more; the FBI is my guest, after all. I nod for the third time, feeling awkward. Am I giving in to the temptation to be mischievous? I'm suddenly nervous about this unannounced initiation; maybe the FBI will freak? It's too late for second thoughts, however. Kimberley sits in Supatra's chair at her desk while Supatra plays with the laptop for a moment. "There. I'm afraid I have to use infrared light, so the images are not very clear. Hard to explain scientifically, though."

The FBI is finding it hard to believe what is happening. Only seconds ago it was a normal sort of day in the life of a cop. I'm watching Kimberley intently while the images start to play. Supatra has done this to me before, so I have a good idea of what the FBI is seeing, even though the screen is not in my line of sight. Kimberley turns pale, puts one hand to her face, stares at me for a moment, turns back to the laptop, shakes her head, then winces. She puts her hand to her mouth as if she is about to vomit. Supatra leans over her to turn off the video clip.

The FBI stands up, anger distorting her features. "I'm sorry," she says, red-faced. "I'm a guest in this country, and I'm afraid I don't think that's very funny."

Supatra shares a glance with me and raises her hands a little. I say in Thai, *"It's okay, Kimberley is doing exactly what I did the first time I saw it. She has to find a way to convince herself that it's not real, things like that don't happen, it must be a trick."*

Supatra: *"What should I do? She's very annoyed. I don't think this was a good idea, Sonchai. Is it easier if I pretend it's a trick?"*

I shrug. *"Whatever is easiest."*

"I'm very sorry," Supatra says to Kimberley in English. "It's Thai humor. I didn't mean to offend you."

Mollified, the FBI manages a smile. "It's okay. I guess it's a cultural thing. Sure, I guess I would have found it funny in a different context. I'm not a killjoy—I just wasn't expecting a practical joke."

"So sorry." Supatra *wais* to indicate sincere regret.

Now Kimberley is anxious to show she's a good sport. "It's very clever," she offers. "I don't know how you did that. Is it part of Thai culture to believe that ghosts fornicate with each other and do those— those, uh, ugly things to each other? I've never heard of that. Amazing the way you got those kinds of effects. You must be a serious amateur filmmaker."

"Right," Supatra says. "It's all camera magic. For the antics of ghosts, though, you have to remember that when the brain dies, many urges are left. Generally quite ugly to look at, I agree."

"Those other creatures, the nonhuman ones—how did you do that?"

"Oh, I use a special kind of animation program," Supatra says, at the same time making a little *wai* to the Buddha sitting in a little shrine halfway up the wall, asking for absolution for telling a white lie.

"It's incredible. I've never seen anything like it. It seems more advanced that anything coming out of Hollywood."

Supatra accepts the compliment and takes us back upstairs. I can tell she's angry with me for encouraging her to share her hobby with a *farang* by the way she doesn't look me in the eye when she says goodbye.

Out on the street I don't want to talk about Damrong, but I'm trapped. I have to take Kimberley back to her hotel in a taxi, and her silence presses on my consciousness like an ever-increasing weight. She doesn't even need to look at me. She stares out of her side window pretending to be diplomatic, while all the time she's adding tick by tick to the great black burden of silence.

"Of course Chanya knows," I say after a long pause. "It was before she and I met. The reason she talked to you about the case is she's scared of the effect it's having on me. She thought you were the one person who could help on a psychological level. She feels helpless herself."

Kimberley doesn't say anything for a while. Then she leans forward to tell the driver to take us to The Dome on the top of State Tower, instead of her hotel. It's a smart choice. A few hundred feet above the city, sitting in an open-air restaurant and cocktail lounge, naked to the stars, an exotic coconut-based cocktail in Kimberley's hand and a Kloster beer in mine, one may feel as if the ceiling of one's skull has been raised to be contiguous with the night sky: a cosmic confessional.

"So it was like this," I say.

3

Unless you've been there, it's hard to understand. If I'd never met Damrong, I too would have remained bemused at the antics of men in that morbid state that you insist on calling "being in love," *farang*. We don't look at it quite like that over here.

Let me get the least embarrassing part out of the way first: she seduced me effortlessly, within a week of coming to work at my mother's bar, which I still help to run. Like all good *papasans*, I had as a guiding principle never to sample our own services, and I had never done so. I was lonely, though, and missing my partner Pichai terribly, after he was killed in the line of duty. Like a fool, I had no idea how obvious were my feelings for the new superstar. Looking back, she probably knew how I felt before I knew it myself. At what point do a man's feelings for a woman switch from objective admiration to the psychosis of possession, against which the Buddha so vehemently counsels? I know only that it was Songkran, the Thai New Year and the hottest time in the solar cycle. *That* Songkran—it was about four years ago—was particularly steamy; while the Sun transited Aries, Mars pursued Venus in the unforgiving sign of Scorpio. In my lovelorn state I was reduced to sharing Proustian paeans with my computer:

Last evening I watched from the door of the bar when she
arrived at the soi on the back of a motorbike taxi wearing some
new, violently colored dress that seemed somehow to embody
the essence of this terrifying season, and with a haughty toss of
her head, almost overendowed with its thick mane of heavy
black hair, so that even her gaunt beauty was overwhelmed by
this dense silken mass of shining darkness, stalked proudly into
the brothel where I had been waiting for her and only her . . .

Oh, dear. I guess every man in that state is transparent to the love object, right? I think it was the night after I wrote those words, around two A.M., when she just happened to be the only girl left in the bar and I was about to lock up. I had already turned off the sound system, and it seemed to me the ugly noises I made prior to locking up—rattling bottles, trash chucked in the bin, glasses sloshing in the sink—possessed the very quality of loneliness that dogged me. I looked down at the floor so as to avoid her eyes as she passed me on the way out. She played a little game of getting in my way, but I refused to fall for it. So she gently placed a hand under my jaw and raised my head until I was looking into her face. That's all it took. In our fever we didn't bother to go upstairs to the bedrooms.

"You're the most amazing lover," she whispered afterward. Standard whoretalk, of course, and like a standard john, I really wanted to believe it.

Indeed, with the benefit of hindsight, the whole affair strikes me as quite horribly standard in its beginning, middle, and end, and I say as much to the FBI, who carefully avoided looking at me while I was outlining the sorry saga. Somehow it seemed to emerge out of the wildness of Songkran itself. Originally it was a holy festival in which sacred water was gently and lovingly poured over monks and respected elders; nowadays, though, *farang* have taken it over in Bangkok: pink-faced juvenile delinquents in their thirties, forties, and fifties stand guard with two-foot water pistols and squirt at passersby; in drink they become quite aggressive, until they get tired and emotional and curl up on the sidewalk with their plastic toys. Everyone who entered the bar that night was soaked to the skin; the wise kept their cell phones in plastic Ziploc bags. Madness was everywhere.

I take a gulp of beer. Now the FBI and I are both staring at Orion in his priapic march across the sky.

"So spare me the middle. How did it end?" the FBI says, with no sign of jealousy or any other emotional response; her voice has gone a little sandpapery, though.

"Do women experience extreme passion the way men do?"

"Total psychic dissolution, identity annihilated, ego shot, not sure if you're one person or two, no sense of security when you're not in bed with them, precious little when you are? Sure."

"And how does it end, usually?"

"The one who is suffering the most ends up with a simple choice: kill the other or get the hell out while you still can." A quick look. "You're a cop—you know better than most there's no violence like domestic violence."

Her harsh *farang* truth-telling stuns me for a long moment. I wasn't expecting to come to the climax quite so early in the evening. I think maybe ten silent minutes pass before I can get it out:

"After that first night I made her swear she would not go with any john. She would just serve drinks and flirt, and I would make up for her loss in income, whatever it was. A classic case of a gaga john buying his girl's chastity. She kept up her side of the deal for at least ten days. Then she got tipsy one night with a muscular young Englishman. He paid her bar fine and took her upstairs in front of my nose." Another long pause. "It's like you say, either you kill them or you get out. I held my guts together for as long as it took to call my mother to have her take over the bar for the rest of the night. The other girls had to tell her what had happened. I took a two-week vacation on Ko Samui. When I got back, my mother had gotten rid of her."

Kimberley shakes her head. A compassionate smile, spiced with wicked humor, plays on her features. "So Mom saved you after all?"

I nod. "Yes, but not only her. When I got back from Samui, Chanya had started to work for us. Spend time with the morbid, and you develop a taste for the wholesome. I don't think I would have appreciated Chanya so well if I hadn't gone out of my mind with Damrong. The universe is composed of pairs of opposites."

In the taxi on the way back to Sukhumvit, the FBI says, "That night, when she went off with the English john in front of your nose, you very nearly went upstairs to the room where they were? You were almost out of control?"

"Yes. My gun was in its holster under the register. I became very aware of it."

"Then when you were on Ko Samui for those two weeks, what you were doing was fighting homicidal fantasies?"

"All the time. They would come in waves. Mornings were my only strong time, when I could handle them. The rest of the time I used alcohol and ganja."

"And what about her? Why did she do that? Wasn't it self-destructive? You were her boss, after all."

"The dirt poor don't actually have selves to destroy. When they get a little power, they know it's only for a moment. They have no practice in preparing for the future. They generally don't believe they have one."

The FBI ponders this. "Is that true?"

"For the poor, birth is the primary disaster: owning a body that has to be fed and sheltered and looked after, along with the drive to reproduce, to continue. Everything else is kid stuff, including death."

She sighs. I know she is thinking of the Damrong video when she says, "I was afraid you were going to say something like that."

When I drop her off at the Grand Britannia, she says, "She would have let you do anything, right, anything at all, any perversion or degradation, just to capture your soul?"

I answer with silence. There is one other little thing, though, that the FBI wants to get off her chest before going to bed tonight.

"That little hobby of Dr. Supatra's—is it typically Thai, or am I right in thinking she's a little eccentric?"

I cough. "All Thais are eccentric, Kimberley. Nobody colonized us. We don't have much sense of a global norm to follow."

"But you've seen that stuff yourself, right? I mean, it wasn't just phantoms fornicating. There were really grotesque things going on, with demons and, like, subterranean creatures. I'm talking seriously *bestial*. It was very clever but very morbid."

I shrug. "She's been a forensic pathologist for more than twenty years. Imagine what her subconscious must look like."

The FBI nods at this convenient explanation, which fits her own cultural prejudice. There's something nagging at her, though. "Sonchai, I'm getting a feeling that there are levels here, levels below levels. Are you being totally straight with me? I mean, if that stuff Supatra has on her hard disk, if that was for real, she would be world famous by now, right? There would have been investigations by *National Geographic* and the Discovery Channel, *Scientific American*, all that?"

I have to suppress a smile at the thought of Supatra allowing herself to be the center of any kind of public attention. "Dr. Supatra is a very private person," I explain. "I think she would rather die than be involved in a media circus."

By now the FBI is out of the cab, the door of which is still open, bending down to speak to me, her forehead a mass of wrinkles. "You mean you're saying that stuff *is* real? Or might be?"

"Depends what you mean by *real*," I say, and gently close the door.

Alone in the cab on the way back to Chanya, my mind insists on replaying the whole of those steamy, intense, impermissibly passionate moments with Damrong. I don't think there was a day when we didn't make love at least three times: *Tell me your heart, Sonchai, tell me your pleasure. I want you to do things to me you've never done to any other woman. Sonchai, make me your slave, hurt me if you like, you can, you know.*

It might look corny in black and white, but it's heady stuff when it comes from a sorceress who has already bent your mind.

When I reach home, I see that Chanya has waited up for me. She is watching a soap on TV (magicians, ghosts, and skeletons add spice to a kitchen-sink drama) and welcomes me with a slow blink and the eternal greeting of country folk: "Did you eat yet?"

"I had a bite."

The first thing I do after I kiss her is caress the Lump. It's a sort of joke between us that the fetus is the reincarnation of my former partner and soul brother, Pichai. Except it's not quite a joke. We have both been dreaming about him almost nightly, and Chanya has described him perfectly even though she never met him in the flesh. So I say, "How's Pichai?"

"Alive and kicking." She studies my face. "Well?"

"I showed Kimberley the video. She thinks she can check the perp's eyes using isometric technology. It's like fingerprints for the eyes. Every foreigner coming into Thailand has to have a digitalized mug shot these days, on the insistence of the U.S. They call it freedom and democracy. We should be able to catch him sooner or later."

She puts a hand on my cheek, then checks my brow for fever. "I've never known you to be so affected by a case. Is it only because you were lovers?"

"What else?"

"What else? The ending, of course. What did Kimberley say about it?"

"She can't quite handle it either. It made a strange atmosphere."

"Even dead, that woman has the power to turn your world upside down."

I take a couple of beats to absorb that penetrating observation. "Not only mine. The FBI isn't exactly naïve, but she's in shock. It's what it does to your faith in life. Makes it that much harder to get up in the morning. You don't want to believe it, but it's hard to ignore the evidence."

By way of answer, she takes my hand and places it on the Lump.

4

I have already checked out her apartment, where the security found her body, of course. It was a quick, cursory visit, though, and I have been feeling the need to return for a more thorough examination. I had plenty of time to do it yesterday, but that was a Wednesday, and you don't mess with the dead on Wednesdays. If all roads in the West lead to Rome, then all superstitions in the East lead back to India; our Brahmin mentors left precise instructions on this and other points, including color coding for days of the week; if you notice a lot of us wearing pink on Tuesdays, that's why. I don't normally follow this tradition unless something has made me nervous. Today there's a tint of Thursday orange in my socks, shirt, and handkerchief; better safe than sorry.

Damrong's condo happens to be in a midrange apartment building in Soi 23, within easy walking distance of my mother's bar, the Old Man's Club, where I slept last night. (Okay, I confess, I didn't want to bring bad luck to Chanya and Pichai on a Wednesday night, when the black god Rahu rules the skies; I figured if I was going to come under attack from Damrong's ghost, it would be better to take the hit at the club.)

It's late morning by the time I've finished getting the bar ready for tonight; most of the chores involve ordering beer and spirits, checking that the cleaning staff have done a good job, and taking care of the Buddha. He's a little guy, no more than two feet tall, who sits on a high shelf above the cash register; he has a huge appetite for lotus garlands, however, and shuts off the luck pronto if I forget. Before I go to Damrong's flat, I find a street vendor in a side *soi* with a trishaw piled high with lotus garlands, *kreung sangha tan* (monk baskets full of goodies like soap, crisps, bananas, sugar, instant coffee; you buy one and donate it to your favorite *wat* as a way of making merit), wind chimes, bamboo chairs, cut flowers. I buy three lotus garlands, take them back to the club, festoon our voracious little Buddha with them, light a bunch of incense that I hold between my hands as I mindfully *wai* him, and hope I've done enough to keep lucky today.

I wait half an hour or so for my mother to appear. She arrives in a BMW with tinted windows. Her driver stops just outside the club to let her out, then drives off to a private car park in Soi 23. She has put on weight recently, with the result that her bum-hugging black leggings and tit-hugging T-shirts have given way to looser, more conservative attire. She is wearing a long tweed skirt with matching jacket (Thursday-orange threads prominent)—top-of-the-range stuff but sadly middle aged—and plenty of gold. She is the very image of a middle-class professional and could easily be a university professor. I give her a sniff-kiss on the cheek when she crosses the threshold and notes with approval that I've fed the Buddha. She sits heavily at one of the tables in the club and lights a Marlboro Red.

"This place is so dated now, Sonchai," she says, taking in the faux jukebox with its galaxy of twinkling stars, the Marilyn Monroe, Sinatra, Mamas & Papas, Doors, early Beatles, and Stones posters on the wall. "We're going to have to do something to pull in the johns. All the other bars have renovated. The girls are dancing naked in Fire House and Vixens. We're losing customers."

I frown and shake my head. The prospect of girls dancing naked strikes me as a step down the slippery slope toward a more calculated form of exploitation. My mother knows my reservations and frowns in her turn.

"Times are changing, Sonchai, and we have to change with them.

You've done well enough from the bar—you could never survive on your cop's salary. It's time you took off the rose-colored glasses. Nine out of ten girls who apply for jobs here *want* to dance naked. They know that's the way to get customers. A john who isn't sure if he wants to get laid, get drunk, or go to bed early to nurse his jet lag will weaken at the sight of nipples and pubic hair. The West is sinking under the weight of its own hypocrisy, and these days more and more Chinese and Indian men are visiting the bars looking for some no-frills action. Let's face it, the girls are too poor to worry about their manners."

"Aren't you worried about what we're going to become, *chart na?*"

"The next life is determined by how generous we are in this one, how much compassion we show, not by the extent to which we're bent by market forces."

I know she's right, but I don't want to talk about it right now. I hand over the keys, tell her how much beer and spirits I've ordered, and kiss her goodbye like a sad but dutiful son. Once out on the street I realize how nervous I am about visiting Damrong's apartment again and think about calling my assistant, Lek, to come with me; I decide to be a *farang*-style man, though, and vigorously suppress the quaking in my stomach as I stroll down Soi Cowboy, where the girls who sleep upstairs at the bars are emerging in jeans and T-shirts, hungry for breakfast and digging into food from the stalls that line the street at this time of day. I emerge into Soi 23.

There are plenty of restaurants down at this end of the *soi*, catering to every Western taste, and a lot of cooked-food stalls catering mostly to Isaan tastes; almost all our working girls come from the poor north and never get used to Bangkok cooking. Farther along, past the Indian embassy, it's mostly apartment buildings, some of them built with Soi Cowboy clientele in mind. Damrong's, though, is of the clinically clean, no-nonsense style designed to attract middle-income locals. On the other hand, since the owners of the units are almost all Thai, quite a lot of attention has been lavished on the guards' uniforms: white jacket, crimson sash, Turkish pantaloons, white socks, dress shoes, and a bijou cap with shiny peak. With that kind of sartorial elegance elevating ego, the guy at the door doesn't allow himself to be too impressed with my police ID and takes a while to write down the number before he calls an equally overdressed colleague to take me up to the twelfth floor. In the lift the guard tells me the reason they broke into the apartment a few days ago: an endless string of men, mostly *farang* and Japanese, had been calling the desk downstairs to say they were worried they couldn't get hold of her. It wasn't like her to spurn business. When they broke down the door, they found the body.

He lets me into the apartment using a key card but won't enter himself. He feels no embarrassment at fessing up to a ghost phobia. He even looks at me a little strangely; maybe it's because I'm half *farang* that I'm prepared to cross the threshold all alone?

I close the door behind me and reexperience the same sense of desolation I felt on my last visit. I've been here many times before, of course, when the heat of passion had the power to turn the white walls rosy. Even then, though, I half notice the barrenness of the place. Every prostitute I ever knew owned at least one stuffed toy—except Damrong. There were never any pictures of her either, which is quite egregious in a beautiful woman.

They found her naked on her own bed with a bright orange rope about a centimeter thick still twisted tightly around her neck to the point where it was half buried in her flesh; I have to screw my courage to the sticking point to enter the bedroom.

A hundred clips of frantic, uncontrolled lovemaking fill my head, producing a stark contrast to the silent, sterile, white room. She was always scrupulously clean; except when in the throes of passion, she confessed to disliking the messiness of sex. When I step to the bedside and look at the opposite wall, I see the elephant is still there. A photograph of a great charging tusker which seems to be bursting out of the plaster; it is the only picture in the whole apartment. When I asked her what it was doing there, as I frequently did after lovemaking, she would laugh and reply with flagrant sarcasm, *He reminds me of you.*

I don't miss her cruelty, but the loss to the world of that unconquerable spirit comes hard, especially when there seems no evidence of it left. The stark white pillow lies on the stark white sheet, folded back and tucked under the mattress like a bandage. She favored hard beds, so the mattress sprang back into shape the minute they took her corpse away. No flowers, no wallpaper, no dirt, no life. *The clue is that there is no clue,* I mutter to myself, feeling Zen-ish; it's true though, in a way. If anything, the kitchen is still more pristine than the bedroom. I open a drawer where she kept cutlery and remember that she, who entertained so many men here, only ever had one of anything: one spoon, one fork, one set of chopsticks. And yet she was not miserly. Unusually for a Thai working girl, she liked to pay for meals when we ate together in restaurants. She managed to give the impression that she had more money than me; quite often I felt as if I were the whore.

At the front door I examine the lock. No sign of forced entry. When the perps came with the body—surely it took more than one to bring her here surreptitiously—they must have used her key card. How did they do it? Was she bundled up in a carpet like Cleopatra, or held up between them like a drunk? Obviously someone bribed at least one of the beautifully dressed guards to look the other way. I doubt that will prove a fruitful line of inquiry, however. My guess is that the bribe was big enough to provide a prophylactic against interrogation, even assuming I can find the right one to intimidate. No, this is not a crime scene, and the presence of her body here was merely a decoy. I close the front door behind me, thankful to have avoided contact with her ghost.

The next step in forensic investigation should be a visit to Damrong's family. She came from Isakit, the poorest part of our poorest region in the northeast, known as Isaan. I'm not ready for that journey, but duty requires me to get a local cop to make the call. I tell the switchboard to find the police station nearest to Damrong's home village. Eventually a gruff country voice comes on the line. He knows the call is from Bangkok but insists on speaking in the local Isaan tongue, which is a dialect of Khmer, so that I have to ask him to translate into Thai, and he makes a cute little protest dance out of that. Eventually he agrees to send a constable to talk to the mother. According to records, Damrong's father died when she was young. Her one sibling is a younger brother who, so far as we know, is still alive. The database shows he was convicted of possession and trafficking in *yaa baa*, or methamphetamines, about ten years ago.

If I didn't already know about Damrong's background, I might consider inviting her mother up to Bangkok for an interview, but I learned something about the matriarch during our brief affair which makes that strategy improbable. In the meantime I need to do some fairly intrusive investigating, using parts of the government database that will require authority from Colonel Vikorn, the chief of District 8. I've given him only a very general outline of the case so far, and I need to see him this morning. However, this is Thursday, and the Colonel and I have a curious ritual that takes place every Thursday.

Call it a consequence of globalism. Like many Thais (roughly sixty-three million, give or take a few freaks like me), Police Colonel Vikorn's interest in Western culture could, until recently, have been described as tepid, to say the least. As he aged, though, and his core methamphetamine business came to involve more and more lucrative export contracts, he decided he ought to know something about his customers and appointed me to keep him informed of important developments in Europe and the United States, changes in the street price of *yaa baa* being chief among them. I found myself justifying my existence by exploring whatever cropped up in *The New York Times* using such keywords as *meths, DEA, drug abuse, porn*. Porn, in this exercise, was originally merely a way of relieving the monotony of the usual bleeding-heart stories of how drugs have criminalized families who formerly could have been relied upon to destroy themselves with alcohol. Something about porn stories intrigued Vikorn, though, who seemed to see beyond mere sleaze. He demanded to know more and more, so that just recently porn has been the flavor of the month. It so happened that I found a masterly article in *The New York Times* archives a few days ago.* I know that Vikorn is not much interested in the Damrong case, so I have to launch into the porn report as soon as I've sat down opposite him at his vast desk.

"Listen to this," I say, and outline the article to him.

The Colonel is so intrigued, I have to translate word for word. In a nutshell, porn's evolutionary spiral can be traced from dirty postcards to video shops to mail order to instant downloads from the Net, all in about a decade during which it grew from a disreputable million-dollar industry to a massive, and therefore respectable, multi-billion-dollar industry. (Seven hundred million rentals of hardcore porn occurred in 2000: that's exactly two and a half movies per U.S.

---

*See Appendix.

citizen, all of which feature, on average, two or more penises penetrating an equal number of mouths or vaginas, which means that the average American vicariously participated in no less than five orgies in 2000, the year the article was published. Word is the number has more than doubled since then. I don't have the figures for homosexual porn.) In other words, as an investment, porn became irresistible to certain grandmother corporations. Like Internet gambling, porn largely survived the dot-com bubble, thus proving itself, along with eating, sleeping, dressing, and dying, as one of those industries in which a young person starting out in life cannot go wrong.

By the time I've finished my translation, Vikorn, a normally laidback sixty-year-old exuding cynicism, is sitting bolt upright like a man who has been injected in the left ventricle with adrenaline. The innocence of fresh revelation has smoothed his brow. He looks ten years younger.

"Read those numbers again," he says; then, with a gasp of admiration, "Amazing. *Farang* are even more two-faced than the Royal Thai Police. You mean those mealymouthed little Western TV journalists, who get their knickers in a twist about our brothels, spend most of their lives in five-star hotel rooms paying to watch people fuck for money?"

"It's a culture of hypocrisy," I offer, sounding rather more judgmental than I intend.

But gangsters of Vikorn's stature are masters at seeing opportunity where mere mortals see only darkness. He shakes his head as if I were a poor, challenged intellect incapable of picking up a half-billion dollars lying on the floor at my feet.

"It's a culture of masturbation," he corrects, rubbing his hands together and assuming the posture of a country schoolmaster. "So, what are you waiting for? Let's make a movie."

I shake my head wisely. "No way. You don't understand. American porn may be full of silicone tits and lipstick on pricks, the acting may be even worse than ours, and most of the women may have pimples on their bums"—Yes, I have added ten dollars to my hotel bills from time to time—just like you, hey, *farang?*—"but the camerawork is first class. The guys behind the viewers once believed they were going to make art-house movies for posterity. They do angles, pauses, use more than one camera, long shots, pans, slow-mo, graphic inserts, unexpected close-ups of bits of your body you've never seen yourself. They're top-notch pros," I explain with satisfaction. "Mr. and Mrs. Jerkov of Utah aren't going to buy stuff shot in a back room on Soi Twenty-six with a single Handycam. They're used to quality."

A pause while my master rubs his jaw and stares at me with those frank, unblinking eyes. "What's an art-house movie?"

I scratch my head. "I'm not sure, it's a phrase they use in the industry. Something that hopes to sell itself by pretending not to be commercial, I guess."

"Where have I heard the phrase before?"

I am about to answer that question, for I know exactly where we both first heard it. Then I realize how far ahead of me the Colonel already is. We exchange glances.

"Yammy," I say. "But he's in jail awaiting trial, at which you've made sure he'll be sentenced to death."

Vikorn raises his hands and lifts his shoulders. "The best moment to pitch him a deal, don't you think?"

With resignation I realize I've blown any possibility of carrying the Damrong case further today. Sorry, *farang*, I feel a digression coming on.

5

As the detective responsible for prosecuting him, I carry the whole of the Yammy file in my head as I sit in a cab on the way to Lard Yao.

He was born into a lower-middle-class family in Sendai; his father was a salaryman for Sony and his mother a traditional Japanese housewife who cooked whale and seaweed like a demon. Decisive in Yammy's early years was his father's access to Sony prototypes, especially cameras. Our hero learned to point and click soon after learning to walk and as a consequence never fully mastered verbal communication. In an introverted culture, that didn't matter much, but his written Japanese was also poor. Never mind: his father, all too aware of the depressing consequences of a life spent toeing the line, saw genius in his son's defects. Sacrificing much, the family moved to Los Angeles, where Yammy's educational flaws went unnoticed. As soon as possible his father sent him to film school. All was going well until the family took a sightseeing holiday in San Francisco, where Yamahato senior was the only tourist in two decades to manage to get run over by a tram. His mother used the insurance payment to finance the rest of Yammy's film education but refused to stay a minute longer in America. All alone with his genius and without his mum's famous seaweed-wrapped whale steaks, nevertheless Yammy had little difficulty in rising in the ranks of Hollywood cameramen.

"You're terrific," his favorite director told him. "You have this Asian attention to detail, your ego doesn't get in the way of business, and you understand perfection in art. You're gonna go a long way in advertising."

"I don't want to go a long way in advertising," Yammy replied. "I want to make a feature film."

The director shook his head sadly. He also had once wanted to make feature films. So had the first, second, and third cameramen, the gaffer, the sound engineer, and the dolly grip. "It ain't easy, kid," the director said, "and it doesn't have a whole lot to do with talent."

Yammy already knew this. If the studios appreciated talent, they wouldn't make the same old junk year after year, would they? Sure, sometimes even Hollywood did something right, but Yammy wasn't interested in the American market. He had plans to go home once he'd honed his talents to a razor edge. His heroes of the silver screen included Akira Kurosawa, Teinosuke Kinugasa, Sergei Eisenstein, Vittorio De Sica, Ingmar Bergman, Luis Buñuel—cinematic geniuses whom most people in Hollywood had never heard of, not even in film school. And he knew there was another, probably insurmountable, social impediment to his success in California. After all, at that particular time he and his team were filming in Colombia for a perfume advertisement that could just as economically and a lot more easily have been filmed on a mountain in Colorado. As Yammy put it in his faxes to his chums at home in Sendai, "Firstly, I do not snort cocaine, secondly I do not use coke, thirdly I do not do snow. Everyone thinks I'm an FBI plant."

Every night after filming, he and the director went through the same ritual conversation while the director arranged extravagantly long lines of white powder on a marble tabletop.

"It's about money," the director said. "To make an independent art-house movie, you need investors who can get hold of as much dough as they need whenever they need it so they don't have to worry about losing a few tens of millions on a risky venture. D'you know who fits into that category?"

"Yes," Yammy replied.

"Dealers," the director said while closing one nostril with a forefinger and bending over the table. "And d'you know who runs the dealers?"

"Yes," said Yammy.

"And d'you know who runs the mob in L.A.?"

"The Bureau," said Yammy.

When they returned to California, the director decided to give the talented young Japanese his big break. The party was at an obscure and secret mansion located in the desert and well known to everyone who was anyone in the film industry. Yammy remembers women and men with eyes the size of flying saucers staring at a white mountain, in the middle of a banquet table, that even Yammy knew was not a wedding cake. Near-naked women, boys, and dozens of spare bedrooms were available for anyone to use, but most could not take their eyes off the white mountain. Within five minutes everyone except Yammy was enjoying impregnable self-confidence while bumping into furniture and talking nonsense.

"You don't have to worry about the chief of the L.A. Bureau," the director explained, coming up behind Yammy and missing his step. "See, they have to get their information about who to murder in Colombia and Bolivia from somewhere, and who are they going to get it from if not the mob in L.A. who buy the stuff wholesale? Bust them, and their intelligence sources dry up. That's why the chief is here tonight." Maybe the director thought he was nodding discreetly as he shook his head like a neighing horse at the short, broad guy on the other side of the table who had just grabbed a handful of the mountain. "This is freedom."

Next day, depressed, for he had made no use at all of the golden opportunity to further his career by socializing with the mob at the coke orgy, Yammy decided he just didn't have what it took to make it in L.A. and packed his bags. Back in Sendai with Mama, he called up his one pal in the film industry in Tokyo, who had managed to make a feature film about a psychotic body piercer who murders everything that moves except his pet hamster, which he ends up dying for. The film had flopped, but so what? At least he'd made one feature film in his otherwise meaningless life. Yammy paid him a visit in the Shinbashi area of Tokyo.

"Listen," his pal said after five bottles of sake, "there's only one way to make a film these days, and that is to find the kind of investors . . ."

Yammy finished the sentence for him.

Well, *farang*, I know you've guessed the rest, although it happened in Jap Time, which is to say that dear Yammy slumped into alcoholic depression for nearly a decade before he succumbed to the inevitable. To be fair to Yammy, he came very close to running a successful business operation, but like a lot of beginners in my country, he made the fatal error of choosing to buy from the army instead of the police. Worse, he bought his modest ten kilos of smack from Vikorn's arch-enemy General Zinna, which, to cut a long story short, is why Vikorn had him banged up and had the boys produce a watertight case that will inevitably get Yammy the double injection. (We changed from the bullet last year in recognition of current fashions in the global execution industry; Buddha knows why, nobody ever felt the slug enter the back of the skull. It wasn't a question of humanity, simply new-wave squeamishness. Personally I would much prefer hot lead in the cerebellum to a slow suck into the big sleep by chemical means. What d'you think, *farang*?)

So, things were not looking so good for Yammy until five minutes ago. Here's my heroic visit to him in his cell in Lard Yao (our biggest, holds nine thousand prisoners, built by the Japs as a concentration camp in World War II):

Imagine a long hot ride to a tropical middle-of-nowhere. Suddenly a not-displeasing display of lush vegetation announces the beginning of the penitentiary's extensive estate. Hold it, though—what is that terrible stench? Oh, that's the raw sewage vat in which they make difficult prisoners stand up to their necks for hours, sometimes days. Not a great place to drown. Hold your nose, and we're being patted down by the rock-faced screws and led to the visitors' room, where we sit on a single wooden seat while they bring in Yammy in cuffs and leg irons: a slim, rather handsome Japanese in his midforties with an attractively receding hairline and the sullen determination of a true artist, in an age when true art is beyond the cultural pale. There's no seat for him so he has to stand. I am delighted to be the bringer of fantastically good news and feel that I must be well in with the Buddha, since I am the instrument of his salvation. Imagine my consternation, therefore, when, after I have outlined in broad strokes Vikorn's irresistible business plan, he says, "No."

"But Yamahatosan," I say, "perhaps I have not expressed myself with sufficient accuracy. Let me be clear. In a few short weeks from now your case will come to trial. It makes no difference if you plead guilty or not—the evidence against you is overwhelming. And even if it wasn't, Colonel Vikorn knows how to get a conviction. You will be sentenced to death, and while spending the usual few years on death row, you will be gang-raped by *farang* and thereafter deemed an unlucky pariah by the Thais, who will cut off your supply of fresh cockroaches, thus depriving you of your only source of protein. You will probably be terminally sick long before they strap you down and get you ready for the long needles—"

"Stop!" says Yammy. "You can't scare me. I've decided to kill myself." He makes a samurai-like gesture with his left thumb across his lower intestine. "I've got the knife already."

"But Yamahatosan," I say, "I thought I'd already explained, you don't need to kill yourself. I'm here to get you out."

"I don't want to get out. What's the difference? You Thais know nothing of honor. I was going to kill myself anyway if I couldn't make a feature film. If you let me out, what will I be?"

"A well-paid pornographer."

"I don't want to be a fucking pornographer. *I'm an artist.*"

Flabbergasted, flummoxed, exasperated—and impressed—I fish out my cell phone to call the Colonel.

"So let him be artistic," says Vikorn. "He can use ten cameras at the same time if he likes. He can cut to the fucking moon landing in between fellatio. He can have flowers and ink-block prints all over the stupid studio. He can have complete artistic freedom, just so long as he gets the cum shots right and the junk sells in America and Europe."

I translate all this to Yammy, whose glower slowly lifts. "I'll think about it."

"Here, take my cell phone," I say with saintly self-control. "If you decide to graciously accept our humble offer of employment, please press this autodial number, which belongs to Colonel Vikorn."

Back in the cab I borrow the driver's cell to call Vikorn, who bets five thousand baht Yammy will call within the next five minutes. I bet the same amount he will not call before I reach the station, because he's a stubborn, suicidal Japanese whose honor will take at least half an hour to collapse.

Vikorn and I sit amazed in his office, waiting until after nine in the evening. Finally the phone rings, and Vikorn hands it to me because Yammy speaks no Thai.

"I want the right to introduce my own story lines. Most porn has the stupidest, corniest story lines, if any. I want real plots."

Vikorn waves a weary hand of resignation when I have translated.

6

Damrong came to me last night. I guess I knew she would whatever color pajamas I wore, and no matter how many times I *waied* the Buddha in our little homemade shrine with fairy lights: Chanya's idea. I was aware of her and the Lump in bed with me at the same time as being out of the body. Furtiveness only added to the intensity of my lust. *We cannot wake Chanya,* I tried to say, even as Damrong's mouth descended on my quivering member. Liberated from time and space, she was able to project a multiplicity of images: naked; half naked; wearing a black ballgown with silver jewelry; topless in tight-fitting jeans with her long black hair intermittently covering her breasts; bent over me in the attitude of total submission; standing above me in a posture of command. The point, really, was the overwhelming sexual power of her spirit, which somehow was able to trigger hormones from the other side. Men, let me be frank, there is no erotic experience that compares to being fucked by a ghost. When she had finished with me, I took myself off to the yard to hose down my feverish body. Thankfully Chanya was still fast asleep when I slipped back beside her.

. . .

Back to the case. I have used Colonel Vikorn's security clearance to penetrate the deeper reaches of the national database. When I plug in Damrong's ID number, I find a curious surname: เบ็เคอ. It takes me a few moments to process this odd couple of syllables. I try out various possibilities before light dawns: the name is Baker. Armed with this clue, I make a few cross-checks and discover that her Thai family name is Tarasorn, and her parents were Cambodian refugees. She married an American named Daniel Baker just over five years ago and, according to the Immigration data, went to live with him in the United States until she returned about two years later. On official documents she was still obliged to sign her name as Mrs. Damrong Baker, which is the name that will appear on her death certificate.

From the database I extract Mr. Daniel Baker's American Social Security and passport numbers. I call Immigration to have them check if Baker happens to have returned to Thailand recently. It's a long shot, but you never know. Then I call Kimberley at the Grand Britannia to give her Baker's Social Security number.

I am afraid the FBI is the first to respond. Within less than half an hour she calls me back, slightly breathless.

"Okay, this could be your big lead. Dan Baker has a conviction for pimping."

"Pimping?" I give this information the reverence it deserves. "No illicit porn videos?"

"No, but these days that's pretty well implied in the act of pimping, at least in the States."

"And?"

"She was prosecuted for running a bawdy house, in Fort Lauderdale, Florida. They both pleaded guilty. He got twelve months plus one year probation. She got six months, but they deported her."

"When?"

"Just over four years ago."

A pause, then Kimberley says, "It must have been right after she was deported that she went to work for you."

Fighting a certain internal resistance, I say, "Yes. We always thought she was way too upmarket for us. I guess she was just using us as a stepping-stone while she readjusted to Bangkok. It must have been quite a letdown after the States."

"I don't know about that. Prostitutes in the States don't have such an easy ride."

"Anything else?"

"I'm working on it. The whole case rings a bell. I think it got a lot of publicity because some of the city fathers were involved."

Mrs. Damrong Baker: the asymmetry in the name might say it all. I have to call Immigration five more times before I am able to convince them to get off their backsides. When they do, it is simply a matter of plugging Dan Baker's passport number into their database. Finally my desk phone rings.

"He's here in Bangkok."

"As a tourist?"

"No. He has a license to teach English as a foreign language. Yearly renewable visa plus work permit, signs in every three months to confirm his residential address."

"Which is?"

"Sukhumvit Soi Twenty-six."

I call Lek, my assistant. While I am waiting for him, I walk to the window to look down. The young monk, whom I've come to think of as "the Internet monk," is crossing the street to enter the Internet café. I watch his vivid saffron robes disappear into the bright shop; then Lek arrives. We take a cab. "I want to know if he's lying or not," I tell Lek. "Just watch him while he answers."

All Bangkok taxi drivers practice witchcraft, but this one is at postgraduate level. Garlands in honor of the journey goddess Mae Yanang hang from the rearview mirror with a bunch of amulets, obscuring the middle slice of external reality. I should mention that there are two ways of avoiding death on our roads: *pop pong* and *pop gun*. *Pop gun* signifies the usual dreary ineffective stuff like wearing a seatbelt and not driving too fast; we generally prefer *pop pong*, with its inviolable spiritual protection. Done properly, *pop pong* not only protects your life, it can also deal out severe punishments to those who threaten it. At this very moment our driver is proudly recounting the tale of a road-rager who cut in front of him last week, only to be flattened by a cement truck five minutes later. "What a mess," he says with glee, and points to the ceiling.

Lek is riveted: "Dead?"

"Sure."

"He didn't have an amulet?"

"Would you believe it? He had a *salika* inserted under the skin."

"And he still died?"

Our driver points to the ceiling again with a beat-that expression. "Accidents don't just happen. The origin is in the past." He jerks a thumb backward to indicate the past. "*Gam*," he says. Karma.

Lek and I study the ceiling, where a kind of astrological chart provides luck, health insurance, and protection from traffic cops. The inscriptions are in, not Thai, but the ancient Khmer script called *khom*, from the time of Angkor Wat. "You use a *moordu*?" Lek wants to know.

"Sure, a Khmer *moordu*. What do Thai seers know? All magic comes from the Khmer in the end." He shifts around to give Lek a quick glance. "I got into this in a big way after the tsunami. Before that I was pretty *choi choi* about it."

"Because of the ghosts?"

"You bet. See, what people don't appreciate is that most of the Thais who died didn't come from Phuket at all. They came from Krung Thep and up north. And of course, the *farang* ghosts wanted to get home as well, so the dead all arrived here trying to get on planes at the airport or buses back to Isaan. My partner, who uses this car on the night shift, said it was terrible. He'd pick up a party of four or five passengers and drive them to Don Muang; then when he turned around to collect the fares, they weren't there anymore. The worst, though, were the ones who boarded in the dark; then when he turned the light on at the end of the trip, they were totally rotted already, eyes hanging by the optic nerve and bouncing around on their cheeks. Then there were the *farang* who don't know diddly about being dead and were still looking for loved ones, crying out and all that. It was just awful. For that kind of stuff, you got to have professional help."

Lek nods gravely in agreement. I'm not sure I'm comfortable with this side of the *katoey* soul, so I look out the side window, where carbon monoxide is laced with air. We're stuck in the usual jam at the Asok-Sukhumvit crossroads, and a kid about ten years old with a dirty face and exaggerated misery picks his way around the stationary vehicles.

He makes a halfhearted attempt to clean the windows with a broken windscreen wiper, then holds out his hand. When I roll down the window to give him ten baht, hot poison wafts in and the driver complains. "There's no karmic benefit in giving to kids like that," he explains. "Better to get the right amulet. How can you walk around without protection?"

Lek gives me a told-you-so nod. He never removes his shamanic plant roots wrapped in yellow yantra cloth, which hang in a small bunch from a cord around his neck. He often chides me for trying to take reality naked, like a dumb *farang*.

The right turn out of Asok into Sukhumvit can be tricky without *pop pong*. Our shaman screeches around almost on two wheels, just in front of a crowded bus, forcing a motorcyclist to swerve and the bus to brake. Then we're speeding along past the Grand Britannia, way ahead of the pack. "Amazing," Lek says, lavishing awe on the ceiling.

I'm pleasantly surprised when the guard at Baker's apartment building tells me the American *farang* still lives here and is at home this very moment. I give the guard (light and dark blue uniform, handcuffs, and nightstick; he was playing Thai checkers with his colleague sitting at a makeshift table using bottle tops when I interrupted) two hundred baht, and by the time I'm standing outside Baker's door, I already know most of the American's private life. Works regular hours mostly from home. Brings a girl back every Friday and Saturday night, sometimes the same one. Speaks Thai quite well. Likes to work out at a local gym. Never has any money to spare but usually pays the rent on time. Not a big drinker but smokes ganja from time to time. Has a sideline in something photographic, but it doesn't seem to make him much money. Never seems to return to America, prefers to spend his vacations in Cambodia. He was quite an argumentative type of *farang* when he arrived about three years ago, but he's learned local ways. He's quiet now, respectful; he walks the walk.

I have to decide what kind of knock to use. Too hard, and I fear I will awaken that *farang* mind-set called Thaicopsyndrome: he could start shivering in his boots and replaying every horror story he's ever heard about our legal system, which is not what I want. Too soft, though, and I could get insolence. I opt for the middle path, which brings him to the door in a pair of knee-length walking shorts, nothing else.

Thirty-seven, male-pattern baldness, gray in his chest hair, an iron-pumper's physique, no tats; he experiences the usual sinking feeling when I flash my police ID. Teachers of English tend to be a subset of the backpacker nation; for us they fit into the poor-and-deportable category of foreigners and tend to think the worst when a cop comes calling.

"I'm here to ask a few questions about your ex-wife, Mr. Baker."

A scowl disguises something more sinister. I think he is not surprised enough. I check Lek with a flick of my eyes. Lek is using feminine intuition, or at least practicing the shrewd, assessing look that is supposed to go with it. He purses his lips at me and shakes his head.

The apartment is built from the same tired building plan that is used all over the world these days: in the hierarchy of concrete caves his owns a window and a toilet, which puts him two points above basic. There are other signs that he is not totally resigned to nonexistence: a laptop opened and sitting on a chair; a corny but provocative poster of a Thai girl sitting topless by a river and a poster of Angkor Wat; some books. I guess Not a Lot to Show would be his category in the global pyramid, a popular level, I have to admit. They have long been a curiosity with me, these *farang* men who come here to be nobody, as if even that role is too stressful in their utopia of origin. Now Lek and I are both staring at Baker, who checks his wristwatch, which looks to me like a fake Rolex. (The second hand jerks instead of rotating smoothly around the dial; for some that's all you need to know during your stopover in Bangkok.)

"I don't want to offend a cop, but I have to tell you I have an English lesson in ten minutes."

"Where is your lesson, Mr. Baker?"

"Right here." He looks me in the eye. "A private lesson. You can get me on nonpayment of tax if you want, but it's the only way I can survive. The school I work mornings doesn't pay a living wage."

I nod. "I don't want to deprive you of income. Let's see how far we get before your student arrives," I say.

"Right."

"Your ex-wife, Mrs. Damrong Baker."

He seems uncertain how to proceed. A long moment passes, and then he comes out with it, in a kind of anger burst: "That bitch—what did she do now?"

I raise my eyes and crumple my brow. "What did she do before?"

A mistake on my part; my response was too smart by far. He quickly erases all expression from his face and shrugs. "I was married to her for a year. We lived together. You might as well ask what she didn't do to destroy me—the list would be shorter."

I exchange a glance with Lek and nod at him. I know he is anxious to practice his interrogation skills—and his English.

"Mr. Baker, how did you first meet your Thai wife?"

Baker takes Lek in for the first time. There are not that many trans-sexual cops in Bangkok; as far as I know, Lek is the only one. On duty he takes measures to disguise his growing bosom and keeps the camp act to a minimum. When he talks, though, his body language says it all. There is shyness and female cunning in the way he does not look Baker in the eye. Baker experiments with an attitude of contempt, then thinks better of it after a glance at me. I jerk my chin: *Yes, you do have to answer that question.*

He grunts, and a native garrulity takes over. "I was early thirties, getting over a relationship, came here for a ten-day vacation, met Dam-rong, caught her disease." I flash him a look. He waves a hand. "Just a manner of speaking. The disease in question used to be called passion. The only officially sanctioned form of happiness known to the West: being in love. What a con. I was gaga. Of course I sent her all the money I could so she wouldn't rent her body to another man. Of course I believed every promise she made about that. Of course she lied her head off. Of course she fucked every dude who was willing to pay her price while I was trying to set up a computing business in Fort Lauderdale for us to live happily ever after. Of course I went through all the damned paperwork U.S. Immigration threw at me, of course I married her, of course she came to live with me in the States, of course it didn't last a full year. Of course she's the only woman who has ever reached me that deeply. Of course it's because she had a better grasp of reality. Of course, of course, of course." Waving a hand: "I'm Mr. Average *Farang*. I got caught the same way they all do, doesn't matter if you're French, Italian, German, British—whatever, it's the same dumb story, over and over again. I don't need to tell you that, right?"

It seems to have been a genuine tantrum, with the usual moment of disorientation straight afterward: *Did I really just say all that?* He grinds his jaw with the determination of the righteous. "Yeah, that's how it was with me and her. Mistress-slave syndrome. Want to know how I got along with my mother?"

"No, thank you," Lek says with a look of revulsion and a glance at me to take it from there. Estrogen doesn't increase attention spans.

"You sound very bitter, Mr. Baker," I say with a compassionate smile which he disregards by turning his head away.

"Comes with the territory, doesn't it? Know any *farang* men in my position who aren't bitter?"

I shrug. "Cultural conflict has its casualties."

He turns to stare incredulously. "Cultural conflict? You mean between a Western man with his pathetic need for a safe womb to crawl into and a Thai whore looking for a gold mine to exploit? I guess you could call it cultural conflict if you were giving a seminar to anthropology students." He scratches his head and shakes it. "Total fuck-up is what I call it. Of me, by her. Period."

I check Lek to see if he is as intrigued as me. I think he is. When a psyche is fragmented, it often experiments with different postures. What posture should we provoke now?

"Mr. Baker, let me be frank. I have checked the national database here in Thailand and sought assistance from the FBI." I smile.

Knowing that I know causes a new Baker to emerge from the old. He snaps his head around to stare at me, then smirks. "The Bureau? They told you about her little scam?"

"Only the criminal record part. I'd love to hear the details."

The smirk becomes a permanent fixture, proclaiming, I think, a defiant pride. "So I did six months' jail time after remission, for pimping. She got deported. That's how it panned out, but it wasn't what I had planned when we married." He pauses to stare at the topless girl in the poster for a couple of beats. "I was still in the walk-into-the-sunset, midpubescent phase when she came to live with me in the States. We hadn't been married a month, though, when she disappears for most of one Saturday night. I'm calling emergency services, I'm going out of my mind thinking she's been raped or murdered or both, or been run over, all the crap that drives a man crazy when he's in love. Then she walks in about four in the morning with a great big grin on her beautiful, cynical face and lays out more than a thousand dollars on the kitchen table. Sheeze!"

This last is a kind of yelp, caused by severe backbite of heartburn. He has to gulp a couple of times. "She didn't care so much about the money as the power, the very liberating act of walking out at about seven P.M. in a big strange land and coming back more than a thousand dollars richer a few hours later. That turned her on a lot more than I could."

He has to pause to steady himself, then appears to regain sovereignty over his mind. "She tossed me half the money and told me how it was gonna be. I'd never seen that side of her before. It was frightening and very unnerving. I cried like a baby for two whole days, but it didn't affect her at all. She had seen men bawling like that plenty of times. No way was she going to change, and she wasn't afraid of violence. I didn't even threaten to hit her—she was way too tough for that. Kick her out? And spend the next months in mental torture wondering about what she was up to in the States?"

He scratches his chest hair, lets a couple of beats pass. "After I'd quit bawling my eyes out, she started talking reality. She told me about her childhood. I mean, she told it like it is in a way you never hear Thai people talking unless you're one of them. I started to see the world with her eyes. It was a total personal revolution for me, what it must do to your head, growing up like that. In the West all our problems are social and psychological these days. But suppose you were programmed in a totally different way, suppose your very existence was constantly under threat, and there was no way out—*no way out.* That was her message. She didn't give a shit that she could make a lot of dough in the States— that didn't alter the fact that all her people, everyone she had ever known and been fond of, they were still there, trapped, hungry, impotent." Waving a hand: "At least that's how she put it at that stage. She admitted she was in America to work, not to play at love. She said she had a family to look after. Turned out she was talking about her kid brother. I don't think she gave a shit about anyone else."

A long pause filled with heavy sighs. He does seem to be going through something. "At first I only went along with it to keep her from leaving me."

"You became her pimp?"

"Not really, but the law saw it that way. In the technical sense I suppose I was, but that lady didn't need a pimp. What she needed was my house and me as a secretarial service." A pause while he fidgets with something on the table. "Then later to hold the video camera while I was standing in the wardrobe and she was performing with the john." Looking me full in the eye: "Within six weeks she had a full diary for every day, starting at lunchtime and going through to about two A.M. Word of an exciting new game spreads real quick in a small town in America. She had the local movers and shakers lining up—the male ones, that is—practically begging for the privilege of hiring her body. Big shots who owned chauffeur-driven limos arrived at our house in hired cars and taxis. Within a few months we were in a position to blackmail most of the leading local lights, including judges and prosecutors. That's why I only did six months' jail time and she only got deported. It was a deal. If they'd have gotten heavy, we would have started flashing video clips. As it was, we made three hundred thousand dollars before they closed us down."

He's walking around his small room, fidgeting with this and that, pretending the poster of Angkor Wat needs adjusting. My eyes rest on it: the vast, sinister jungle temple with its five phallic towers at the center. I think we have arrived at yet another psychologically interesting moment, when there's a knock on the front door. Baker cannot disguise his relief and says with an apologetic smile, "That's my lesson." Hurriedly he grabs a T-shirt from a drawer and pulls it on.

I nod for him to open the door, and Lek and I both examine the new arrival: a slim Thai in his early twenties, respectfully dressed in white shirt, black pants, and polished black lace-up shoes, an innocence in his eyes that you rarely see in *farang* of that age. What unreal ambition has brought him here today, probably on his day off from some dreary office job? What stories has he believed about the global economy and language skills? When he sees me, he makes a respectful *wai* and says, in excruciatingly correct English, "Excuse me, am I interrupting a conference?"

"We're just going," I say in Thai. In English to Baker: "Perhaps we might return at a more convenient moment?"

Baker gives a helpless shrug to say, *A Thai cop can make me do whatever he likes.*

"Say seven P.M.?"

"Tomorrow evening would be better. I've got another private lesson at six, and then another at nine, plus I'm working at the school all day."

Lek and I stand up. "Tomorrow then." I cough apologetically. "Mr. Baker, I'm afraid I must ask for your passport in the meantime. I will return it to you tomorrow."

The Thai student makes big eyes. He hadn't realized I was a cop, and to see his respected *ajaan* hand over his passport suddenly changes the dynamics. He's ready to flee from Baker, so I say to him in Thai, "Just an immigration matter," and smile. He smiles back with relief. Downstairs I slip the guard another hundred baht on condition he keeps an eye out for Baker's comings and goings.

In the cab back to the station, I check Baker's passport, then pass it to Lek. We exchange a shrug. Baker was out of the country at the time of Damrong's killing. It would seem he flew to Siam Reap in Cambodia, the nearest airport to Angkor Wat, several days before the event and did not come back until after the approximate time of her death. Damrong owned an American and a Thai passport; both documents indicate that she had not left Thailand for more than a year before her death. Forget Baker.

7

Without any leads other than Baker, I decide to spend quality time with the ladies in my life. I take my mother, Nong; Chanya; and the FBI for a buffet supper at the Grand Britannia on Sukhumvit, just near the Asok Skytrain station. A gay waiter charms Chanya with his concern for her condition and makes her laugh when he admits he envies her. The FBI also is solicitous and insists on fetching her whatever food she wants, while Nong casts a shrewd eye over the clientele.

"See that whore from Nong Kai? Her name is Sonja—she works at Rawhide. I've been trying to persuade her to work for us, but she's happy where she is. You know how they are."

"Friends are everything. If she has plenty at Rawhide, she'll never come work for us. How can you blame her? They're as lost as *farang* in Bangkok—even more so, since they don't have any money."

"Well, she certainly seems to have her customer under control. She's giving him the marry-me treatment. Look, she's brought her family down from Isaan to meet him."

"Must be serious," I agree.

A big muscular Australian in walking shorts, long white socks, and sandals, in his fifties with a gigantic beer gut, is bringing his plate back to where the girl, her mother, and a few other relations, who are proba-bly siblings or cousins, plus a boy about five years old, have occupied the table next to us.

"That's her son by a Thai lover," Nong explains in a whisper.

The Australian tries to make conversation with the family who are keen to adopt him, but his true love is enjoying speaking her native tongue, a dialect of Laotian, and cannot resist gossiping with her family. Every now and then she casts the Australian a warm, comforting smile, presses his thigh with one hand, and says a few words to him in English, then returns with renewed enthusiasm to the gossip. The Australian perhaps does not realize it, but his future in-laws are behav-ing exactly as if they were at home in their wood house on stilts and sit-ting barefoot on the floor nattering, probably with the TV on at full volume and a dozen kids beating one another up in the background. Nong understands Laotian better than I do and has started to grin. When the FBI comes back with a plate of oysters for Chanya, my mother enthusiastically explains in English for Kimberley's benefit:

"Her aunt just asked what color the *farang*'s dick is, and her mother wants to know how they do it when he has that huge gut. The girl's explaining that his dick is white most of the time, but after sex it turns bright pink. She says she asks him to take her from behind except on special occasions, because when he gets on top his flab kind of splodges all over her stomach like a ton of Jell-O and she gets indigestion in the middle of *boom-boom*. Anyway, it's not usually an issue because most nights he's too drunk and falls asleep on the sofa while she watches TV in bed. It has the makings of a successful marriage."

While Nong is talking, the family bursts into raucous laughter. The FBI looks down at her oysters. "Is this, like, normal suppertime conversation?"

Chanya, Nong, and I share grins. "We are mostly peasants, chil-dren of the earth," I explain. We all keep our heads down when the Australian starts to speak.

"I wouldn't mind knowing what you and your family are talking about, Sonja," he says to his girlfriend with just a touch of chagrin. She has no idea about Western etiquette so decides to tell him straight, word for word, in good but somewhat wooden English. He turns pale for a moment, finishes his beer, and orders another. I admire his power of recuperation, though, when he says, "You're gonna do just great in Queensland, Sonja, just great. Ever seen a dwarf-throwing competition?" He explains the sport to Sonja, who has a bright gleam in her eye when she translates into Laotian. The family listen with big eyes, then bombard her with a dozen questions about dwarf-throwing, which she translates into English. Do the dwarfs get paid? How much? How short do you have to be? My aunt's older brother is only four feet ten, does that qualify? Can you gamble on it? Can throwing dwarfs get visas easily? Her family had been quite bored with him, but now they are warming. Delighted that he finally has a topic that interests them—he had tried income tax, the world economy, standard of living, his new Toyota four-by-four, his giant refrigerator, health care and life insurance, the Middle East, et cetera, without much response—he launches into plain tales of the outback, including 'roo-baiting and yarns about man-eating crocs and the lurid wounds inflicted by blue-ringed octopus and box jellyfish. Suddenly he's a hit, and they have decided to welcome him into their hearts. "You're half Isaan already," the girl tells him. Beaming, he downs his beer in one gulp and orders another. Thailand's not so different from Queensland after all.

I stand up to fetch more seafood. Oysters, prawns, and shrimp sit in trays under an ice sculpture of a seahorse. Elsewhere in the middle of the huge room Chinese, Thai, Italian, French, Middle Eastern, and Japanese cuisine is piled high around a vast circular island. Standing near me are delegates to some convention with large name tags clipped over their hearts and Best Behavior software controlling their facial expressions. In their hygienic anonymity they form a quite distinct tribe, prompting me to ponder that perhaps Bangkok is located on some cosmic intersection where visitors from different galaxies mingle but never communicate. As I reach our table with a plate piled high with sushi and prawns, the FBI returns with ice cream for Chanya. She is fascinated by her, almost like a lover. I cannot take my mind off the case for long, though, and by coincidence (of course it's not really coincidence, it's cosmic intervention), just as I'm thinking about Damrong, my cell phone rings.

"I can't say for sure, but I might have something," Lek says. "There might be more than one copy of the DVD."

I have to disguise my relief that the case might be moving again. "I'm so sorry," I say to the table at large, "I'm going to have to dash."

When I take out my wallet to pay in advance, Nong makes me put it away, saying she'll charge the bill to the Old Man's Club as business entertainment. I check the FBI's face to see how she likes benefiting from the profits of prostitution, but she's enjoying the food too much to make the connection.

Out in the street I use the Skytrain bridge to walk across the road, then take the escalator down to the new subway at Asok. It's been open only a couple of years and still has a brand-new feel about it. I get out at Klong Toey, where Lek is waiting.

"You'll never believe this," Lek says, excited and cautious at the same time, "and it may be a long shot, but there's a rumor going around the clubs about a snuff movie with a masked man and a Thai whore. I tracked the story down to a *katoey* who's famous all over Soi Four for having a HiSo lover."

The shantytown at Klong Toey is our biggest and in many ways our tidiest. Most of the huts are of similar size and height and the narrow walkways are kept *riap roy*, or spic and span, in true Thai style. There's plenty of extreme squalor, of course, if you want to look for it, but generally people are getting on with their lives in near rent-free accommodations, which can be handy if you want to do a course in higher education, are a professional girl nearing the end of her shelf life, prefer recreational drugs to reality, or just plain hate work. Lek has been here before and takes me down a path that follows the railway track, with the endless line of wooden huts on our right: scratching dogs, shy cats, naked kids getting bathed in oil drums, teens with orange and green hair, families eating together in the cool of evening. "He's an artist," Lek explains. "That's why the HiSo master likes him. I came to a party here once. Actually, he's totally *ban-nok*, worse than me, but he has this creative streak, so he gets these upmarket lovers." *Ban-nok* translates roughly as "country bumpkin" but is a lot more insulting. We stop at a front door that bears a magnificent dragon in scarlet on black. "See what I mean?" There's a playful element in the rampant posture, the feminized, elongated claws, the malicious grin.

"It's very well done," I say, which makes Lek beam with pride at *katoey* talent. He knocks on the door. "Pi-Oon, it's me, Lek." No answer, so Lek knocks harder. "He likes to smoke ganja, all artists do. Never touches anything else, not even alcohol most of the time, but he can go into a dope-trance for days." Embarrassed in front of me, he knocks more aggressively, then, muttering *Fucking katoey bitch*, fishes out his cell phone. He speaks into it using his Isaan dialect based on Khmer, sounding much like a whore in a temper. "I told him I was bringing you," he says, folding the phone and putting it away. "Now he's all shit-faced from the ganja." Then he offers me a pained smile. "He'll open up in a minute. He has to get back from the moon."

Finally we hear sounds of life from the other side of the door. A couple of bolts are drawn back, and he opens a crack. Then he reveals himself in his full glory, wearing only a pair of cycling shorts: a surprisingly bony, masculine face with purple eyeshadow and lipstick, long ink-black hair drawn back in a ponytail in the ancient way, and a magnificent tattoo of a chrysanthemum adorning his hairless chest, where two small new breasts are budding. His gestures are exaggerated in the tradition of his tribe, but there's something else: it is not difficult to believe there is a real woman behind the prizefighter's features. When he drops the *katoey* posturing, he can seem genuinely female.

"Darling," he manages, and bends forward from the hips to allow Lek to peck him on the cheek.

"You're stoned," Lek chides.

"I'm in the middle of a major work, love. I need the meditation aid."

"This is my boss, Detective Jitpleecheep," Lek says with a slight pout.

"*Ever so* pleased to meet you," Pi-Oon says, and beckons us inside.

Now I'm thinking: *Gauguin.* Pi-Oon has used those same tropical purples, morbid mauves, and old golds to adorn the walls and roof of his wooden hut with images of *katoey* nightlife. A cabaret star with similar features to his is holding a microphone in the centerpiece of a triptych. I realize that every human depicted in his work is a transsexual. I'm most fascinated, though, by the frisson of his big boney tough-guy face, which seems to beg for love and tenderness. He gestures at the floor, which is unencumbered by furniture save for a few cushions. We all sit in semilotus with our backs against the wall. "We've come about the snuff movie," Lek says, still irritated.

The words cause a dreadful pain to corrupt our host's features. He places a palm against one cheek, his eyes great bulbs of horror. "Oh my Buddha, oh my, I never thought it was *real*, you know." Looking at me:

"It's was only when Pi-Lek told me you were investigating that I thought, oh, oh, oh, Pi-Oon has got himself into hot water here. Pi-Oon, I said to myself, Pi-Oon honey, you've got the biggest *mouth* in Krung Thep. I wish I'd never got *drunk* and *told* everyone. I never drink, normally, so it went straight to my head, and I just spilled my *guts.*"

"Tell us what you saw," I say.

"Well, at first it was just a big yawn, don't you know, because the girl's a *real* girl, and who wants to watch a *tart* do it nature's way like a *farm animal*, you know, but my man's *bi*, so I watched it with him to be polite, you know. And of course it made him horny as hell." Glancing at Lek with a wink: "What a *punishment* he gave me afterward, you wouldn't *believe.*" Turning back to me while Lek suppresses a smirk: "So it's some silly whore doing a fairly elaborate *boom-boom* with a dishy stud in a black gimp mask, and at the end he snuffs her with a rope around her neck, but it never occurred to me that it was *for real*, you know, I thought it was *virtual*. Of course I did. I mean, why wouldn't it be virtual in this day and age? Why go to the expense of snuffing the tart when you could fake it and use her again? *Common sense* says it's virtual."

"Who's your man?" Lek demands, drawing a scowl from both Pi-Oon and me.

Pi-Oon casts me a helpless glance. "Isn't our Pi-Lek direct? Doesn't mince words, comes straight to the point." Frowning: "You know I can't tell you that. It's against the rules."

"You've told the whole of Krung Thep everything about him except for his name." Turning to me, Lek says, "He's very big in advertising, practically runs the industry here. He's in his midforties and wears tons of gold. Keeps very fit, prefers *katoeys* to women but hates regular gays. Always uses a condom. Right?"

Pi-Oon seems genuinely put out. The palm presses the cheek again with the head on one side. "Oh my, did I really say *all that*?" Proudly: "It's true he's incredibly rich." He giggles and makes Lek smile despite himself. "*Very* well endowed. On the first night I said, darling, there's nothing for it, I'm going to have to charge you by the *inch*. Of course he loved that. *Laugh?* We have *such* a great time together, we're even thinking about marriage, maybe in Canada where it's legal. He's a tiger in bed but gentle as a lamb the rest of the time. I'm sure he didn't know it was a real snuff movie."

"Course he did," from Lek.

Stoned, Pi-Oon turns gray. "D'you think so? Oh my, I'm *sure* he didn't have *anything* to do with it. Some rich buddy of his must have loaned it to him, someone *straight*, you know, because let's face it, straight sex can be very very weird these days, what *women* will do with their bodies—well, I don't need to tell you, you're all cops."

"Tell us his name, or we'll whip you to within an inch of your life," Lek says, looking firm.

"Promise?"

Now both *katoeys* have collapsed with laughter, and I'm scratching my jaw, feeling out of place. When Pi-Oon has recovered, he says, "Would you two honor my humble home by smoking some export-quality stuff with me? My man gave it to me, and you know what they say about money? It attracts the best."

"I don't smoke," Lek says. "But *he* does."

"Do you, darling?" Pi-Oon says, looking at me. "Don't worry, I won't tell the cops." More giggles.

Naturally I refuse, but while Pi-Oon is getting his kit out from a box in the corner of the hut, Lek whispers to me that his friend is even more loose-tongued on grass than he is on alcohol. If someone doesn't smoke with him, though, he'll get self-conscious. I am also amazed to see Pi-Oon produce a homemade vaporizer, using a soldering iron stuck into the top of a large bell jar from which a long transparent tube emerges.

"I'm *very* health conscious," Pi-Oon explains. "My father was a chain-smoker, and I had to watch him die, poor lamb. I said to myself, Pi-Oon, you're never going to smoke *anything* in your life, *ever* again, but they say the vaporizer is totally safe. I got the instructions on how to make it from the Internet."

He plugs the soldering iron into a socket, and within seconds a little wire basket of marijuana has started fuming inside the jar. Pi-Oon takes a couple of tokes, offers it to Lek, who refuses, and passes it to me. I have never used a vaporizer before and simply suck as if it were a joint, taking it all down as far as the esophagus and beyond. There is very little odor or taste, so I think it cannot be very strong and is maybe not exactly export quality as Pi-Oon insists, so I take a couple more tokes, which amazes Pi-Oon. "Wow! *Well*, you're a real smoker, I can tell. Frankly, any one of those puffs would have been enough for me." He takes a surprisingly modest toke himself, before passing it back. To be honest, I'm a little frustrated that the stuff doesn't seem to have much effect, so I suck up a few more bottles of fumes, then sag against the wall. I know that I've misjudged the strength of the product when the guy in the mural starts to play the saxophone and I can hear one of the riffs from *Blade Runner.*

"Paul," I hear myself saying in English, "I'm so impressed with your decision to reject the materialism of contemporary culture in favor of a more spiritual lifestyle." Lek giggles while Gauguin seems to be giving me a perplexed look. "But tell me, how do you make them move?" It's true, the saxophonist on the wall is swinging his instrument up and down while he belts out the meanest version of "Bye Bye Blackbird" I've ever heard. Now I realize it is the colors that are playing the tune, the complex structures of tropical russets, extravagant sunsets, overripe jackfruit, heavy brown men and women who seem to have only half emerged from the earth, the cries of the human spirit that has trapped itself in matter—all are transmuted into an intense, tangible aural landscape by the sax on the wall. Then Damrong appears. By an extraordinary shake of the kaleidoscope the whole wall swirls and twists until her form emerges. She is topless in a sarong of Tahitian design, and her brown skin fits the color range of the painting perfectly; but her slim body is lithe and Thai, and a superior energy gives her power over those around her. Her black hair is flying, and there is a mystic gleam in her eye. *Hello, Sonchai. What are you doing here?*

"I'll call for a taxi," Lek says, half amused, half ashamed.

8

Of course Lek and I know very well who Pi-Oon's lover is. His mug adorns the pages of the HiSo zines in both Thai and English versions. Here he is with the usual suspects at some ballgown and black-tie function, having his pic taken with deep-cleavage wives of deep-pocket movers and shakers. Round-faced with porcelain skin, laden with filigreed gold on his neck, wrists, and—according to Lek—ankles, he has shrewdly cultivated the banking sector of the aristo circuit, which is said to be the real reason his advertising business thrives. His name is Khun Kosana, and he is known throughout Bangkok as a true *na yai:* big face. His bizarre affair with the poor, ugly, but wildly gifted Pi-Oon has been the talk of the gossip industry for over a year; it seems they get on famously and really are considering a marriage in Canada or Amsterdam, and to everyone's amazment Khun Kosana, the *na yai* playboy par excellence, really does seem to adore his paramour, has paid for all the medical fees pertaining to his gender reassignment, and most incredible of all has so far been faithful to him.

I'm at my desk, thinking that things are falling into place rather well. All I have to do is find a subtle way to put the squeeze on Khun Kosana to find the origin of the Damrong snuff movie. I have no doubt one of the advertising mogul's HiSo buddies earned himself some street cred by giving him a copy; no doubt it's doing the rounds of the jet-set circuit, and so long as I play by the rules (never threaten law, only blackmail), I'll be able to force one of them to reveal the true source. I'll need to have Vikorn behind me in order not to get snuffed myself, of course, but that can be finessed by letting the Colonel do some milking of these expensive cash cows who run the country. All in all it was a good move to get stoned with Gauguin—I'm still thinking of him in that incarnation (which I rarely revisit, I mean the Tahiti lifetime a century ago; it was a mistake, the whole back-to-nature thing; I was a French doctor, which is how I got to know Gauguin, who, as we have seen, has not yet clawed his way out of the third-world trap he set himself over a hundred years ago—but never mind, it's not part of the plot). Now my cell is playing Dylan's "Tonight I'll Be Staying Here with You": it's Lek.

"They're dead," he says. "Both of them."

"They tortured Pi-Oon in front of him, then shot them."

Lek has called a couple of uniform cops to secure the hut while we're waiting for the forensic team, but there isn't going to be anything we don't know already: Pi-Oon, his great prizefighter face still in a howl of agony, his artist's hands twisted and torn, fingernails ripped out, a hole between his eyes and a bigger exit wound at the back of his skull, is propped against the lower part of his self-portrait in the middle of the triptych. Khun Kosana seems to have been executed standing up, because there is a vertical trail of blood on the painting, pointing down to where he is collapsed on the floor. He too bears the entry and exit wounds of a single professional shot.

"Nobody knows anything, of course?" I say to Lek.

"The shots were heard about three this morning. Yesterday evening about seven a tall, well-dressed *farang* paid a visit. He asked someone for directions, so it must have been his first time here. He spoke Thai with a thick English accent." Lek is avoiding my eyes. When I try to bond with him, he says, "I'm going to the *wat*," and leaves me in the hut to wait for the forensic team. When they arrive with their plastic gloves and video equipment, I go to find Lek at the *wat* at the entrance to the shantytown. He is sitting in semilotus facing a gold Buddha on a dais, straight-backed, his eyes closed. I light a bunch of incense to stick in the sand tray, sit with him for half an hour, then leave. In the street outside the *wat* I fish out my cell phone to call Vikorn. When I describe the scene of torture and murder, he grunts; when I tell him one of the victims is the famous playboy Khun Kosana, he says without missing a beat, "It didn't happen."

"But—"

"It didn't happen."

"What about his family and friends?"

"He was tragically hit by an untraceable truck."

I take a deep breath. "Colonel, this is a murder. We're cops."

"This is Thailand, and I got a phone call five minutes ago."

"Just a phone call is all it takes? The one who made the call—how much is he going to pay?"

"Mind your own business."

"You have no sense of responsibility at all?"

"Cut it out, mooncalf. If you hadn't investigated, nobody would have wasted them. If I'm taking money, it's in return for covering for your fuck-ups. Maybe you're the one who needs a course in responsible behavior. Who told you to get so intense about a little old snuff movie in the first place? Nobody cares about that whore except you."

He is using Teflon Voice, preempting all argument. I'll have to use Baker, I'm thinking as I close the phone. He's the only lead left. But does he know anything?

9

Three hours later I take a cab to Soi 23, where Lek is waiting for me on the corner. On the grounds of Baker's apartment building the guard tells us the American *farang* has received three visitors that afternoon, two of them young Thai men who were probably English students, and one a tall, well-dressed Englishman in his early forties. The Englishman stayed for only ten minutes and came away looking concerned.

This time when Baker opens the door to his flat, he is dressed in an open-neck shirt and long white pants. He is barefoot, however. We settle down in his plastic chairs, and I decide to resume where we left off.

"So your wife, Damrong, is deported, you do some jail time, and the next thing that happens is you arrive here in Thailand teaching English as a foreign language. Want to fill me in?"

He shakes his head and frowns. His posture is one of heroic struggle with demonic forces of pride, which he defeats with a theatrical groan. "I'm here because of her, of course."

Stifling an embarrassing sob: "I'm that kind of guy—I'm turned on by life in the raw. I'm not really a jerk, I just live like one. When it comes down to the wire, there's only one kind of woman who can deliver the total experience, and I'm ready to admit that to myself, ready to be humble. I came halfway around the world and stayed four years just for the crumbs she was willing to toss me from time to time, and I'm not even ashamed."

Looking at me with a strange, twisted smile: "I envy heroin addicts. It must be so easy to kick that habit, in comparison to the habit of the most alive woman you've ever met."

"Most alive," Lek repeats, then clamps a hand over his mouth at a stern look from me. Baker's eyes flick now from Lek to me and back again. I let silence tell the story. I'm thinking that if he already knows she's dead, it will be hard to fake a reaction to the news. Lek and I are watching carefully, trying to sift maya from reality. With a slowness that may or may not be theatrical, he grabs the back of a chair and shifts it so that he's looking out of his window while he leans on it.

Softly: "How did she die?"

"What kind of death did you have in mind for her, Mr. Baker?"

His head snaps around to glare at me. "What the hell is that supposed to mean?"

I shrug. "You admitted to feelings of extreme bitterness, to being a kind of emotional slave. The condition of psychological slavery is invariably a precursor to homicidal thoughts. In your fantasies, from time to time, how did you kill her?" He stares, speechless. "I fear my interrogation technique is not quite up to Western standards, Mr. Baker. You must forgive me. You know how we Thai cops are, virtually no training in the finer points of forensic investigation, nothing but our crude third-world intuition to go by—and what little we've been able to glean of human nature in our folksy way. You did dream of killing her from time to time, didn't you?"

I seem to have broken through to another, more interesting Baker when he says, "She was murdered? Yeah, okay. Guilty of homicidal thoughts against her, so long as you include half the johns in Bangkok in that category."

Then all of a sudden another fragment takes over; there is nothing to forewarn us of the flash storm. "Dead? Goddamn it, you people just make me want to puke. You come here to tell a man his ex-wife is dead, and that's it, you just say it like that, like a weather report, like it's just a fact like any other." He is wild-eyed and challenging me with outrage. Perhaps in a newcomer it would have been a convincing response, but this man has been here nearly five years. Finally he makes a show of controlling himself. "Are you going to tell me how she died?"

"First tell me how surprised you are," I say. Just the quirky, dumb question you'd expect from someone like me, right? Hard to answer though.

"How surprised? What kind of question is that?" He studies me for a moment. "Maybe I need a lawyer."

I look around the room. "By all means. They're expensive, though, and it can be quite difficult to find one who, let us say, has your interests at heart. You could spend a long time in jail waiting and then find you have to answer my questions anyway. Up to you."

He thinks about this and says, "I am personally shocked that she is dead, but no one who knew her would be surprised that she met an early end."

"Good," I say, "now we're getting somewhere. What sort of early death would you have envisioned for your ex-wife? Give us the whole story. Take your time."

A pause, a groan, then what looks like an honest response: "Nothing you can't guess. Really."

I let a couple of beats pass while he wrestles with his heart. "When did you last see her?"

"A couple months ago." He raises his eyes to look into mine. "Of course I'm not going to demand a lawyer. For what? You don't have a system of justice—you have a system of extortion. This is a kleptocracy. Everyone who stays here long enough finds that out." I raise my eyes in a question. "So it would give me some comfort if you would disregard some minor infractions, in the interests of bringing her killer to justice." There is no self-consciousness now, no posturing; he's looking for a deal.

"I can't promise because I don't know what you're talking about. I can be very lenient for the right person though."

"How much d'you want?"

"I'm not talking about money. I want information. Everything you know about her life here."

Shocked: "You don't want money?" He sighs and purses his lips. "After they let me out of the penitentiary, I came over here looking for her. I found her working in a bar in Soi Cowboy, run by a cop and his mother. She was quite pleased to see me but explained that our relationship was going to be a little different over here. It was business only. I started to do porn shots of her, mostly soft stuff for some American magazines and the Net. Sometimes it was hard porn—it's a specialist niche these days, anonymous clients put in special requests for a particular girl on the webpage. If the request wasn't too complicated—you know, a blow job or something—I would supply the cock, using a delayed action timer on the camera. That's what we met for. Sometimes I would have the business connection, and sometimes it would come from her. She liked to use me as stud and cameraman because we worked well together. We didn't make a lot that way, but it sure helped supplement my income." He waves a hand at the apartment to indicate the extreme simplicity of his life.

"Webpage?"

A shake of the head. "You won't find it. We would change it from week to week. Punters these days know how to follow the trail, download, and move on. Then the webpage ceases to exist. Some have a twenty-four-hour life cycle." A shrug.

"This was only a sideline for both of you?"

"Sure. She got eighty percent of the dough, but it still wasn't exactly big bucks. We were both working." Looking out the window: "She wasn't the type to stay anywhere for long. I gave up asking her where she was working. She generally liked to move upward though. She said something about a very upmarket men's club, somewhere off Sukhumvit in a side *soi*, but like I say, she never stayed anywhere long. She despised that downmarket bar run by the cop and his mother. She had fun seducing the cop and watching him grovel for the right to lick her cunt—she was hilarious when she was on the rice whiskey. She would give these brilliant imitations of a jerk in love—apparently this cop fell for her real hard." Turning his face to me with a frank, humble smile: "Just like me in the beginning."

Now my head is spinning, blood has rushed to my face, and Lek is wondering why. Perhaps Dan Baker already knows about my affair with Damrong and is needling me, but I doubt it. That would be counterproductive from his point of view. I think he told it straight.

"That'll do for now," I tell him in a tight voice. "I'm keeping your passport for the time being." I'm looking out the window, not able to face him all of a sudden. "I'll issue an official receipt when I get back to the station and have a cop bring it around to you tomorrow."

I give the room a final glance, then remember I've not yet visited the bathroom. He doesn't seem too keen that I should do so; I'm following the line of his discomfort all the way into the cubicle. Jammed into a small space next to the toilet is a tall, cheap-looking set of drawers in a free-standing frame. I open them one by one, aware that he has come to stand in the doorway. Each drawer is full of photographic equipment of what looks like the highest quality. The main object is a sleek, professional-quality Sony movie camera. When I turn to him, a tic flutters under his left eye, and sweat has broken out on his forehead.

"You keep this stuff in the bathroom?"

"Where else? You can see how much space I have."

"Don't leave Bangkok until I say you can, Mr. Baker," I tell him at the door. Now I feel a little impatient with Lek, who suddenly points at Baker's left wrist and asks, "Who gave you that bracelet, Mr. Baker? It's elephant hair, isn't it?" A fine burnished virility aid, Baker looks at it curiously, as if he hasn't thought about it in a while.

"A monk gave it to me a few days ago when I was walking down Sukhumvit. He said it would bring me luck. He wouldn't take any money for it, so I figured he meant what he said." He is as bewildered by Lek's wayward mind as I am. At the door I ask the question I've been saving for last: "Who was the tall well-dressed Englishman who came to see you this afternoon, Mr. Baker?"

I was hoping for some telltale panic reaction to the question, but instead he smiles ironically and says, "A lawyer. He's helping me with an immigration problem."

When we reach the ground floor, I walk casually over to where the guards are playing checkers. They look as if they've not moved for a while—a week at least—but surprise me with a grin and a nod. Without a word the one I bribed takes us around to the back of the building and points up to something on the fifth floor. "That's Baker's window," he explains. Hanging from the window by a rope: a shiny black laptop. "He hung it there at about the time you knocked on his door," the guard explains.

Lek and I look up at the suspended laptop and scratch our heads. "Do you want to hire a ladder?" the guard asks. "Better hurry—he's sure to take it in again now he thinks you're gone."

I negotiate a price to hire both a ladder and a guard with scissors and leave Lek to supervise the operation while I return to Baker's apartment. He is shocked to see me again and cannot disguise the foxy look on his face. I pretend a renewed fascination with the photographic equipment in his bathroom, which keeps his nerves on edge for a good ten minutes, then politely take my leave.

Downstairs Lek is hugging the laptop, beaming. "That was so exciting. I was sure Baker was going to catch the guard at the top of the ladder and kick the ladder away." Lek gives an elegant demonstration of kicking the ladder, apparently while wearing high heels. I give the guard my cell phone number and tell him to keep an eye on the window and call me when there's some reaction from Baker. We're in the back of the cab, halfway to the station, when my phone rings. "He went totally crazy. First he opened the window to pull the rope and saw that the rope had been cut. He stuck his body halfway out the window and seemed to go haywire. Next thing he's down on the ground, below his window, scrabbling around in the dark, as if the thing fell down. Then he saw me looking at him and guessed what happened, and he looked like he'd seen a ghost. I mean, I've never seen anyone go like that. He crouched down against a wall with his head between his hands. I don't know if he was crying or not, but he was very upset."

"Where is he now?"

"Back in his apartment."

Half an hour later he calls again. "That Englishman came, the same as before. He's with him now."

"Describe him again."

"Tall, very fit-looking *farang*, dressed in smart business suit, striped, stiff white collar, and flashy silk tie. Good-looking like a film star."

"Did he speak to you?"

"Sure. I asked him in Thai where he was going. He said to Baker's apartment."

"How was his Thai?"

"Good, with a thick English accent."

I drop Lek off at his apartment building and take the cab home. As soon as I get in, I open the laptop. Judging by the lights below the keyboard, there is enough battery power to boot up, but a PIN number is necessary to access it. I don't know how to bypass the PIN, and I can't risk leaving it with the nerds at the station—Buddha knows what salable images they might find there. I guess I need the FBI.

"I'll need a can opener," she says. "That's what the nerds call them. I'll have them courier one over to me. I should have it by tomorrow."

Chanya has seen my impatience with the computer, and I assume she is staring at me in order to provoke an explanation. When we lock eyes, though, she presses her lips together to make an apologetic face, at the same time as she raises her eyebrows in a question. I grunt. The last thing I feel like doing is hunting around for a supermarket that is open at this time of night.

"Ice cream?"

"No. *Moomah* noodles."

"You're kidding. There's no known form of nutrition in them, you could eat them until you're as round as a football and still die of malnutrition."

"It's what my mum ate when she was pregnant with me."

I extract maximum points by emphasizing how tired I am, then drag on a pair of shorts and a T-shirt. One shop I know for sure will be open is Foodland up in the Nana area, so I take a cab. I see from the cab's dashboard that it is one twenty-nine A.M. All along Sukhumvit food stalls have appeared to cater to hungry hookers and their johns. It's quite a jolly street atmosphere, with people eating or sitting in the door-ways of shops and nattering, telling stories of the night. A few drunken *farang* weave shakily between the stalls, but generally everyone is behaving themselves. When I reach Nana, it's quite crowded with girls who work the go-go bars and have just finished for the night. The supermarket itself serves food at a small bar near the checkout counter, and this is packed too. The aisles of the shop itself are relatively empty, though: only a couple of *farang* men deciding what wine to buy to fin-ish the evening off, some working girls buying provisions to take home with them, and some Thai men shopping for rice whiskey. It takes me a while to find the *moomah* noodles; even the packet is probably better for you to eat than the contents, but who is going to argue with a pregnant wife? I grab five packs, just in case she gets the urge again, chuck them into my plastic basket, and make for the nearest checkout counter when a familiar profile catches my gaze. Of course it could not be her, and anyway she has her back to me so it could be almost any-one; but something in the way she moves . . . you know that Beatles song, *farang*? "Something in the way she moves, attracts me like no other lover"? I have goose bumps on both forearms and shivers down my spine. I don't really want to risk the elaborate maneuver of peering at her while she examines a bag of chilis, so I decide it's late, I'm tired, and I'll feel better in the morning. Proud of myself for kicking the superstition habit, I walk past her to the checkout counter, stack up my five packs of *moomahs*, fish out my wallet—then become aware of the young woman, who has come to stand behind me. Why can't I look at her? Why am I insanely focusing on the pack of chilis she is waiting to buy? Why is my hand holding the five-hundred-baht note shaking like a leaf? The checkout girl has noticed and decided I'm one of those dangerous men of the night. I want her to hurry up with the change, and in my haste to grab it, I knock over one of the noodle packs. Now it is lying on the floor between us, the other shopper and me. Both she and the checkout girl are waiting for me to pick it up—what kind of gentleman am I that I expect a woman to pick up something I've dropped? We're still old-fashioned like that. I manage to avoid her eyes as I bend down, but she permits no such strategy on the way up. Now I am staring into Damrong's face, no doubt about it, down to the last nuance. There is even a familiar, triumphant smile playing over her lips. "Good evening, Detective," she says softly, lowering her lids, feigning shyness.

I'm gibbering. Unable to wait for the plastic bag, I grab the five packs and hug them to me as I make for the door. Naturally, once I'm out in the street, I cannot resist waiting across the road for her to come out of the shop. Twenty minutes pass with no sign of her. Nothing for it, according to the rules of the haunt, but to return to the shop. She is nowhere to be seen. When I ask the checkout girl what happened to the woman who bought a pack of chilis, she gives me that look.

"Thanks," Chanya says with a breezy smile when I reach home. "I'll make some right now. Want to join me?"

"No," I say equally breezily, "I'm not hungry."

When we lie down to sleep, I close my eyes and observe my mind slip into denial. *Of course, it didn't happen, right? Right. Such things are impossible, they are the imaginative creations of bored and ignorant peasants, right? Right. You're only half Thai, for Buddha's sake, you don't need to be sucked into this primitive sorcery, right? Right.* By the time I fall asleep, the incident has been dismantled and stored somewhere dark and deep.

10

I am at my desk watching Lek weave between the other desks on his way to me. He is carrying a plastic bag of iced orange tea, of a hue I associate with Chernobyl, and sips from time to time from a straw sticking out of the top, which is tied with an elastic band. I note with approval that he avoids the desk of Detective Constable Gasorn, who has developed a crush on him. Well, perhaps not a crush exactly, for Gasorn's private e-mails to my assistant, while affectionate, hint at something more radical than a passionate affair. There are statistics and theories in great measure concerning the tendency, troubling to some, of young Thai men to change sex. In a nutshell, the ancient system, by which a Thai man has to worry about Everything while his Thai wife gets to live on a more hospitable planet at his expense, may be breaking down. DC Gasorn is one of those who incline to the view that it would be better to have the lot chopped off and find a sponsor: let some sucker of sterner stuff fight it out with market forces. He's not sure, though, and I've instructed Lek not to talk to him or reply to his e-mails. Lek survives only because I protect him and Vikorn protects me. If it looks as if we're starting a subversive fashion, Vikorn will hang us both out to dry.

Off duty, Lek has started rolling his buttocks *à la* Marilyn Monroe, but he controls his gait in the station. Nevertheless, he is unable to avoid a quick glance at DC Gasorn on the opposite side of the room. The more he takes of the estrogen, the less defense he possesses against idle flattery. On the other hand, he's coping much better in so many ways these days. He has passed through the ordeal of accepting that even in Thailand he is a freak in the eyes of the world; now he's much harder inside and stares down villains effortlessly: gender reassignment has been good for his career, in a sense. Not that he'll ever get promoted beyond humble constable.

When he reaches my desk, he takes the straw out of his mouth long enough to *wai* me with the straw somehow—miraculously—held between his hands. I tell him I want to know where Damrong was working at the time she died, and hand him a photograph. It must be the most recent, because the FBI showed me how to make a still from the video, using her laptop. The face in the pic has about three minutes left to live. Lek will flash it around the bars, starting with Soi Cowboy, then up to Nana, then across to Pat Pong; if he hasn't gotten anywhere by then, we'll have to dig deeper, perhaps try the escort agencies. I guess about twenty percent of women who are eligible to sell their bodies in Bangkok do exactly that; it makes for a big haystack in which to go looking for a needle. Damrong was special, though; people will remember her. Me, for example. I remember her very well. I think there must be quite a few other men who might be able to help with inquiries. I'm thinking about saving time by doing some of the footwork myself, when Colonel Vikorn calls me into his office.

On my way up the stairs I'm preparing a summary of the Damrong case, on the assumption that the Colonel has finally developed an interest in it. When I'm sitting opposite him, with the big anticorruption poster behind his chair and a little to the right, and the photograph of His Majesty the King in full regalia immediately above his head, I start into my report. Vikorn imposes a mask of patience while I speak, but it doesn't last long. When I tell him about Baker's high-tech equipment in his squalid little rented room, and the laptop I stole, he sees an opportunity to cut short my report.

"So, it was him. You've cracked the case in less than a day. No wonder you're our best detective."

"But he wasn't even in Thailand when she was killed, and I haven't checked the laptop yet."

Vikorn gives a benevolent smile and wags a finger. "Don't spoil a great case with too much perfectionism. Of course Baker did it. He knew her, he'd been married to her, he'd pimped for her, he'd sold her porn for her. Why don't you charge him, offer him a deal in exchange for a confession? I could probably get the death sentence reduced to eight years if he gives us the names of the accomplices. If he resists, you can copy that snuff movie onto his laptop. It's a wrap."

"The laptop will show the date when the movie was copied."

"So don't let the defense team examine the laptop."

"Suppose he didn't do it?"

"Then you've imprisoned an honest man. How likely is that?"

I don't want to argue. He knows I'm not satisfied and that I'll work my buns off before I charge Baker, and in his eyes this makes me profoundly pathetic. Any self-respecting Thai cop would be in a girlie bar congratulating himself on having solved the case in a matter of hours. My Colonel doesn't much care if Baker did it or not—he's the kind of *farang* who gets into trouble anyway, adds no value to Thai society, and would probably benefit from a third-world course in social responsibility at the university of Lard Yao.

Now that he's got my business out of the way, he rubs his hands.

"Sonchai, I think we're making progress with our project. I had someone check out what that Jap Yammy is up to in his new studio. Did I tell you I rented a property in Chinatown next to the river?"

"No. That was quick."

"You got me all excited with that report in *The New York Times*. I had no idea there might be more dough in porn than in *yaa baa*."

"Great."

He leans forward confidentially, the way he does when he needs a favor. "Sonchai, I'm appointing you as my eyes and ears. I'm sorry to have to add to your duties, but you're the only cop in District Eight who might have an idea how a good porn movie gets made. I want you to pay regular visits to Yammy, make friends with him. Will you do that for me?"

No one says no to Vikorn, so I nod. Out in the corridor I figure I should probably consider myself lucky—at least I'm allowed to carry on with the Damrong case undisturbed. Down in the canteen, over a 7UP, it occurs to me that it might be fun to take the FBI on a field trip to the river. Before that, though, I want to check out Baker's laptop. I tell Manny I'm going to the river on a special assignment for Vikorn and I'm not to be disturbed. I call the FBI at the Grand Britannia, who has just received the gadget she calls the can opener, then call my partner, Chanya, on her cell phone. She is just returning from the temple so she should be back by the time I get home.

As it happens, both women have arrived at our little house before me. This is the first time they've been alone together for any length of time, and I'm curious to see how they've been relating. So far each has been in awe of the other. Chanya can hardly believe that a woman can cope with the world in such a masculine way and achieve such authority and power; the FBI still gapes at the effortless elegance with which Chanya walks, talks, and smiles; she really cannot understand why my true love isn't in Hollywood making billions. Nor is she sure her serenity is entirely terrestrial. *Nothing bothers her,* the FBI complained after the first couple of meetings. *She has the sangfroid of a leopard.* And then, of course, Chanya is heavily pregnant, which mystic state the FBI seems to find disturbing.

Sangfroid translates literally as *luak yen:* same phrase, same concept. I thought about that. The two most important women in my life have *luak yen* to an unusual degree: my mother, Nong, and Chanya. The thought leads naturally to the Third Woman. Damrong possessed an effortless sangfroid: cruel, enticing, immense, a real leopard. But there was nothing petty about her. Both my mother and I expected her to act superior to the other girls when she first came to work for us, because she so obviously outclassed them; not so. She humbled herself, bought them presents on their birthdays, showed many kindnesses, gave free advice to those who wanted to ply their trade overseas, loved them. The general consensus was that she possessed *jai dee,* or good heart, in great measure. My stomach is fluttering because I don't know how I'm going to react to scenes of her naked and performing for other men. "Hi," I say, "I'm home."

At some level I was expecting them to be talking about me. It's a little humbling to find them huddled together in the kitchen listening to the radio. The program is called *Thinking in Modern Ways,* and for Chanya listening to it has become a religious ritual. She is translating for the FBI: "You see, instead of just starting cooking and then looking for all the ingredients, you gather all the ingredients together first and put them in proper order on the bench. Now they're talking about washing clothes. Instead of just putting all the clothes in a pile, you use three laundry baskets: one for whites, one for colors, one for delicates. See?"

Chanya turns to Kimberley with a triumphant beam. The FBI has trouble hiding her confusion. She knows Chanya is no fool, so why is it necessary to have instructions on such primitive time-and-motion issues? "Great," she says. "Efficiency makes life easier." She's relieved that I've appeared and looks at me expectantly. How to explain that a nation which has been surviving on intuition and custom for a thousand years doesn't pick up Aristotelian logic just like that? The revelation that "A cannot be not-A" does not come naturally to undivided minds.

It's easier to change the subject. I go to a suitcase in the space under the stairs where I have locked Baker's laptop. Both women stop to stare when I take it out. I bought a charger for it in Pantip Plaza so now I plug it into a socket in the living room. So they *had* been talking about me after all. The FBI has explained that the laptop will likely contain clips of Damrong performing with other men. The looks on their faces are a fine expression of puerile curiosity: *How's he going to take it? How much suffering are we going to see?* We don't have any chairs, so they huddle around me on the floor at the coffee table on which I have placed the computer. The FBI fishes a gadget out of her pocket that is about six inches long with a plug that fits into the USB port of the computer. The FBI switches on the gadget at the same time as pressing the boot button on the laptop. An LCD display on the gadget, which has space for about thirty digits, starts racing through numbers, letters, and punctuation marks at lightning speed. Eventually it stops at: {{jack***rongdam\\\29===forty. I never would have thought of that. Now the Windows icons come alive, and we are welcomed with the cheery music.

In the MS Explorer screen I experiment with a few files before I realize that Baker uses the prefix X for his porn stuff. "Original," the FBI says.

A double-click, and there we are: a close-up of Damrong with an erect penis in her mouth. Probably Baker's, for the clip, which lasts only forty seconds, seems experimental in nature. It is quite a jolt to be taken so rapidly into the unbearable frisson of a beautiful woman practicing an obscenity with such joie de vivre. She grins at the camera whenever she takes it out of her mouth. "I'm okay," I tell the two women, who are even more interested in my reaction than in the porn.

"She's not even pretty," Chanya says. This is not merely a reflex of jealousy; I think Chanya sees a very different image on the monitor: a common Cambodian face, browner than Chanya's, with the somewhat pouting lips of the Khmer. To me Damrong's is a gaunt, haughty beauty, whereas Chanya's is full-bodied and jolly. But the FBI too is shaking her head. "Only men think that's irresistible," she grunts.

We go through all of Baker's X files, starting with the shortest. In about ten minutes we have covered Damrong's full sexual repertoire, without observing any demonstration of passion on her part. The men's faces rarely appear; when they do, it is by way of hairy pink foils to her performance. I have shrugged, inwardly, and bought myself a certain amount of cheap immunity thereby. I am even congratulating myself on my Buddhist self-control when I start into the first of the two longer clips.

The atmosphere is quite different. One senses immediately that this recording has been made furtively, without the john's knowledge. At first the couple move in and out of camera range, until Damrong has maneuvered her client to a specific position on the bed. Here she is giving oral pleasure with great enthusiasm; indeed, there is an intensity to her performance that hacks a hole in my guts. (Sexual jealousy started in the reptilian incarnations and is firmly embedded in the brain stem; its distorting effect on the personality has been studied for millennia.) "You okay, Sonchai?" the FBI says. Chanya stares at me in disgust: "He's still in love with her, look at him."

"I'm okay," I croak. "Really."

"So why have you turned green?" my pregnant partner wants to know.

"I haven't" is the best I can manage by way of reply. I'm struggling with an internal tornado during the first five minutes of the clip, though, and don't start to come out of it until we begin to get flashes of the man's face.

"Look," Kimberley says, "look how she's moving under him to bring his face in range of the camera."

It is very subtly done, each pelvic shift on the bed made to look like a reaction to the exquisite torture of sexual frenzy. Now he is in full view. It does not help that he is a handsome *farang* with a strong jaw, auburn hair, hazel eyes, and a masterful manner. "You sucker," I mutter, avoiding the women's eyes. "That's the way she worked," I explain hoarsely. "She's let him think he's dominated her mind, that he's so good and his cock's so big she's totally fallen for him, body and soul."

"That's not a technique she invented, Sonchai," the FBI advises. Chanya nods in agreement, still maintaining a sneer for my benefit. It's the postcoital sequence that grabs all three pairs of eyeballs, though.

"Amazing," the FBI says.

"Genius," from Chanya, former bar queen.

I'm rubbing my eyes. "Play it again," Chanya instructs.

"Real tears," from the FBI.

It's true. Damrong has managed a delicate, reluctant trickle from both retinas, which she quickly, bravely wipes away. She pretends she cannot look him in the eye when she says, "Tom, you're just amazing." A slight wobble around the chin, then: "I don't think I can stand the thought of you with another woman. I just can't."

"Don't worry about that," Tom says with a lump in his throat. "There wouldn't be any fucking point, would there?" Now his eyes too are weepy. They blend the salt for a while, before starting again. This time she manages to get both his face and groin in camera range while she works on him.

"Did she use that trick on you?" Chanya wants to know. So does the FBI, to judge by the way she's looking at me.

"No," I say, not sure how I feel. "Not at all. I guess he has a lot more money than me."

"Hm," the FBI says thoughtfully, "kind of over the top, somehow, unless she wanted more than just money."

"Like what? Not marriage, surely."

"No," Kimberley agrees, "not that."

I take a deep breath. "Last one," I say.

It is the same room, but the atmosphere is quite different. The man is clearly Oriental, and that is all we know about him for the first seven minutes. Damrong has adapted perfectly to her ruthless Asian master, absorbing his remorseless thrusts with helpless cries and groans. When he becomes too aggressive, she bites him hard on one hand: a warning shot or an invitation to still more combative sex? Certainly, without antique fragments of the courtly love tradition to cloud his judgment, this client is not so easy to maneuver. When she finally has his mug in the camera lens, Chanya and I exchange a glance, and I freeze the frame. There he is, face turned beautifully in full frontal ecstasy while she works his member. The sexual angle is suddenly quite irrelevant, however.

"What?" the FBI wants to know.

"I'll need a still of that," I say.

Kimberley shrugs, plays with the software for a moment, downloads the still, and folds her arms. "Will someone tell me what's so different about this guy? I mean, I can see he's Asian with a lot of Chinese blood. Quite a dish, actually."

"It's Khun Tanakan," Chanya whispers, careful, even in the midst of her contempt, to use the respectful *Khun* in accordance with feudal law.

"Who?"

"He's big in banking," I explain with a gulp. "About as big as they get. We're talking HiSo all the way to the top of the pyramid. Him and his buddies control the economy. All big deals go through them."

Chanya and I switch to Thai for a telling moment:

Chanya: *What are you going to do? This could get you killed.*
Me: *I know that.*
Chanya: *You'll have to tell Colonel Vikorn.*
Me, gloomily: *How safe d'you think that will be? You know what he'll want to do.*
Chanya: *I'm pregnant, Sonchai. I don't want to bring up our child all on my own.*
Me, passing a hand over my brow: *I'll have to think about it. I'll do whatever's safest.*
Chanya: *Start by getting that laptop out of here. I'm scared, Sonchai, I really am.*
Me: *Okay.*

Now I'm hurriedly unplugging the laptop and sliding it into its case under the gaze of the FBI.

"Wow," Kimberley says when I'm finished and about to leave the house, all in less than five minutes. "When you guys spook, you really spook. How about letting me in on some background?"

"In the cab," I say.

Now Kimberley and I are standing in the street, hailing a passing taxi. Chanya has remained in the house. "I'll let you off at the Grand Britannia," I tell the FBI.

"Where are you going with that thing?"

"The police station," I grunt.

In the back of the cab I explain, "Damrong had that stuff shot for blackmail purposes. There can be no other explanation."

"I agree. So what?"

"If she had started putting on the screws, Tanakan will have his people looking all over the city."

"But you're a cop. Doesn't that count for anything over here?"

I smile ironically. "Sure."

"So?"

"So, Chanya's right. The smart thing has to be to tell Vikorn. At least I'll have him on my side that way."

"Why is that a difficult decision to make?"

I turn to her. "What d'you think he'll want to do with the video?"

I think the FBI has mastered this little cultural conundrum by the time I let her out at her hotel. She pauses while the door is open and pops her head inside for a moment. "Kind of strange, don't you think?"

"What is?"

"That two or three easy steps is all it needed to get you this far. You did no more than the obvious, right?"

"Looked up Damrong's name on the database, which led to Baker."

"Which led to the most dangerous scoop of your career. Strange. I don't know about Bangkok, but policing is rarely that simple stateside."

On the way to the station, with the laptop next to me on the seat, I'm thinking, *Simple?* I fish out my cell phone to call Vikorn on his. He's cavorting at one of his clubs not far from the station. When I tell him in coded language what I have sitting next to me, he says he'll get dressed and be with me in thirty minutes. At the station I'm so nervous about the laptop, I don't release it from my grip. Once I read about a courier who brought two bottles of Mouton Rothschild '45 from London to Hong Kong and for secuirty reasons had the briefcase containing them cuffed to his wrist. Well, this is the porn industry's equivalent of Mouton Rothschild '45. I have to wait about an hour before I get the call: he's arrived.

We're sitting in his office now, having carefully reviewed Damrong's performance with Khun Tanakan. It's around midnight. When Vikorn turns to me, I cannot read the expression on his face. There is a frown of sorts, but it is complex and nuanced by what might be a smile flickering over his lips from time to time. I've known him so long, though, all I need do is check his eyes: bright and shiny. He speaks very softly, like a lover. There is gratitude and caress in his tone.

"Sonchai, I might need a witness."

"Yes?"

"Someone with the smarts to understand what's going on, and at the same time the foresight to realize that any breach of confidence could be fatal."

"I'm not following, Colonel," I say.

"You know the way our country is, Sonchai, *ti-soong, ti-tam.*" The reference is to the Thai feudal system, called high-low or, if you prefer, top and bottom. "If I do this alone, he'll find a way of pulling rank."

Light breaks in my frontal lobes. I feel a delicious frisson of fear and excitement. "You want me to be there when you put the squeeze on Khun Tanakan?"

Vikorn raises a finger to his lips. "He won't know you're there."

"Why don't you video it?"

"Because he will insist on meeting in his office."

"So how can I be present?"

"You'll come as my assistant and bodyguard. He will not allow you into the room during negotiations, so I'll be wired. You'll have the recorder. You will also listen over a headset so you can claim to be a live witness if things go wrong. We'll make it look like you're listening to music—what are those stupid things called?"

"iPods."

"Right. You'll be one of those switched-on cops, like in the recruitment posters."

"This could put my life at risk, Colonel."

He raises his eyebrows, then looks away. "Ten percent for the relief of poverty."

"Twenty."

"Done."

I shrug. If it is the Buddha's will that Khun Tanakan's wealth be more equitably distributed, who am I to argue? Anyway, I wouldn't want to miss Vikorn doing what he does best.

"You better tell me about the case again," Vikorn says. "It's a murder investigation, isn't it, or have I got that wrong?"

"Sort of."

"Anyway, one thing is for sure. We can't let this Baker character hang out unprotected. Have someone arrest him on pornography charges. I want him in the cells, where I can keep an eye on him."

"Okay," I say, "okay."

As I'm preparing to go home, with most of the station in darkness, I realize I've not given much thought to Baker these last few hours. Hanging the laptop out of his window like that was humorously amateurish, the kind of dumb reaction of a born loser. But losers scare easily, and now I know what is on the hard disk. I call the guard at Baker's apartment building.

"He left with a rucksack more than an hour ago, after that Englishman left."

"Why didn't you call me?"

"You only bribed me for one call." I groan, hang up, then dial the station operator to get me Immigration.

"He can't get far without his passport," a cheery voice advises.

"He's running for his life. Maybe he has a forged passport. Maybe he bought a spare one in Kaosan Road."

"Okay, send me a good copy of his passport mug shot in the morning, and we'll send it out in digital form to all major entry points."

I say something sarcastic that repeats the words *all major* and *in the morning*. Thais don't react well to sarcasm, though, and he grunts noncommittally before closing the phone. I call Vikorn, who promises to kick ass; after all, he's the one who wants Baker arrested.

11

I expected Vikorn to use his Bentley, which only goes to show how vulgar and unsophisticated I am. Of course, he is visiting the great Khun as Humble Cop, so we sit in the back of a particularly banged-up patrol car. Fortunately, the journey lasts only ten minutes, which is just about the upper limit of the Colonel's tolerance as we bounce around on the torn-up backseat. He is in full police colonel uniform, though, and looks quite trim in the brown tunic with gold shoulder boards. Throughout the journey he has been making curious, delicate hand gestures, which are an expression of the infinite subtlety of his mind. I follow him into the vast lobby of the bank. He uses charm, not authority, on the receptionist, who makes a call. From the look on her face when she puts the phone down, the instruction must be to get the two cops out of the banking hall and into some private room, pronto. We are taken in a lift to an oak-and-green-leather conference room on a high floor, where we sit at the board table. Normally, one would expect a secretary to appear at this stage, but Tanakan didn't get where he is today without knowing how to play every gambit of the game. The door opens, and there is the man himself. The Colonel and I both stand immediately, hands held together at our foreheads in a high *wai*.

The Khun shows his humility by giving us a high *wai* back. This cookie is way too smart to try to defend the indefensible.

Chinese genes are taken for granted among Thai high society, especially in banking. Khun Tanakan's porcelain skin, small intense dark eyes—more slitted than those of an ethnic Thai—jet-black hair, sophisticated manners, and beautifully cut suit all place him at the highest level of Thai-Chinese movers and shakers. But Tanakan has something extra: surely his forefathers were not all diminutive Chiu Chow from the Swatow region of fishing folk, for he is almost six feet tall, indicative of ancestors from the north, Manchuria perhaps. It is nearly impossible to imagine uncontrollable passion in this man, but I've seen Baker's video; I have watched that intense, focused ambition morph into a lust of reptilian intensity. In his early fifties, he owns an excellent physique and—ref. the video—a smooth ivory member of respectable dimensions.

"Allow me to introduce my assistant Detective Jitpleecheep," Vikorn is saying. At the subtlest shift of the banker's eyes, Vikorn adds, "He will wait here, or perhaps in your own suite, while we chat."

Tanakan nods. Graciously: "He can sit wherever he pleases. My secretary has her own office. He can sit there, or he can stay here."

"I think he would prefer your secretary's hospitality," Vikorn says, thinking of the range of his equipment.

"Yes," the banker says, turning to me with a smile of such warmth and hospitality, I could be his favorite nephew. Once in his suite, he introduces me to his secretary at the same time as he shows Vikorn into his office, then firmly closes the door.

She is, I am afraid, quite amazingly attractive. If Tanakan is banging her (which I bet Wall Street against a Thai mango he is), you have to wonder why he needed Damrong.

Or do you? Her long black hair floats on the air when she moves, exactly like a shampoo advertisement. She is dressed in the very latest HiSo business combination (black and white with a dash of color in the jewelry). I'm sure that's Van Cleef and Arpels distributing subtly perfumed vectors into the air-conditioning. She does not make a single move, or even blink, without reference to some beautician's code of conduct, and she seems able to type. On the other hand, I have my own insight into the kind of service Damrong provided to the master banker, the likes of which might have shocked this girl into confessing all to her mother; unlikely that she could satisfy Tanakan's darker needs.

Her instructions include seducing me, at least to the point of bringing me to heel. She has never flirted with a cop before, though, and is having trouble covering her revulsion. I have not helped her dilemma by fishing out my iPod and my Bluetooth earpiece and lounging on the Italian leather sofa under the porcelain lions with my feet stretched out like the yobcop she had me down as from the start.

"Welcome to my humble office," Tanakan is saying in my right ear.

"It is a great honor, Khun Tanakan," Vikorn says. "I don't think I've ever seen an office of such beauty. Your taste is impeccable, Khun Tanakan."

"Oh, you must not be so modest, Colonel. What am I? A banker, a moneyman. Compared to the service a senior police officer of your caliber renders to society, I am the one who should be congratulating you."

"Ah, Khun Tanakan is too kind. Let us be frank, we belong to different classes. You are porcelain, and I am earthenware."

"Even if I were to accept that admirably modest statement, Colonel, I would have to add the rider that when porcelain collides with earthenware, it is the porcelain that suffers the most damage."

"I was coming to that," Vikorn says softly.

Meanwhile Tanakan's secretary has started to worry that she might not be following instructions to the letter. She has found an excuse to stand up, turn to the side, inhale, and square her shoulders; her breasts are, of course, perfect, but what am I supposed to do about it? Now she has emerged fully from behind her desk and sees an urgent need to tidy up the glossy magazines on the coffee table just in front of the sofa. She frowns in concentration with *Fortune* in one hand, then finds she has to explain herself by turning to me with a confused smile. When even that fails to bring me to my knees, she swallows before speaking. "I can't remember where this goes," she says sweetly. More than ever I can see why Tanakan needed Damrong.

"Of course," Vikorn is saying, "there is an attraction between opposites, as the Buddha taught."

"Correct," Tanakan admits.

"It goes without saying that humble earthenware feels awe, admiration, even passion for porcelain, not to mention envy, but the attraction that porcelain feels for earthenware is less well documented."

"Colonel Vikorn's forensic genius is well known. Your insight into even the subtlest shades is amazing."

"Of course, what the world does not know is the true nature of the service rendered to society by men like you. All day and most of the night you are laboring to keep our economy healthy. At Khun Tanakan's level, the pressures are enough to kill a lesser man. You must have some rest and recreation, perhaps of a kind not entirely accepted by piety and ignorance."

"Not only is the Colonel a great policeman, he is a connoisseur of human nature and the embodiment of compassion."

"I like to practice compassion whenever possible," Vikorn says. "However, is it not one of the great insights of the Buddha that even monks need to be sustained? Even compassion needs material help."

"Certainly. A great deal of help, and it is my deepest wish that I might be able to contribute in some small way."

"For example," Vikorn says, "suppose at this very moment a servant entered this office, perhaps an ignorant and uneducated young woman, and in the process of cleaning dislodged that beautiful vase, which, let us say, is about to fall unless a person of practical ability were there to see the danger and save it."

A pause. Tanakan replies, "Such a service of compassion would be rewarded to the value of the vase and beyond."

"What is the value of the vase, Khun Tanakan?"

"It is a long time since I had it valued. The Colonel is no amateur when it comes to evaluating such items, however. What value would the Colonel put on it?"

"May I?"

"Certainly."

I assume Vikorn is now holding the vase. "Look how perfectly the potter designed these dragons more than a thousand years ago. No one in this modern age would have that kind of skill and patience, much less such an eye for beauty. Exquisite. I would say a million dollars, wouldn't you?"

An audible sigh of relief. "Certainly, I think the Colonel has valued the vase with great precision. A million dollars, no doubt about it."

"I'm afraid Khun Tanakan misunderstands," Vikorn says with irritating humility. "I was referring to each of the dragons being certainly of the value of one million dollars."

Tanakan, dully: "How many are there?"

"Quite a lot, Khun Tanakan, quite a lot."

"Would the Colonel do me the great service of counting them?"

"Not today, Khun Tanakan, not today. I would need to study the vase in much greater depth to be able to make an assessment."

Voice cracking a little: "Greater depth? I am afraid I do not understand."

"Well, Khun Tanakan is known to be a very prominent collector of such objets d'art. Therefore would he agree with me that two vases may look and even be identical and yet one may fetch a far greater price because of the stories associated with it? Is that not so? Fame, even notoriety, adds so much false value these days, like Elvis Presley's guitar. Is it not so?"

"I am afraid I am no longer following Colonel Vikorn's brilliant train of thought."

A polite cough. "Suppose we change the analogy somewhat. Suppose that the servant girl herself were holding it up high and threatening to smash it. Certainly Khun Tanakan would, in such circumstances, be entitled to take whatever measures necessary to protect his property."

"Yes?"

"On the other hand, if Khun Tanakan's measures were unfortunately to result in the untimely death of the girl . . ."

A strange silence. "Death of the girl?"

"I am afraid so, Khun Tanakan. I am profoundly sorry to be bringing such sad news at such a time. I think it would be insensitive of me to attempt to evaluate your exquisite vase at this moment. Another day, if Khun Tanakan will be gracious enough to spare the time?"

Defeated: "Whenever the Colonel wishes. I am at your disposal." A hesitation, then: "Is the Colonel aware that I was in Malaysia on business for the whole of last week?"

"I was not aware of that, Khun Tanakan."

"Might that be a factor in reducing the value of the vase?"

"It might, Khun Tanakan, it might. Clearly, the whole valuation needs mature consideration. Good afternoon, Khun Tanakan."

"Please, let me show you out."

As her boss opens the door, the secretary leans toward me to offer the most brazen come-on I've seen outside of the Game.

In the back of the old patrol car, Vikorn says, "How did I do?"

"Brilliant as usual. You saved his face with that vase thing. But he can say he never admitted anything."

"Sure, he could say that in court and bribe the judge to make sure he got away with it. But nobody would ever believe a word he says again, especially in the international banking community, and he loves being Mr. Big-in-Banking more than he loves life."

Vikorn and I look out of separate windows while thinking the same thought.

"Was he convincing?"

"About not knowing the girl was dead? Unclear—he's so *luak yen*, anything he says is going to sound artificial. And he's probably telling the truth about being in Malaysia last week. Anyway, what does it matter? The point was to show him there is more than an indiscretion for him to deal with—there's a corpse as well. I'm selling absolution from a higher crime." He passes a hand over his great wise head. "Tell you what, Sonchai. This case is getting to be one of your greatest gifts to me, and that was just so much fun with Tanakan. How about I give you *twenty-one* percent for charity?"

"Fine."

"Oh, I forgot to ask. Have you been down to the river to see Yammy yet?"

"Not yet. I'm still looking for Baker, remember?"

Vikorn grunts. "Oh, I forgot to tell you. We found him."

"We did? That was quick."

My Colonel taps his forehead. "Some of us are still cops, Sonchai. I told Immigration to identify all those crossings to Cambodia that don't yet have isometric software to check mug shots. There are only five, and only one of those is commonly known to *farang* crooks. So I told the boys over there it was worth a hundred thousand baht." His smile is the embodiment of wisdom and compassion. "Motivation is everything in human resources. I had to let them soften him up a bit, as part of the bribe. He should be pretty compliant by the time you reach him." A couple of beats pass while he wrestles with irritation caused by the upholstery. "No hurry—he isn't going anywhere. I want you to check up on Yammy before you go."

12

When Superman morphs into Godot, you can be sure you have reached a deeper, more nuanced level of the American initiation: ask the Iraqis. It's been one excuse after another from my biological father, aka Superman. I contacted him more than a year ago, in the teeth of outraged objections from Nong ("If he wanted to know us, he would have got in touch decades ago"), and to my astonishment he replied with true Yankee enthusiasm and promised to visit as soon as his legal practice gave him a break. Since then it's been one excuse after another. Nong has begun to doubt that he really intends to come see us at all, and now we've just received an e-mail to say he's had to postpone again on the advice of his doctor. We're in the Old Man's Club at about six-thirty in the evening, and Nong is ranting about *farang* men in general and him in particular: "Why do they make these stupid promises they don't intend to keep, as if we're children who can't take reality straight? This is the problem with their whole culture—they think the rest of the world is as childish as they are. A Thai man would have told us to get lost, and we would have forgotten about him by now."

We are sitting at a table near the bar that is empty except for Marly, who is taking a break from her new porn career with Yammy, and

Henri the Frenchman, who has sneaked in early because he's heard that Marly is here. Henri is one of those who decided tragically early in life that they wanted to be an author and didn't notice the passage of time until it was too late. Now he is short, bald, and forty-three. As is often the case with literary genius, especially the unpublished sort, Henri has no disposable income at all and just about makes ends meet through a little English-to-French translation work over the Net, which he considers a serious threat to his psychic health and intolerable for more than an hour a day ("another fucking microwave manual, *mon Dieu*, I don't have to translate the *fuckeur*. I know by heart a fucking large fucking potato takes *cinq minutes*, and if you wrap it in aluminum, you can expect a wonderful little firework display with lots of fine crackles and pops—there are days when I would give my *membre virile* for a little ambiguity, *double entendre*, obscure literary reference, even a well-placed adjective, *nom de Dieu*"), and lives in a tiny room on the notorious Soi 26, a stone's throw from the still more notorious Klong Toey area (they almost pay you to live there). He is, for reasons of impecuniosity, therefore not the most popular customer among the girls, which might explain the pining quality of his prose. He does, though, to give him his due, own not a little of the elegance of the nineteenth-century Paris he so much wanted to inhabit and when sauced can charm them with his silver tongue:

Henri to Marly (I suspect the secret heroine of his perpetual work in progress): "When they told me you were going to be here tonight, I abandoned my work and rushed over."

"*Lork?*"

"Yes, and what is more, this anguish seems to have sharpened my perception, because when I saw you, I experienced all over again that joy, that leap of recognition which I experienced the very first moment I set eyes on you."

"*Lork?*"

"And I even love the way you say *lork*. On the lips of another Thai woman it is just as dreary as that pathetic English word *really*, but from you it possesses the intangible quality of nirvana."

"Do you want me tonight? I have time for a quick one, before I start filming down by the river."

Henri forces his features into an exaggerated beam. "I'm saving up.

Three more microwave manuals and five DVD players, and you will be mine, *chérie*. On the other hand, why don't you extend to me a little credit? The orders are in, I just have to do the work."

Marly, who thanks to Yammy's irresponsible encouragement has set her sights on Hollywood, raises her eyes to the ceiling in disgust and turns away. I smile at her and invite her to join us, in the hope it will put an end to Nong's moaning. "How's the filming going?"

"Fine, I think. Yammy's *ting-tong*—I mean, the guy is *totally* nuts—but he really knows what he's doing." She checks her watch.

"Give me a *ting-tong* Jap any day against a two-faced *farang*," Nong growls. I feel sad because I know where her anger comes from. She didn't expect much from renewed contact with the young American soldier she fell in love with more than thirty years ago, only a certain belated sharing, a pride in the son they made together—I haven't turned out that bad after all, compared to most *leuk kreung* from the Vietnam War—a chat about old times. It's his meanness of spirit she resents with its racist implication: would he have been so neglectful of a white American girl? Marly looks at me, and I raise my hands to convey helplessness. Luckily, at that moment Greg the Australian walks in. Nong has the same soft spot for him as I have for Henri, and she gives him a big welcoming smile. He responds with an inept *wai* that makes Nong grin and shake her head. Without waiting for his order, she goes behind the bar to open a cold bottle of Foster's and hands it to him without adding it to his slate; she is using this gesture to change her mood. "Love the way you look after me," Greg says. "You're better than twelve mums." The idea of someone having twelve mothers tickles Nong's funny bone, and she cackles at him.

A word about Greg. Endowed by nature with a metabolism that keeps him slim no matter how much Foster's he drinks, he looks quite a bit younger than his thirty-eight years. A product of what I believe his countrymen call "the tall poppy syndrome," he manifests normality to a morbid degree. He drinks beer with men, has sex with women, loves rugby, football, cricket, and gambling on what he calls the *jee-jees*, and is always bright and friendly with a ready "G'day" in all stages of inebriation except the last.

It is Lek, usually, who rescues dear Greg from his fits of uncontrollable sobbing at the end of a Foster's-intensive evening, usually in the lavatory, when he feels no embarrassment at being hoisted from the pit of suicidal despair by an exceptionally effeminate transsexual:

Greg says to Lek, "I'm all in fragments, mate, atomized. Me mum drove me dad away when I was a kid. Then she worked on me mind, mate. She hates men, see. All Australian women do—there's something in the food down there. Must be the mushy peas."

Lek shudders in revulsion. "Mushy peas? Oh, you poor thing."

"I never really had a family," says Greg, "grew up all by meself. I'm like the product of a Saturday night bunk-up. You're the only family I've got—that's the god's honest truth."

"How awful. Don't worry, love, we'll take care of you."

"I love the girls—they're terrific. They do more for me in an hour than anyone else ever did for me in thirty-nine years."

"Well, that's because you're all man, dear," Lek says.

"Am I? You're looking pretty good from where I'm sitting right now."

"You're drunk, love." He giggles. "Don't do that—you can't have me, darling. I'm a cop."

"You're rejecting me?"

"Me? I don't reject people, darling. I'm at the bottom of the bottom of the bottom—getting rejected is my role. Don't make me jealous, now."

Having won on the horses today, Greg is feeling generous and doesn't mind buying drinks for Henri, who is nursing his thousandth rejection by Marly. It doesn't take long for them to rebond in the medium of alcohol (they had a fight last week that neither remembered the next day), and as they get drunker, their voices get louder. I'm pinned to my seat at the table with Marly and Nong, who try not to look at me while my guts are laid out for public consumption by the two drunks.

"D'you remember her?" Greg asks Henri. "She worked here a few years ago."

Henri glances quickly over his shoulder, apparently believing we cannot hear him. "Of course, she wasn't a common prostitute. She was a born courtesan, a creature of the Belle Epoque stranded in this age of functional barbarism. I felt a certain camaraderie, but she was so formidably *elegant*, I didn't dare even speak to her. I was afraid of what her starting price might have been."

"I did. I saved up. She was terrific between the sheets, but she had a way of screwing your head up. After the second time I was depressed for a week. She was way out of my class."

"*Shush.* The boss's son had her too."

Greg is surprised. "Sonchai? He never goes with his girls."

"He fell for her. It was the original *coup de foudre, avec* bells and whistles."

Greg says conspiratorially, "The beat on the street is there's a snuff movie. That's how she croaked."

"*Mon Dieu,* I didn't know that."

"Sonchai, why don't you check upstairs to see if the cleaners did their job properly today?" Nong says, avoiding Marly's eyes and casting a furious glance at the backs of Greg and Henri.

I go upstairs to lie down on one of the beds to let my mind wander. Musing: prostitutes were the world's first capitalists. The ancients understood very well that men need sex more urgently than women. It was natural, therefore, that this imbalance should be redressed by means of cash, which hitherto nobody had had any use for. Later, of course, whores found other things to sell, and many were reincarnated as lawyers, doctors, dentists, merchant bankers, presidents, sweetshop owners, mayors, et cetera. Commerce was born, and war became just a tad less fashionable. Hey, if it wasn't for prostitution, the human race would never have got beyond the siege of Troy. Many haven't, of course.

I didn't intend to do anything more tonight—I was in lazy-Thai mode—but Henri and Greg have stirred up a gut full of bile, and now I'm restless. When I check my watch, I see it's only eight in the evening. There won't be any airplanes flying to that part of the Cambodian border where they are holding Baker, but there will be plenty of buses. I don't think I can quite stand a long, hot, uncomfortable bus ride tonight, though, so I make a call to Hualamphong railway station and manage to book a first-class overnight sleeper. It's one of those third-world treats I like to accord myself from time to time, and I'm quite excited when the train starts and the uniformed orderly comes around with his crisp white sheets to make up my bunk. Suddenly I'm a boy again taking a first-class trip up north with Nong, who is flush with dough from our sojourn in Paris with the ancient Monsieur Truffaut. *Clickety-click, clickety-click,* I might not have the most respectable mum in the world, but I definitely have one of the smartest. *Clickety-click, clickety-click*, we have money in the bank and medicine for Granma's eyes, and we've paid the rent—nothing to worry about for at least a month. *Clickety-click.* To know how to cheer oneself up is a first step to enlightenment. It's fun to be disobeying Vikorn, who thinks I'm checking out Yammy at this very moment.

I wake up to a dawn in cleaner air. It's a two-track, two-platform country station, but there are a few cabs waiting for passengers. I agree on a day price with a driver, and off we go for a picnic in the country.

13

Sleepy Elephant village is a large hamlet with no municipal buildings at all. You distinguish it from the countryside because there is a slight increase in the density of population. The police station where they are holding Baker is hardly more than a large shophouse with a five-cell jail attached and a half acre of land, where a silver buffalo is inexplicably tethered. The young cop behind the desk is feeding a pet monkey when I walk in. I flash my ID and tell him I'm investigating the murder of one Damrong Baker, which doesn't ring a bell with him at all. I tell him the *farang* Baker, her ex-husband, is a key suspect in my investigation. He blinks at me: *So what?*

"Immigration," I explain. "You are holding a *farang* who tried to cross the border illegally yesterday. They don't have any holding cells—that's why Baker is in one of yours." His brow is like a piece of wood with fixed furrows. It occurs to me that stupidity can be exaggerated for strategic reasons.

The problem with rural policing is that there is no such thing as a rural policeman: the best you can hope for is boys and girls who can wear the uniform without getting themselves into too much trouble. Their loyalties are always local, however, and I'm from the despised big city. By all the rules I ought to bribe him, but I resent the idea. Anyway, he's too young to help. I decide to concentrate on the monkey for a moment. It's a baby and emotionally dependent on the young cop. It looks at me with big moist eyes, then scuttles away to cling to his neck, then climb up on his head, holding his hair in bunches in its tiny hands.

Now the cop with the monkey on his head is finally looking directly at me. He's not at all sure I'm safe to talk to, and I'm not at all sure he can speak standard Thai; all I've got out of him so far is a few mumbles in the local Khmer dialect. I've got his attention, though. "Get the boss," I say softly. He nods and picks up a telephone to say a few words.

Just as I thought, the boss was on the other side of a door, listening. Now he appears, doing up the buttons on his sergeant's uniform, wiping his lips. He's in his midforties and looking at me with drunken belligerence.

"Are you holding a *farang* in this station, a *farang* named Baker?"

He is at the point of shaking his head, so I intervene with a narrowing of the eyes and a concentration of the sixth chakra. When that doesn't get his attention, I say, "Colonel Vikorn, Chief of District Eight, Bangkok, is going to be very angry with you if you took his money and then double-crossed him. Did you let Baker bribe you last night?"

The sergeant was not expecting to be put on the spot in this lifetime. His survival strategy in this body has been to take money and then kick the can a little farther down the road for someone else to pick up—or kick. His police station is ten miles from the smallest, most obscure, least used, and technologically most backward immigration post in all Thailand, so he's had plenty of opportunity to develop this MO into an art form. Now he's having trouble with the sudden delivery of the karmic bill about two hundred years before he expected it.

"You never heard of Colonel Vikorn before yesterday?" He shakes his head. "And you thought he was just some fancy-pants city slicker who would throw money at you, then let you resell Baker back to Baker, or Immigration, or whoever, and come up with some flimsy excuse like he broke out of his cell last night and managed somehow to cross the border, and isn't it terrible how insecure these rickety little country holding cells can be. Right?"

The idiot blinks and nods: *Isn't that what everyone does?* I also nod thoughtfully. There is really nothing for it but to call Vikorn and confess that I'm not masterminding his pornography venture right now but rather moonlighting on police business. The sergeant watches with slow, frightened eyes while I fish out my cell phone.

To Vikorn, I gloss over my dereliction of duty and come to the main point: the local cops are making a fool out of my Colonel. They've taken his money and then allowed Baker to bribe them to let him go, probably in cahoots with Immigration, whom Baker would also have had to bribe. I figure the pressure on the line has reached about a thousand pounds per square inch when I hand the phone over to the sergeant. I watch with interest while his face turns red, then white, then gray. He is blubbering *Yes, yes, yes,* and the hand holding the cell is shaking violently when he gives it back to me. Now he grabs the desk telephone and dials a number that seems to consist of three digits. He starts yammering down the line in Khmer and very quickly ratchets himself up to a full-throated scream. I have no Khmer at all, but I'm willing to bet Fort Knox against a jackfruit he's saying, "Fucking get him fucking back or we're all fucking finished." Or words to that effect. Now he's beckoning me to follow him with an impatient gesture, as if I'm the cause of delay. I follow him out the back of the police station to a carport, where a four-by-four is parked. It's not a battered old police Toyota, though, such as we have to put up with in Krung Thep; no sir, this is a Range Rover Sport TDV6 4WD in metallic russet. Five minutes later I can see why he might need a real off-road four-by-four. The brand-new, metaled road leading to the border post is for wimps, obviously; this guy charges down a well-worn set of ruts that cut through dense jungle. In less than five minutes we have passed through a broken razor-wire fence and ignored a skull-and-crossbones warning about illegal border crossing, and we seem to be heading toward the border post on the Khmer side. Just as we draw up, an officer of the Thai Immigration service arrives in *his* Range Rover Sport (in metallic gray). He immediately identifies me as the source of his problem and scowls. On the other hand, he dashes into the Khmer border post. When the sergeant and I arrive inside the small building, we see the Immigration officer leaning over a desk and yelling in Khmer at one of the Cambodian officers. Once again I am reliant on intuition to interpret.

Thai Immigration official: *Give him back immediately. We
   have a problem.*
Cambodian Immigration official: *Go fuck yourself. We've been
   paid, and we've stamped his passport.*
Thai: *It's a false passport.*
Cambodian: *Well, I know that. Why else would he have
   bribed us?*
Thai: *Do you realize this could sink the whole scam?*
Cambodian: *Only for you, bud. Your successors aren't going to
   be any more honest than you are.*
Thai: *Please.*

The Cambodian looks out the window at the two Range Rovers.

Thai: *Which one do you want?*
Cambodian: *Both of them.*
Thai: *How are we going to get back?*

The Cambodian nods at two mopeds parked near the four-by-fours
and smiles.

Thai: *Can the* farang *walk?*
Cambodian, mulling the question for a moment, then: *We'll
   give you a lift.*

Outside the Cambodian Immigration post, I watch while the two
rather worn mopeds are stashed in the back of one of the four-by-fours;
then they bring Baker out from some dank place under the building. It
takes two of them to hold Baker up, and even then his head lolls and
rolls dangerously. There is a large angry bruise on the left side of his
face, under the eye. "Fucking Cambodians," the Thai Immigration
officer says to me in standard Thai. But the Cambodian also speaks
Thai. "They did this," he says, pointing at the Thais.

"We didn't do that," the Thai says, pointing at the bruise. "We use
telephone books—no signs of bruising. Only you barbarians do stuff
like that."

"So why couldn't he walk last night when you brought him over?

You knew who he was. The only point of beating him up was to get more money out of him."

When they have laid Baker in the front seat of the four-by-four, I check his pulse, which seems surprisingly robust. Other vital signs show promise, and now I'm wondering if he, also, is not engaged in some kind of strategic pantomime. Maybe his health is not as bad as he is making out? "Just lie doggo until we're out of here," I tell him in a whisper.

We take the same route back through the jungle and arrive at the rear of the Thai police station in five minutes. I watch while they drag Baker out and prop him up against a wall while they unload the mopeds. The Thais are looking pretty sour when the Cambodians take their remaining four-by-four back over the border. Suddenly the sergeant has got his balls back. "Get him out of here," he says. "You'll have to pay for a taxi—we don't have any transport." He looks dolefully at the mopeds.

Now I'm looking at Baker and wondering if he's up to a twelve-hour journey back to Krung Thep. "I need some painkiller," I say. When the sergeant merely scowls, I threaten to call Vikorn again.

"What about opium? It's all we've got out here."

I shrug. The sergeant pops back into the station and returns a few minutes later with a long pipe with tiny brass bowl, a wedge of black opium between two transparent plastic squares, and a few pills. The pills are paracetamol, which he grinds up with the opium to make the drug less viscous; then he places a tiny drop on the side of the bowl, heats it with a butane lighter until it fizzes and bubbles, takes one toke himself, then hands the pipe to Baker, who sucks on it with unexpected enthusiasm. Baker keeps up the malingering for fifteen pipes until he can no longer disguise the feeling of supreme well-being that has overwhelmed him. "I guess he's ready to travel," I tell the cop, who helps me slide him into the back of the taxi.

Baker is deeply into his opium dream by the time we reach the country station, and I have to pay the driver to help me drag him to the train and dump him on a bench in the first-class compartment. It's a relief when the train starts and I pull the blinds over the door. A few hours later Baker shows no sign of forsaking paradise for this sterile promontory, so I insert the name *Damrong* into his dream by whispering it slowly and clearly over and over again in his ear. Suddenly his eyes open full of that light which has not been much seen in *farang* since the sixties, and says:

> *Age cannot wither her, nor custom stale*
> *Her infinite variety. Other women cloy*
> *The appetites they feed, but she makes hungry*
> *Where most she satisfies; for vilest things*
> *Become themselves in her, that the holy priests*
> *Bless her when she is riggish.*

"School play," he adds with a smug smile. "I was Enobarbus." And closes his eyes again.

It is not until we are on the outskirts of Krung Thep that the drug's high tide begins to recede. He starts to rub the angry bruise under his eye and other parts of his body where they beat him. His mind seems to be working on a more powerful distraction than pain, though, when he begins to narrate his inner journey:

"Monochrome, shades of gray, white floor with gigantic tiles, maybe ten feet square, with black between them, like a giant chess-board. On each square a gray spiral staircase leading to a gray platform. She is *color*: gold and green mostly, dazzling, with dark purple, crimson, orange, a blaze of colored light in some kind of silk robe, stepping off the platform into the void. Go to the next tile. Again, spiral staircase, this time taller than the last; same thing, she is the only colored object, stepping off the platform into the void. And so on, for infinity, staircase after staircase, each one taller than the last, Damrong after Damrong—a different robe every time, do you see? *Always about to step off into the void.*" He grasps my forearm. "She comes to me every night, glowing gold-green. She controls my dick, my orgasm, everything. She can make it last for hours, literally all night, or make me come in five seconds flat. Every night, *every night!*" Digging his nails into my flesh: "I want to jump off into the void with her, but I just don't have the guts."

I have called ahead, so Vikorn has arranged for a police van to meet us at Hualamphong railway terminal.

14

We are tiny figurines hanging from the charm bracelet of infinity. When these bodies wear out, we will migrate to others. What will I be next, tinker, tailor, tiger, fly? Demon, Buddha, mountain, louse—all things are equal in their essential emptiness. But will there be a planet worth living on in fifty years' time? *Chart na* means "next life," and if you're Buddhist you worry about it. Not only yours, but the earth's too, for it, also, is a living being with its own karma with which our own is inextricably entwined.

Well, it's getting hotter year by year—that's finally official. Even scientists employed by the United States government now agree: we will be the only species in cosmic history deliberately to fry itself to extinction. I happened to be watching the BBC on our cable link this morning and half expected the newscaster to adopt an urgent tone, but he used the same smooth voice as for births, deaths, and football results. It's not his fault, of course; he knows better than most how retro normality can be, but what is the appropriate reaction when the mind relies on denial to balance itself? Carry on as normal, I guess: just keep burning carbon. Environmental fascism will come eventually. When the Himalayas are melting, leaders of English-speaking countries will threaten to nuke to a crisp those third-world nations still relying on fossil fuels. That'll help global warming.

So now the FBI and I are in a cab on our way at last to a warehouse in Chinatown by the Chao Phraya River, which Vikorn has rented and is in process of buying for the purpose of developing the arts side of his empire. It was, clearly, a blunder on my part to mention to Kimberley this amendment to my job description, for I happen to loathe this new role of mine and need a couple of beers before I can steel myself to enter Yammy's atelier.

I order a Kloster at a riverside café, and to my surprise Kimberley joins me. We both spare a moment to take in the river, which as usual is roaring with human life. In the midstream brightly painted tugs tow barges with big eyes on the bows, while longtails with gigantic former bus engines mounted on davits with outboard propeller shafts about fifteen feet long roar up and down, packed with tourists. The river is still the only jam-free thoroughfare for a lot of people commuting to work and back, so the long, thin passenger ferries are packed; they arrive and depart the floating docks amid a frenzy of hysterical whistles from the pilots at the stern, who like to give the impression of catastrophe narrowly averted.

The FBI almost never drinks alcohol, but I know from various telephone conversations that she's been in a strange state ever since she arrived. Why is she here, *exactly*? Sure, she's interested in the case, and from what she has disclosed so far, it really does tie in with her work in Virginia. But even razor-sharp FBI agents don't just jump on a plane overnight on the basis of a call from a friend. Delighted though I am to have her around, I've been wondering about her. As a matter of fact, our friendship went on hold for more than a year, before it restarted with one of those telephone calls *farang* make out of the blue: "Hey, Sonchai, how's it going?" as if she were just around the corner and we'd been constantly in touch. It was the middle of the night, my time, and it took me a while to wake up. I had to take the cell phone out into the yard so as not to awaken Chanya and the Lump. (No, I did not say, "Kimberley, do you realize it's two A.M. over here?" Thai courtesy.) My attitude changed when I started to realize how unhappy she was. As her voice slowed and drooped, compassion kicked in. When she tried out a few amorous gambits, I had to tell her about Chanya and the baby; that gave her pause for a while. She didn't quite admit that she'd been fantasizing about living happily ever after in Bangkok with that weirdo half-caste cop she'd sort of bonded with on the python case. (A transsexual Thai—M2F—murdered a black American marine with drug-crazed cobras and a giant python. We refrained from potting her/him for reasons of compassion.) Not quite, and anyway it started to emerge that her need was extrahormonal: "I'm hitting a wall over here, Sonchai. I don't have a lot of friends outside the U.S.—only you, really. Just because America is a big country doesn't mean the walls don't close in on you from time to time." We carried on like that, with middle-of-the-night chats, until the Damrong case gave us something practical to talk about. I really didn't expect even a supercop like Kimberley to jump on a plane, though. So, the case aside, I've been waiting for signals that she's ready for the deep and meaningful. It's taken me a whole week—there are parts of the *farang* psyche with which even I am unfamiliar—to realize that under the tough, relentlessly extrovert, take-no-prisoners carapace, there lives quite a shy girl who doesn't have a lot of practice in sharing her heart.

The conversation, at this minute, however, is not about her mood but mine.

"It's kind of funny how much you dislike pornography—you know, considering," the FBI says.

"That I've been involved in the Game all my life and run a brothel? It's just not the same thing."

"What's the big moral difference?"

I search for words. Actually, *moral difference* is the right way of putting it. "Spontaneity. A girl arrives in Krung Thep from Isaan feeling lonely, terrified, inadequate, poor. A middle-aged man arrives from the West feeling lonely, terrified, inadequate, rich. They're like two halves of a coin. All my mother's bar does is facilitate their inevitable congress, supply the beer and the music, the short-term accommodation, and rake off a little profit. The whole thing is driven by a good healthy primeval human need for animal warmth and comfort. In all my years with the Game I've only come across half a dozen serious cases of abuse of one party by another, and I figure that's because the whole thing works perfectly as an expression of natural morality and grassroots capitalism. The way I see it, we're like a real estate agency that deals in flesh instead of earth. Setting it all up artificially, though, in a film set, choreographing the whole thing so flabby overweights in Sussex and Bavaria, Minnesota and Normandy, can jerk off without having to tax their imaginations—that strikes me as downright immoral, a crime against life almost. I guess the real difference is that in the bar people actually *do* it. There's a reality input."

She smiles and shakes her head. "You're just too much, Sonchai. Some people would say you were slightly insane. But when you come out with that kind of stuff, it makes sense, at least for the moment that you're saying it. How did your mind get so free? What happened to you? Are all Thai pimps like you?"

"No," I say. "I'm strange, I guess."

She has drunk a bottle of Kloster rather quickly and seems to be sinking into depression. She orders another, though, and drinks it rapidly, straight from the bottle. *"Actually doing it,"* she says in a musing voice. "I guess that's exactly what we're not good at. Maybe that's why we love war so much: reality starvation."

Now she's giving me one of her most puzzling looks. "You've changed," I say. "Big time. What happened?"

Another gulp from the bottle. "I hit thirty-five. The midway point. It finally dawned on me that my whole description of reality was secondhand. My generation of women never rebelled—we felt we didn't need to. We inherited a message of hate and simply elaborated it a bit. I never saw much of my father—my mother made sure of that. I think I went into the only important relationship of my life in order to be a bitch. In order to express hate. Isn't that sick?"

How to answer that? By changing the subject. "Why did you come to Bangkok, really?"

A sigh. "I think I came for this conversation. We don't have them at home anymore, you know? Maybe it's modernism: we trade tribal sound bites so we can feel we belong to something. I came for your mind, Sonchai. Chanya can have your body—she deserves it. That is one very smart woman. I can hardly stand to see the two of you together. The cozy, unspoken, genuine love makes me want to have you both arrested. I don't think it exists stateside. There's a very powerful taboo against it. Think of all the hours you spend loving when you could be making money."

I say, "Let's go."

"I want another beer."

"No."

In the cab we enjoy silence for a while, then: "I did marry. I lied to you." A pause. "And divorced, of course."

"Any kids?"

"One. A boy. I let his father keep him. His father said if the baby stayed with me, I would destroy him. I was like a smart bomb programmed to destroy anything male. I was afraid he may have been right." Another long pause, then: "It was a hell of a long time ago. I was barely out of my teens. When it all fell apart, I joined the Bureau. I figured if I was a natural-born man-killer, I might as well get a license."

Somehow she sneaked an extra can of beer into the cab, which she opens. Raising the can to her mouth: "I don't know, Sonchai, the minute you start to search for meaning, you're lost. But without meaning, we're lost also. *Who am I, where do I come from, where am I going?* Fuck knows. I can't handle marriage—that's way beyond my tolerance level. But a lover who lasts more than a weekend might help my emotional stability." She takes a swig of the beer. "So now I masturbate," she says with Tragic Mouth, "every fucking night. Maybe I need a toy boy?"

The best way to check if you're in Chinatown is by counting gold shops. If there's not one on each corner, chances are you've taken a wrong turn. The shop signs are invariably yellow on red in Chinese characters, and the gold is of the extra-shiny variety that screams at you from the windows. Many of them are not technically shops but *hangs*: warehouse-size affairs with scales on the counters and turbaned Sikhs with pump guns on guard, all ablaze with neon light bouncing ferociously off the interminable stretches of gold Buddhas, gold dragons, gold belts, gold necklaces, gold bracelets. Clothing is the other industry: crowded narrow lanes made still narrower by stalls selling every kind of cotton or silk garment at astonishingly low prices.

The FBI has managed to get drunk on a few beers and stays my hand when I try to pay the cab driver. "Do you know I've never known simple joy? Darker, more complex emotions, yes, but joy, no. Nor have any of my friends. We were infected by the psychosis of winning at the age of five. But *you* know joy. That's what blows me away. You're the son of a whore, a pimp, you run a brothel, you're an officer in one of the most corrupt police forces in Asia, but you're innocent. I've never broken a law, cheated, lied, or presided over a crooked deal in my life, but I'm corrupt. I feel dirty twenty-four hours a day. Does anyone on the planet recognize the significance of that apart from me? The material you're made of is fifty percent lighter than ours. Why?"

"We don't have original sin," I explain as I hand a hundred-baht note to the driver. "That iron rod through the skull. We just don't have it."

Vikorn has posted a couple of plainclothesmen outside the warehouse. They recognize me and let us into Yammy's studio, where Marly, Jock'nEd are sitting around discussing the Iraq war in white silk dressing gowns with crimson trimmings. I feel the FBI's sexual frisson when she clocks Ed. Excuse me while I explain Jock'nEd:

They are a team, famous throughout the Bangkok porn industry, and the invariable performers whenever the script requires a *farang* male to flesh out the skeletal story line. Ed is, well, simply magnificent. A natural six-two male animal with superb pecs that gleam under the lights when rubbed with Johnson's baby oil, power thighs that could do justice to a lioness, a rocky-handsome bone structure, one of those aquiline noses that emit erotic fire with every exhalation, relentlessly seductive baby-blue eyes, and a telltale cleft in the chin that is so distinctively American it could have been invented by Ford. (Actually, Ed is a Cockney who hails from Elephant and Castle.) On the other side of the karmic balance, lamentably—well, how can one put it? Even tumescent his dong is not of the Big Mac dimensions your randy granny in Omaha is accustomed to ogle over a TV dinner. He has to be supplemented, in other words, using the magical techniques of the silver screen we all love to be conned by. Enter Jock. He is a five-foot-nothing Scotsman with a consonant-free burr, bald, pot-bellied from a heroic beer habit, almost chinless, with slurpy lips you wouldn't want your worst enemy to be kissed by, but armed with—you guessed—a gigantic member of positively pneumatic obedience.

They are inseparable pals and true pros, who eye Kimberley up and down as if she were a mare in a horse market. The assumption that she has come to work is, in the circumstances, forgivable.

Now Marly: you will recall she works for us at the Old Man's Club and was handpicked by Vikorn for her stunning visuals. Her excellent English enables her to understand Yammy's stage directions—which, I am told, tend to be complex beyond the industry norm. Seeing a potential artistic rival, she does not immediately respond to Kimberley's big and somewhat inebriated woman-to-woman smile. I leave the FBI to launch a charm offensive—she is clearly fascinated by the boys, the girl, the bed, the lights, and the cameras (well, *something* is making her lips curl lasciviously)—to go find Yammy, who apparently is taking a creative break in his office in back. I find him huddled over a bottle of sake.

"Hello," he manages from measureless depths of depression. "Come to make sure I don't leave out the raw meat?"

"Don't make it difficult for me, Yammy. I'm only doing my job."

He gulps the rice wine straight from the bottle. "Listen, I have this fantastically surreal plot, with a cobra and a tiger cub, white kimonos, a Kyoto backdrop straight out of Hokusai . . ." Catching my eyes, he mimes futility with one hand and lapses back into despair.

"And? What's the problem?"

"It's so much more erotic with the kimonos left on, don't you see? Sonchai, I'm begging you."

I shake my head in total sympathy. "He won't go for it. Look, it's not his fault—blame the consumer. The big respectable hotel chains won't buy it if it's not brutally obscene."

"I knew you would say that."

"Can't you do both? Subtle erotic with the kimonos on, then the standard stuff with them off?"

Shaking his head but resigned: "You lose aesthetic balance that way. It ends up like a dog's dinner."

"There's no point in my trying to persuade him. He'll say it's all about money."

Silence. Then: "I've been thinking. I've found a couple of investors in Japan. They'll go fifty-fifty on a modest, fifty-million-dollar all-Nippon art flick. I just need to come up with the other half, twenty-five million."

"Yammy, we've been through this before. It's not that he's against you—you simply don't fit the profile."

"So what the hell does a successful trafficker look like?"

I gaze at him for a moment: neurotic, twitches like a horse plagued by flies, desperate and hurtling toward middle age, the unmistakable stamp of jail in the hollow of his cheeks, the hardness under the eyes. "Not like you, Yammy. Any customs officer would get the sack for not searching you on sight."

From experience I know there is no point sitting and trying to be persuasive. Yammy does everything in his own time or not at all. I return to the set, where the FBI is interrogating Marly.

"I would have thought a woman like you would have done fantastically in the States," Kimberley is saying with an ambiguous smile. "What happened?"

"It's not as easy as they make out," Marly explains. "I did Third World Pathetic, I got a bleeding-heart eunuch. I did Thai Whore in a G-string, I got a geriatric on Viagra." With a hint of aggression: "Why, what's your game?"

"Postmodern," Kimberley says. "I got a dildo."

"We're shooting in one!" Yammy yells as he exits from his office, suddenly oozing authority. Immediately Marly, Jock'nEd slip out of their dressing gowns and are now stark naked. Marly walks over to the bed and bends over it, careful to lean on her hands so her breasts dangle. "It's okay, we can still talk," she tells Kimberley. "It's just a bum fondle."

Right on cue, Ed begins with the oil on her apple-shaped behind, as if polishing a Greek urn. "What are you looking at?" Marly asks the FBI, then casts a glance over her shoulder. "Oh, Jock. He's amazing isn't he? You wouldn't give him a second glance if you saw him in the street, but he's such a pro, the best in the business. He can do that even when he's drunk. It's like he's got an electric inflator or something. And it *is* gigantic."

Kimberley seems to be suffering hormonal overload. Hoarsely: "Tell me, when you do this, d'you feel like you're screwing the whole feminist matriarchy?"

"No," says Marly with a frown. "I feel like I'm screwing the whole Thai patriarchy."

Kimberley, nodding: "Even so."

On a signal from Yammy the FBI steps back. "Scene twelve, take one," Yammy snaps. Marly immediately starts moaning. "Cut!" yells

Yammy. "He isn't inside you yet, honey," he explains. "If you start with the kettle drums, what'll you have left for the crescendo?" He goes to a laptop on a table to check something. "And you're not quite in position, Marly darling," he says distractedly, working the mouse. "I've got your clitoris and the top of your pussy in the floor camera, but we're going to miss half of Jock's dick for the fuck cut. Shift your bum about half an inch backward. Good. Perfect. Now, get your body memory to lock onto that. Jock, are you drooping?"

"Ah wah jus' wai'in' on hold," says Jock, looking down.

"Okay now, when you enter her, don't use too much thrust, or you'll push her out of position, and all we'll get is your hairy balls. Make it look merciless, but don't use any real horizontal pressure. Smoothly controlled grinds come out best on the celluloid. Clear?"

"Och aye," says Jock.

"Good man." Yammy's mood has swung. With the Promethean will of a true artist, he has conquered despair. He casts me a grin. "I wish mine was that reliable. Okay now, Marly love, you have this gorgeous Ed here polishing your ass like it was Sung dynasty, and you know what's going to happen next, but you don't know when, and he's teasing you to the point of madness. Anticipation agony in every facial muscle, please. Good, keep that. Now give us a little tongue—no, don't stick it all out, we want only the teeniest pink tip sneaking between those hungry lips. Perfect. Okay, take two."

Take two is the penetration shot, starring Jock. I cast a glance at the FBI. "Can we go now?" Kimberley groans. "I need to sit down somewhere cool, or find a man."

It is as we are leaving that I see the tall athletic forty-something Englishman for the first time. He is sitting in a far corner of the studio in a plastic chair, watching everything, wearing smart casuals of impeccable cut; his open-neck linen shirt reveals a filigreed gold chain. I already know what he looks like naked and that his name is Tom. I feel exactly the same jolt of sexual jealousy as if Damrong were still alive:

Tom, you're just amazing. I don't think I can stand the thought of you with another woman. I just can't.

Don't worry about that. There wouldn't be any fucking point, would there?

Why is he here?

. . .

On the way back to Sukhumvit I tell the FBI I have to pick Lek up from the hospital, where he has his monthly check. Kimberley immediately assumes he must be HIV positive and considers taking precautions, like getting out of the taxi and taking another, so I explain he's in perfect health. The checkup has to do with his gender reassignment. Basically, the procedure is not to cut his goolies off all at once but to ease him into his new identity using the estrogen. The surgery is almost the last stage. Now the FBI is a helpless doomed creature caught in an overwhelming mudslide of curiosity and cannot help staring at him when he gets into the backseat next to her. "You're so beautiful," she tells him, taking in his long black hair parted in the middle, his big oval eyes with just a hint of mascara, his gaunt high cheeks, the adolescent litheness that is still upon him.

"*Lork?*" says Lek, trying to catch my eye.

As she gets out of the cab at the Grand Britannia, there's a catch in her throat: "My first angel."

Back at the station I'm thinking about the Englishman named Tom and trying to work out what the hell he was doing at Yammy's atelier, when my cell phone rings.

"It isn't going to happen," the FBI says.

"What?"

"We're not going to let him go through with it. I'm having nightmares about the knife, and I'm not even asleep yet. Ugh!"

"Of course he's going through with it. For a true transsexual, the surgery is the most important day of his life. It is the birth of his real self."

"It isn't going to happen," the FBI says in that tone Americans use when they intend to bomb the future into submission. "He's too beautiful. Give me his phone number."

"No," I say, and close the cell.

15

Next day Lek comes to see me at my desk at about four in the afternoon. He has something of the weary professional about him, which he manages to feminize by passing his hands deftly through his long inky hair and shuddering. He has not been able to resist adding a touch of rouge to his cheeks. He takes out a *yaa dum* aromatherapy inhaler and sticks it into his left nostril.

"I've been chasing leads all day," he explains, switching nostrils, "and it's hot and stinky. That whore has been everywhere, really everywhere, but she never stayed long. I tried to follow what her ex-husband, that American Baker, told us about her, and he was basically right. She was steadily working her way upmarket."

"Was she attached to any bar at the time she died?"

"That's what I'm coming to. She'd done Soi Cowboy, Nana, and Pat Pong, where she was one of the best earners on the street. Then she moved to the Parthenon Club." A pause while he searches my face.

"The Parthenon," I repeat, swallowing. I guess it was inevitable, but it hardly simplifies the case.

He looks at me to make sure I'm aware of possible obstructions to further inquiries.

"And? Who did you talk to there?"

"I needed a disguise, didn't I?"

"Lek, what did you do?"

"Pretended I was looking for work. How else was I going to get any-one there to talk to me? If I'd told them I was a cop, you would have had the male half of Bangkok's HiSo on your back."

"They take on *katoeys*?"

A proud pout. "Of course. No bar is complete without us these days."

"Who did you talk to?"

"A low-ranking *mamasan*. I told her Damrong was my cousin, and I was using the connection to look for work. She told me Damrong worked there for the last two months. She said she didn't know why Damrong hadn't turned up for work recently—she assumed it was because Damrong had found a highflier to look after her. That's what all the girls and boys at the Parthenon are looking for, of course."

"You didn't find out which members she'd been with? Anyone spe-cial in her life?"

"I had to keep it all on a gossipy level, you know, emphasizing my cousin's amazing success in her work. The *mamasan* didn't exactly spill her guts, but she did let on that Damrong had been the favorite of two club members."

"*Farang* or Thai?"

"One was *farang*, the other Thai."

"You got their names?"

"No. If I'd started asking questions like that, I would have blown my cover."

"Right."

"By the way, that female *farang* in the cab yesterday—is she a hun-dred *satang* to the baht?"

"The FBI? Why?"

"She got hold of my number from the station switchboard and says she's interested in gender reassignment and wants to take me out to lunch to discuss it with me. I told her F2M is very complicated and nothing I'm going through has any relevance to her case, but she insisted, and out of *greng jai* to you, I said I would go."

I am blinking rapidly. "When's the date?"

"Tomorrow."

"I'd like a full report," I say, not meeting his gaze.

I'm pondering and frowning, not sure if there is going to be any way to penetrate the Parthenon Club without committing professional suicide and wondering if this is the case that will finally reveal my secret martyr complex, while I take the stairs down to the cells. The word from the turnkey is that the *farang* Baker is more than ripe for interrogation.

He is sitting in a peculiar position at the end of his bunk with his forehead pressed so hard against the bars, he seems welded to them.

"He's been like that for hours," the turnkey says. "He stopped eating and drinking. I think we've broken him already."

I nod for him to open the cell door. I tell him to leave it open and to disappear from view, while keeping an ear out in case the *farang* turns violent. When a personality splits like this, you never know which way the particles are going to fly.

I step inside the cell, which is to say I step inside the psychology of its inmate: a meltdown at the center. Reaching out with open hand, I grab the hair at the back of his head and pull him away from the bars. He is shivering and twitching like a rabbit. I have to caress his head and face to calm him down. The bruise under his left eye is healing well but has turned dark. Now he's looking at me with helpless eyes. I grab a chair and sit directly opposite him on his bunk.

"Why are you here, Dan?"

A blink. The challenge of verbal communication is lifting him from a mood that is sustainable only in solitude. It is, of course, exactly solitude combined with classic Thaicopparanoia that has broken him. He blurts and blabbers at first.

"Why am I here? Because you put me here. Because you're a Thai cop who's found a fall guy and doesn't give a damn about truth, or justice, or freedom, or democracy. You're all about sending me to death row so you can get on with the next case. So I ran away, and now you have an even better excuse."

"You know a lot about the Thai system of justice?"

Bitterly: "I've been here four years, man. I've seen a lot. You don't have a justice system."

"If it's so dreadful, why are you in Thailand?"

Suddenly: an avalanche of words that must have accumulated in his feverish brain during the couple of days he's been down here. His tongue races to keep up with the thoughts:

"I'm here because there is no such thing as rehabilitation in the free world: one criminal conviction and you're out, no jobs above subsistence level for you. I'm here because marriage doesn't work. I'm here because I'm bald and almost middle aged—sounds silly, but I haven't come across a single Thai girl who gives a damn if I'm thirty or forty, bald or not, divorced or not. You're a nonjudgmental people, and it's taken me four years to find out why. You've got a massive underground hell called the prison system that devours anyone who falls off the tightrope. It's amazing, it's the most outrageous institution in the world. It isn't really a prison service—it's a Stone Age money factory owned and run by cops and prosecutors. No one is safe. It could happen to anyone, Thai or *farang*, male or female, old or young: you're walking down a quiet street one night, a cop emerges from nowhere, plants an Ecstasy or *yaa baa* pill on you, and takes you off to jail. You have a choice: pay his fee for freeing you, or watch the system gobble up the whole of the rest of your life. In your society there is only one judgment to be made: has he fallen into the pit or not?"

"This pit—does it have a way out?"

"I don't have the money to pay you to let me go. I just don't have it." Looking me in the eye: "I didn't kill her."

I nod gnomically. "Suppose I tell you you've lucked out with the one cop in Bangkok who doesn't take money? Suppose I tell you I really am interested in finding out what happened to Damrong?"

I guess I should not have used her name in that tone. It causes him to flash me a look. An idea is slowly rising to the top of his mind. "How would I know that?"

"You were married to her, you two had been business associates— to some extent you still were. Maybe she confided in you more than anyone else. Maybe you didn't kill her but have a shrewd idea about why she had to die."

I think the choice of phrase *why she had to die* was quite serendipitous. It seems to have triggered some internal narrative that takes him off into another space. Finally he says, "Did she have to die? You haven't told me how it happened."

"I want you to tell me."

"I don't know. You haven't even told me when she died." Looking me in the eye again: "When did she die, exactly?"

"Good question," I admit. "But not strictly relevant. Thanks to technology, many things can be done by remote control today that needed a hands-on approach in more primitive times."

Now he is assessing me in a different way. Now he is more scared than ever. I was fishing, though, and have no idea why my words should have had such a profound effect. The expression on his face is of a drowning man. I shift my chair a little closer. "Tell me," I say softly, "tell me. Maybe I can help."

A shrug. "Help? I'm between a rock and a hard place. You let me out today, I'd be lucky to even make it to the airport."

I nod sagely, then abandon the chair to stand up and pace a little while I speak. "I see. So you weren't supposed to keep those clips on your laptop. Am I right?"

Shaking his head in wonder at my understatement: "Yeah, you could say that."

"So why keep them there?"

"Knee-jerk opportunism. It's been a problem all my life. Great tactics, no strategy worth a dime. It was dumb. I've been beating myself up ever since. Discipline is what I don't have. If I did, I'd be rich and free."

"You thought having the clips might give you leverage one day when you needed it?"

"Right."

"Do you know who the Thai Chinese player is?"

"Not exactly. Someone big. A *jao paw*."

"Yes, a godfather. You could say that. You weren't supposed to keep him on your hard disk, so I suppose the drill was for you to set up the cameras, record onto a DVD, and give it to her so she could choose when and how to turn on the screws. Why did you disobey orders?"

Looking away: "Who trusts anyone in this town?" A pause, then: "I didn't think about it all that clearly. Like you say, I was looking for leverage."

"You took a great risk for an illusory security. Fear? Yes, I can see how that might work. Perhaps you were too used to her tantrums, her shifts of plan, her sadistic way of playing on your heartstrings. Yes, I can see how the revelation that you have kept a life-threatening record of her performance with a *jao paw* might swing things your way at a crucial moment in time. And there was the Englishman too. I guess she must have been blackmailing him?"

He shrugs. "Some yuppie jerk who kept his brains in his dick. No great challenge. Especially not for her."

I place a finger against my nose, not for the posture but because I'm torn between two paths. I know the Englishman has twice been to look for him at his apartment over the past few days until one of the guards divulged that Baker was in jail. Instinct chooses reticence. I cough and change the subject. "The *jao paw*, though—he was different?"

He almost sniggers. "I've never seen her even slightly nervous before. She was with *him*, though. You saw the clip. She pulled out all the stops for him. I've filmed her working a hundred times—I never saw her perform like that before." Giving me a suddenly less fearful look: "Send me down. I'm not buying into your game. You can't scare me the way he can, whoever he is." His jaw is set, his mind made up.

What I have to say next will cost me a lot, but I find I don't have a lot of choice.

"She wasn't a woman, she was a disease," I say, still pacing, "a disease that infected the blood of half the men she ever serviced." He raises his head to stare at me. "In her hands your body was a pennywhistle that she could play anything on. But it wasn't what she did to your body alone, it was what she did to your heart—right? She knew how to set it on fire. She was an addiction worse than crack, worse than *yaa baa*—worse than heroin. Isn't that the way you put it at our first meeting?" He seems to be daring me to carry on. I pace the cell, allowing my anguish to show. "How did she do it? Is the sex instinct in men really so all-powerful? Or are we talking about something else, I ask myself, something even more fundamental? Had she discovered something most women are only vaguely aware of? Had she found a way of suggesting, ever so subtly, that she could cure even the base anguish of being alive? That between her thighs you would find the peace you crave? That she actually *understood you*? The holy grail, in other words, that no man ever really finds?" I pause to stare at him. "Was it really the sex, Dan, that hooked you, or was it the surprising, uncanny way she had of soothing you, as if she understood your problem?"

He is staring at me in amazement. Perhaps I should stop here, but once you've started on the path to crucifixion, you may as well suck it all up. "Of course, the final experience was the very opposite of that. What you got was a lethal dose of heartburn after all, when you realized she'd been playing you along like the top-notch pro she was, right? How sorry are you that she's dead?"

His features have quite altered. Malice has returned to his eyes. "So it *was* you. I figured it might be, but it seemed too much of a coincidence. You're that cop who fell for her like a sack of potatoes?"

"I want to find the people who did this, Dan," I say, avoiding his gaze. "Even if you were an accomplice, you were pretty minor. There's money and organization here, Dan, way beyond anything you're capable of. I would bear that in mind when the time comes to prosecute. I could probably make sure you didn't do more than five years, and I'd try to make sure it was somewhere, shall we say, survivable? With luck you would even be able to avoid rape, HIV, and tuberculosis."

With sudden contempt: "You don't know what you're asking. The interview's over."

He turns away, so I have to go up to him to twist his head around. "He hasn't come to see you while you've been down here, has he?" To his look of blank incomprehension, I add, "Of course, you didn't expect him to. Strange, though, don't you think? You're on excellent terms with a Brit called Tom who dresses too much like a lawyer not to be one—unless of course he's an estate agent—who likes to visit you as much as I do. In fact, he visits you *after* I visit you. That must be either because he is having you watched, or because you call him like an obedient slave whenever the law comes knocking on your door. He stars in your private movie collection too. Indeed, he seems to have more than an amateur's interest in the ancient art of pornography and enjoys a privileged seat at rehearsals." I let Baker throw me another of his wild looks, but he does not follow up with a verbal response. "But when you're in trouble with the law, he doesn't lift a finger to help you." I offer a contemplative stare. "At least not a visible finger."

He has folded his arms in a tight, prolonged shrug. He is shivering again. "Go fuck yourself."

"Ah! When you have known the scorpion, you are not afraid of the toad, right?" To his aggressive frown: "That's what the Tibetans said when the British replaced the Chinese as their chief tormentor. Now they've got the scorpion back. It's called progress. I think you find yourself in similar straits: better a toad like me than a scorpion like Tom the Brit, Tom the Lawyer, Tom the Yuppie—Tom the Enforcer, perhaps?"

He thinks I want him to look at me, but I twist him in the opposite direction, toward the open cell door. "I'm condemning you to freedom, Dan. If you want to stay here, you'll have to come up with some serious answers."

He gives me a wild look and shakes his head. "Jailor," I call in Thai, "throw this bum out of here."

"They'll kill me," Baker says, suddenly frantic.

"I know. That's how we'll catch them, isn't it?"

"I'll run away again."

"Doubt it. Your mug is on every Immigration computer in every Immigration booth all over Southeast Asia—and let's face it, your last bid for freedom was a little uncomfortable to say the least. Try to escape again, by all means. Maybe next time I'll let the Enforcer get to you before I do."

16

I'm about to pay a visit to the Parthenon Club for Men.

I'm in a four-button, double-breasted blazer by Zegna, a spread-collar linen shirt by Givenchy, tropical wool flannel slacks, and best of all, patent leather slip-ons by Baker-Benjes, which uncoplike wardrobe is entirely thanks to my junior share of profits from my mother's bar. My cologne is a charming little number by Russell Simmons. I am a humble self-effacing Buddhist, so you can believe me when I say that I look—and smell—sexy as hell. The Thai genes give me a haunted look; the *farang* genes provide an illusion of efficiency: a high-tech dick or a third world ghost buster? These concepts are not mutually exclusive.

Although the *soi* is narrow and ends in a brick wall, the Parthenon itself is a gigantic, neo-Roman affair: four blinding white stories of columns, kitsch and camp, with, I am afraid, a great many red lights. A crescent gravel drive leads to the Doric uprights and the crimson, brass-studded double doors. Over the threshold we find an Oriental identity crisis.

For a moment I'm in the Paris of Truffaut, an old French roué who hired my mother for a few months when I was still a kid. He loved

Maxim's in the rue Royale, and for a moment I'm distracted by the Parthenon's lady lamps. These lamps are five times the size of those in Maxim's, though, and factory products: the gigantic bronze women are identical in every case. Never mind—my brain is finally processing the décor in a more global way. Louis XV bowlegged chaises longues, gilded coffee tables, tassels in purple, velvet, and old gold; a domed ceiling where plump cupids hunt; Venus de Milo and other amputees on pedestals; and tiered balconies leading upward to the heaven of private rooms for rent by the hour. And there is a stage, empty at the moment save for an unnerving stream of electric blue lighting that might herald the arrival of a UFO: fusion, I suppose.

A *mamasan* arrives, heavily rouged and wearing a kind of eighteenth-century ballgown; the body inside is not much older than twenty-seven, however. I am sitting on one of the sofas facing the stage, and she kneels down next to me, careful to keep her head below mine. She explains that since it is officially a club, I need to become an official member, a chore that is completed in five minutes and consists mostly of taking a print of my credit card, during which time she has repeated over and over that the member list is secret and kept in an encrypted form on one single non-LAN computer.

I have come early; it is a few minutes past eight in the evening. I am the only man in sight, and now that I am a fully paid-up member of this exclusive club, rewards appear. They come stealthily from many directions; before I know it, I'm surrounded. Four are sitting with me on my sofa, about six others are sitting on chairs, watching and listening with respect, interest, and a certain glassy-eyed look that would morph into adoration if I gave the slightest sign of encouragement. All of them are wearing different kinds of ballgowns with the usual emphasis on powdered cleavage, rouge, and purple eyeshadow. I'm thinking of Damrong while I scan the faces. They are all young and beautiful, of course, but none exhibit that kind of radiance, not even the *katoey*: it took me a while to spot her/him, all trussed up like Marie Antoinette. Only a very particular kind of self-consciousness gives him away—I would never have been able to tell from his/her face. I am conscious, however, that this Oriental club will doubtless follow a feudal hierarchy, and sounds of female voices come drifting down from the higher balconies. As discreetly as I can, I beckon to the *mamasan* and point upstairs. A couple of soft words from her make my new friends disappear. As she accompanies me up the velvet staircase with gilded handrail, she mentions, sotto voce, that the girls on the second floor are particularly highly valued, by which she means they charge double up here. Once again we go through the beauty parade. Here the flesh is somewhat whiter, indicating a larger component of Chinese genes, and there is a good deal more shrewd life behind the fluttering eyelids, but I do not see the kind of awareness I am looking for. No *katoeys* either.

The *mamasan* is standing nearby and sees that I'm not entirely satisfied. I catch her eye, and she subtly beckons me to take the stairs to the top floor. On the way up I take more notice of her: efficient, hardworking, but far too young and attractive to be a glorified usher. She notices, of course, that I am looking at her, but gives no come-on. I understand. This millionaires' club follows the same basic ground rules as my mother's humble establishment. It is a matter of great political importance that the *mamasan* does not actively promote her own services unless all the available professionals have been rejected. On the top floor there are five prima donnas on chaise longues with suspiciously perfect bosoms, China-doll faces, and the indolence of movie stars. Here the only *katoey* is truly queen; s/he lounges languidly at the center of the group and offers me a bitchy stare. The *mamasan* and I exchange the subtlest nod. The private rooms are a mere flight of stairs away.

She has undressed, showered, and appeared in a bathrobe. Her name is Nok. She clearly expected me to have undressed while she was showering. Since I am still fully clothed, she applies herself to unbuttoning my shirt. I have not yet formulated a plan of action and find myself torn. I know that Chanya would not mind if I slept with Nok in the line of duty; she would probably not think it worth mentioning. Nor would I feel any particular qualms in doing so; I am prevented, however, by a very Thai interpretation of Buddhist teaching. Both Chanya and I have become quite pious since we knew she was pregnant; we do not want to generate any negative karma at this time that might affect the child. My problem, therefore, is how to get Nok to talk without sleeping with her.

While she is working on my fly, she allows her robe to fall open, and I figure it would be impolite not to caress her breasts. The immediate flash of intimacy causes us both to relax. When she has pulled off all my clothes except for my shorts, I explain about Chanya and her condition. A Buddhist herself, Nok understands but does not falter in her attentions.

That is pretty much how we remain during the interview, with her gently massaging my cock through the shorts, using the palm of her hand, and me studying her breasts, paying particular attention to the network of veins leading to her large brown nipples, which I begin to rub slightly nervously between finger and thumb. In view of the fact that I have decided not to let my attentions follow the usual hackneyed path downward, I have to be more than usually inventive with regard to the mammaries. I try both alternating and simultaneous jiggles of each breast, underclutches and overgropes, squeezing-with-fingers-apart, squeezing-with-closed-hands, and other borrowings from the martial arts. I study her expression to ensure that humor does not trespass into offensive satire, but she's a good sport, and the only objection she makes from time to time is *jikatee*: tickles.

"Do you want me to suck you?"

I make a face expressing a polite and reluctant *no thank you*. She smiles, pleased with me. "You're a good man. There aren't many like you left."

"Well, the circumstances of my own birth were not ideal. I want the kid to have every chance."

She nods wisely and watches my fingers while they rub her nipples as if they were money. "I know what you mean." She beams. She had assumed I was a spoiled rich boy, like all the others. There is a subtle change in her use of Thai: more countrified, more idiomatic, lower class. Before long, we're exchanging stories about growing up in poverty in Thailand and the problem with financing smallholdings. Her parents own more than twenty acres of not-bad farming land in Isaan, near Kong Kaen, but it is virtually impossible to make a profit because of the agricultural subsidies in the G8 nations, a topic on which she seems to be an expert. I decide to deepen the interview by decisively taking both her breasts in my hands and holding them for a moment in the way of irresistible objets d'art. She looks down at my hands and smiles. "*Siaow*," she says: horny. "Are you sure you don't want to do it?"

"Sure," I say, but she has noticed a certain stirring. Vanity requires her to play the temptress, but I catch her chin gently and raise her face again to look into my eyes. "I know you don't really enjoy this kind of work," I say.

There is no better phrase to get a whore talking. Now I am receiving in great detail the saga of her fall, and how she might have enjoyed a wonderful loving marriage with a wonderful loving man and been able to live a good honest Buddhist life, were it not for her parents' indebtedness and the need for her to send at least ten thousand baht per month home just to keep them and her siblings alive and well. People don't realize that having enough to eat is not even half the story—what about medical bills, school fees, all the things that you need to be fully human in this world? I say I suppose all the girls working here come from similar backgrounds. She agrees, most are poor country girls who managed to get enough sophistication to be eligible to work here; otherwise they would be working in bars very much like my mother's. Except for the Chinese prima donnas on the top floor, who have spent small fortunes modifying their bodies and often come from more affluent backgrounds. I say that a friend of mine also belongs to the Parthenon, which is what prompted me to join. He was particularly impressed, I say, by a girl called Damrong.

There is a momentary hesitation in her caress, before the hand resumes the mesmeric massage. "You're *his* friend?" Her tone is more formal, tinged with fear.

I cough, taken by surprise. "You mean she only had one customer?"

She stops immediately and challenges me with her eyes. "You've come to check up on her for him, haven't you? That's really why you're here. Your friend is the most possessive man I've ever known. Well, I'm afraid she hasn't been seen here for more than a week. We all thought she'd gone to live with your friend."

Now I'm in a fix because I can't think of a way to get her to name him. "Hasn't he been here for a week either?"

"No."

"Maybe he went home."

"To England? He hates England, he told me as much."

"Ah." I take a long shot. "He never told me that."

"Really? Khun Smith told me his life didn't start until he came east."

"Actually, I don't know him that well," I explain, "an acquaintance more than a friend. A business associate, actually."

She seems relieved that Khun Smith and I are not close.

After ten minutes I seem to have exhausted her stories about the possessive Khun Smith—on two occasions he became quite uncontrollable and had to be restrained—and ascertained that he is an English lawyer working in Bangkok for an international law firm. He uses the club to entertain certain kinds of clients, met Damrong here two months ago, and became obsessed with her. He is tall, dresses well, and speaks Thai with a thick English accent. I have one more question: "You know Khun Kosana, the advertising tycoon who's always in the HiSo magazines? He's a member here, isn't he?"

She says nothing, exactly as if she didn't hear what I said. I thank her for her caresses and tell her I have to go. I pay her exactly the exorbitant amount she would have charged if we had done it, and take my leave.

Outside on the gravel drive I stare up at the surreal fantasy that is the Parthenon and fish out my cell phone. I could certainly find out the details of Khun Smith's law firm with a bit of legwork tomorrow, but something about the club irritates me. I call Vikorn to ask him to order a drug bust—I cannot believe that such an establishment could be entirely cocaine-free—the main purpose of which will be to get the Parthenon's secret member list. I tell Vikorn to tell the troops to look for a single, isolated non-LAN computer.

17

"Come up," Vikorn says. "There's someone I want you to meet."

Outside his office I experience a tiny frisson in my guts. I have a feeling that Vikorn has been up to something with the member list that our brave troops grabbed from the Parthenon last night. I'm told by his loyal and ferocious secretary, Manny, that an extraordinary number of phone calls from high-level movers and shakers have been received this morning, despite that no cocaine was found and no charges laid. All I want is the coordinates of Khun Smith, the English lawyer who obsessed about Damrong and is beginning to look like some kind of consigliere, but suddenly Vikorn has bigger fish to fry.

I'm quite taken aback, therefore, when I find a tall, pink *farang* with auburn hair and hazel eyes in a business suit sitting opposite the Colonel.

"Allow me to introduce Khun Tom Smith," Vikorn says with unusual courtesy.

Smith has already stood up to *wai* me and shake my hand with overwhelming enthusiasm. "Very pleased to meet you. Saw you at Mr. Yamahato's studio the other day," he says.

"Sonchai Jitpleecheep," I say. "Yes, I saw you sitting in a corner watching."

Vikorn grins. "He wasn't there for a cheap thrill—he was protecting his clients' interests. Is that not so, Mr. Smith?" Vikorn speaks only Thai; I am surprised that Smith speaks it well enough to reply, "That is correct, Colonel," using exactly the right form of address.

"Really, really great to meet you," Smith says, offering me his business card with both hands; he has been here awhile for sure.

"You're going to be working together," Vikorn says. I frown, but Vikorn waves a hand to shut me up.

"It's going to be a pleasure," Smith says in English. His is a synthesis of London accents: some BBC, a lot of Thames Estuary, and traces of authentic Cockney from way back; also just a touch of Los Angeles here and there. "A very, very great pleasure."

On Vikorn's unsubtle cue, I say, "I look forward to it," which provokes a gigantic beam from Smith.

"Well, Colonel, sir," Smith says, "I guess that's as far as we can take it today. Great talking to you."

When Smith has gone, Vikorn allows himself a smirk of undiluted triumphalism. I've not seen him like this since the last victory over his arch-enemy General Zinna.

Rubbing his hands together: "They love it, Sonchai."

"Who love what?"

"The syndicate that supplies the international hotel chains. Smith is their lawyer over here. He used to work in California, and he's very well connected. He's very impressed with Yammy's professionalism and says the work in progress is already the best-directed porn he's seen after nearly ten years in the game. It was brilliant of us to use Yammy."

"Right," I say.

"There's going to be some kind of contract, and they want to hook up a video conference with their big honcho. I said you would represent me at all times."

"Meaning I'm the point man, not you, if anything goes wrong? Thanks."

Vikorn gives a stern look to indicate that maybe I need to remind myself of my feudal responsibilities. Back-scratching is not merely built into the system, it *is* the system, and didn't he order that raid on the Parthenon in response to a mere whim of mine? And now he has to deal with a dozen high-flying senators and members of parliament, senior bankers and industrialists, all very nervous about publicity. I do not say, *And willing to pay whatever you ask to keep their names from the media.*

"Okay," I say, "whatever."

"Just do what he wants, check whatever contract they offer, translate it yourself, don't use any official translator, and report back."

"Certainly, sir," I say. "Can we talk law enforcement for a moment?"

"Sure," Vikorn says, not missing a beat. "You mean the raid last night? How much of a cut were you thinking of for yourself?" He asks this question ironically, knowing I won't take the money.

"I wasn't," I say. "Did you know the man you were just talking to is an active member of the Parthenon? He had an affair with Damrong. He's the john in the other blackmail clip, the one that does not star Tanakan. He's some kind of enforcer for a snuff movie gang—did you know that?"

Vikorn freezes for a telltale second. "We need to stay focused on our core industries," he explains. "We don't need to concern ourselves with minor distractions."

"Just tell me one thing. Is Tanakan a member of the Parthenon? Is his name on the member list?"

He resorts to a serious tone, usually reserved for matters of life, death, and money. "If I were you, I wouldn't go there, Sonchai. Let me handle Khun Tanakan."

A tiger grin tells me the interview is over.

At about eleven o'clock that morning a document appears on my desk. It is a computer printout of about a hundred and fifty names. The name in question is Thomas Smith, and the only other detail on the Parthenon's member list is his credit card number. I take out Smith's business card. The firm's name is Simpson, Sirakorn and Prassuman. When I check the Net, I see its webpage emphasizes private international law, corporate law, real estate, and trade. It is particularly skilled in facilitating import and export projects and can obtain letters of credit even in the most difficult circumstances. I'm on the point of picking up the phone to call Simpson, Sirakorn and Prassuman when my cell phone starts ringing. It is Tom Smith. In the friendliest, humblest, and most unctuous way, he more or less orders me to go see him at his law offices, where he has scheduled a videocon. The urgency is a function of a difference in time zones, he explains.

At reception I pick up a copy of *Fortune* and exchange it for *House and Garden*, then settle for the *International Herald Tribune*. There are a few Thai newspapers, but they are out of date. When Smith emerges from the secure area, he greets me warmly and shakes my hand again. His French cuffs with gold links slide back, revealing a handsome elephant-hair bracelet which I had not before noticed. He catches me admiring it. "You were not wearing it yesterday," I observe.

He smiles. "You're a real detective. That's right. Weirdest thing, I was catching the Skytrain at Asok when a young monk bumped into me. He gave me this as a kind of apology." He holds up the burnished hairs that have been twisted together. I do not wonder aloud why a monk would be handing out virility talismans at a Skytrain station. On the other hand, I think such a charm would be irresistible to a man who valued his erections as highly as Smith.

He takes me into the heart of his firm's suite of offices: a window-less room with a small boardroom table, a desktop computer, and a large flat-screen monitor on a stand at one end of the table. Smith is an expert on the gadget; at least he knows how to switch it on and adjust the controls. Now he picks up a telephone. "I have a videocon scheduled with Mr. Gerry Yip for—exactly now. . . . He's on the line? How long has he been waiting, for chrissake? Okay, *now* make it happen."

He barely has time to sit me and himself in front of a digital video camera on a miniature plinth on the boardroom table before the screen brightens to reveal a short, skinny Chinese fellow in his fifties with a potbelly, wearing only a pair of swimming shorts. He is standing on a beach with his legs apart looking bored. A strong Australian accent: "Am I on or not, for fuck's sake? On? Well, why didn't you say so? Tommy? You there, mate?"

"I'm here with Mr. Sonchai Jitpleecheep, as arranged, Mr. Yip."

"Good on yah. Trouble is, I can't fuckin' see yer." Hitching the shorts. "Right, now I can. G'day, Mr. Jitpleecheep, thanks for coming."

I say, "Not at all."

"Good, right. Listen, 'cos there's not a lot of time, I've got the fuckin' prime minister first thing tomorrow, and I 'aven't prepared, so this is the deal. We're very impressed with your product. Ain't that right, Tommy?"

"Oh, wildly, massively impressed. World class."

"Now, you've seen the contract, Mr. Jitpleecheep. What do you think of it?"

"My Colonel and I have not yet had time to go through it," I reply.

"Your Colonel? This is the Emperor Vikorn, right? Too bad he couldn't make it to the videocon. Listen, I might talk ocker ozzie, but I'm Asian to the bones, mate, Chinaman to me marrow, me, I speak fluent fucking Putonghua. I know why this Vikorn character didn't want to come. I've checked him out—he's a smart cookie, no way is he gonna expose himself. So he sends you, and anything you negotiate he can repudiate if he wants to. No, please, no need to deny—I'm talking with respect and admiration, as an Asian. I like it. So look, Asian to Asian, and not meaning any disrespect to Tommy there, who worked his balls off drafting it, but fuck the contract, right? You send us the product of the same quality as your trailer, and we wire the dough to whatever offshore bank you name. If we default, you stop supplying the product; if you default, you don't get paid. If there's a prob with any of the product, we'll give you a chance to fix it, but if you miss a deadline, you're penalized. How much a day, Tommy?"

"Ten thousand U.S.," Smith replies.

"Right. That okay with you? Course it is. Your Colonel has no intention of ever paying a penalty to anyone, and there's no way I can go after him in Thailand 'cos he'll just have me bumped off if I try to enforce, right? So it's as well to know what our leverage really is here." Hitching the shorts: "I represent a large consortium of interested parties worldwide, not only hotel chains but other outlets in every civilized nation on the planet, especially media. So if you do default, you may as well start looking for another business to be in. Clear? Good. Now Tommy, you had a problem with one of the member corporations?"

"A certain oil company that is closely connected to—?"

"Oh yeah, the kid in the White House. Just to fill you in, Mr. Jitpleecheep, the oil companies are interested in your product as a way of keeping the men entertained during the long boring days and nights on the rigs. They've all had enough of the usual cock-and-pussy show, so they might be ready for your wacky stuff. But there is a whiff of S&M that's got a few knickers in a twist. That right?"

"That too, but according to some secret protocol, and considering the senior members of government who are associated with this oil company, they have reservations about showing actual penetration."

A groan from the little Chinaman. "Fuckin' wimps. See, Mr. Jitpleecheep, this is what we have to contend with. The rules change from corporation to corporation, government to government, and from one fuckin' month to another. There's no industry standard, as I pointed out in a meeting of the top producers of this type of product in Manila couple months ago. I said, 'This is crazy, mates. We're going to be as big as oil in ten years, and there's no bloody industry standard for anything. You can see the girl's pubic hair but not her nipples, or depending on the time of day, you can see her nipples but not her pubic hair. You can see the couple rolling and humping, but you can't see the actual pumpin' dick, or you *can* see the pumpin' dick but the tart keeps her bra on'—well, fuck it. Have someone tell the kid I might just start thinking about ordering a global return to reality-based journalism. That'll put the wind up the fucker."

"I'll make it happen, Mr. Yip," Smith says.

"On yer. Anyway, time's up, thanks for the trailer, Mr. Jitpleecheep. Tommy, you and I need a private word about the other thing."

"Certainly, Mr. Yip. If you don't mind, I'll just show Detective Jitpleecheep out."

The Chinaman stares blankly out of the screen as Smith shows me to the door. In the corridor Smith turns to me. "Isn't that a great guy? You ever meet a genius of that caliber before?" He is good at reading faces and sees it as part of his job to accommodate me. He raises his shoulders, points his palms at the ceiling. "What can you do? The pathologically greedy have inherited the earth."

Once on the street I fish out my cell phone and the card the *mamasan* gave me at the Parthenon Club last night. She agrees to meet me at Starbucks at the Nana end of Sukhumvit. I have to go back to the police station before the meeting, but there's not a lot of time, so I take a motorbike taxi. There are about fifty riders gathered at the mouth of the *soi*, slouching around, playing checkers with bottle tops, talking about money and women in their well-worn *seua win*, sleeveless orange jackets with their numbers on back in huge spiraling Thai digits. I want to choose number nine, which is everyone's lucky number, but I have to take the next in rank, number four, considered the number of death by the Cantonese and everyone they ever influenced, including us. Well, I guess this guy has lived with the number for long enough and still seems to be breathing. By the end of the journey I'm revising that view, though. Every motorbike trip makes you fear for your kneecaps when they overtake into oncoming trucks and zoom down the *corrida de la muerte* with no margin for error, but this guy knows no fear at all. It shows that whereas the number four isn't necessarily lethal in all circumstances, nevertheless it is not a number to be taken for granted. I'm quite shaken when I get off outside the station, pay him—then turn right into the Internet monk.

"*Kawtot*," I say automatically at sight of the saffron, but as I step into the station, I'm thinking that it was his fault. He must have seen me getting off the bike and simply stood behind me so that I would bump into him. Strange, because monks are meticulous about how they present themselves to the world. The moment passes, I attend to a few chores and note that Lek and I are on "red spot" all afternoon, which means we have to respond to whatever comes in over the radio and our caseload is more or less suspended for the day.

I call Lek over to my desk for a quick brainstorm. In his honorable opinion we should concentrate on the bracelets. "That's twice, and both from a young monk. And it just so happens that we have a young monk in the area who has started to bump into you. Could this be a clue, d'you think? Sorry if it's difficult."

"You don't have to get sarcastic. Of course I've thought about the monk and the bracelets, but what am I supposed to do? You can't just drag in a monk for questioning in this country without having the Sangha down on your neck, and this one hasn't done anything wrong so far as we know."

"How come he's handing out elephant-hair bracelets to everyone who ever got involved with Damrong?"

"You're exaggerating, and we don't know it was him. I want to let the monk play his full hand first, I don't want you to start nagging him."

I watch as a new idea penetrates and blossoms in Lek's mind. He is more intuitive than me—indeed, intuition dominates the whole of his mental organ, so that once he is convinced of something, it is very hard to dissuade him. Now he is staring at me in fear and awe. "You're going to let him win, aren't you?"

I should, of course, say *Win what?*, but I guess that would be to deny a subtle truth. I have no idea what the young monk is up to—I'm just sure it's more honest than any work Vikorn may have for me. I refuse to engage Lek's eyes and look away.

Now I'm on the back of another bike on my way to Starbucks. My cell starts ringing, and I have to answer it because it might be Nok calling to cancel the meeting. The traffic noise makes it hard to hear, and the signal is intermittent.

"Is it true you're giving him the money for the surgery?" the FBI wants to know. I have to use both hands for a moment to grab the strut behind the seat because the driver is taking a bend at about forty-five degrees; the trick is to keep the cell between one's central digits without pressing any buttons, while clinging to the strut with thumb and pinky. "Hello, hello?"

"Sonchai? You still there?"

A little breathless after a near-death experience, I say, "Lending. Did you two have lunch already?"

"He switched to a coffee break because he says you all are on call this afternoon. How could you do a thing like that?"

This is one of the worst drivers I've ever had, and he's a number nine, would you believe? Sometimes you have to wonder if there's been a paradigm shift equivalent to climate change, causing nine and four to switch in terms of luck distribution. I had to hug his back with my head down when he overtook a taxi just now. "What? Lend him the money? Because he practically went down on his knees and begged me. When I said yes, he made me the most important person in his life. Now we have *gatdanyu*."

"What?"

"Never mind. I'll explain when you've got a week to spare."

"I want to know. If you didn't lend him the money, there's no way he could go through with it, right? There's no one else in the world going to put up that kind of dough for him."

I sigh. "Kimberley, if I didn't lend him the dough for a first-class operation, he'd go downmarket. Can you imagine what that means in Bangkok?"

"Sonchai, I just don't understand you. That's one of the most beautiful male specimens I've ever seen." I have a disgusting feeling that the tough hide of the FBI is being corrupted by the worm of do-goodery. "You're such a compassionate man. How can you do this? He'll never be happy."

"Hang on." With all the optimism in the world, it is difficult to believe I am going to survive the oncoming cement truck. Well, I did. "Without a dick? I don't know about that—you seem to manage. The male member doesn't bestow any privileges anymore. A lot of us owners wonder if it's not more nuisance than it's worth."

"Stop trying to be funny. This is serious. We're talking about a young person's future here."

Irritated because I have to get off the bike before my destination in order to carry on talking, I say, "Wait a moment. I'm going to tell you something." I have the driver stop at a cooked-food stall so I can grab a 7UP and sit down to drink it. "It's like this." Handing a reality sandwich to the FBI is not going to be easy, but there seems to be no alternative. "When Lek was five years old, he had an accident. He was jumping onto the hind legs of a buffalo to spring onto the animal's back the way they do in the country, when the animal jerked his legs and sent him flying. He was lucky not to land on the horns and be gored to death, but when he hit the earth, he split his head open on a rock. They had no medical facilities, nothing at all. They assumed he was going to die. He looked dead already. Are you listening?"

"Yes."

"So they called the shaman, who built a charcoal fire near the kid's head and blew smoke over the boy to assist the shaman's seeing. The parents were called. The shaman told them their son was as good as dead. There was one hope and one hope only: they had to offer their child to a spirit who would fill his body and bring him back to life. But after that the child would belong to the spirit, not to the parents."

"Huh?"

"There was only one downside. The spirit was female. Strictly speaking, Lek is not entirely human—he's a female spirit who inhabits a male body."

I take a sip of the 7UP and wait for her response, which doesn't come. I don't think she has hung up, though, because after a while the line starts bleeping until I close my phone. When, a few minutes later, it gives the double-bleep that indicates a message has been received, I open it again with great curiosity. The message is not from the FBI, however.

Did you know that since the NATO invasion of Afghanistan poppy production in that country has increased more than 500%? Cost of raw sap has halved. My contacts can take the stuff as far as Laos. It would be up to us from there. What do you say? Yammy.

In the reply window I tap out two letters, *no,* and zing it off.

18

I sit upstairs in Starbucks on a sofa with a good view of the street, wait-ing for Nok. I am only vaguely aware of other patrons; I'm pretty much glued to the window. I know what she thinks our meeting is all about, and I'm feeling guilty to be deceiving her, but at the moment she might be the only real lead I have. I'm also feeling disloyal to Vikorn, who would obviously prefer that I don't investigate the Damrong video too carefully. Amazing how easy it is to divide one's own mind. There's a fanatic in me who will not rest until I've got to the bottom of that snuff movie; he lives in the same house as the other guy, who would be happy to go along with Vikorn's game plan and live happily ever after with his pregnant wife. The fanatic is winning.

Now I see her and know exactly what she expects by the way she is dressed. In tight jeans and T-shirt, she could not be further from the eighteenth-century *mamasan* of last night. She has assumed that because I've chosen the Nana area, with its profusion of cheap short-time hotels, we'll go straight into sex: no need for her to dress up. There's a bounce in her step: anticipation of making a little on the side in what will probably be a pleasurable encounter that may lead to something more enduring: maybe I'll even make her my *mia noi*, or minor wife; give her a salary and a room to live in. Also, since I seem to have decided to betray my wife after all, I must have found her irresistible: pride and dominance in her quick smile at me when she arrives.

"Did you know we were raided last night, just after you left?"

I shake my head. "Really? Did they find anything?"

"No drugs, but they took away the computer with the member list. The boss has been on the phone all day talking to members who are scared the press will get hold of the list. Someone called Colonel Vikorn is taking money. Fuck cops."

"Right," I say, giving up on the idea of coming clean. "Well, it's not your problem."

She smiles. "Not right now anyway." She waits expectantly. When I do not begin bargaining regarding the price of her services, she examines my face more closely. Maybe I'm one of those confused men who got into a marriage he's not enjoying but is not sure if a mistress is really what he wants? I have not prepared properly for this interview, and I'm conscious of exceeding my authority. I feel more like a bandit than a cop when I take out my wallet and start to lay out some thousand-baht notes on the coffee table. There's a flash of anger at my indiscretion which diminishes as I continue putting the money on the table. She has counted ten thousand baht and now checks my eyes. No one except a *farang* would offer that kind of money for a midday romp: *Okay, I'm special, but I'm not that special.* I roll the money up into a tight ball.

"Let's say I'm an investigator," I say. "I work with banks."

Her shift into the new reality is pretty well immediate. "You're trying to protect the members? That's why you were there last night and didn't want to do it? The bankers are paying you?"

"No. Someone else is paying me."

I make a face that she construes as affirmation of her suspicion. Her features have hardened, and there is a new clarity in her gaze. "I'll want more than that."

"I'll double it."

"More."

"No."

"Then I'm not talking."

I puff out my cheeks. Twenty thousand baht would probably be what she averages per month. Most girls would grab it—unless they were frightened.

"Look," I say, "how do I know you have the information I'm looking for?"

"I can guess. If you're not working for the bankers, then you're into some kind of blackmail scam. I don't want to get involved, but I need the money. I'll talk for fifty thousand."

There's finality in the tone. "Okay. I'll have to go to an ATM."

"We'll go together, then we'll go to a short-time hotel. That way everyone who sees us will think you're hiring my body." She pauses to look around the café. Three middle-aged white men are sitting with girls they probably picked up in this area the night before. The others are mostly *farang* men and a few *farang* women taking a break from the third world and reading newspapers and magazines over a caffè latte or machiatto. We go to the nearest ATM, where a couple of young *farang* men with eyebrow hatpins watch with amusement while I take out a wad of notes with my whore standing beside me.

She knows the Nana hotels better than I do because she worked some bars here before she went upmarket to the Parthenon. We take a cab to a drive-in, where there are curtains to draw around your car if you brought one, and a hastily constructed set of rooms that give directly onto the underground car park. I pay a guard three hundred baht. Once in the room he asks if I want to watch porn on the DVD player while I'm humping, but I tell him no. Meanwhile Nok has started to feel horny. She sits on the double bed with a teasing smile and looks up at us in the ceiling mirror. I smile and shake my head. She holds out her hand. I give her ten thousand baht and promise to hand over the balance if she has useful information.

There is a gynecological chair in one corner. In use, it must offer access to the captive vagina from virtually every point of the compass. Nok jerks her chin at it with a complex smirk: *Look what we could be up to if you didn't insist on asking stupid questions; maybe we could multitask?* I shake my head again. She sighs and lies flat on her back. I join her, so we are both looking at ourselves in the ceiling mirror, which distorts somewhat. Perhaps the purpose is erotic, for everything appears longer.

"What do you want to know?"

"How the Parthenon really works."

Her elongated features in the ceiling mirror give me a shrewd look. "Why don't you tell me what you know so far?"

"I know that there are only a hundred and fifty official members. The subscription fee is not that high, and there's no way such a small number can keep a place like that going. A membership that small couldn't even keep you in your silk gowns."

In the mirror a female demon nods gravely. "You're pretty shrewd. So how do you think it works?"

"Secret membership," I reply. "There are some impressive names on the membership list, but not half as impressive as they could be."

She nods. "Correct. Not many people know about it, not even the girls. Nothing is written down."

"Tell me how it works."

"We call them the X members. Actually, they are the founders. It's their money that keeps the place going. For them it really is a private club. They get the pick of the girls, anytime, anywhere, any kind of service, on call 24/7. One of the *mamasans* gets a message from the manager: such-and-such a girl is to go to such-and-such an address at such-and-such a time. The girl does as she's told—she doesn't know anything about X members. She doesn't mind because she gets paid double and is given the next night off. Sometimes the assignation is upstairs at the club. Usually she won't know who she's sleeping with. We're all simple country girls—we don't know much about HiSo."

"You mean a private room like we used?"

"No. These are the *real* private rooms. You get to them by private elevator."

"Who are the X members?"

"Who do you think? The highest fliers in Thailand—senior army officers, very senior cops, bankers, businessmen, politicians. Pretty much the same sort of men as the official members, but much more senior."

"So the official members are basically fall guys?"

A shrug. "They get their money's worth. Very often they're business associates of the secret members, so it pays for them to join."

I turn to examine her face. "Do I need to ask you how you know all this?"

A shake of the head. "I'm quite popular with the X members. I talked them into making me *mamasan* so I didn't have to go with the official members anymore. Better one big bastard once a week than a little jerk every night."

"And Damrong?" I ask. "She was popular with the secret members too, no?"

She turns away and speaks to the wall. "Tell me what happened to her. Is she dead?"

"Yes."

"I thought so. Are you investigating for her family?"

"Not exactly."

She turns to study me. "She wasn't popular with everybody. A lot of men saw through her, and women didn't think she looked special."

"But the rest, among the X members?"

"Suppose she was popular with one of them, what about it? What difference if she's dead?"

"It's my job to investigate."

A pause, then: "She was a kind of genius prostitute. The genius was all in her instinct, which was so fast, so accurate, she was more like a wild animal. She would know in a single glance if a man was going to fall for her or not. The ones she couldn't reach in the first ten seconds, she ignored. They ceased to exist for her. That gave her time and energy to concentrate on the others. The suckers. She understood what a lot of girls don't, including me." I raise my eyebrows. "The bigger they come, the harder they fall. I never would have believed it if I hadn't seen it with my own eyes." As she speaks, her left hand seeks out mine. "She was my friend, though. She was very kind to me. She protected me."

Now we are looking at each other eyeball to eyeball. "From what?"

"A pig. I told her I didn't think I could carry on with him. I was losing all self-respect—of course I was never told his name. He paid big money, but he was brutal. She seduced him herself, got him away from me. She didn't seem to mind sadism. Maybe she was kinky that way. Or maybe I'm just too sensitive. She even shared with me the money he gave her the first time he had her. That's the kind of woman she was. *Jai dee mark mark.*" Shaking her head: "But I didn't think anyone could reach him the way she did. For me he was hard as diamond."

"What does he look like?"

"Thai Chinese, tall, slim, about fifty, still very handsome in a vicious kind of way."

I let a couple of beats pass. "I think you know who he is."

"I found out."

"Khun Tanakan?"

She seems reluctant to repeat the name and gives only the briefest nod.

"But at the same time one of the official members was crazy about her—the lawyer Tom Smith. You told me about him."

"That moron. He has no idea how close he came to being bumped off by the Thai Chinese. He didn't know who his rival was, or he would have kept his mouth shut. He would go crazy whenever he came to the club and she wasn't available, started making threats. *Farang* are like boys—they have no self-control."

"Did Tanakan know about Smith?"

"Sure. That kind of guy knows everything. He pays."

"But he didn't do anything about Smith?"

"Smith is still alive, isn't he?"

"Did he do legal work for the Thai Chinese?"

"How would I know a thing like that?"

"Of course. Sorry." I hold up the remainder of the banknotes. "Who organizes all this? There has to be someone in control?"

"The footman at the door. Take a look at him. He's smart. He carries the names of every secret member in his head, and he's the one who takes the girls to the assignations. The secret members pay him big bucks to keep his mouth shut. Of course, he wouldn't dare to talk anyway."

I'm holding out the wad of notes but clamp it between my fingers when she reaches for it. "Khun Kosana, the advertising mogul, he is an X member, isn't he?"

She blinks for a moment and swallows. "Yes. He was a close friend of Khun Tanakan."

"Was?"

"He's disappeared. Everyone thinks he's dead."

"Did Tanakan do it?"

A flash of anger. "How the hell do I know?" Calming herself. "Khun Kosana was the main reason the club hired *katoeys*. I think he only pretended to like girls—I only ever saw him hire *katoeys*. He was a kind of slave to Tanakan. They say he didn't really have a head for business, Tanakan had to bail him out plenty of times. But he was very clever with the media. Tanakan used him to buff his public image."

I hand over the balance of her money, then peel off some more notes and hold them up. "Get me into the secret part of the club, where the escalator leads to the private members' rooms."

"What for?"

"Just to look."

Now she has changed her mind about me all over again. "I think you must be a real cop. That's where she was killed, isn't it? In one of the private rooms."

"How would I know without taking a look?"

She snatches the money out of my hand. "I would do it for nothing. Come to the club tonight. Call ahead to ask for me personally, and reserve a room for us."

We leave the short-time hotel separately. Lek is calling me on the cell phone, asking if I'm coming back to the station because the duty calls are starting to come in. I say I'll be there in twenty minutes. Sergeant Ruamsantiah is running the response teams today.

I'm in a cab when my cell phone starts to vibrate in my pocket. It's Ruamsantiah with a bust. "It's a damn funeral casino," he says, his tone full of apology.

"I thought we stopped busting them."

"Unofficially. We got a report from a cop—must be a disgruntled relative who wasn't invited. It's not something we can ignore. You can go as easy as you like, just make sure you take down names and keep notes so we can say we acted promptly on the information." I call Lek to tell him to meet me at the Skytrain station nearest the address.

Sorry to lay a culture shock on you halfway through the yarn, *farang*; funeral casinos work like this:

You are a newly minted ghost all alone on the Other Side without a body, feeling understandably disoriented. There is still plenty of connection with your living relatives through subtle lines that science will not be able to detect for a few hundred years yet, but after your loss of vital functions, the communication operates largely through transfer of emotional energy: urges outlive reason. Without a body, though, you are dependent on a certain residual awareness filled mostly with separation anxiety. Now, what do you most not want? Answer: you most don't want to be alone. Relatives who might have irritated you profoundly before you became a corpse now acquire an important—nay vital—function. It is the duty of close family to surround you with as many people as possible for the duration of the wake, which can go on for forty-nine days, at the end of which you will have found a new bivouac in someone's—or something's—womb. Now, there is one activity and one activity alone that will keep your average Thai coming to your home day after day for seven weeks, especially if they didn't much like you in the first place. The other advantage to buying a few roulette wheels and offering a private gambling service is for the bereaved spouse to use the profits to pay for the monks, the food, and the roulette wheels and to put together a fistful of baht to see close family through the difficult postwake period.

All of which explains why Lek and I find ourselves outside Nang Chawiiwan's third-floor apartment in a modestly appointed building on Soi 26. Lek snooped around and confirmed there is a fire escape from the apartment by means of the back door. By banging loudly on the front door, therefore, and yelling, "Police," we are able to cause an immediate evacuation. Sounds of Sunday-best shoes slapping on the wrought-iron fire escape on the opposite side of the apartment, excited whispers, some giggling. The exit goes on for about ten minutes, which probably indicates that more than a hundred guests are now legging it down the *soi*. We bang again on the door, and this time it opens on an exhausted, tearful, but spirited woman dressed in traditional Thai costume; Nang Chawiiwan is all of five feet tall.

I don't want to cause offense at her time of mourning, so I let her play for time while the last of her guests make their getaway, then she leads us into the flat. She has not troubled to hide the roulette wheels; there are five of them. Cleverly, she has left small piles of cash next to one of the wheels. She glances from the cash to me to Lek to the cash.

"This is a very serious offense that carries a prison sentence," Lek tells her sternly, while taking a peek at the deceased, who is lying with his arms folded over his chest in a brightly varnished pine coffin: the gaunt, humble face of a workingman. Indeed, he is so gaunt, I'm wondering if Nang Chawiiwan starved him to death. An ignoble thought, perhaps, but that is one skeletal cadaver.

"Sorry," Nang Chawiiwan says.

Unable to maintain stern for very long, Lek stares with infinite compassion at the corpse. "Poor thing's lonely already," he says, "I can feel it."

A sniff from Nang Chawiiwan. "That's why I did it, I had to make it worth everyone's while to keep him company. How else was I to fulfill my obligations as a wife?"

Lek finds this question too troubling and turns to me for instructions. I am afraid I am somewhat transfixed by the corpse, like a cadet with his first cadaver. Death is hitting me strangely this week.

"Take the money," Nang Chawiiwan says, losing patience and jerking her chin at the cash next to the wheel.

"We don't take money," Lek says, again checking my eyes.

"That's right," I confirm. I smile. "Better put it away—it's a little incriminating lying there like that."

Nang Chawiiwan makes big eyes. "You don't take money?" A grin breaks over her features. "I knew my Toong was a good man, but I never knew he had that kind of karma. Imagine, busted at his funeral by two cops who don't take money!" She shoves the cash down her bra for now. "He was practically an *arhat*, a saint, and this proves it."

"You'll have to give us your ID card," I say, "and if anyone asks, this was a serious bust that went wrong because we didn't know there was a fire escape."

"Right."

"And you're never going to do this again, are you? I mean, you're not going to call around to all your guests to tell them the coast is clear as soon as we're gone, right?"

"Of course not."

"Promise?"

"Promise."

"Just this time then."

Locking eyes with me for a moment: "Are you sure you won't take some money? I would feel safer."

"No," Lek says, all firm again and pointing a long finger at her. "You'll have to trust us."

Old Toong's excellent karma has her all excited. She's remembering all over again what a fine man she married and how well he took care of her, even after death. It's not often a ghost gets so lucky at his own funeral casino. Indeed, Nang Chawiiwan is now so fortified with his spiritual power, she has fished her cell phone from out of her costume and started calling the guests back before we're out the front door.

While we're walking down Soi 26, though, in search of a cab, I'm starting to feel dizzy and have to stop at a café. Normally I don't drink on duty, but I need a beer and order one. Lek orders a 7UP, then goes to a street vendor who is pushing his glass-and-aluminum trolley along the gutter. I watch while the vendor opens the hinged glass, stabs at a sour green mango, dunks it onto a cutting plate, and slices it up so fast his hands are a blur. Now he's using the funnel end of the steel plate to slide the slices into a plastic bag. He chucks the first plastic bag into a second, into which he adds pink sachets of chili, salt, and sugar for the dip. The final touch is a cocktail stick with which to eat the mango slices.

"What's the matter?" Lek wants to know when he returns, chewing.

I felt the blood drain from my face, and I'm sure my skin was gray as I sat down hard on a plastic seat outside the café. It's a street that caters mostly to the housing needs of workers in the entertainment industry. There are plenty of *katoey*s around, a lot of *farang*, and girls in jeans and T-shirts on their way to work.

"Death," I say. "Every cop builds up a resistance from the first day on the beat. You can lose it, though, just like that." I snap my fingers while he makes big eyes. He does not understand, and there is no way I'm going to confess to a shameful event of last night that the bust has brought back to mind. I swallow the beer quickly but fail to block the memory:

I woke up with a jolt so hard, I could feel it in my joints. Chanya was my first thought, but she was already awake, staring hard at the ceiling. She only does that when she's angry.

"It was her again, wasn't it?"

I waited as long as I could before saying, "Yes."

"Sonchai, I don't know how much of this I can take. I'd fight any living woman for you, but the dead? D'you know what you've been doing for the last half hour?"

I was unable to answer.

"You've been fucking her, haven't you?"

I turned my head away. "Yes."

"On and on. That's the third time in as many nights. Then you came. You're all sticky."

I didn't realize. Now the whole dream came back to me. Except that it wasn't a dream. It was a visit. I couldn't move for trembling.

With an effort my darling overcame her anger and went to fetch a damp cloth. She wiped me down as roughly as she could without removing surface skin. "A normal man has a real *mia noi*. You have to have a fucking dead one."

"I'm so sorry."

"This has been going on since you went to her apartment the last time, hasn't it?"

"I better have a shower."

"It's the middle of the night."

I went out to the yard to hose myself down like an elephant. We couldn't face each other this morning.

I finish the beer and stare at Lek.

"It's the Damrong case, isn't it?" he asks with that uncanny sixth sense of a *katoey*. I nod without meeting his gaze. "I want you to come to see my *moordu*, master, please?"

Lek discovered his infallible seer about a year ago and has been trying to get me to meet her/him ever since. Lek is convinced that he and I have been circling around each other for hundreds of lifetimes, fulfilling various intimate roles for each other: mother/father, sister/brother, husband/wife. What he's particularly interested in finding out, though, is when I was last a *katoey* like him. It is a tenet of our Buddhism that all human souls go through the transsexual experience from time to time.

"When I'm stronger, Lek," I say, "not today."

While I'm paying for my beer and Lek's 7UP, my cell phone buzzes with a text message. I fish it out, read it, then show it to Lek. It's another from Yammy, the fifth this week:

I've found a mule so I won't have to carry myself. Please talk to the Colonel. I don't think I can take much more of this. I must practice my art. Yammy.

I groan, show the message to Lek, and put the phone away, only to take it out again because it's bleeping. This time the message is from the FBI:

You live in a magic-ravaged land.

19

Nok ordered me to arrive after eleven P.M., when the Parthenon would be at its busiest. The sofas are all occupied by men in dark suits with two or three overdressed girls to serve them. Nok, in her upholstered ballgown, is quite busy introducing customers to girls, taking men up to the second and third floors, returning to welcome yet more eager sperm-spenders. Even when I look directly at her, she avoids my eye. She did manage a quick grasp of my wrist as she passed by, however. It seems the big moment has arrived when the stage will finally be put to use.

The house lights darken, and an invisible orchestra is playing something saccharin-based from the fifties, the kind of music that justifies fifty girls in low-cut swimming costumes kicking their legs in unison. The show is a perfect copy of the stuff you see in old Hollywood movies featuring elaborate dance routines, with a finale that showcases the girl with the biggest breasts—these are truly gigantic—standing on a circular dais, and everyone else on their knees paying homage. Unlike in other bars five minutes from here, the choreography forbids the baring of nipples and pubic hair; it's almost family entertainment. To keep up appearances, Nok has provided me with three young women who are delighted that I speak Thai despite my somewhat Occidental features, and they have been nattering to me about their lives to pass the time. I think they are aware that I am the *mamasan*'s man, however, because not one of them has made a single erotic pass. Finally, when the show has reached its inevitable crescendo and people are clapping in a distracted kind of way, Nok comes up beside me to ask if I want any of the girls sitting with me. I say no in a polite, embarrassed tone, and the girls immediately disappear. Nok takes me up to the second and third floors, where we go through the same routine as on my last visit. She then ostentatiously takes me to one of the private rooms and locks the door. She leans with her back against it, thrusting her Louis XV bosom at me.

"I thought we were going to the secret rooms."

She raises a finger to her lips. "Don't worry, I have a key card." She dips into the depths of her gown to show me a plastic card with a magnetic strip. "The doorman owes me some favors. I told him you are my very special boyfriend and I wanted to make love with you in one of the secret rooms. This card is the master key: it opens all the doors over there." I smile. "Maybe you'll change your mind about having sex with me when you see the room."

She leads me down a fire escape to a utility area on the ground floor, then uses the key card to open a drab door that leads into a heavily carpeted area and a lift with a padded red-leather door. The lift also has a thick red carpet and zips up to the top floor in seconds.

The doors open out into a fascinating playground. TV monitors show alternating scenes of Paris, Venice, Rome, and fellatio. Nok shows how to change channels to get the erotic image of your choice: any position from the Kama Sutra and many more not contemplated by even that optimistic text. The ceilings are high, gilded but less ornate than the public area. All in all there has been an input of improved taste in the decor, with less emphasis on velvet and crimson. The centerpiece is an Olympic-size indoor swimming pool, from which steam rises in elusive wisps. It is amoeba shaped with plenty of Davids, Zeuses, and Poseidons slouching around the edges and a couple of live nymphs naked and splashing each other. I guess they got active when they heard the lift arrive. Nok waves to them through the magic mist, and they wave back.

"This is my boyfriend," she explains.

"Want to share him?"

"No."

She tosses her head with a defiant smile and leads me by the hand down a corridor off the pool area. Silence save for the bustling of her gown and dripping water from the pool. I count only three doors here, and Nok confirms that there are indeed only three private rooms. There isn't enough space for more.

I see what she means when she opens one of the doors. The room must be more than a thousand square feet with a large kidney-shaped Jacuzzi in the middle. Towels, soaps, gels, and massage lotions with Parisian pedigrees are neatly set out around it, and there are mirrors everywhere. On high shelves what look like priceless antiques in porcelain and jade stand guard. My eyes rest for a moment on a jade reclining Buddha of exquisite workmanship about eighteen inches long, which amounts to a lot of jade. "Everything's authentic," Nok says, following my gaze. The bed, which is larger than king size, waits about ten yards away. What impresses, however, are the LCD monitors, some of them enormous, that populate the walls like paintings. I see there are plenty of closed-circuit cameras too. I guess that armed with a remote one could zoom in on genital activity, whether one's own or someone else's, from any point in the room. We exchange a glance, Nok and I.

"This is Tanakan's room," she confesses, finally bringing herself to pronounce her tormentor's name.

I'd not heard her attribute any of the three private rooms to any particular member before; now that she has done so, many things clarify. I want to ask more, but she takes my hand to the edge of the giant Jacuzzi and starts to undress me. "We can at least bathe together," she says. I want to refuse, but her tone has changed from erotic banter to sad and needy. When I am naked, she quickly strips herself, leaving her gown in a heap by the side of the Jacuzzi, and pulls me behind her into the warm water.

"He brought you here often, didn't he?"

She looks away. "You're so intuitive. That's how you survive, isn't it? Pure instinct. I believe you when you say you come from a poor background. Only the poor and people in jail develop such instincts."

She sighs. "Yes, a lot. At one time I was his favorite. He has a kind of clockwork lust. Each girl lasts almost exactly six months, before he dumps her and finds another."

"But I thought—"

"I know what I told you. I have my pride. He was a sadistic bastard, but he was also"—she waves a hand—"incredible."

"Damrong took him away from you?"

She gives me a sharp look. "It doesn't work that way with the X members. The men call the shots." A sigh. "I was coming to the end of my six months anyway. The *mamasan* told him about a new girl. I got the push the next day. But Damrong was very gracious about it, and she did give me half the money he gave her on her first night. A real pro and a good heart. It was a joke between us that she took my Saturday-night whipping for me."

Suddenly, without warning, the water jets all around the circumference of the huge Jacuzzi switch on at full power. My heart rate doubles, and Nok is in my arms, naked, wet, scared, pressing her face into my shoulder. "It's okay," I say. "We must have triggered a switch or something."

She clings to me for a full minute before I can disentangle her and set her down again. I have to let a few beats pass while she recovers. "You don't know him," she says by way of explanation.

I let a couple more beats pass. "Six months is quite a long time to be intimate with someone. You must have talked about more than the price of massage oil." Her pain is haunting and far more attractive than her standard seduction routine. I hold one of her fingers under the water, which causes her to flash me a glance. "You were in love with him, despite his sadistic tastes?"

"He knows how to do that. How to make a woman have strong sexual feelings toward him. How to make her lust for him."

"A lot of men would like to know how to do that."

"With his money and power, it's not so difficult. Little by little he takes over your whole life until there is nothing but him. You become obsessed with him, whether you want to or not. A lot of women like to be forced to focus. I suppose I'm one of them." Looking away at the reclining Buddha: "I guess what makes it all bearable is feeling his pain, even while he's hurting you. It's a kind of twisted love, I suppose."

"Is that what happened to Damrong?"

A wan smile. "No. She was different. She was stronger than him." A quick glance at me, then away: "That's why she had to die, isn't it?" She suddenly decides to duck down, then rise up again with the water dripping from her body, as if she has been baptized.

"I don't know," I say. "That's why I'm here. I think Tanakan's psychology is the key. You must have learned something about him."

"Wait," she says. I watch while she gets out of the Jacuzzi. As with the exquisite vases and jade works, her body and limbs are in perfect proportion, just like Damrong's. "Let's have some music." She goes to an electronic touchpad near the door, and a long, low note seems to emerge from everywhere. I recognize a Zen flute, with its long, dry, haunted yearning for infinity. She comes back to the Jacuzzi, smiling. She beckons for me to put my head under water, where the sound is still more haunting; a liquid pleading for a borderless eternity whose center is everywhere.

She nods with a grave expression and picks up where the conversation left off. "Oh, yes. He's smart enough to realize that even a whore needs something to go on if the affair is going to last six months. He's quite good at sharing his heart." Her left hand emerges from the water for a moment, caresses my chest, before giving up and returning to the water. "That's the other side to him, what makes you forgive his rage when he fucks you. You have to understand, he's no charging bull. More like a python waiting to strike."

"So, who screwed him up?"

"I think Thai society did. His father was a Chinese businessman who operated on the borders between Thailand, Burma, Laos, and China."

"Opium?"

"I think so. Tanakan didn't go into specifics, I think his father traded whatever he could sell. Jade was one of his principal plays." She waves a hand at the high shelves. "Tanakan is a world authority on jade."

"I see. And his mother?"

"A Thai whore, of course. She was third or fourth wife, I can't remember which. All the wives lived together in a big house in Chiang Rai, and he and his mother came last in the pecking order. He showed me a photograph of her. I thought that meant he was really serious about me, but when I checked with the other girls who had been with him, they told me he showed them the picture as well. She was incredibly beautiful. You can see it, even in the snapshot. One of those Isaan girls, you know?"

I nod. The rare Isaan beauty, product of hardship like a wild rose growing out of a crevice, is one of those phenomena people in the Game often talk about. It is as if nature takes revenge on a thousand years of feudal repression by occasionally producing fruit of a quality no upper-class girl ever comes near.

"According to him, she was hard as nails. She didn't show a lot of affection, but she knew how to get enough dough out of his father to send her son to the best schools. Of course, everyone in his class knew what his mother was. He developed a need to win at any price." She waves an elegant hand to take in the priceless vases on the shelves, the jade, the astonishing opulence. "He's proud of that. He thinks his mother made a real man of him, a warrior. He doesn't think she screwed him up at all, merely prepared him for reality as she saw it. Maybe she was right. How should a woman like that—like me, for example—bring up a boy, knowing what we know about the world? Should we pretend it's all Disney?"

"My mother was on the Game too," I confess.

She wrinkles her brow. "Somehow I knew that."

"Statistically, it's quite likely. Prostitution has been a major industry in Thailand for three hundred years. Most family trees are dominated by courtesans." I want to stop her needy hand from sliding any farther down my body, so I say, "Excuse me, I have to pee," and get out of the Jacuzzi.

The bathroom is at the far end of the room and crammed with shiny stainless-steel gadgetry. I examine the power shower for five minutes to kill time and control myself: that's quite a stalk she was provoking. When I try to leave the bathroom, though, I find the door locked. Gently at first, then with greater ferocity, I pound on the door, kick it. Finally I ram it with my shoulder, and it bursts open. When I reach the Jacuzzi, she is floating facedown. Somehow the jets have turned themselves on again. At first I think she must be listening to the music.

I squat down by the edge of the water, waiting for her to raise her head. Little by little the color of the water turns to a delicate churning rose. I turn wildly and run naked around the huge room. I can find no entrance other than the one we used, but this is a smart bedroom, with clever devices everywhere. At the pad near the door I press a rectangle named "water jets," and the turbulence stops. A long diaphanous pink stream emerges from her throat in harmony with the infinite yearning of the Zen flute. I slip into the water to turn her over and examine the fatal gash just under her Adam's apple.

Fresh corpses are hard to maneuver. It takes me more than ten minutes of clumsy clutching and sliding before I can get her onto the side of the Jacuzzi. The best I can do is to lay her out respectfully with her arms crossed and to cover her with a silk sheet from the bed.

By the time I reach the door, depression has set in which quite eclipses fear. I am profoundly sorry to have been the cause of her death. When I emerge into the central area where the nymphs are still hanging out in the pool, they observe the expression on my face.

"What happened? Did you come too soon?"

Without answering I take the elevator down to the ground floor. The footman, I'm thinking—he must have told Tanakan what she was up to.

In the back of a cab I call the FBI. "At least we know where the crime took place," I tell her. "Damrong's death was filmed there—I recognized the reclining jade Buddha."

"What are you going to do?"

"Nothing."

"A woman's murdered in front of your eyes, and you're not going to do anything? Why don't you arrest Tanakan?"

"Vikorn wouldn't let me," I explain. "He's blackmailing him already."

"He's that corrupt?"

"You don't understand. It's a question of honor—that's why Tanakan is playing along. So long as he does, Vikorn is bound to protect him. Even though it's expensive, it's actually to Tanakan's advantage to accept the squeeze."

"You're right, I don't understand."

"Just think Wall Street," I say, and close the phone.

Standing on the sidewalk outside my hovel, I think about making a second call. It's two forty-five A.M., but the person I'm thinking of calling is notorious for her insomnia. She answers on the second ring, not a note of sleepiness in her voice. Because it's so late and the street so silent, I whisper, "Sorry if I woke you."

"Sonchai? It's okay, you didn't wake me. But why are you up so late?"

"Sometime today a corpse will be delivered to you. It will be of a young woman whose nickname is Nok. Her throat will be cut just below the Adam's apple."

A long pause. Something in her tone tells me this is not the first time she has received this kind of call. "What do you want me to do? Please don't ask me to cover up."

I'm overwhelmed by a flashback: Nok, naked, floating facedown, a pale pink stream from her neck like a gossamer scarf undulating in the water. "The opposite, Dr. Supatra," I say. "I want to know who is in charge of the cover-up."

I'm exhausted and wired both. The processing unit between my ears is buzzing like a hornet's nest, but my limbs are so weary I can hardly move them. I know I'm not going to be able to sleep whatever happens; why put off until tomorrow the humiliation that could be mine tonight? The only precaution I take is to enter my hovel silently, careful not to disturb Chanya and the Lump, take my service revolver out from under the mattress where I left it, and go out again into the street. When a cab stops, I tell the driver to take me back to the Parthenon. I get out about a hundred yards before the club, though, pay off the driver, and wait. It is four twenty-three by the clock on my cell phone. The last of the girls are leaving, wearing jeans and T-shirts, saying goodnight to one another in tired tones. The men who work mostly behind the scenes are going home too. From a dark corner I wait until everyone has gone; almost everyone. A tall, closed van of the kind used for wholesale food deliveries draws up. In the blaze of the Parthenon's entrance lights I recognize the doorman, who has changed out of his uniform and is now in shorts and singlet. The arrival of the body bag from out of the building and its delivery into the back of the van takes less than twenty seconds. Now the van is gone, and only the doorman is left, staring after it. He fishes a cell phone from his pocket, listens to it for a moment, then stares down the *soi* in my direction.

Suddenly the hunter is hunted. I wait like a scared rabbit while he unhurriedly walks down the *soi* until he has found me. I know that the distortion in the right pocket of his shorts is caused by the cell phone; a gun would be bigger. Nor does he look especially lethal in his physique: a couple of inches shorter than me, about forty-five with a potbelly.

Now he is peering curiously at me. "Are you going to assassinate me tonight?" he asks. He reaches out with both hands to pull me by the lapels of my jacket. It's not an aggressive move, and I wonder what he has in mind until I realize he is dragging me toward a streetlamp. He positions us so that I can get a good look at his face. It is twisted in spiritual agony. He prods at the gun in my pocket.

"Why don't you kill me? I would consider it a favor." I stare into his anguish. He swallows hard. "My wife and daughter are both servants in his mansion. He treats them well. They're not beautiful, so he never lays a hand on them. But I'm his slave. I hope you understand."

20

"A body fitting the description you gave last night arrived at the morgue at six this morning," Dr. Supatra says. She has called while I'm getting dressed. Chanya is at the *wat* begging the Buddha to overlook her former profession and provide a healthy, happy, and above all lucky baby.

"Who brought it?"

"Detective Inspector Kurakit."

"Where did he say the body was found?"

"At an apartment rented by the deceased."

"You were not invited to investigate the scene?"

"No."

"Thanks," I say, and close the phone.

I call Manny, Vikorn's secretary, to ask her to put me through to the boss. I can tell by her tone that she's been primed already. "He's out at a meeting."

"No, he's not."

"He's very busy, Detective. I'm not sure he's got time for you today."

"I want to know why I'm not on the new murder case that came in this morning."

"Do you want me to ask him for you?"

"No. He'll say it's because I have my hands full already. I want to speak to him."

"I'll see what I can do."

No call comes, of course. Our protocol is of such rigidity that he might as well have taken a trip to the moon—there is no way of getting to him if he doesn't want to see me. I guess I'll have to try to deal with Kurakit. It would have to be him, of course.

We don't hate each other, for the simple reason that to hate another person you have to understand them on some level. Kurakit is as baffled by me as I am by him. From his point of view, I'm an idiot who should never have been recruited in the first place. A devout Buddhist and a former soldier, to Kurakit and millions like him, life is very simple: find a billet, identify the boss, do whatever he tells you to do, and accept the promotions that follow. To him, my complicated psychology is a sure sign of insanity. He has, of course, been warned that I might call.

"How are you?" I ask with as much bonhomie as I can muster.

Suspiciously: "Okay."

"I hear a new case came in early this morning."

"Who told you?"

"Is it a secret?"

"It's *my* case. Colonel Vikorn called me at home at four o'clock this morning. You're too busy to deal with it."

"I'm not trying to steal it from you. It might be connected to something I'm working on—maybe we should brainstorm together."

"Brain what? What are you talking about? It's not connected to anything you're working on."

"How do you know?"

"Vikorn said so. He said if you called, I was to tell you it's not connected."

"Did he tell you who did it?"

"No."

"But he told you who didn't do it?"

"Maybe."

"Did he tell you a certain senior banker named Tanakan had nothing to do with it?"

"Yes. No. I don't want to talk to you anymore."

He hangs up. I call again. "At least let me have the address where the body was found."

"No. I'm not allowed to."

This time *I* hang up. I call Dr. Supatra instead to ask her for the address on the admission form that Kurakit must have completed. She's too busy to deal with it right now but promises to fax the form to me, which includes Nok's ID number and her original address in her home village. While I'm waiting for the fax, the FBI calls.

"Sonchai, d'you know I think what you're doing is evil? I've thought about it—there's no other word. It's so medieval, like castrating choirboys or something. He's only doing it to sell his body, isn't he?"

"I told you why he's doing it."

"I don't buy it. It's an Oriental cover-up. You people, I'm starting to get the picture here, you still play this game of making ugly things look pretty so you can sell them."

"Advertising is a Western invention. Ever watch a cigarette advertisement? They used to feature pure mountain streams, so they could sell poison that gave people lung cancer. I was bombarded with them throughout my youth. So were you, probably. You've just got a dose of culture shock, that's all."

"It's so grotesque. Cutting everything off like that, then giving him a phony vagina. Ugh!"

"Do you feel the same way about breast implants? If you do, you could start a nice new pressure group in your own country, keep yourself occupied for decades."

She fumes over the telephone. "You think I'm just another lost *farang* woman looking for a soapbox to bitch on, don't you?"

"I think you're in love with Lek," I say.

Two beats pass. Cautiously: "Is he gay?"

"For Buddha's sake, no. He's never had sex in his life and likely never will. With his kind of *katoey*, the lust is all in the conversation. They can be quite prudish when it comes to the crunch. I told you, he's a female spirit in a man's body. All he wants to do is express his inner truth. Sorry if it's difficult." Exasperated, I hang up.

She calls again in the time it takes to press an autodial button. "Did you say express his inner truth? Well, that's what I want to do too. That's why I'm here. You wanted to know, that's why. I never thought of it like that till you used that phrase."

"If it involves seducing him, you'd better not use precision bombing—it tends to antagonize. Try a little sympathy. Try taking him seriously. He's the one with the guts to have the surgery—give him a little credit."

A pause. "Has he really never had sex? How old is he?"

"Twenty-two, and I'm busy." I hang up, then turn off the phone and go to lunch.

When I check with the telephone company, I am given the number of Nok's family home. Now I hesitate. After all, she died because of me—how easy will it be to face her people? I decide to check the apartment first.

The address is way out of town, quite near the new airport, which is not yet open. When I arrive in a cab, after more than an hour stuck in traffic on Sukhumvit 101, I realize that she lived in a standard one-room accommodation in a project intended as a dormitory for airport drudges. The apartment building is designed much like a prison, with ten-by-fourteen-foot cells giving onto an internal corridor. She lived on the fifth floor, which is the top, and there is no lift. The doors of the cells are secured by means of crude padlocks, but when I arrive at Nok's, I see that her door is open. I knock anyway and enter. Five people are in the room, including a couple in their midfifties who must be her parents, a young man in his early twenties, a young woman who may be still in her teens, and a boy about seven years old. There is nothing else in the tiny room apart from a futon and some women's clothes on hangers that are hooked over a length of molding. My eyes fixate on the boy for a moment; I hope he is not Nok's son. In her conversations she never mentioned she had a child. "I am Detective Jitpleecheep," I say.

There is no hope at all in the five sets of eyes that stare at me. As a rule, cops don't offer it. There is fear in the mother's and daughter's expressions, anger in that of the son. Neither the father nor the grandson seems to understand what is going on. I say, "May I ask why you're here?"

"Our cousin called us—he lives downstairs. He told us some men brought our daughter here on a stretcher last night, and he could see that she was dead. Then some other men came to take her away. We don't know where she is." It is the mother who spoke. Now the brother: "She was our only hope. She kept us alive. What will we do now?"

Suddenly they all seem to be silently accusing me. I have to admit there is some justice in that. As a rule, fifty percent of problems suffered by the lower income levels are caused by cops.

"She was a good girl," her mother says. "She didn't sell drugs, and she didn't sell her body. She worked in a restaurant." I look at the young boy without asking the obvious question. "Nok was married to his father, legally, but he found another wife and stopped sending child support."

"I see," I say. Of course, there is no way Nok could have kept five or more human beings alive on wages from a restaurant job, but protocol requires these necessary illusions. Maybe only the mother is smart enough to realize what Nok really did for money. Certainly no one in the family would ever have discussed the matter out loud. Without breaking the omertà, though, it is difficult to discuss the case.

"She sent home ten thousand baht a month," her mother explains, "and I have to feed all of us plus my parents on that. We spend all our time growing rice to eat. We have no cash at all. My mother has diabetes. We get her drugs cheap on the government system, but she needs a special diet. My father has health problems too—something is wrong with his brain from farming in the heat all his life. My son here wanted to finish high school, but we didn't have the money. My younger daughter here is a virgin, but she meets only local boys who have no money and usually drink whiskey and do drugs. Nok wanted to help her find a good husband, but she needs to finish high school as well or only LoSo men will look at her. Nok said she was pretty enough to find a *farang* husband in a year or so, when she might come here to Krung Thep. Nok said *farang* have so much money, one man would keep us all. Now what will we be, just beggars?"

I see my own family here. Thank Buddha my mother had the smarts and the ruthlessness to get out for long enough to make a pile—and start a brothel of her own: nobody escapes the cycle of karma, not even a Buddha.

Now the brother speaks. "Our cousin thinks it was cops who brought her and took her away again. We think maybe some rich man used her and killed her, then paid off the cops." He stares at me accusingly.

"I know that she was killed," I say. "I don't think she was sexually assaulted."

Now the father speaks. I recognize him as a type who might be termed the backbone of our country. He speaks slowly, carefully, and very politely, in a voice that has never told a lie. "We are a devout family. We give so much to the *wat* for *tambun*. Nok also made merit whenever she could, even here in Krung Thep. I have worked the fields all my life. When I was young, I ordained for a whole year. When I die, I will go to nirvana. I do not want to think about my daughter being killed by a bad man. It makes me feel crazy." As he speaks, he holds his head between thick calloused hands and twists it one way then another. The gesture somehow completes my feeling of helplessness. I want to say that I will hunt down Nok's killer and bring him to justice, like you hear in the movies, but I doubt even this unworldly family would believe that. Gentle they may be, but they have already absorbed and discarded Nok's murder; what they want is some security for the future, some substitute for their only breadwinner. There is no tragedy that compares to an interminable tomorrow without rice. The mother seems to have followed my thoughts.

"It cost us more than a thousand baht for all of us to come here today," she says, fixing my gaze. I fish out my wallet, hand over two thousand, cast my eye around the room (not a sign of blood or struggle), nod, *wai*, and take my leave. Outside I trudge around for a while, feeling bad. The apartment building is only one of dozens that have sprung up on land speculation, and they are all the same: long five-story structures composed of identical cells. Blink once, and it could be a concentration camp. Blink twice, and it could be anywhere in the third world. Blink three times, and it might be all our futures in this age of functional barbarism. I have to get out of here.

When I'm back at my desk, Vikorn calls. "Where have you been?"

"I'm investigating a murder."

"Sonchai, I'm not asking this time, I'm ordering. Don't go there. Let Kurakit deal with it. As it is, you're lucky to be alive. I know you don't give a shit about anything except your piety, but if you won't keep your nose out of it for me, at least do it for Chanya and your unborn child. Tanakan will squash you like a bug and never give you a second thought. Do you want Kurakit investigating *your* murder? Where will that get you?"

I think of Nok's father and want to say, *Nirvana*. But I don't have the innocence or the guts. Instead I grunt, "Okay."

In the circumstances, the company of a frustrated drug trafficker–cum—movie director feels like light entertainment. Yammy has just messaged me:

I'm at the Kimsee, drinking. Come join me.

The Kimsee is a Japanese restaurant on Sukhumvit, opposite the Emporium and under a Skytrain bridge. It looks as if it were carefully removed from somewhere quaint in Tokyo and reconstructed here in Bangkok under strict Japanese quality control. I've been there a couple of times, and apart from the Thai waitresses everything about the place strikes me as authentic Nippon, including the heavy-drinking salary-men who all have their own reserved bottles of best sake with their names printed on them, waiting on a high shelf.

Yammy's is not waiting, though. It started out as a liter but has lost half its contents. As I sit down at the dark-stained wooden table, which perfectly matches the dark-stained wooden decor, Yammy beckons to one of the waitresses, who comes to pour some of the sake into a stone jar for heating. A few minutes later it comes back warm, and she pours a couple of shots into the tiny mugs. Yammy is halfway through his bento box, gloomily picking at yellow tofu with his wooden chopsticks.

"I don't think I can go on any longer, Sonchai," he says in that soft California accent. "This is it, I resign."

"Okay," I say, taking a slug of the sake. "I'll speak to the boss."

I cannot tell yet if this is the correct strategy. Maybe he's too far down the line with his depression to be tricked out of it? He gives me a sly glance. "The third movie in the series is only one-half shot. You'll have to find someone to take it over."

"Right."

Peering over his chopsticks: "You don't care? The whole contract is at risk."

"I realize that, Yammy, but you're an artist—you're temperamental. If the working environment is not right for you, you cannot work. Vikorn will have to understand that."

"He won't snuff me?"

"He might. But we already know you have no fear of death. After all, you were on death row for a while, and we practically had to beg you to leave jail."

He manages a smirk and drops the pretense. "Look, I'll finish this one and do the other ten, but after that—"

"Yammy, forget it. If you want to be difficult, Vikorn will dump you anyway. Maybe he'll kill you, or maybe he'll send you back to jail. Maybe you really do have that kind of integrity, but so what? The movies are going to get made, Yammy, if not by you then by someone else. I'm only afraid Vikorn will want me to take over the production."

He hadn't thought of that. He lays down his chopsticks to stare at me. "You? You don't know scat about making a movie."

"I agree. Just think how awful they'll be if I make them. How is an amateur like me going to get a penis to slide into a vagina? It must take decades of practice."

He maintains radio silence for about ten minutes—at least, that's what it feels like. Finally, forcing me to stare back into those bottomless pits of morosity: "You have to babysit me, don't you? That's your job. So, we're going to get drunk." He tosses back some sake and nods at me to do the same. I'm still nursing guilt and mourning Nok and cannot think of a better thing to do. I'm not sure how many times we knock back the rice wine, but the sake bottle with Yammy's name on it in elegant Japanese calligraphy is empty by the time we leave. Outside it is early evening. On the street, with the Skytrain rattling overhead and the static traffic chugging out airborne poison down below, the cooked-food stalls of the day, with their hundred varieties of sweet snacks, have been replaced by more serious stalls serving noodles and other dishes suitable for hungry commuters on their way home. Generally speaking, though, the landscape is more fluid than I remember. Yammy is in worse shape and can hardly stand. He claws at my left arm, which he is using to support himself. "You think it's so easy to slide a penis into a vagina, when neither bit belongs to you? It's not as easy as you think. You know who are the biggest prima donnas in the porn industry? The studs, my friend, the studs. One harsh word, and they droop."

"But you have Jock?"

He grunts. "If not for him, I really would resign."

That night Chanya surprises me. We are in bed together with my hand on the Lump, and I have just finished telling her how Nok died. I was expecting another fear reaction, followed by a demand that I listen to Vikorn and forget Nok. Chanya, though, is quiet for a long time. Finally she says, "Do what you have to do, Sonchai."

"But what about you and the child?"

"We'll have to take our chances. Too many people in Thailand are in denial. Keeping quiet in the Thai way doesn't work anymore. Maybe one day a rich man will decide to rape and kill me, then pay off the police. Change has to start somewhere."

"That's not the way you talked last time Tanakan's name came up."

"I know. Now another woman is dead. Perhaps our Buddhism has made ordinary Thais too humble."

"And the others too arrogant," I mumble.

21

All serious crime starts with a plausible excuse: terrible childhood, fell down the stairs at a tender age, emerged from urban squalor, et cetera. The one I plan to commit needs nothing more than the murder of Nok, Pi-Oon, and Khun Kosana *qua* motivation; let's not dwell on any residual outrage I may feel at the manner of Damrong's demise. Nok, at least, did not conspire with her killer. I want Tanakan's head, and to hell with Vikorn. I shall have to be a fox, though, if I am to survive. I have grudgingly to admit that it must have been precisely my connection with Vikorn that saved my life: if Tanakan bumped me off, the nature of his deal with the Colonel would alter in Vikorn's favor; the Colonel would, of course, have shown no mercy.

I don't have much of a plan as yet, which puts me in one hell of a mood. All I can think of is to grab the footman at the Parthenon on some pretext and do whatever is necessary to get him to talk, but if I do that, Tanakan will find out and snuff me. Anyway, that man does not fear death or jail; Tanakan holds his women, who are everything to him. He won't talk unless he wants to. Sometimes I envy my Western counterparts the simplicity of their lives; presumably they have no care in the world beyond bringing perps to justice? A little schoolboyish, though, and lacking in moral challenge. I doubt you can burn much karma that way.

Still furious, I decide to take a walk around the block. I'm in no mood for social niceties when the Internet monk manages to get in my way as I'm crossing the road. I glare and pass on.

It is about eleven-thirty, the time when all good hawkers get cooking in readiness for the midday rush. They have set up their stalls opposite the police station especially for cops and staff, which earns them a special dispensation from arrest. You can tell what they are selling depending on the utensils: a simmering brass basin probably means a beef-based soup; a big enamel basin will have pigs' legs simmering in it; a dark brown burnt-clay mortar with wooden pestle will produce wickedly hot *somtan* salad; a wok over charcoal means a fry-up, and so on.

I've cooled down a bit by the time I'm returning to the station, and I'm wondering if this might be the time to bring the monk in for questioning when he reappears out of the Internet café just as I am passing and bumps into me all over again. I turn on him with a sarcastic comment on my lips but freeze because he is standing with his hands in the air, palms facing me. The expression on his face is quizzical, almost amused. Mad monks are as common in Buddhism as in other monastic traditions. I think he must be really crazy, though, when he maneuvers to stay in front of me until I can find a way around him. I'm still thinking about him when I reach my desk and Lek joins me.

"D'you know what that Internet monk just did? He deliberately bumped into me and went like this." I hold up both hands, palms toward Lek.

"He did the same thing to me yesterday." I've noticed that Lek is less keen on the monk than he once was. "Maybe he is nuts. Did he show you his scar?"

"What scar?"

"I thought that was why he was holding his hands up. He has this scar on his wrist, like he once tried to commit suicide or something and maybe now he's obsessing in some way."

"But the bracelets?" I say.

"Maybe he's giving bracelets to everyone he meets. Maybe there is no connection."

"He didn't give me one."

Actually, I did see the scar but paid it no attention. We both shrug. Nobody wants to be the one to get a monk put away in a mental asylum. It's a shame, though, for one so young to be in such decline. I dismiss him from my thoughts as I refocus on how to pot Tanakan, whether Vikorn likes it or not. I don't think about the monk at all for the rest of the morning, and it's only when Lek and I are sitting at a cooked-food stall for *kong kob kiao*, something to chew, that I think of him again. I am holding half a dozen fish balls on a stick, which I put down on the table.

"The scar," I say.

"What scar?"

"On the monk's wrist."

"What about it?"

"I want you to check the Internet café to see if he's still there. I'm going back to the station. If he's in there, ask him if he wouldn't mind coming up to see me at his convenience. Be polite."

Lek shrugs. Maybe I'm the one who will soon end up in the nuthouse.

I watch from the window next to my desk while Lek emerges from the Internet café, pushing his hair back with both hands. He appears at my desk a few minutes later, alone.

"Well?"

"He said he would be delighted to come and see you here in about an hour. He is going to the *wat* to meditate for a short time."

I feel a twinge of annoyance, then let it pass. I remember that no one is more meticulous than a fraud. I'm recovered by the time he does show up, only to get irritated all over again at his self-conscious monk-at-the-shore-of-nirvana posing. I have to take myself in hand not to use an aggressive interrogation technique. Since he likes to wear monk's robes, he obviously enjoys seeing others grovel.

"Phra—I'm sorry, I do not know your Sangha name."

His sangfroid is imperturbable, I have to give him that. "It doesn't matter. From the look on your face, I suppose you believe I do not have a Sangha name. Is that not so?"

Irritated all over again, I ask, "How many precepts do you follow?"

"What a childish question, Detective. You know very well every monk must follow two hundred and twenty-seven precepts."

"I'm sorry," I say, "foolish of me." I am taken aback at the educated quality of his Thai. I expected a lost, unlettered young man from the poor north.

"I understand. You think that I have not been behaving like a monk, therefore I cannot be one. This is called clinging to fixed images or, more generally, ignorance. Do you always behave like a detective, Detective?"

The elegance of his answer startles me into playing a poor hand. "For a monk you spend an awful lot of time in an Internet café. Are you a modernist Buddhist?"

A smile—not quite patronizing, but close. "Of course not. Modernism is largely a form of entertainment, and a superficial one at that. It doesn't survive environmental disasters or oil shortages. It doesn't even survive terrorist attacks. It certainly doesn't survive poverty, which is the lot of most of us. One flick of a switch, and the images fade from the screen. Ancient questions begin to torment us all over again: Who am I? Where do I come from? Where am I going? But without wisdom, these questions turn toxic. Confusion seeks relief in bigotry, which leads to conflict. One high-tech war, and we're back to the Stone Age. This is the connection between modernism and Buddhism. In other words, there isn't one unless you posit the latter as a cure for the former." A sudden charming smile: "On the other hand, it's convenient to download Buddhist texts without having to spend hours searching for them in a library. Until recently I'd had no idea how limited Theravada is. If I were to ordain today, I think I would do so in Dharamsala, where the Dalai Lama lives."

I push my chair back. It has dawned on me that the case has taken an unexpected, even a shocking turn. In my surprise I find I am mesmerized by this young *phra,* whose true identity seems to grow more elusive whenever he opens his mouth. Have I mistaken his mannerisms for those of a fraud exactly because he is so advanced that he is no longer conscious of the effect he has on others? Perhaps he doesn't give a damn. Real monks don't.

"I'll take you to a private room."

. . .

In our smallest interrogation room I say, "You have been watching me for more than a week now. Why?"

"I wanted to tell you about my sister," he says with that same balance of compassion and detachment that may or may not be authentic.

My tension collapses in a grateful sigh. "You sister's name is Damrong?"

"Yes. You guessed anyway from the scars. I made it obvious enough."

"You have information regarding her death?"

"No, none at all."

"So why come to me?"

"Because *she* has information she wants to give you. She visits me every night. Her soul is not at rest."

I take a moment to absorb this forensic bombshell. "Why play games? Why not come to see me like a normal person?"

"I am not a normal person. I am a monk."

"Or does it have something to do with that?" I point to his left wrist, where a short white scar exactly replicates the scar on Damrong's wrist.

"Not what you think," he says with a smile. "A teenage prank, nothing more."

I grunt in resignation. "Please tell me all you know," I say with a sigh.

"Not here," he says, looking a little fastidiously around the small bare room. "I prefer the outdoors. I think you do too, is that not so?"

He leads, I follow, out into the blinding light and the never-ending business of the street. I remain half a step behind him, as protocol requires. We keep pace with a man in a straw hat pulling a cart piled high with brushes, brooms, and dustpans while I bend my ear to catch the monk's every word.

Damrong, according to her brother, was something of a female *arhat*, or Buddhist saint. Born with the name of Gamon, now using the Sangha name of Phra Titanaka, he was a sickly child. Even at that time their mother was a *yaa baa* addict and losing her mind, given to sudden bouts of irrational violent anger. Their father was a career criminal whose body was covered in tattoos bearing magical incantations in *khom,* the ancient Khmer script, who was ritually murdered by local police when Gamon was seven years old. Both parents were Khmer refugees, who fled after Nixon bombed the eastern half of their country and destabilized the whole of it. Both children were born in a refugee camp on the Thai side of the border. His reverence for his sister is impressive.

"I would never have survived without her. She took all my beatings when our father was still alive—she wouldn't let him touch me. She was so fierce, he was afraid of her. And she saved me from our mother too."

"She paid for your education?"

"Yes. All of it."

Our eyes meet. My own education was funded in the same way. I cannot help asking, "You knew where the money was coming from?"

"Not at first. Of course, I grew up and could not help knowing."

His discipline is excellent. The single trickle down his cheek from his left eye must surely cause an itching sensation, but he makes no attempt to wipe it away. From his level, even his emotional anguish is simply another misleading phenomenon, like everything else in the world. He is amused that I admire him. He has no idea how tempted I used to be, perhaps still am, by the monastic life. I spent a year in a forest monastery in my midteens. It was the most peaceful year of my life, and the simplest.

We stop at a crossroads to let a motorcycle trolley pass; it is festooned with lottery tickets and brightly colored magazines, to the extent that the guy riding it is invisible. The cop in me has a cruel question: "Do you know how good she was at what she did?"

He suppresses a shudder. "Of course. She was very beautiful and had a brilliant mind. That's how she paid for my education, from the time she reached sixteen and could sell herself. The way she saw it, she could provide me with the chance she never had. But I was never that clever. I think in another country, or if she had been born into a different class, she would have been a great surgeon."

"A surgeon?"

"She had a natural healing gift and was a supremely unselfish person. She learned about nutrition and drugs so she could stop our mother from killing me." He allows himself a gulp. "She was very gentle."

"When did you hear of her death?"

A shrug. "She came to me in a dream."

Since his information is voluntary, I have no way of forcing him. I am intrigued, though.

"There is nothing more you can tell me? You've gone to a lot of trouble to check me out."

"I needed to know if you would be receptive. I'm overjoyed to have found such a devout man as you."

A thought wings its way into my mind, perhaps originating in his. "You knew she was dead because she came to you as a ghost. How could you be so sure?"

He has turned to face me, with exactly the same abstract elegance as all his other movements. "I have said enough for the time being. I came to make contact."

"How shall we proceed?"

"When I have more information, I will find a way of telling you. I would not like to meet at the police station again, though. We shall meet at the local *wat*, if you don't mind." I experience a sense of loss, a fear I might not see him again. He offers a compassionate smile. "Don't worry—whom the Buddha intends to bring together, nothing can keep apart."

I smile, quite seduced by this extraordinary saint. "That's true," I say enthusiastically. Then the cop within starts with his annoying doubts, which I suppress.

It is pathetic, but I cannot help wanting this young man's approval. Nor can I help feeling the need for some kind of absolution. "Did you know your sister worked at my mother's club for a while? We knew each other, Damrong and I."

My question seems to cause a shift in his consciousness. There is a contraction of his brow, a frightening concentration at the chakra between his eyes. His look is quite merciless, and there is no need for him to say, *I know everything.*

"She said you were a holy fool," he mutters before he crosses the road.

Only when he has gone do I realize I forgot to ask which monastery he ordained at. I call Lek to ask him to check with the Sangha. Half an hour later he arrives at my desk to tell me the Sangha have never heard of Gamon, aka Phra Titanaka. Lek's manner is ambiguous as he plays with his *yaa dum* stick, then pushes his hair back with both hands. He coughs.

"What is it, Lek?"

Another cough. "That *farang* woman. You remember?"

"Lek, you could at least call her 'the FBI.' It's more polite."

"Well, she took me to lunch yesterday while you were out."

I push back my chair, not quite sure what expression to use. "I see."

"She wants to marry me. On condition I don't go through with the surgery." He is staring directly into my eyes. Suddenly I am the outsider, the one with *farang* blood; perhaps I can explain? Nothing in his manner suggests that he has even considered the FBI's alarming offer; the cultural gap is far wider than that. He simply wants to know if I have a clue as to how an Earthling should behave in the presence of a particularly pushy Andromedan.

"If you married her, you would be entitled to half her income. I think the FBI at her level get about thirty-five thousand dollars a year gross."

Casually, Lek shifts the calculator on my desk toward him and punches in the numbers with one finger while he shoves the *yaa dum* stick up his right nostril, then blinks at the result. I think it is more than he expected. He raises his shoulders helplessly. "But then I wouldn't be able to be a woman, would I?" He walks away, shaking his head in despair at the level of education on Andromeda these days. At some level I'm furious with the FBI, but I have to leave her on hold while I focus on Damrong's brother.

The problem with an unknown and perhaps unknowable quantity is that your imagination will make anything of it. Fraud or madman? For once I share my self-doubt with Lek. "He had me fooled. For a moment I really thought he was the real thing."

"He is," Lek says with total confidence, now that he's sure the monk is not loony after all. "And you're crazy about him. He's what you

were supposed to be, master." He adds the last word by way of cushion-
ing the impact of his *katoey* truth-telling.

"But the Sangha have no knowledge of him."

Lek puts his aroma stick away to give me one of his rare frank looks.
"You know as well as I do that he is a real monk who has spent years in
a monastery. If he hadn't, he couldn't walk and talk like that. He's very
advanced. He must have ordained in another country."

"Cambodia, where his parents came from? How could someone
like him ever come out of Cambodia?"

I frown and get up to leave the station and go for a walk. For want
of direction I follow a *saleng* as he slowly pedals his flatbed trishaw
down the street, looking for trash. *Saleng* are our sorcerer-scavengers;
in their hands beer cans turn into toys, plastic bottles become painted
mobiles to hang in shopwindows, Coke cans are stitched into sun hats,
and grilles from truck radiators transmute into garden gates. I watch
him stop to dip into a garbage bin and triumphantly return to his
trishaw with a broken umbrella. Without his sublime humility, I cannot prevent my thoughts from turning back to Damrong's brother.

I am afraid my identification with him is too great for objectivity. I
don't need to read his biography—I can smell every detail. He had it
tougher than me, but it's only a question of degree. We too were inches
away from disaster, my mother and I. Nong took the relocation path, by
deliberately cultivating clients who took us overseas, but Gamon stayed
home while his sister sold her body. The price he paid for survival
was the abuse of his sibling by armies of rampant men of every race
and creed; on his own admission he was a sensitive child. How many
nights did he spend in torment before someone told him about methamphetamine? It's expensive, though; if you're poor and need it, you
more or less have to trade in it.

I pass over my intimate knowledge of his misery; no point playing
those old tapes on his behalf; what has impressed me is the degree to
which he rose above it all. I never scaled such heights. My late partner,
Pichai, and I spent a year in a forest monastery as a deal to keep us out
of jail. Apparently Gamon ordained voluntarily, for life. His supervisor
must have been as ruthless as my own, probably even sterner. He could
not have survived long as a novice monk without putting himself
through that form of destructive testing called *vipassana* meditation. I

know he must have started from some hell of frustration, with its complex trap of poverty, crime, drug abuse, and the selling of his sister: an authentically lost soul only a membrane away from despair and madness.

When I get back to the station, I find Lek standing at the window near my desk. "He went back to the Internet café for ten minutes, then crossed the road in the direction of the *wat*," he says in a dreamy voice. "That's a very holy brother."

My cell phone bleeps twice:

We could start small, just to test the mule. Or I could risk everything on one big consignment. I'm willing to die for my art. How sincere do I need to be? How desperate? Yammy.

22

"He told you, didn't he?" It is the FBI's voice, a tiny, nervous hiss in the cell phone.

"Yes."

"How pissed are you, on a scale of one to ten? Don't say eleven."

"Eleven."

"Okay, with you that means going back to biblical times. You think the Western mind is some Frankensteinian product of a botched religion and a bunch of ancient Greek pedophiles, the same unholy combination of schoolboy logic, lust for blood and glory, we-know-best, and destroy-to-save that slaughtered three million in Vietnam, most of them women and children, all in the name of freedom and democracy, before we ran away because it got too expensive. Right?"

"Right."

"Well, you're wrong, dead wrong. I had no idea I was going to say what I said to Lek. It wasn't in my head at all. I took him to a good Thai restaurant that even Thais respect and watched him using his fingers to eat the *somtan* salad with the sticky rice, and I saw that you were right: that is one totally innocent soul." I do not dignify the pleading tone with a reply. "But it didn't make any difference. I felt this flood of love, compassion, lust—the whole nine yards, totally overwhelming. I didn't know such emotions could happen to a woman like me. I adore him. Totally, helplessly, ridiculously. I'm head over heels in love, Sonchai. Isn't that what you once told me was the secret to understanding the Buddha: that he was head over heels in love with the whole universe?"

"Then you won't have any problem in loving him after he's had the surgery, will you?" I say testily, and close the phone.

Forget Wat Po and the Temple of the Emerald Buddha; most *wats* are ramshackle affairs where hungry cats, flea-tormented dogs, and dispossessed humans take advantage of the Buddha's compassion under bhodi trees, along with a motley crew of monks of varying degrees of commitment. (Some are hiding, some are weeping, some are frustrated, some are ambitious, some are gay, most are devout, and some are almost Buddhas.) It is above all a community where *looksits* in white pants and shirts clean and wash robes for their monk mentors in return for a fast track to enlightenment, *chart na*; handymen gain merit by repairing the roofs of monks' shacks; and there is always someone cooking and eating, except for monks who are not allowed to eat after noon. Kids whose parents cannot afford fancy schools where Mandarin and business English are taught are left to absorb whatever wisdom the monks offer; people who may or may not be passionate about Buddhism come and go.

You might think it medieval, but it's far more ancient than that. We are a deeply conservative people at heart. Our version of Buddhism, called Theravada, is two thousand five hundred years old, and we haven't changed a word of it. The robes our monks wear are stitched together from the same template Siddhartha himself used, and we follow the same Four Noble Truths the Greatest of Men expounded when he began his ministry, the first being: *There is suffering*. Only *farang* ever argue with that one.

I pass through dilapidated but majestic wooden gates onto consecrated ground, and it is as if he is waiting for me. A young novice, all bright and earnest, points him out where he is sitting on the balcony of an old wooden *kuti*. He is not surprised to see me.

"Welcome to my palace," Damrong's brother says with a smile, hitching his robes and waving a hand at the particularly tumbledown shack the abbot has loaned him in the name of hospitality. I *wai* him, as if he were a real monk. Now he's smiling modestly. "You checked with the Sangha? They've never heard of me, right?" He laughs. "I ordained in Cambodia, brother. The Thai Sangha wouldn't have me. Something about a criminal conviction." He offers a shrug to lose the world.

"Oh," I say, as if I didn't know.

"Does that bother you?"

"I'm a cop."

"No," he says, all-knowing, "you're a monk, like me. You just signed the wrong form. You'll be in the robes, *chart na.*"

I settle down in a semilotus with my back against a flimsy wooden wall, facing him. Down below a dog with almost no fur left on one leg is ferociously scratching. In the middle distance two senior monks are talking softly in the shade of the huge bodhi tree that forms a sort of center to the complex. "It's true we have a lot in common," I concede. "You lived off your sister's prostitution all your life before you ordained, I lived off my mother's. You traded *yaa baa*, I watched while my buddy Pichai murdered our dealer. I spent a year in Buddhist purgatory. For three months my abbot had Pichai and me breathing death."

Perhaps it is melodramatic of me to use this colloquial phrase. While I have been speaking, he has allowed a smile of affectionate amusement to flicker back and forth across his mouth, a master watching the clumsy gropings of one who has never passed intermediate level and likely never will.

"Breathing death is good practice," he says. I want him to say more and find myself fidgeting, wishing he would continue. It seems the perfect expression of compassion when he finally starts speaking again.

"In Cambodia it is still possible to use real corpses. I lived with one in my cell for a year, experiencing its dissolution from the flies-and-stench stage all the way to dry bones. While I watched I identified: every attachment, every aversion dropped away as the organ that created it disintegrated."

"A year? I would have gone mad."

A tolerant smile. "Of course I went mad. For a monk, what the world calls sanity is a whorish compromise."

"But something saved you. You seem okay now."

A curious expression. "Saved? There is nothing to save, my friend. You are talking like a Christian. You cannot cast yourself into the Unknowable in the hope that gesture will buy you salvation—you have to jump for the hell of it. In a nirvanic universe there can be no salvation because we are never really lost—or found. The choice is simply between nirvana and ignorance. That is the adult truth the Buddha urges upon us. We are the sum of our burning. No burning, no being."

I accept defeat in awe, a mere B-plus student effortlessly demolished by a true yogin. I decide I may as well give up testing him, since I am only making a fool of myself. I sneak back into forensics.

"If that is your enlightenment, why did you trouble to seek me out?"

"I told you, my sister's spirit is not at rest. As a monk, of course, I have nothing to do with her dharma at all anymore, but particles of my debt to her remain." For *debt* he uses a word which has no counterpart in English but invokes the most serious obligation known in my culture: *gatdanyu*, a kind of blood debt.

"But to a near-*arhat* like you, how can a cop help?"

Perhaps it is my imagination, or perhaps that really was a wince that distorted his features for a moment.

"Her spirit craves justice" is all he will say.

A few beats pass. He is the one who finally breaks the silence to prompt me: "Why don't you ask me questions that will push the case along? Isn't that what you're here for?"

A pause. "Okay, do you know about the video?"

More beats, no answer. I say, "Someone sent it to me anonymously. I think it must have been you." Still no answer. "I thought you wanted to help with the case. You do know about the video?"

A long pause before he says, "I am still in touch with my village. Monks are allowed e-mail." A very long pause, during which he seems to dwell in another universe, then: "The function of the West is to turn bodies and minds into products. It cannot understand that the rest of the world holds this to be an obscenity, a corruption of our nirvanic nature." He follows this statement with a scowl.

I find I am cast into doubt about him all over again, perhaps by a twitch or gesture, a subtle alteration in his diction, which turned vulgar.

I cough apologetically. "Phra Titanaka, may I be permitted one very personal question?"

"For a monk there are no personal questions."

"Then for the sake of forensic inquiry, would you tell me how close you and your sister were?"

His eyes dart, but he says nothing. Instead he stands up abruptly—inexplicably—and leaves me on his balcony to cross the compound to the *bot*. I remain in a semilotus, watching that elegant, measured walk in the flowing saffron robes until he enters the temple. I think he expects me to leave, and I'm half tempted to do so. I wait, though, feeling foolish and distracting myself by watching the muted but incessant life of the *wat* until he returns about an hour later. He makes no sign of surprise to see me still here, slips down into a semilotus a couple of yards from me, and says with that peculiar abruptness that I suppose is a consequence of his mental discipline:

"We were closest when she was in her early twenties and I was a teenager. She always said she was sorry for using me as a pillow to cry on, but it was the only way she could cope. She said maybe if she paid for my education, I would be able to figure it all out better than she."

"She used to talk about her customers?"

I stare in fascination while his serenity morphs into hatred. It is as though he has peeled off a rubber mask to reveal an alien monster from a denser planet. "Every sweaty, pink, brown, black, overweight, desperate, lovelorn, emotionally crippled, fucked-up, shit-eating one of them. It took all she had to pretend enthusiasm. She even had to pretend to love them sometimes—that's the kind of assholes they were." A scowl at me: "That was before she became a numb professional."

I am struck dumb not only by the sudden change in personality but also by the way he seems quite unaware of it. Something else, too, has made the hairs on the back of my neck stand on end. He sounded exactly like Damrong; same voice, same tricks of speech.

Thoroughly unnerved, I say, "I see." He is still scowling and turns his head away, perhaps aware that he has said something inappropriate but is not sure what. He has lost his serenity and fidgets with his robe. He clearly wants to get rid of me.

Now it is my turn to stand up, *wai* him, and leave, telling myself that the man who pronounced those bitter words in a growl of the most vulgar slang was not the monk Phra Titanaka; it was someone else.

In a state of shock I wander across the compound, past the great white *chedi,* which is the oldest part of the temple complex, and ask a senior monk where I might find the abbot. The monk replies that he is in the same *bot* from which Damrong's brother just emerged.

The abbot sitting in semilotus under the dais is fat, almost the perfect image of a laughing Buddha, and acknowledges my high *wai* with a nod. I use the most polite form of address from a hierarchy of dozens as I sit, careful to keep my head lower than his. In the jolly face shrewd eyes examine me. I explain I am a detective investigating the death of the monk's sister. The abbot confirms that he is extending hospitality to the Khmer monk, who arrived last week and seems very devout.

"Have you noticed anything strange about him?"

"Strange? We humans insist on inhabiting a charnel ground—isn't that strange enough for spiritual creatures without splitting hairs?"

"He seems to be two different men. His personality switches from moment to moment."

"Only two? Perhaps there is something wrong with your eyes. Look more closely and you will see he changes with every exhalation. So do I. So do you."

I *wai* once again, thank him for his wisdom, and take my leave.

23

The monk's sudden entry into the case has brought me to an emotional dead end. The intensity of my guilt over Nok's death is tempered by the great mountain of suffering this young man has climbed over; and anyway this afternoon has *long massage* written all over it. I use a fairly large, well-known establishment on a side *soi* which joins Sukhumvit and Soi 45. A lot of people use the *soi* as a shortcut, and it has plenty of cooked-food stalls with specializations that can be known from the shape of the stall: braised pork with rice; boiled chicken with rice; *som-tan* salad with sticky rice; and mango and sticky rice plus a lot of *kong wan*, sweets. Don't miss the crispy pancakes with coconut cream fillings, *farang*. I'm watching a hawker prepare Thai coconut pudding in the old style, pouring the batter into tiny hollows of a large round pan, then pouring sweet coconut milk into them. You don't often see it done properly these days; sometimes I'm driven to steamed banana cakes, thanks to globalism and the fast-food fad.

I have brought the FBI by way of developing our kiss-and-make-up strategy. We had it all out yesterday in a hurricane of calls, text messages, and e-mails, only the most hurtful of which are really worth recording:

Me: It's just hormonal consumerism. You're no different from the middle-aged johns roaming Nana Plaza.

The FBI: Oh, and what about you and Damrong, huh? When it happens to you, it's Cupid, it's Orion marching across the night sky, it's chakras and lotus petals in the head. When an American woman falls in love, it's hormonal consumerism.

Me (aware that I am about to make a serious tactical blunder): Exactly—that's the cultural difference.

The FBI: So you are a cultural chauvinist, exactly what you're always accusing the West of.

Having duly noted the magnificence of each other's claws, we found something else to talk about, and I invited her to the massage parlor so we could sign off on our peace treaty. Now the FBI, all bright, smiling, and looking professional (I know she took Lek out for a drink on Soi 4 Pat Pong last night, however; Lek called me afterward; she was a little fresh but took no for an answer after an aborted grope), tells me she has good news which she will share during the massage.

"I don't know if I'm going to stay awake, Sonchai."

"You're not supposed to. If you don't nod off, the masseuse isn't doing her job."

It's a relief to step out of the crowded *soi* into the air-conditioning. The girl at reception asks if we want traditional Thai or oil massage, I say "Traditional Thai" without consulting Kimberley. I order two hours each. Two hours of pure mental emptiness: at three hundred baht I see it as a bargain.

As many as thirty masseuses are sitting around reading magazines or gossiping in low voices, which causes the FBI to turn to me. "These girls, some of them could be . . . are they straight or on the Game?"

Ah! The simple mind of a *farang.* "When they work the second floor, they are totally straight. When they work the third floor, they are on the Game at the client's option."

"Are we talking morality by altitude, or am I missing something?"

"The second floor is traditional Thai massage, the third is oil. It is very difficult for a young woman to oil a man all over without arousing him, and we are a compassionate people."

"Compassion pays better too, huh?"

"Three times the price of a straight massage, but the expense is all in the tip. The girls love the third floor, but we are on the second."

"Got it" from the FBI.

Before we are allowed to climb the stairs to heaven, however, we must have our feet washed. The FBI is ill at ease when her girl tells her to take off her shoes and come sit down in front of a bowl of warm rosewater. No one to arrest, shoot, or interrogate here; Kimberley sees no outlet for her talents, and her forehead is a mass of stress wrinkles. She is afraid that having her feet washed in this way might be anti-American, like cricket and Communism. Five minutes later she turns to me with a clear brow. "Amazing what a lift a simple little thing like that can give you." Her eyes are sparkling.

I tell the two masseuses that the FBI and I will have adjoining mattresses. Actually, the whole of the second floor consists of mattresses divided one from the other by thin curtains, so we can talk in low voices while the masseuses work on us. We change into thin cotton pants and shirts. A grunt of satisfaction from Kimberley next door as she hits the mattress.

My girl has already begun working my feet, untangling knots of nerves and muscles with their mysterious connections all through the body. A sudden gasp comes from the FBI side. "Wow, it's like something popped. This is reflexology, right? Isn't the theory that every organ has a connection to the soles of the feet?"

"And every emotion arises from an organ." I realize that in some way I am echoing the words of Damrong's brother. I think of him alone in his cell with the corpse. I could never do it myself, but I understand enough to see how it might work: the disintegration of the cadaver was the liberation of his spirit. It's a radical technique, though, frowned upon by orthodoxy these days, because the Sangha doesn't want to be responsible for the cases that go wrong. No such qualms in Cambodia, apparently. How wrong did Phra Titanaka go?

"Yeah, I know that theory. Love is all chemical reactions."

"Not only love. What the blind call life is virtual reality for those who see."

Another grunt. "You're losing me. I'm a nuts-and-bolts *farang*, remember. Want to know what I found out?"

"Of course."

"The masked man, the monster in the black gimp mask, we know who he is. His name is Stanislaus Kowlovski, Stan for short. Both parents were second-generation Polish immigrants." She groans suddenly. "My god, I don't know what organ that corresponded to, but a vivid clip of childhood memory just passed across my eyes. Where was I?"

"So we have the killer?"

"Not yet, but we have his Social Security number, fingerprints, everything. That isometric hardware you've got at the airport works fine. All I had to do was give the nerds the challenge of using the DVD to get a still of his irises. Took them less than five minutes."

"How did they react to the DVD?"

A pause, then softly: "Same as me, Sonchai. Except maybe for a man it's even worse, to see a beautiful young woman, full of life, do a thing like that. When I told them it wasn't just a sick fantasy, she really died like that, they couldn't take it. Hardened agents had to hold back the tears. Amazing."

"So you're hunting for him?"

"Sure. Everyone's excited. International sex offenders are the flavor of the month all over the West. We'll have him for sure in a few days, unless he has strong connections in another country, which I doubt. He might hail from Kansas, but he's a California boy through and through."

"Any rap sheet?"

"No form at all, but plenty of reputation. The LAPD know about him as a male porn star. There are dozens of low-rent movies with his dong in a supporting role."

"All heterosexual?"

"Yes."

"All sadistic?"

"No. Not a single one. He was a mainstream stud—you know, the obliging, smiling, baby-oiled, irresistible jock who fades into the background early in the flick while the camera homes in on the girl's body. They showed me a few pix of him without the mask. A handsome male animal, strong jaw, toothpaste smile. If I didn't know better, I would have categorized him as harmless beach-bum type—you know, the kind of Ivy League iron-pumper who makes a point of *not* kicking sand in other guys' faces because it's uncool and blue collar."

We both take a break from the investigation while the girls go deeper into the torture. Mostly these are country girls from Isaan who were tough enough even before they took up massage and are built like miniature brown tanks. I'm getting the elbow in the liver and trying to think of the next question.

"So, it must have been money that made him do it?"

"What else? It fits in a kind of way. Male porn stars fade as quickly as their female colleagues. He is forty-three, broke, technically bankrupt, and when that happens, you can bet loan sharks are making circles somewhere under the surface. We're liaising with the LAPD. Ouch! Is it healthy to get an elbow in the gut like that?"

"Helps with digestion. Did any childhood clip come up when she did that?"

"Ten years of car sickness. We lived in Florida, but both sets of grandparents lived in New York. Reunions four times a year. We drove every time."

A pause while my feet are bent inward and pressed. "So, what we really want is a lead to the paymasters?"

"I'm optimistic. Porn stars of either sex tend not to rate so high in IQ tests. A couple days of interrogation should give us everything."

We both fall silent under the power of the Wat Po massage technique. There comes a point where the masseuse must confront the sex organ if her client is male. Usually one is totally relaxed and the girl delicately shifts your dormant member from one side of your groin to the other. Often there is humor in the moment, especially if the client has been finding the massage stimulating and the girl gives a *why-are-you-so-big?* twist to her lips. This time, though, in my relaxed and vulnerable state, the sudden erotic connection triggers off the nightmare I've avoided replaying all week. I block it, though, somehow, and now that the massage has reached the relaxing stage, I start to nod off.

I wake in a state of total disorientation. Despite what I told the FBI, I myself do not normally fall asleep during massage. Why has Kimberley opened her curtain? Why is she kneeling next to me, stroking my cheek?

"You started screaming, honey. You were scaring the staff." Her face is the very picture of compassion when she says, "You're a passion-ate man, Sonchai. Anyone can see a part of you kept on loving her, bad as she was."

After we have dressed and paid, standing together in the narrow *soi* at something of a loss, I finally have the courage to say, "Kimberley, I have a favor to ask. Can you guess?"

"Sure. You need to watch the video again, and you need me to hold your hand."

I touch her shoulder. "Thanks, Kimberley."

24

The video and Stanislaus Kowlovski's performance in it weigh on my mind all the way home. Knowing I'm going to have to put myself through it all over again is a little like the second parachute jump. I've never done it, but I've heard people talk: the first jump is tolerable because you don't know what to expect. On the second something deep in the mind rebels, a feeling like, *Why am I driving myself through this terminal horror?* After all, Vikorn wouldn't bat an eye if I gave up investigating the Damrong video altogether. In fact, he would prefer it.

I'm asking myself this question as I reach home, kiss Chanya, pat the Lump, and eat the food she puts before me with love and devotion in her eyes. She catches my gaze with hers for a moment, then swallows hard. I think, *Oh Buddha, she has seen into my heart.* Then a lover's intuition kicks in, and I grab her and kiss her. The darling was feeling threatened because I had a massage with my *farang* friend. Chanya would never be challenged by a Thai girl, but she is overawed by Kimberley, whom she believes to represent the Western side of my mind: much as she loves me, Chanya can never forget I am a *leuk kreung*, a half-caste, and must surely have *farang* tendencies and *farang* preferences lurking somewhere.

It is almost comic, how accurate the heart can be and at the same time how mistaken. Of course I spend most of my time thinking about another woman, but it isn't the FBI. My vow—which I make with a mixture of tears and giggles, to the effect that I volunteer to be reborn a hungry ghost if I ever have so much as thought of sleeping with Kimberley—is so forceful, so convincing, that Chanya now is ashamed of herself and wants to compensate for doubting me. She promises to cook my favorite, *pla neung menau*, steamed fish in lemon sauce.

We make love as best we can in her condition. She is anxious to please me, needing comfort and reassurance. She uses some of her old tricks from her days on the Game, which causes us to share a smile or two. I make her feel how much I love her, force that certainty upon her, and there is no hypocrisy here, only a haunting. Afterward, perhaps from subtle signals she has interpreted, whole packets of information transmitted by the subtlest alteration of pressure in the touch or intonation of voice, now processed properly through her encyclopedic experience of men, gives the right answer: "It's her, isn't it?"

I grab her to hug her, but she turns away.

"I have to see the video again, my love. It's quite a chore for me. Kimberley is going to be with me."

"Why not me?"

A long silence full of the anguish of separation: "Because of what you would see."

"You think I can't handle a video like that?"

"Of course you can. I can't handle you watching me watch it."

Neither of us wants an argument, and Chanya has grown too used to serenity to squander it on something trivial like a snuff movie. I watch while the kind of divine sleepiness which is the privilege of the pure takes over.

I take the opportunity to caress the Lump, full of wonder, fear, and anticipation. *Vipassana* meditation affects everyone in different ways. Although I was never any kind of master, I penetrated to that part of the psyche where memories of the womb lurk. These have returned to me since I've known that I will soon be a father. I can easily relive the fear of birth that afflicts us in that transient security: that first agonizing acid-breath of oxygen, air burning your skin like napalm, hanging upside down like a bat while someone in a white coat smacks your ass, then—and here's the first taste of the police state—if you've seen enough already and decide to turn back because corporeal existence is not for you, it's the oxygen mask: *It ain't optional, bud—you're here to be processed.* Who would fardels bear? Pichai seems still to be quite merry in his shrinking domain, though. According to the ultrasound, he is kicking and flapping his arms about and showing commendable faith in the future. In my less confident moments I fear a sports-obsessed brute. I reluctantly decide to pay a visit to Lek's *moordu*, when I have the time.

"Want a painkiller?" Kimberley asks the minute I've settled on the sofa in her suite at the Grand Britannia. "I don't have any coke, but I guess you could get that if you wanted it. How about a single-malt Scotch? They have miniatures in the minibar."

She goes to the minibar and hands me a tiny bottle, keeping one for herself. We unscrew the tops and clink. "Good luck," the FBI says. I take the video out of my jacket pocket and hand it to her.

At first I think I've cracked my inner resistance, that I've got my objectivity back. I am able to watch the prolonged foreplay with a certain distance and professional eye. I have to admit, Damrong pulls out all the stops. With her, fellatio is developed into an art form, complete with elegance, romance, humor, drama, tension, and an attention to the visual side of the thrill which is nothing less than masterful; a sorceress at the top of her game. The masked man, too, is no amateur. He understands that he is the foil to this extraordinary performance and does not permit ego to intrude. Kowlovski is particularly courtly on his knees during the cunnilingus scene. Advanced camera techniques allow us to participate in the versatility of his tongue, the anguish of her pleasure. Kimberley pauses the disk for a moment, freezing Damrong with the tip of her tongue just touching her upper lip with her eyes half closed, to say in a philosophical tone, "I've been thinking about it, and the way I see her, she's a kind of Madonna phenomenon. A basically plain face, nothing special at all, which somehow highlights the sexual charisma. A paradox, really. But you can see how it works." The FBI presses the button that makes Damrong come to life again. "Look, she's actually enjoying it. She's not faking. *She's excited.*"

Which is very hard to take; her excitement, I mean. Accepting how real her enjoyment is ten minutes or so before she dies does something to my head. She isn't even slightly frightened; she is in a state of ecstasy. I tell Kimberley to turn it off, but she refuses.

"Tough love, kid," she growls. "You're going to suck it up this time."

"At least give me another shot."

She pauses the video to get four more miniature bottles from the minibar. With the action frozen, it is possible to take in a little of the scenery. Just as I recalled, a shelf with priceless objets d'art is visible: the jade reclining Buddha. Now that I know what I'm looking for, it is easy to identify the decor of Tanakan's room at the Parthenon Club. We swallow the miniatures quickly, and she unleashes the rest of the flick.

"Wait," I say. She pauses again, using the remote, with a what-now look on her face.

"I'm not going to be able to look at it again, after the ending, so let's rerun the story so far. I need to know more about Kowlovski, but that damned mask is in the way."

"Watch his hands," Kimberley says. "They're all we have of the human in him."

We replay the foreplay in slo-mo. The FBI is right—the only clue to the psychology of the masked man lies in the way he uses his hands.

"There," Kimberley says. She freezes at a point where he is attending to Damrong's left breast.

I say, "What?"

"The shaking. You can't see it when I freeze. There."

It's true—her female eye saw it probably from the start. I myself was too transfixed by Damrong. "It doesn't prove anything," I say.

"No, but it's all we've got. Virginia sent me some porn stuff he did not long before. In the narrow confines of mainstream porn, he was something of a master."

"No shaking in the hands?"

"No."

The FBI backs up a few frames and freezes again. Now we are looking at three fingers lightly supporting Damrong's left breast, while bearing in mind that those fingers are actually shaking rather wildly. Indeed, we must bear in mind that the whole hand is shuddering from the wrist. I exchange a glance with Kimberley, and she presses play.

Now that the FBI has shared her wisdom, it is not difficult to pick up on other clues. When their foreplay is almost over, he lays her on her back to begin the first of five intercourse intervals before the final countdown (on her back; doggy style; with her on top; plus a couple of rather complicated maneuvers that have him penetrating her from behind while she twists around for him to thrust his tongue down her throat).

The FBI takes us through the first penetration scene again in slo-mo. Now that I'm focused, I see that the hands that dramatically part her unresisting thighs are hardly under his control at all. At one point Damrong herself reaches down to grasp a bunch of his fingers in a comforting way: one professional to another. She also whispers something in his ear.

"STOP!" I yell. This time Kimberley obeys. She goes to the mini-bar and brings all the miniatures she can find, about ten in all, a mixture of brandy, whiskey, vodka, gin; necessity is the mother of anesthesia. I gulp two; *my* hands are the ones shaking in this scene. I have no choice but to let Kimberley see my pathetic, tearstained face.

"Stay with it, trooper," she says, which only makes things worse. She has to hold my head in her arms, as she would comfort a child.

"*She's giving him moral support,*" I say, hardly able to get the words out.

Even the FBI is having trouble with self-control. "Say what you like about her, that is one amazing woman."

"It's almost as if she loves him."

"Why not? He definitely loves her, though he might not know it."

"How can you be so sure?"

"Why else would he be suffering like that?"

"If he's having so much trouble with his head, how can he still perform at all?"

"Viagra is the lifeblood of the porn industry, Sonchai."

She presses play again. We are deep into intercourse territory now, with the camera somehow zooming in on private bits that, at this level of magnification, could be any part of the body at all; could even be the genitalia of some other anthropoid species; at one point the shading of flesh from deep crimson to light pink reminds me of carnivorous vegetation, say the pitcher plant.

"Look!" He is taking her from behind again, but with such trembling in his knees that he is unable to maintain intimacy. Three times in this scene her small, elegant brown hand reaches down to reinsert his member.

"Sonchai, for god's sake!"

"I bought her that ring," I sob. I have just remembered. Our affair was so short, there was hardly any time for presents, and I recall how cheap I felt, buying her a silver ring from an antique stall at Wat Po for a few thousand baht, knowing she had slept with billionaires. It strikes me that it might not be a coincidence that this is the only jewelry she is wearing; that at this moment, exactly three minutes twenty-five seconds before her death according to the counter on the DVD player, she is perfectly aware that I would one day be watching this hand of hers, with my ring on it, giving comfort and aid to her executioner.

When he finally takes her to a kind of trestle for her to lean on, so that no detail of the finale will be lost to the camera lens, and fumbles with the orange nylon rope so badly that he drops it and she has to pick it up for him, I grab the remote and switch it off.

Kimberley looks at me with disappointed eyes. "Sonchai—"

"I can't."

"If you don't, it'll haunt you for life."

"I'm Thai. All Thais are haunted for life."

"Sonchai!"

"Fuck your tough love, Kimberley. It's destroying the world, haven't you noticed?"

Suddenly I'm outside her suite, slamming the door. It is a genuine tantrum, complete with amnesia: I have no idea how I got out into the corridor at this moment. I do know that I'm running, though. There is really only one thing to do at a time like this.

I take a cab in the direction of the police station but have the driver stop at Phra Titanaka's *wat*. Just outside the massive doors a string of stalls sell candles, lotus wreaths, and monk baskets. I am still shaking when I buy all the paraphernalia you need for a serious exorcism. The baskets these days are no longer wicker or bamboo but the same semi-transparent buckets of lurid hue you would use for washing the car, although these are all saffron-tinted. Inside, ready-packed by the stallholder, I find all a monk needs to survive a day or two in that spiritual desert called maya: a pack of instant coffee, biscuits, Lux brand soap, two cans of 7UP, a box of *yaa dum* aromatherapy sticks, toothpaste, toothbrushes, and incense. The whole idea of *tambun* is to store up treasure for *chart na*: give flowers, you'll be beautiful; give money, you'll be rich; give medicine, you'll be healthy; give candles, you'll be enlightened. It's a long wait for the next life, though, when you're only thirty-five.

The magic is more powerful the more senior you go, so I seek out the abbot and offer him the goodie-crammed bucket, which he accepts with a nod. Now I'm in the temple kneeling before the great golden Buddha on the platform, holding my trembling hands in a high *wai* and begging for mercy. My mother, Nong, *in extremis* has been known to promise a thousand boiled eggs and a couple of roasted hogs' heads, but I am of a different generation: *I'll be a better husband, a perfect father, a better cop, a wiser teacher to Lek, a more devout Buddhist—I'll do anything, anything at all, just to get this THING off my back.*

You never know immediately if it's going to work or not—it all depends on the unpredictable compassion of the Buddha—but for the moment I'm satisfied I've done what I can. I try to meditate for twenty minutes to give more power to my supplication; then, pretty much exhausted, I leave the temple. I'm on my way to the great gates, when a familiar figure catches my eye. Lek is sitting with Damrong's brother, Phra Titanaka, on a seat under the banyan tree. Lek is careful to keep his head below that of the monk's, while gazing at him with adoration. Phra Titanaka is speaking slowly, with a beautiful, compassionate smile on his face.

Did you know, *farang*, that the ancients saw jealousy as a greenish horn-shaped intrusion of the astral body directly into the physical sheath? The cuckold's horns were independently witnessed all over the world even before the age of sail: the Maya, the ancient Egyptians, and the Japanese all knew about them as well as the Elizabethans. I know because I checked the Net. Well, *Arbeit macht frei*, they say, so I stroll back to the office projecting nonchalance to see if I can push the case a little further along. However, I find conventional forensic analysis unhelpful: there is no evidence to link Smith the suave lawyer and Baker the less-than-suave pornographer either to the snuff movie or to Nok's murder. Tanakan is only implicated to the extent that both atrocities took place in his very own perfumed garden—a circumstance he could argue away with a thousand-baht note. If, on the other hand, I unlock my bottom drawer and take out the old Burmese wooden phallus which I use only *in extremis*, like Green Lantern's light—mostly because it's embarrassingly large, with the glans painted a lurid crimson—and hang over it an amulet that Lek claims he got from a Khmer *moordu* of towering seniority—thus producing a kind of altar on my desk underneath the computer monitor—lean back on my chair, close my eyes, and let go of all extraneous thought, what do I find? Three blind mice propelled by tight little spirals of karma that go back many hundreds of years, and a black cat whose pleasure it is to toy with them.

So much for clairvoyance; but the exercise does seem to have provoked a more mundane line of inquiry. I check the data Immigration sent me this morning. It is a curious fact that Baker, Smith, and Tanakan all arrived back in Bangkok from their various destinations overseas on the same day, some twenty-four hours after the end of the period during which forensics says Damrong must have died. Coincidence, or the inevitable response of three blind mice who had no reason to be elsewhere once the cat was dead?

THE MASKED MAN

25

The FBI is staring at a tureen of fat snails cooked in their own juice with a brown sauce. We are eating at D's, just off Silom, an open-air restaurant popular with those who work the Pat Pong bars.

"You don't have to do this," I tell her. "Really. It's quite a risk you're taking."

"I want to. I got into Thai food in the States, right after I met you the first time."

I cannot comment because I never ate Thai food on my one trip to America. (To Florida; the john was a muscular seventy-something who meant well. I remember massive hands that were always fixing things, long hours while Mum and I stood around watching and applauding on cue at the Bathroom Leak Triumph, the Victory of the Fuse Box, the Battle of Flat Battery, et cetera. But he bored Nong so badly she had to invent a terminal illness for her mother so we could leave after a week. Back in Bangkok I had to deal with his pleading phone calls because Nong couldn't bring herself to speak to him. I was twelve.) I'm not as worried about the snails as I am about the *somtan* salad, which also has caught Kimberley's eye.

"At least have some sticky rice with it. Roll it into a ball like this."

She watches a little resentfully, having graduated in spice already. She copies me, however, dips her ball into the sauce, and munches merrily with no ill effects. "Delicious." I see no advantage in pointing out there were no chili fragments at that end of the salad.

"We think he's in Cambodia," the FBI says. We are still doing Bright and Cheerful around each other, by the way, careful not to mention Lek.

"Who?"

"Kowlovski, the masked man. His isometric image was recorded entering Phnom Penh airport about a week ago. Meanwhile the LAPD has come up with a whole bunch of background data. It's like looking at a fly caught in a web. That guy was in deep trouble." She doesn't really want to eat any of the snails but feels honor bound to give one a go. "How do you do this?"

"Suck."

She does so, and after a moment of resistance the snail shoots out of its shell into her mouth. She starts to gag but masters herself manfully.

"Money?"

Covering her mouth and speaking through her fingers: "It all comes down to that. It's the California Catch. To be marketable you got to be glamorous and to be glamorous you got to be hip, and to be hip you got to have dough, and to have dough you got to be marketable."

"Cocaine?"

"Whatever's in style. This guy is a cipher. He has the mind of a whore: *Whatever you want me to do for money—just make sure I look sexy while I'm doing it.* He owes dealers and loan sharks, he owes back payments on child support for an ex-wife and two kids in Kansas, and he owes lease payments on some SUV he never drives far because he can't afford the gas. Threats pouring in. This is just stuff the guys on the ground over there picked up in one quick trawl through the porn industry. There are no secrets—it's a very transparent business."

"So why Cambodia? If he was paid as much as we think for the flick, he could have settled all his debts and resumed the lifestyle, gone back to the more humdrum kind of studding."

A shrug from the FBI. "We don't know. We only have one witness who saw him in the last couple weeks. It's an old girlfriend who he keeps in touch with. She says she's the only person in the world he's ever had a relationship with that went below the skin. She thinks he's a troubled soul, with everything repressed. That certainly fits the pattern for prostitutes, male and female."

Kimberley rolls another ball of sticky rice and this time plunges it deep into the *somtan* salad, pressing it down to absorb more of the sauce, then takes a bite. I dare not get technical at this stage by explaining that the intense but transient suffering she is about to inflict upon herself has directly to do with the overstimulation of her second chakra, which of course is the prime mover in her passion for Lek.

"Did she say anything else?"

I have to wait for the answer because her mouth is on fire, she is hiccupping, a sweat has broken out on her forehead, and her face is heart-attack crimson. Cold water is the worst therapy, but she takes a gulp from the bottle in the ice bucket. Now she has to visit the bathroom. I munch on the *somtan* and pick off a couple of snails while I'm waiting for her to return. The chili in the *somtan* goes well with my cold Kloster beer. (The two streams come together in a riotous clash somewhere in the back of the throat, sending a delicious shock wave through the taste buds.) Now the FBI is marching back to the table, her face set.

"Yes. She said he came back from a trip somewhere overseas a couple weeks ago and was real quiet, then disappeared altogether. Usually he's always ready with the latest friendly sound bite, normally a very personable guy in a Lycra kind of way. This time, though, he seemed depressed. She was surprised he had the depth to get depressed. I don't think I need any more snails or *somtan* salad."

"I think they'll cook you a steak, if I ask them nicely."

"I'm suddenly on a diet. How about I watch you eat, and I'll munch on some nice bland sticky rice if I get hungry?"

"Okay. Did he seem to have money the last time she met him?"

"Yes, she said he made a point of paying off some back rent on his apartment in Inglewood, cleared the slate with a grocery store, and gave her a silk shirt and skirt. They asked her if it was Thai silk, and she said she didn't know."

Finally the braised duck has arrived in a pot. The FBI eyes it suspiciously, but when I assure her there are no spices in this dish, she takes a tentative bite, then digs in.

Her cell phone rings, except nothing rings anymore. The gadget explodes with an old Thai number she grew fond of when she was here a few years ago: "Sexy, Naughty, Bitchy." She says, "Kimberley," and listens. Then she says, "Shit," and closes the phone.

"He committed suicide in Phnom Penh yesterday. Apparently he used an AK-47 and a piece of rope tied around the trigger, which is not easy to do, but I guess if you're really determined to go that way . . ." She casts an eye over the remains of the meal, then looks at me. Hard to say what is causing my sudden loss of appetite: death; the manner thereof; the fact that the Masked Man will never be brought to justice; the memory of what he did to Damrong; the thought, only now surfacing in my mind, that I might have to make a visit to Phnom Penh. All of a sudden the energy has gone out of the day, and it's not because Mercury is retrograde (though it is, and our prime minister is on record as observing what a corrosive effect it is having on political life; for me, Mercury can come or go, but Jupiter conjunct the Moon in Scorpio— now that's a curl-up-in-bed-with-a-spliff day for yours truly).

This case has a trick of remaining perpetually out of reach, like a mirage. And no, I do not want to go to Cambodia; they hate us over there. Both sides have made so many land grabs over the centuries that no one really knows who started the feud, which shows no sign of diminishing no matter how many Thais cross the border to gamble. I guess they've never really forgiven us for defeating them at Angkor Wat that time: even in those days about seven hundred years ago, the Khmer were so reliant on magic they stopped bothering with combat training; the Thai invasion could be likened to a motorcycle gang smashing its way into an undefended sweet shop. We took everything they had: women, boys, girls, slaves, gold, their astrology and their temple designs, music, dance—it was an early example of identity theft. Not their cuisine, though, which was way behind ours and still is. If we'd known how long they were going to hold the grudge, we might have shown more mercy.

Suddenly the FBI and I don't want our eyes to meet. Without the illusion of work, or at least a case to discuss, we are left to wonder what to do about each other. We sneak glances when we think the other is not looking, bestowing wonder and pity at each other's karma. Finally Kimberley plays with a spare spoon on the table prior to getting something off her chest.

"Maybe it's something about your country. I'm starting to feel like those middle-aged Western men you see walking up and down Sukhumvit with a girl on their arms half their age and looking like the cat that found the cream. I know I'm kidding myself." Looking me in the eye at last: "I know that, or at least the left lobe does. But I can't stop myself. Suddenly it's spring again, the kind of spring I never had—there were always too many goals to aim for. When he's around, I experience a deep sense of love, of affection, of compassion. What can I say? It's what I was always supposed to experience as a human being, right? That's what we're here for, even though it's totally impossible, isn't it? Don't tell me you didn't go through this with Damrong."

I inhale deeply. "Of course I did. When you notice light seeping into your coffin, it's hard to go on pretending you're dead. You know the promise of life is not entirely hollow. Ecstasy is not just the name of a drug—there *is* something behind stories of paradise." I try to look at her with compassionate eyes. "If even a tiny part of you is still alive, you can't refuse the challenge."

She looks up with humble eyes. "So you forgive me?"

I slide my small hand over her big one. "Just be careful."

"You think I'll destroy him?"

"The other way around."

She looks up into the trees that surround the open-air restaurant. "He hardly even notices me, right? He's not aware of me at all in that way."

"How do you think the girls feel, when they walk down Sukhumvit with those *farang* men who grin like Cheshire cats? Do they feel like they found the cream too or merely a dirty job that pays better than factory work?"

She nods. "But the surgery, Sonchai. That's just plain wrong."

I shrug. No point getting back into that. We let a good ten minutes pass, during which the restaurant has started to play some old rock music on the sound system. At other tables a young Thai couple are looking as if they intend to spend the afternoon in a hotel nearby; five male middle managers in their twenties are having a lunchtime booze-up on rice whiskey; some *farang* tourists are poring over a map; and cats roam under tables looking for scraps. The FBI says, "I'll come with you. You need to go to Phnom Penh—a detective like you has to see for himself. I want to go too—I'm here for the case, after all. Anyway, I need a reality check. Maybe if I'm in a different country, I won't think about him so much."

The FBI leaves me at Sala Daeng Skytrain station to go pack. I call Lek and tell him to meet me early this evening at his favorite *katoey* bar, called Don Juan's. I go back to the station to deal with a pile of paperwork, then go home to change and to tell Chanya I'm going to Cambodia for a day or so with the FBI. She toys with jealousy for a moment, but it's not enough to distract her from the soap she's watching. Her egg-shaped center of gravity provides an imperturbable complacency these days. "I'm also going to see Lek's *moordu*," I admit.

She looks at me for a moment to make sure I'm serious, then smiles. "About time. Tell me if he's any good."

"It's a *katoey*," I explain.

She makes big eyes. "Even better." *Katoeys* are known to make excellent *moordus*.

There are plenty of different expressions to denote transsexuals: *second women, third sex, the different ones.* I like *Angels in Disguise* best. Don Juan's is crammed with them. Smooth brown feminized flesh, padded bras and silicon-enhanced buttocks, plenty of jewelry—especially silver necklaces—shapely legs, lascivious laughter, cheap perfume, and sophisticated camp combine to lift desperate spirits for a night. You have to admire their guts. I hardly recognize Lek in his lipstick, rouge, and mascara; a tight T-shirt emphasizes his budding breasts. I think he is wearing jeans rather than a skirt for my sake. He squeezes between sisters to reach me, beaming. I don't think he's given the FBI a single thought since her last lovelorn call to him.

"This is my boss, my *master*," he tells his friends with unrestrained pride. "We're working on the most *terrifying* case you can imagine." He clamps a hand over his mouth. "But I can't tell you *anything* about it, it's so *secret*."

"Pi-Lek is such a tease!" a *katoey* in long imitation-pearl earrings exclaims. "It's such a *privilege* to meet you. Pi-Lek has told us *all* about you—we know you're the most *compassionate* cop in Bangkok, in the whole world probably. Pi-Lek says you're already a private Buddha and stay on earth only to spread enlightenment. It's such an *honor.*"

"He exaggerates," I say. "I'm just a cop." It's hard not to be borne along by the avalanche of charm.

"Come," Lek says, "let's go find Pi-Da." To his friends: "You can all run along now—my master hasn't come to waste time with silly girls." He waves a dismissive hand at them, provoking imitation tantrums and stamping of feet. He takes me by the hand to lead me through a crowd near the bar, then across to the other side of the room. His voice is considerably less camp when he says, "Pi-Da, this is my boss, Detective Jitpleecheep."

Pi-Da clearly belongs to the other category of *katoey*. In his forties, with a big round face, a paunch, and heavy legs, he was never beautiful, but his womanly soul must have yearned for self-expression all his life. Lek has explained he is a performer in the "ugly drag" cabarets that feature in most *katoey* bars, when they send up their own camp culture. He is also a kind of wise aunt who eschews campspeak and all the usual trappings of his kind. His voice is high and naturally feminine, though. He is assessing me shrewdly even while we *wai* each other. Then he takes my hand to maneuver me to a table, where we sit down. I watch him clear his mind while he stares at me and I sense his penetration of my heart. He shudders, makes big eyes, stares at Lek for a moment, then back at me. Lek's face collapses when he says, "I'm sorry, this is too big for me, I can't go there. This haunting is too powerful." He makes a gesture to push me away. Lek and I share a moment of confusion; then Lek says, "You have embarrassed me."

There is hardly a greater cultural sin. Pi-Da's face collapses under Lek's relentless glare. When Lek turns away in disgust, Pi-Da says reproachfully, "You don't know what you're asking."

"You're supposed to be clairvoyant. You're supposed to look fearlessly into the Other Side," Lek says more in sorrow than in anger. The whole of the *katoey*'s resentment at not being taken seriously is suddenly at issue here: if Pi-Da can't handle heavy-duty hauntings, what kind of *moordu* is s/he anyway? Just another aging queen?

Pi-Da's expression has changed. No longer the flabby aunt, he is now rather a man whose adulthood has been called into question. "We'll have to go upstairs," he says in a grim tone. Staring at me: "There will be no charge."

"Upstairs" is a collection of rooms used for the storage of alcohol and boxes of snacks. Pi-Da clears a space, and the three of us sit on the floor. Pi-Da holds my hand again and closes his eyes. After about a minute he opens them again, but they seem to be unseeing. I watch with horror and fascination as he stands, places his hands on a wall, and bends forward with his backside sticking out. "Sonchai, why don't you have me from behind like this? Whip me if you like." It is Damrong's voice to the last nuance. "You're such a great lover, Detective, you remind me of a charging elephant." A hysterical cackle.

Pi-Da shakes his head violently as if to break free. When he turns to us, his flesh is gray and he seems exhausted. "I can't do more than that—her energy is too crude and too powerful. She'll kill me if I let her take over. You have no idea what you've got involved with. This is Khmer sorcery, not a party game." Without another word he leaves us to go back to the bar. Lek is staring at me with huge eyes.

"Yes," I say, "it's true. I had an affair with her." I cannot face Lek any longer. I leave him to rush down the stairs two at a time into the anonymity of the busy Bangkok night.

26

There are lots of bankrupt states and plenty of kleptocracies; there are a few failed states; and there is Cambodia. After the Nixon holocaust: Pol Pot, generously supported by the CIA. Almost two million die in a civil war, except it's not like other civil wars. Everyone here remembers the knock on the door in the middle of the night and relatives taken away in an oxcart, usually by a teen with a machine gun, never to be seen again except as corpses, often mutilated. Then there is Tuol Sleng, where the torturing took place, and the skull mountains in Choeung Ek. Among the Cambodians themselves, a universal numbness hides psychic scars that go to the marrow. Many appear to be sleepwalking, random thuggery is an everyday hazard, "girls, guns, gambling, and ganja" are the economy, corruption is the work ethic, child abuse a national sport. You can use the local currency if you're feeling quaint, but everyone prefers American dollars. Naturally the capital, Phnom Penh, attracts NGOs like flies; pale pampered European faces look out from the tinted windows of four-by-fours. A lot of the city is crumbling. At the police station Kimberley flashes her credentials. Neither of us has any investigative rights here, but then nobody here obeys the rules. It's not difficult to get them to cooperate for a hundred dollars.

The apartment where Stanislaus Kowlovski died is on a side street about two hundred yards from the Mekong. We duck out of a blinding sun, following a cop whose uniform may be the only legal thing he owns. A short, stooping brown guy with some fingers missing from both hands, he believes we'll be excited by the blood and goo on the wall. He is. The stains are buried under a swarm of flies, though. He sniggers, "*Big American, what a body, dead now. Crazy. What kind of pain could he possibly have, a white man? All over the country there are people who can hardly walk for the anguish they feel; others cannot walk because their legs were blown away by land mines. This guy had everything. With a body like that he could have had any woman he wanted, even* farang *women. Crazy.*"

They showed us the gun at the police station, a Chinese-made Kalashnikov. You can buy them almost anywhere here: if they charge more than two hundred dollars, they're ripping you off. When the cops took the gun, though, they left the cord he used to pull the trigger, via a pinion he had fixed in the stock, which he must have held between his feet. A bloody way to go—it took out the whole of his lower intestine and snapped his spine—but it did the trick. The FBI and I pay no attention to anything except the cord. You have to believe Kowlovski was making a statement here, perhaps a confession: it is bright orange, about a centimeter thick, just like the rope he used to kill Damrong.

"You okay?" the FBI says.

"Sure."

"What are you thinking?"

"Get him to show us the belongings."

He takes his orders from her rather than me, obviously, and shows us out of the living room (linoleum, one dirty sofa, a TV) to the bedroom, where a suitcase is lying on the bed. Naturally anything valuable he might have owned will not be found. We rummage around a collection of clothes all designed to showcase his outstanding physique and way too big for any Cambodian cop, then find his money belt buried at the bottom. There's no money in it, of course, but there are a few spent airline tickets and something else. The FBI looks at it quizzically and hands it to me. It is a varnished elephant-hair bracelet. I tell her about the one Tom Smith was wearing, last time I saw him, and that Baker also had one. "Smith said an eccentric monk gave it to him at a Skytrain station."

Kimberley shakes her head and looks at me for guidance. "I thought your monk friend was in Bangkok?"

"Only an hour away. Monks are allowed to fly, just like us."

"Don't they take a vow of poverty? They're not supposed to have cash?"

I nod and repeat, "Not supposed to have cash." She jerks her chin at me, but I don't want to say more. The implications are, after all, somewhat radical.

"Why Cambodia?" she asks.

"Yeah, why Cambodia?"

"You said he ordained here?"

I nod.

Kimberley shrugs and picks up a pair of shorts to shake them upside down. A second elephant-hair bracelet falls out. The hairs on the back of my neck stand on end.

"It's like he's making a point, this monk," the FBI says.

"Right."

"But who to, if not you?"

We get thorough in our search after that, but find nothing else of interest. At the morgue we're able to identify Kowlovski from pix that Kimberley brought. The body collapsed in two when they picked it up, and the two pieces are laid in the drawer with a gap between them.

"In this country it's a miracle they managed to get the head at the top and the feet at the bottom," Kimberley growls.

The FBI needs a beer, and so do I. The best place I know is the Foreign Correspondents' Club, which is right on the Mekong (old colonial building, fans and high ceilings, well renovated, brilliant snapshots of war on the walls). From the balcony I'm watching a boy wheel a crude barrow near the river, looking for tourists. The twisted human form strapped to the board, which is bolted to two bicycle wheels, must be a brother or other close relation, because the boy and the quadriplegic appear very close when they are not panhandling. He kisses the distorted human form with the extra-large head repeatedly, coddles him, and presents him to a middle-aged Western couple, perhaps Americans, dressed in smart casuals, as they stroll past. He and the cripple are very polite, to judge by the smiles and pleading eyes and tragic frown on the quadriplegic's big twisted face, but the message is clear, calculated, and direct: *How much is it worth to make this universal icon of guilt disappear?* A few dollars, as far as I can see. After an embarrassed glance, the couple resume their walk by the Seine while the kid wheels his brother back toward the Mekong. *What else could we have done?* the couple seem to ask each other; decent people cannot stand very much reality.

"About this monk, Damrong's brother," Kimberley says, sipping her draught lager, leaving a white mustache around her mouth which she wipes with a sleeve.

As it happens, I'm not thinking about the monk—I'm thinking about Kimberley. I know she's never been to Cambodia before, but I think something in her culture makes the detritus familiar; she's more relaxed, more sure of herself, than in my more demanding country. She is also wearing military-style pants and a light khaki vest with a hundred pockets. "Anything could happen here," she says with relish. "Are you sure he's for real?"

"As sure as I can be. He's definitely a meditator familiar with *vipassana*. There's no other way to get that weird." I tell her about Phra Titanaka's personality changes.

"Bipolar," she diagnoses. "A true psycho could never be that organized or that coherent. Maybe he forgets to take his lithium from time to time. You think he got to Kowlovski?"

"Looks like it, doesn't it? One elephant-hair bracelet might have been a coincidence, but two—"

"Is downright provocative. Somehow he found out who the masked man was before we did? But I thought you said he never saw the video."

"That's what he said. Monks don't lie."

A snort from Kimberley before she quaffs more beer. She is shaking her head. "Wasn't Pol Pot a Buddhist monk?"

"For a while. It didn't seem to take with him."

"A Khmer Buddhist monk?"

I shrug. "It's obvious he didn't do it—he's not any kind of suspect."

"But he seems to know more about it than we do. Sonchai, why are you protecting a religious nut you hardly even know? He got to Kowlovski. He distributed elephant-hair bracelets to all major suspects. Maybe he sold his sister? Maybe he's behind the snuff movie?"

I flash Kimberley a look of incredulity. "You just don't get it," I say. It would be a rude response in Thai, but Kimberley's mood is impregnably buoyant.

"Get what?"

"*Gatdanyu.*"

"Huh?"

I take a deep breath because I've been down this alley before; trying to explain *gatdanyu* to a *farang* is like trying to explain the DNA helix to a Sumatran headhunter—the reception is inevitably superficial.

As best I can, I describe the hidden structure of a society few foreigners would recognize as Thailand. When Buddhism first came to our shores, our ancestors accepted its message of generosity and compassion with enthusiasm. They also saw the need to adjust it to take account of a quirk in human nature which they had noticed during the ten thousand or so years they had passed without Buddhism. I guess the objection they had to the naïveté of their new faith could be expressed in one word: *payback.* How do you make generosity worth anyone's while? By making sure it pays is how. As a result, every Thai is the center of an endless web of moral credits and debits that will end only in death. Naturally every favor must be valued against an unwritten accounting system which uses the Big Favor of Birth as its starting point, a debt that takes priority over all others.

"Superficially, Thailand can seem like a male chauvinist culture; scratch the surface, and you'll see we're all controlled by Mother. I sure as hell am."

"That's really why you work in your mother's brothel, against all your finer instincts?"

"Yes," I confess, unable to look her in the eye.

"And when I see all you Thais running around as if everyone is a successful business center, what they're actually doing is working out how to get a favor out of A to use to pay back a favor owed to B maybe from childhood, et cetera?"

"You've got it."

"Wait a minute—what about the girls who work the bars? Are you telling me they're paying back the debt to Mother by selling their bodies?"

"Yes. That is exactly what they're doing."

"And the mothers know?"

"There's an omertà about it, but in reality everyone knows."

Kimberley is looking at me over the rim of the pint glass of beer she just ordered. She shivers as she puts the glass down. "Wow." She shakes her head. "They may not be cut out for the Game at all. It's emotional blackmail pure and simple? They dump their chances for a successful marriage, childbirth, everything?"

"Now you're going too far. What chances? We're talking poor, Kimberley."

"But how does this apply to the case? I thought Damrong and her brother hated their mother."

"That's the point. *Gatdanyu* is very practical. You owe the one who actually does the favor. In reality, the fact of birth aside, Damrong was her brother's mother. She is the one who saved his life over and over and put him through school."

"And she wasn't a girl to stint when it came to reminding him of how much he owed her?"

"We don't know, but that would be my guess."

"Programmed him from early childhood?"

"Probably."

"My god, that boy must have some problems."

"So do we," I say softly, and jerk my chin toward the Mekong. Tom Smith, also in smart casuals, is strolling along the river this morning. He suffers no culture shock when accosted by the kid and his quadriplegic brother, however. The smiles and pleading eyes freeze on their faces as he gives them the brush-off with a snarl. Since he is wearing short sleeves, it is easy to spot the burnished brown bracelet on his left wrist. I haven't told the FBI about Smith's client the Chinese Australian yet, so I tell her now.

"We've got to get out of here," Kimberley says when I've finished.

"Why?"

She shakes her head. "He's a consigliere, Sonchai. That Chinese Australian, I know who he is. So do a lot of FBI agents with international experience. This is exactly the international dimension I'm over here to check out." I wrinkle my brow. "We think he's the front man for a syndicate of rich psychos. We call them 'the invisible men.' They seem to be behind a lot of things: gladiatorial fights to the death in the

Sonora desert, snuff movies filmed in Nicaragua with the victims picked off from helicopters just for the hell of it, sadomasochism for sale in Shanghai, boys from broken homes kidnapped in Glasgow and shipped off to the Middle East for the pleasure of oil sheikhs—the kind of stuff that never gets investigated because it happens offstage as far as America and the West are concerned and the people behind it are too rich and important to be captured."

I'm not entirely surprised, but I don't see why we need to panic and say so. "Even if Smith is here on the same business as us, it doesn't mean he's going to call up an assassination squad."

The FBI shakes her head. "I can't believe I'm reading this place better than you. Don't you get it? It is lawless. *Lawless.* Know what human beings do when there's no law? They waste other human beings who are in the way, or look like they are going to be in the way, or have potential to be in the way. It's called Cain's First Law of Survival. Think about it: you are the consigliere to a powerful international syndicate whose public face happens to be mainstream pornography but whose premier product is for the delectation of psychotically morbid billionaires. Know what kind of power that gives you, to have the goods on a dozen or so of the richest perverts in the world? Imagine what's at stake here. Smith's people made that video of Damrong; now they're very nervous because the costar did himself in less than a mile from here. About thirty minutes from now Tom Smith will bribe the same cops we bribed and go see the place where Kowlovski butchered himself. On the way the same cops we bribed will tell him about our visit. Tell him we checked out the crime scene. Tell him we are still here. Tell him we plan to be here until tomorrow. What does Smith do in a country where there are about two hundred thousand retired Khmer Rouge on the breadline? How long would it take to put a small squad together? Hell, he'll probably use the cops as recruiting agents— they could call up a dozen contract killers in ten minutes. Maybe the cops are contract killers themselves, who like to do a little policing now and then. Don't you see? He's got to hit us here in Cambodia. It's an opportunity a guy like him can't afford to miss. Look what happened to Nok. Sonchai, let's say I've been here in a previous life, I know where I am, okay?"

"It wasn't here," I say. "It was Danang in Vietnam. You were male then, of course. And black." I smile sweetly while she looks at me in shock. "You'd better fly back to Bangkok. I need to check out Damrong's home village, and it's easier to do that by going overland and crossing the border at Surin province."

We decide to stroll by the Mekong; everyone does. Blood-brown, myth-laden, I guess it means something different to all people. Even the FBI carries a piece of it inside her—deeds of derring-do by Navy SEALs thirty years ago, perhaps; it's our Ganges and was created by a dragon, naturally. There is none of the traffic you see on the Chao Phraya, though; at Phnom Penh the Mekong is still a quiet, lazy liquefaction that merges into the red earth at sunset in a blaze like a fallen firework writhing in mud. It sustains a dozen dilatory fishing craft during the day; most of the canoes don't have engines, and those that do are so small and quiet that, what with the motionless heat and the Pleistocene fishermen throwing skeins, you'd think that peace had prevailed here for a thousand years. That's maya for you.

"I love him," the FBI declares softly, looking away downstream, reserving the right to deny what she has just said, but high for a moment, having first dared herself to say it. "Sorry," she adds, with a hand on my shoulder reasserting control. "I've never been sixteen before. It won't last long."

"You'll be with him by tomorrow," I say with a smile.

"Tonight," she corrects, still looking away. "I just text'd him." She allows her hand to drop so that it first brushes, then grasps mine. "You don't know how clairvoyant you really are, Sonchai. I had the most vivid dream of my life last night. Vietnam. Danang. You're right, I was black and about nineteen years old. The only thing I thought of as I lay dying was a girl in Saigon. All I cared about in the world was that I wouldn't be seeing her again. I died staring at a passport-size snapshot of her."

"Lek?"

"To the last nuance, as you would say." She looks me full in the face for a moment, then faces upstream, toward Laos. "You're the one who is always explaining that we humans are simply the visible ends of karmic chains, intimately interwoven with others, that stretch back thousands, even millions, of years. You just didn't want to apply that to an American in love, did you?"

Touché, and I would not mind leaving it at that. But Kimberley is *farang*, after all. "Sonchai, you don't have to answer yes or no to this question. I'll know by the way you look. Is this—this thing I'm feeling—is it *really* just the reflex of a sexually frustrated thirty-something? I mean, you don't *really* think it's all about dominance, money, power, and exoticism? You were just angry when you said all that? He's more than ten years younger than me, I know, and very feminine . . ." She coughs. "Yeah, well, he's totally irresistible. That beauty, that sensitivity—to an American cop like me, it's a miracle he exists at all in this world. Two nights ago I watched him put his makeup on before he went to that bar of his. All my life I've been bored by women's makeup rituals, but I could have watched him all night. What is happening to me?"

27

Five A.M.: the bus station at Surin is as big as an airport, with buses going everywhere but mostly to Bangkok. Even at this hour my nomadic people are on the move. We keep our restlessness hidden under serene exteriors, but check our life itineraries, and you'll see we never stop moving from country to city and vice versa. Like temple dogs, we carry our fleas with us and never stop itching. I left the FBI at the airport at Phnom Penh; she was retrieving a picture of Lek that she had captured on her cell phone. He is beautiful, of course, but also very ethnic; he looked out of the FBI's cell phone as if he were peering at her from another planet and knew it. She looked at him as if there were not a single thing about him she did not understand.

I'm lucky to get a seat at the back of the bus to Ubon Ratchathani. There's that usual feeling of relief, of a journey finally started, when the driver climbs in and starts the engine. At the same time he plays a noisy video on the monitor, which is on a bracket above his head. Unfortunately it's a sickly romance full of empty beaches, long sultry looks, and sustained close-ups of teary eyes; an ophthalmologist's vision. I close my own eyes and drop off in seconds. I must be exhausted because I do not normally sleep on buses. The seat is quite uncomfortable, and I have to continually adjust by bracing my knees against the seat back in front of me; then when that position becomes intolerable, I twist around so my head is resting on the window; and so on. In the waking intervals I observe a hybrid landscape of failed development projects, sprawls of poor quality housing that looks unfinished even though it's been there for decades, ragged streams, and sultry remains of jungle. The wasteland continues for a few miles, but by the time we reach Pak Cheung, there's been a subtle change. Nature is not so cowed out here: the ramshackle settlements are like barricades against the dense creeping green of the hinterland.

After lunch I get into a conversation with the young woman next to me. We beat about the bush for a couple of minutes before we admit to each other we're both in the flesh trade. She works in Nana Plaza and has been doing quite well these past few months. She's going home for a few days to be with her five-year-old daughter by a Thai lover whom she hasn't seen since she told him she was pregnant. She doesn't say it, but I can see she is also looking forward to the respect her fellow villagers will show her for taking care of her parents and siblings; it will make a change from being just another whore on the Game in the big city. I ask her if she knows Black Hill Hamlet, where Damrong came from. She nods: Yes, she's visited there a few times. Even for Isaan, it's a very poor village. She saw children eating dirt there; they really are on the breadline in that area.

From Ubon Ratchathani I hire a four-wheel drive with driver to take me to the hamlet. Now I'm in true Isaan country. It's starting to get dark, but there's enough light to observe the mystically flat landscape that makes you feel like you're at the lowest point on earth. Wild-looking day workers with T-shirts wrapped around their heads flash by in the back of pickup trucks. Regular tree lines form windbreaks for the smallholdings where women prepare food over charcoal fires; the mystic green of the paddy is immeasurably enhanced by the inexplicable presence of elephants. The pachyderms graze or stand impossibly motionless, relishing the emptiness. I'm reminded that Surin province is the elephant capital of Thailand. During the last weekend in November there is a festival, called the Elephant Roundup, in Surin town, and the roads are crowded with the beasts for weeks on end. In the country it is considered lucky, even vital, that children should run under the lumbering animals as they trundle past.

It's dark by the time the four-wheel drive gets to the hamlet. I don't bother to ask anyone about Damrong's folks—I'm too tired. I find a woman who is prepared to let me sleep in her house for a modest fee of one hundred baht, including breakfast. Like every other house in these parts, it is on stilts. When I've climbed the wooden stairs, I see it consists of one huge room with a few futons on the floor and all the owner's worldly possessions piled up in a corner. Being a widow and middle aged, there is no stigma in putting a man up for the night, nor any suggestion of impropriety. The house is in a compound surrounded by houses belonging to her relations. I don't think she has ever experienced urban paranoia in her life. She shifts her futon to the other end of the room, though, and I fall asleep gratefully. In the morning she gives me rice gruel with a fried egg on top. Starting off gently, I ask her as obliquely as I can about Damrong and her family. I haven't told her I'm a cop.

She has heard about Damrong's death, of course—the whole hamlet has been talking about it for days. How did she hear about it? She shrugs: grapevine. I guide the conversation to Damrong's home life. What kind of people?

Despite the labyrinthine forms of politeness and diplomacy with which country people broach delicate subjects, I've clearly hit upon some subtle level of the whole affair known only to the villagers. I see from her face that my hostess believes that magic, karma, or even divine vengeance were involved. When I open my wallet to offer to pay a little more for a cup of coffee if she can manage one, she understands immediately and, in a sudden change of mood, starts merrily and loquaciously to spill her guts.

Damrong's family were hard people, my hostess explains. She uses a particular Isaan word which indicates a combination of fear, respect, and doubt: even in the country it is possible to take toughness too far. Damrong's father died when she was in her midteens, but he was quite the country gangster in his day, who used sorcery to protect himself during his midnight raids on other villages. His tattoos kept him safe for years. In those not-so-distant times there were very few cops around, and those few were not exactly diligent. Damrong's father killed five men during his life, mostly in brawls or simply because they got on his nerves—generally with the upward thrust of a knife under the ribs. The courting of Damrong's mother consisted of abducting her and keeping her in his house for three days. Whether he raped her or not during that time is irrelevant; at the end of the three-day period, she was ruined as far as any other man was concerned, so she had to marry the country gangster. She didn't much mind, so the story goes, for she had that extra tough—some would say criminal—streak herself, which is why the gangster chose her in the first place. Nobody liked doing business with them. A darkness hung over that family. Damrong's violent death was seen hereabouts as simply one more chapter in a black family history.

My hostess pauses in her compulsive nattering and looks at me. "You know the tradition of making children run under elephants during the festival? Well, I happened to be there when her mother made Damrong do it. Personally I think it's very cruel—some kids are so terrified they're mentally scarred for life. Think of what it must mean to a six-year-old, seeing those enormous legs, those terrifying feet, and being told by your own mother you have to risk your life by running underneath them. Elephants are not gentle giants—they're vicious and unpredictable."

"How did Damrong take it?"

"That's the thing, I never saw a child so terrified. But her mother beat her. I mean, she just kept on hitting her until she was more terrified of another smack than she was of the elephant. She ran under it, but I'll never forget the hatred in her eyes—not of the elephant, of her mother. She didn't run to her for comfort, she just stood there on the other side of the street totally traumatized. Such a pretty girl too. You could see what she was going to become even at that age. What choice did she have?"

We're interrupted by a shout from below. One of the neighbors has heard that a stranger is staying here and wants to take a look at him. "We're talking about Damrong!" my hostess yells down. "I'm coming up!" yells the other.

She is a very short country woman, perhaps no more than four feet nine—a diastrophic dwarf, the smartest kind of little person—in a worn sarong carrying a plastic bag containing a large spiky green durian that she no doubt hopes to sell somewhere today. To see her as poor, though, might be missing the point. I recognize her as belonging to a specific type which is fast disappearing. Even today, all over rural

Thailand, especially here in Isaan, there are still people like her who live off the land in a literal way, people who are sufficiently familiar with the woods and jungles to survive there without much external support. Her face is deeply lined with a great forehead and young bright eyes under the sagging lids. This woman has never experienced depression in her life; she lives on some elemental level and shares her mind with spirits.

"The gentleman was asking about Damrong," my hostess explains.

"Oh, of course," says the dwarf, not at all surprised that someone should appear out of nowhere and demand to know all the gossip. "So sad."

"I said she comes from a hard family."

"Hard?" The dwarf also uses the Isaan word. "You're not kidding." Looking up at me and, I think, quickly identifying me as some kind of authority figure: "They say her brother, Gamon, is heartbroken."

"Oh, yes," says my hostess, distressed at having left out a dramatic detail. "They were so close. But of course, he is a monk, so he will know how to take it."

"We'll be lucky if he doesn't kill himself," says the dwarf in a contemplative kind of way, "monk or not. She was the only backbone he had."

When we hear yet another voice downstairs, a curious neighbor wanting to see the mysterious visitor, I know it's time to go. I dig out my police ID to flash it. No one is particularly surprised. The dwarf undertakes to lead me to Damrong's mother's house.

The house—actually a large shack—is the only one without a flower garden; garbage is heaped up in a corner in front. Unlike the other houses, the stilts supporting this one are entirely of timber, with no concrete support; they are rotting along with the stairs that lead up to the front door. I have to knock a few times. When she opens the door, I see one large, almost-empty space populated by plastic buckets to catch leaks from the roof. In a far corner a small black-and-white television flickers in front of a futon.

She's drunk already and very thin in the way of terminal alcoholics: worn gray sarong wrapped around her skeletal form, black T-shirt. Whatever it is that happens to the legs of drunks has happened to hers: she walks stiffly with a jerk, as if there's a broken nerve in the link between leg and brain. I've never seen a face so black with fear and loathing. No doubt she was hard as nails twenty years ago, but now the hardness has disintegrated, leaving only a rickety body and a damaged brain as processing unit; there's been no higher consciousness here for decades. I know there's no point questioning her, so I have to change my plan on the wing. I flash my ID. "Your son, Gamon, says hello."

She glares at me, apparently not understanding the word "son." I look for signs of him from the doorway and see, of all things, an old publicity photograph for a Harley-Davidson motorbike pinned to a wall. If I am not mistaken, it is a Fat Boy. A flicker of light passes through her eyes. She makes a shooing gesture with her hands. "Fucked off."

"He joined the Sangha."

She glowers. "Fucked off."

"And your daughter, Damrong?" The name seems to have no meaning for her at all. Perhaps she would remember her daughter's family nickname, but I don't know what it is. From my pocket I fish out a still from the video: Damrong's beautiful face about five minutes before she dies. It has a strange effect on the old woman, as if evoking not memories so much as a parallel world. She points at a flimsy structure in one corner of the space, which seems to form a separate room made of thin plywood, with a door that is locked by means of a cheap padlock. "*Borisot,*" she says: virgin.

I know the country tradition of building a special space for a daughter who has reached puberty and whose honor needs to be kept inviolable until a husband can be found. It is a custom which is emphasized in every second soap that appears on our TV screens. By a fantastic psychological maneuver Damrong's mother must have decided one fine day to protect the virtue of her absent daughter, whom she forced into prostitution and from whom she has not heard for years. I have to give her two hundred baht before she will fish out the key to the padlock and open the door. Inside, the tiny room consists of two-by-four studs holding up plywood walls. There is nothing else at all except for two photographs, both of Damrong. One is about eight by twelve inches, old and yellow, pinned to the plywood: the kind of romantic pic only country photographers produce, with softened lines, starry eyes, and a stiff white dress with plenty of lace. Damrong could not have been more than thirteen years old when it was taken; she has been told to look skyward to a TV heaven of handsome husbands and air-conditioning. Despite the photographer's efforts, her classic beauty shines through, and there is no denying the power of it. The other photograph is of a child running under a huge elephant. The old lady sees me stare at it and starts into an incomprehensible babble in her native Khmer. I think this hopelessness I feel, intensified by a factor of millions, must have been exactly what Damrong decided to combat one fine day when she was still very young.

"Just one thing, Mother," I say, putting a finger to her lips. To my surprise, she stops ranting on the instant, like an obedient child. Gently I turn her around so she has her back to me and lift up the T-shirt. She yields as if she's undergoing a medical examination. Sure enough, the tiger tattoo begins somewhere in the small of her back and leaps up so that its head is just peeping over her left shoulder. Interesting. The other tattoo is an elaborate horoscope. Both are very faded and wrinkled, I would guess she's had them since her teens. I examine the horoscope for a while; it is written in ancient *khom*, of course. I don't think there's much more to be gained here, so I say goodbye and descend the stairs to the ground. Outside, looking up at the rickety hut with its rotting stumps and the black madness of the old lady who is at this moment slamming the door, I experience an overwhelming rage. What psychological mountains did Damrong have to climb just to function, just to get up in the morning—merely in order to believe in herself enough to work? What superhuman power enabled her to do it all with genius and panache? They knew nothing of all that, of course—Baker, Smith, and Tanakan—when they made use of her charms. I knew better but carefully concealed that knowledge from myself while I took my pleasure; just like them, *mes semblables, mes frères.*

The hamlet is a sprawling affair that takes up a surprising amount of land because each family owns a smallholding which separates it from the others. A few of the homesteads are quite affluent, even boasting carports with pickup trucks; most are at subsistence level. Everyone has heard that a stranger, a cop, has arrived, and ragged kids emerge blatantly to stare. Nobody wants to be seen talking to me in public, though. I decide to try my luck with the family who live next door to Damrong's mother. A woman in a sarong is squatting under her long roof, using a pestle and mortar to make *somtan* salad. She has been watching me from the corner of her eye, and when I pause at her gate, she calls out, "Have you eaten yet?"

"Not yet."

"Eat with us."

There is a sliding iron gate, which I push open. At the same time three kids appear, the youngest about three years old. A bent old man, probably in his eighties, emerges from the house on wobbly legs, holding a bottle of moonshine. Behind him nagging abuse streams from an old lady. Now a young woman appears, walking very slowly. It is almost a perfect replica of Nok's family. The first woman, who is in her fifties, has been watching my face as I gaze with a professional eye on the young woman.

"Medication," she says.

"*Yaa baa?*"

"Her second husband was a dealer. The police shot and killed him, but not before he'd screwed up her head with his drugs. One half of her brain is mush. The mental hospital was going to keep her locked up for seven years if I didn't guarantee her. I have to pay for the medication every month or she loses it completely."

"Those are her kids?"

"All by different fathers. If it wasn't for my first daughter, I don't know what we'd do."

"Your first daughter works in Krung Thep?"

She turns her eyes away. "Of course." She begins serving the *somtan* and places a wicker basket of sticky rice between us.

I regret the insensitivity of my question and change the subject even as I stick my fingers into the rice and make a ball out of a handful. "I've been talking to your neighbor."

"I know. You're here because of Damrong."

"How long have you lived here?"

"Forever. We're villagers—this is the only land we own."

I decide to let her talk in her own time. She rolls her ball of rice around in the sauce of the salad, which is crimson with chili, and eats for a while, then says, "So, you're a cop investigating poor Damrong's death. That's one family with very bad karma." Shaking her head: "What other explanation could there be? We are poor too, we suffer just the same as them, but we don't go bad. We're good people, we go to the *wat*, we make merit, we keep a clean house, we never break the law." A pause while she shakes her head. "What's that mother going to be, *chart na*? She can't even talk properly anymore. She's going to hell. When she gets out, she'll be lucky to be reborn a human. I've never seen anything that dark, that hopeless. What people do to their minds, hey?"

Suddenly the dwarf woman has appeared from nowhere. She is peering around the open gate, looking in. My hostess catches her eye. "Have you eaten yet?"

"No." The dwarf joins us, lowering herself onto the rush mat we are eating off of and sitting upright with the straight back of a child.

"He's asking about poor Damrong."

"I know," the dwarf says. She looks me full in the face, as if she has decided it's time I knew the truth. "She was a very strong spirit with very bad karma," she explains. "That's why she incarnated into that family. She was very strong."

"The mother's spent a long time in jail," I say.

"Yes."

"There's Khmer writing under the tiger on her back."

"Yes."

"And I think the horoscope is in the black tradition. Did she belong to some criminal cult?"

"Yes." She nods without casting me a glance. Even in the midst of such a dark subject, her fifty-year-old child's eyes are dancing over the house, the kids, the catastrophe of poverty, a smile always on her lips.

"Black sorcery?" I ask.

She shrugs. "It's not good to think about what they did in that family. It will bring bad luck."

"Did they use their own children?"

"Yes."

"What about her brother?"

For the first time a moment of concern appears in her face, then is quickly erased. "She loved him. She's the only reason he survived. A very weak spirit. Perhaps he cannot survive on his own without her." Casting me a glance: "Do you know how her father died?"

"How her father died? Why don't you tell me?"

"Very unlucky to talk about a violent death like that." She lays a hand on my forearm. "I'm a non-Returner."

It's odd to hear a Buddhist technical expression used by someone who is obviously the product of some shamanistic cult, but when the Indians brought Buddhism to Thailand, much of it was absorbed into local animism. Nowadays it is quite common to hear people like the dwarf talk about "non-Returners." Buddhist monks who believe they have achieved this level are careful not to commit a blunder that will land them in the flesh yet again. Even talking in an inappropriate way can ruin your disembodiment plans.

There are few proprieties to observe in the country. When I've finished eating, I get up to go, casting the dwarf one last glance. Without looking at me, she says, "They made the children watch, you know. Both of them, so they wouldn't turn out like their father. The girl was just about old enough to take it—like I say, she was very strong. But the boy . . ."

"They watched their father die?"

She raises a finger to her lips. As I leave, the hostess calls to me in an urgent voice, as if there is something vital she forgot to tell me. "They're Khmer, you know, not Thai people at all."

At the main road I manage to wave down a pickup truck that will take me to the nearest bus station for a hundred baht. My driver is the best kind of country man: silent, devout, honest. In the delicious emptiness that surrounds him, my mind will not cease its endless narrative:

A *Third-World Pilgrim's Progress*

   1. *Born into karma too daunting to contemplate, you decide to go to sleep for life.*

   2. *Mother does not permit option 1: you do run under the elephant, whether you like it or not.*

   3. *Ruthlessness and rage at least produce reactions from society, unlike good behavior, which leads to slavery and starvation. Only sex and drugs pay a living wage. You have seen the light.*

4. At the top of your game and winning, you regret aborting love. Too late, you have reached thirty and demons are massing on the horizon. Only death can save you now. One question remains: who will you take with you?

Welcome to the new millennium.

28

"Where is he, Lek?"

It pains me to use this tone, to reduce my protégé to a sulky child, but I'm at the end of my rope. I've been back two days and seen no sign of Phra Titanaka.

"I don't know," Lek says camply, pouts, and looks at the floor. We are at the station in one of the small interrogation rooms, which hardly helps Lek's mood.

"I'm sure you got close to him while I was away. I think you're lying. I know he's got you involved somehow. I saw you talking to him at the *wat*."

He jumps up, his face exploding with hurt. "I've never lied to you in my life, I couldn't lie to you—I have *gatdanyu* with you. You protect me every minute of the day. If you stamp all over my heart, I'll kill myself."

I pass a hand over my face. "I'm sorry, Lek. There's no way I can pretend to you that I'm strong enough for this case. You'll have to bear with me. I think you must have seen him while I was away. You were getting on so well."

Now his mood has changed. He comes over to comfort me. "Master, I'm so sorry for you. I would do anything to help."

"When did you last see him?"

"He came to say goodbye when you were in Cambodia."

"That's all?"

"He asked me for your cell phone number. I gave it to him."

I nod. Somehow it is inevitable that I must turn in the wind, awaiting a young monk's pleasure. There's karma here: I'm paying one hell of a price for those ten days of ecstatic misery I spent with Damrong.

Apart from the sudden spat with Lek, I've been listless all day. Just to get out of the station, I tell Lek I'm going for a massage, but I don't really intend to have one. Outside, though, passing the Internet café—which has entirely lost its magic now that Damrong's brother no longer uses it—I decide I may as well have the massage anyway. A wicked impulse of pure self-destruction suggests I should go to the third floor and have the works; that maybe two hours of luscious, aromatic, oily, slippery, seminal, orgasmic self-indulgence might be exactly what I need. I know it won't help my self-esteem in the longer term, however, and I think of Chanya, even though I know she wouldn't mind, would even encourage me if it would improve my mood. So I go for my usual two hours on the second floor.

All through the first hour my mind is hopping like a louse on a marble floor, and I hardly notice the massage. I calm down eventually, and I'm able to retrieve just an echo of the peace that once was mine by right. Then the cell phone rings. I left it in the pocket of my pants, which are hanging on a hook above the mattress. Even while the masseuse is pressing her knee into my lower spine, I grab my pants and feverishly fish out the phone.

"I need to talk," Phra Titanaka says.

The cop in me recognizes a weakness finally, perhaps even an admission. "Talk."

I beckon to the masseuse to go to something less strenuous—maybe tie my feet in a knot—while I'm talking. In reality it doesn't matter what she does; my mind is focused on the monk's slow, deliberate, cool tone.

"They sold her when she was fourteen," the disembodied voice says into my ear. "It was a family decision. I wasn't included in the discussion, but Damrong was. She agreed to work in a brothel in Malaysia as indentured labor on condition they look after me properly."

"I'm sorry."

"Your sorrow is a teaspoon of sugar in an ocean of bitterness."

"I'm sorry for that too," I say.

"It was one of those sixteen-hour-a-day jobs. She had to service twenty customers every twenty-four hours, minimum. The first night, though, they auctioned her virginity to the highest bidder. He was by no means gentle."

"Oh, Buddha, I'm—"

"Cut it out, or you'll miss the point. The contract was for twelve months. When she came home, she wasn't the same at all. Not at all. But she checked on how well they had treated me. She asked me and everyone in the village, and she checked my body, my weight, everything. No one had ever seen her like that before. Totally efficient, totally cold." A pause. "Of course, they hadn't treated me very well at all. They'd spent her money on moonshine and *yaa baa*." A long pause. "So she made them pay. Can you guess?"

No, I tell him, I cannot possibly guess how a helpless, impoverished, used and abused, uneducated fifteen-year-old girl could punish two hardened criminals.

"She snitched on our father to the cops. She arranged for him to be caught red-handed during one of his burglaries." I know from his tone that he heard my intake of breath. "It worked better than she could have imagined. The cops were sick of him for his endless crimes. They killed him with the elephant game." Another pause. "She was ecstatic. I remember the shine in her eyes. Next time she took on a contract of prostitution, in Singapore this time, my mother treated me very well for the whole six months. When she was sober."

He has closed the phone.

When he next calls, the massage is over and I am in the process of paying the masseuse.

"I forgot to tell you, Detective. There was a written contract— Damrong insisted on it."

I swallow. "I see."

"Don't tell anyone. Don't tell Vikorn."

He has hung up. I'm thinking, *Don't tell Vikorn—betray my master?* I am simultaneously thinking, *Yes, screw Vikorn.*

· · ·

A written contract sounds unlikely, but if it exists, I'm prepared to bet Tom Smith drafted it. His masters surely would never have trusted any other lawyer. The possibility of getting hold of it seems remote. Was Damrong allowed to keep a copy? If so, where is it? Why didn't she give it to her brother for safekeeping?

I'm at home watching Chanya cook when he calls again. I know that Chanya has grown concerned by my state of mind, that she is watching me as I fish the cell phone from my pants, which I already hung up on a hook on the bedroom door because I changed into light-weight shorts. It is almost as if I can experience her heart when my features alter at the sound of his voice: sorrow, fear, sympathy, a touch of anger because I seem to be slipping away from her.

"Can you talk?"

"Yes."

"Talk about *gatdanyu*. What do you think of it?"

I scratch my ear. "It's all we've got. There's no other way to organize Thailand. It's not perfect, people abuse it, especially mothers, but there's no other way for us."

"You're half *farang*. You must look at it from a different point of view sometimes."

"My blood is half *farang*, but I think like a Thai."

"You've been abroad. You speak perfect English. You even speak French."

"So?"

"I want to know."

My tone expresses the beginnings of exasperation. "Know what?"

There's a long silence. Perhaps he has never formulated this thought before. "What I'm doing."

"I don't know what you're doing."

"I think you do. I want to know, from a *farang* point of view, am I going too far?"

"Too far?"

"The price she's making me pay—is it too high?"

"What is the price? Did she give you instructions?"

A pause. "Perhaps."

"And money. She gave you all the money she made out of the contract, didn't she? How much? A lot, I think—she was very shrewd.

That's what you don't want to face, isn't it? Two weeks ago you were a helpless monk; there was no point in dwelling on the horrors of your childhood; you were penniless; the most you could hope for in this life was to be left to pursue your meditation practice. You were already very advanced, almost an *arhat*. You were able to dissolve the past because the present offered no way of—" I stop deliberately in midsentence. I want to know if he's hooked or not. When he says, "Go on," I'm sure that from now on he will not be able to stop speaking to me.

"Revenge," I say.

Apparently this word has not yet crystallized on the surface of his mind, like a virus that does not reveal its true nature unless magnified and photographed.

"Revenge? Where would I start?"

"You would probably never start. You were never the one to start anything, were you? It was always her. She knew how to survive, you didn't. You spent your life as a second-stringer. You still are a second-stringer. Sure, you wouldn't know where to start when it came to revenge, but she would. Tell me what she is making you do."

A pause. "No, I'm not going to tell you that. Anyway, I think you have already guessed."

"She would never have left the strategy to you. I think that nothing has changed. In death as in life she is controlling you."

"If you think like a Thai, you must know I owe her everything. If she had left instructions for me to hang myself with my robe, I would have followed those instructions to the letter."

"How easy that would have been for you," I say gently.

He takes a full minute to reply, then: "Yes. That's true."

"And how hard this is for you, whatever it is she is making you do."

"I have to do it."

"How? Will you hire foreign mercenaries? You can certainly afford them. But it would be difficult for them to understand. Even mercenaries have rules." Listening to my own thoughts, I suddenly realize where the help will come from, when the moment arrives. "They'll be Khmer, won't they? I don't know why I didn't think of it. Retired KR foot soldiers have many advantages. One, they will do anything for money. Two, they obey orders instantly and to the letter. Three, they are plentiful and inexpensive. Four, they know all about elephants.

Five, they will be able to disappear into the jungle, or more likely Poipet, where geriatric generals in wheelchairs will protect them."

He is full of surprises. "Poipet?" he says with an intake of breath. "You've been there?"

"Yes. Once." Memory clip: a drab Cambodian town near the Thai border, roughly the same latitude as Angkor Wat. A terrible coarseness everywhere, even in the faces of children, most of whom were prostitutes. I really did see the famous retired KR generals in wheelchairs sucking on tubes attached to oxygen cylinders. "Have you been there yourself, Phra Titanaka?"

"I ordained there."

He closes the phone, but the number he was using is recorded on my own. I think he will not answer, but I try anyway.

"Yes?"

"At least tell me about Kowlovski."

"Who?"

"Her costar in the movie."

"Ah, yes. The masked man."

"You worked on him, didn't you? I think you abused powers you had acquired in meditation. You didn't raise a finger, but you killed him by making him kill himself, didn't you? I think that would have been very easy for you. His tiny, shallow, ersatz heart was open to your gaze."

A long pause, then: "I'll send you the video." He hangs up.

Chanya has pretended not to listen the conversation, or to see the intensity of my involvement with Phra Titanaka. She serves the *pla neung menau* in a tureen. The delicately textured fish is cooked perfectly, with not a touch of rawness or dryness, and the lemon sauce balances the natural taste of the fish to produce that wonderful tang on the palate. When we have finished, I pat the Lump, delighted to have the opportunity to play happy family. Our little rented house seems so small, though, and the walls so thin, our existence here so precarious. But it is not outside where the storm rages; it is in my head.

When we go to bed and make spoons, with Chanya curled up against my stomach, my mind flips back not to the case but to the womb. I reexperience that moment of total panic when we must break out at all costs; perhaps the most primeval of all human memories, and the one that always remains deep down inside us, like a door god at the gates of maya. Without that desperation born of claustrophobia, we would never leave that safest of safe havens; but the memory of those months of oceanic peace ensure we spend our lives trying to get back in. Damrong knew that about men.

I nod off for a couple of hours, then awaken with a single phrase on my mind: the elephant game. It resonates for anyone who has ever been involved in criminal law, but how can I be sure a simple Cambodian monk is reading from that hymnbook? Surreptitiously I slide out of bed, fish out my cell phone, and go into the yard.

"The elephant game," I whisper when he picks up the phone. "Tell me about it."

A sigh. "You don't know? I thought all Thai cops knew about it. The cops built a ball out of thatched bamboo, just big enough for a small human being to be placed inside. My father was not tall, maybe five-four at most, and very slim in a vicious kind of way. There was a hatch with a lock on the outside. On the day we were taken to the police station, we stood against the wall of a compound at the back. Some grinning cops brought my father out into the yard and made him lie down while they tied him up hands and feet like a hog. Then they slid him through the hatch in the bamboo ball, locked the hatch, and pushed him around the compound for a while, just for some fun before the main event. Then they led a young elephant, maybe eight or nine years old, into the yard and they started to teach the elephant to kick the ball. That's when my father started screaming. He was always so hard-boiled, I was sure he would keep his cool right to the end; after all, he'd wasted plenty of people himself. But he lost it after the elephant's first kick. That made the animal curious. It sniffed around the ball with its trunk and discovered that every time it rolled the ball, the human thing inside would start screaming its head off. The cops thought it was hilarious. Pretty soon the elephant got addicted to football. It kicked to move my father a few feet along, then pushed with its trunk, then kicked. I guess this went on for maybe ten minutes until the ball stuck in a corner of the compound and the elephant lost patience. People don't realize, elephants can have quick tempers. It whacked the ball with its trunk a few times, making a big dent in it; then it started trying to bring its foot down on it. The ball was too big for the elephant at first, but after it made a few more dents with its trunk, the ball collapsed to half its size, and the animal was able to stamp on bits of it. My father was screaming out of control by this time. Then he stopped screaming, but I could see he was still alive. I guess the animal had damaged some part of him that stopped him from screaming. He managed one last howl, though, when it stamped on his lower back. Next thing I knew, there was just a mess of spiky bamboo splinters all mixed up with my father's remains."

During the long pause I'm trying to think of what to say. It's hard to say nothing, but he's too smart, too mentally advanced, for any normal condolence. He saves me by speaking again: "There's a picture."

"What do you mean?"

"Of him being crushed by the elephant."

"Who took it?"

"Who do you think? Actually, there are lots of pictures. She used up a whole roll of film. I'll scan a few and send you a sequence."

29

He sent me the pix by e-mail. I was expecting a few amateurish snaps in which an out-of-focus elephant steps on something indistinguishable. Not so. Whatever camera she used, it had an impressive zoom. Here's Jumbo close up, sniffing around a gigantic bamboo latticework ball with a clearly discernible human form inside. Now she's homed in on her dad, all trussed up. He was naked apart from a baggy pair of shorts; his elaborate esoteric tattoos are clearly visible. Now here's a cruel sequence: the elephant with trunk upraised; elephant bringing trunk down on helpless human; close-up of helpless human's big terrified eyes; split-second snap of furious elephant with trunk raised high in the air; trunk splintering the ball with bamboo shards flying; right foreleg lifted as high as it can manage; right foreleg squashing human.

I cross-examine myself thus: *You of all people must have seen some clue, some pattern of behavior, that would have revealed her true nature. You, who have spent your whole life with women, who understand women better than you ever understood men, who have been known to cause hardened prostitutes to fall in love with you exactly because you're the only man they ever meet who does understand them, you of all people: why couldn't you read her?*

Because I was in love is a pathetic reply, but it is probably no more than the truth. We didn't talk much, few thoughts and feelings were shared, but she did not give the impression of a bored professional going through a pantomime of love. She was interested in me; with hindsight I guess the interest was that of a praying mantis for her doomed lover. She was interested in me as food; I invented a heart for her.

After sex, usually, when she had really made an effort to deliver the experience of a lifetime—not for my benefit, of course, but with exactly the same meticulous self-criticism a world-class ballerina might apply when dancing in front of a mirror—her long black hair would end up tangled and wild. She could get wild-eyed too with the frenzy of sex, and I have a snapshot of her in that state: black hair flying, madness in her eyes, naked, hunched like a witch over her breasts, her brown skin glistening with sweat, the room redolent with the stench of our lovemaking—even at such times to deny her power would have been as futile as denying our pagan origins. A hundred thousand years our ancestors spent carefully adding to the stock of irresistible allurements in the collective subconscious: her real art was to take men back to that forbidden jungle of lethal pleasure. Choosing the most vulnerable men was easy after a lifetime of practice.

Generally I was too intimidated, too concerned that my perform-ance was not up to scratch—terrified, I guess, that she would come out with some cutting remark, some comparison with another lover that would destroy my face. She never did—she merely had to look as if she were about to.

This morning, in addition to the elephant pix, the monk sent the DVD of his conversation with the masked man.

The scene is Stanislaus Kowlovski's apartment in Phnom Penh where he killed himself; I recognize the rip in the sofa. I think Phra Titanaka bought a DVD camera with his new wealth and learned to screw it to a tripod. It does not move throughout the interview, so that the monitor is full of our handsome buck, who is no longer so hand-

some after however many hours and days spent with a merciless inter-
rogator of the soul. It is impossible to know if the camera is hidden or
not. Perhaps the monk didn't read the handbook too well, because the
disk seems to begin in the middle of the interview. Phra Titanaka's
English is surprisingly grammatical, although his accent is thick Thai:

S.K.: *I want to know how you found out about me, how you
knew where to contact me in L.A. You still haven't told me.*
Monk: *I have contacts on the other side.*
S.K.: *Oh, yeah, we're not getting into that spiritual thing again
are we?*
Monk: *Not necessarily.*
S.K., shaking his head: *This is weird, man, very very strange.
First I thought you were putting the squeeze on me. That's
how you got me here. You know stuff about me, but I don't
know how much you know. Let's say you convinced me it was
in my best interests to get a plane to Phnom Penh. Then I
thought you were going to kill me. Then I thought just for a
moment you wanted to save my soul—you are wearing a
monk's robes after all.*
Monk: *Why would I want to kill you? You've been dead for a
thousand years already.*
S.K.: *Shit, man, I don't know if I can do that again today. Just
tell me how much you want. I'll borrow the dough.*
Monk: *Let's say I'm a collector of stories of cause and effect.
Let's go back to that moment—that white-out we're calling
it, I believe—when you were, how old?*
S.K., with a reluctant grunt: *Thirteen. Yeah. I was pubescent
all over. I finally knew what I was. A prick. A big, hard—*
Monk: *But why?*
S.K.: *I told you, sport was the only official way out, but I wasn't
any good at it. Gigolo was the only role left. It was the
Columbine syndrome.*
Monk: *Deeper, Stan, please.*
S.K.: *Deeper? What can be deeper than that?*
Monk: *Was that the moment you decided there was no morality
in the world?*

S.K.: *Yeah, that was it. I didn't really give it a second thought. I would have had to get into some born-again racket if I wanted to do moral. For what?*

Monk: *I think there was something else.*

S.K.: *What else?*

Monk: *I think there was a certain taste of nausea. Wasn't there?*

S.K.: *Nausea? You mean like after sex with a bad performer?*

Monk: *More like a feeling of despair, but actually in the stomach.*

S.K., surprised: *Yeah, I remember that. How'd you know? Nauseous, yeah, that's how I felt most of the time in a small town in Kansas. It disappeared the day I hit L.A.*

Monk: *How was it, this nausea?*

S.K.: *Everybody knew about it. We called it small-town blues, but it was more than that.*

Monk: *Something missing inside?*

S.K., nodding: *Yeah. A vacuum on Main Street as far as the eye could see.*

I realize I have underestimated the monk's electronic prowess. He has edited the interview at least to the extent that it is in two parts. We jump now to the second part. Kowlovski is quite transformed, sweating, extremely nervous. A dozen twitches work his face. He gives the impression of a man in a state of chronic terror.

Monk: *It's okay, you're still here, aren't you?*

S.K.: *No. I'm not still here. I'm in a thousand pieces. You've fucked my head, man.*

Monk: *Did I? What did I fuck it with?*

S.K.: *My crime, fuck it, my crime. How in hell did you find out? How?*

Monk: *You really want to know?*

S.K.: *Yeah, I really want to know.*

Monk: *Are you sure you really want to know?*

S.K.: *Fuck you.*

A long pause.

Monk: *She was my sister. Before she died, she sent me an
e-mail with the names and addresses of all the major players.*
S.K., aghast but disbelieving: No!
Monk: *Here, this is a snapshot of her in her prime, aged about
twenty-four.*

The monk hands over a passport-size photo. The masked man stares at it.

Monk: *Of course, her neck is in a lot better condition than
when you last saw it.*

Screams come from Kowlovski. Then the picture dies.

Miraculously the camera switches on again. It is impossible to know how much time has passed, perhaps a minute, perhaps hours, but the sequence makes a kind of emotional sense. Kowlovski is slumped on that cheap sofa. He seems quite exhausted, but there is no peace in his baby-blue eyes. They dart from one place to another even while his body rests immobile.

"*How often did you work with her?*" the monk's voice asks.
"*That was the only time.*"
"*Is that the only snuff movie you ever made?*"
"*The only one. I don't do that kind of stuff. I don't even
understand it. Someone was squeezing me.*"
"*Who?*"
"*You have the list, don't you? She sent you a list of all the major
players.*"
"*Names only. I'm a simple monk—how do I know what these
names represent?*"
"*Well, that's one question I can answer. Big, is what they
represent. Power. Money. Not them, but what stands behind
them. The invisible men.*"
"*Invisible men?*"
"*Sure. Why else would the world be so fucked up?*"
"*Ah! You only recently began to think like that, am I right?*"
"*You and her—you're so alike, you could be the same person.*"

"So you did talk to her before you strangled her?"

"Don't keep saying that. If you'd seen the movie, you would know."

"Know what?"

A pause while Kowlovski licks his dry lips. "She had to encourage me. I was permanently on the point of chickening out. We were supposed to film the thing in under two hours, but I couldn't do it. I couldn't control my bowels, and I had to take so much Viagra I couldn't stop farting. I had this ridiculous erection I was too stressed to use. I kept bursting into tears, and I kind of collapsed, and they seemed to think about abandoning it all, but she insisted. It was incredible."

"What was?"

"Her will. The Asian will, it's truly amazing."

"It's not Asian. It's third world. Two hundred years of misery and degradation can produce some strong spirits."

"She was the strongest I ever met. She wasn't human. Maybe you are, but she wasn't."

"I was human before you killed her."

Screaming: "I didn't kill her! She killed herself! Can't you face that?"

A pause.

"So, you collapsed, the invisible men were thinking about cutting their losses and getting out, but she took you in hand. Tell me about that."

"She told them we would start again same time next day. She didn't ask, she just told them. The whole thing was falling apart, and she was the only one with a plan, so they said okay, talk to him. Take him home and sleep with him. Do what you have to do."

A long pause.

Monk: "I see. You spent the night with her."

It is a statement made in a compassionate voice. For a moment the monk seems to sympathize with Kowlovski, causing him to raise his eyes and steady them.

"*Right. I spent the night with her.*"

"*She did something to you to strengthen your resolve. What did she do?*"

"*She explained the world to me, as she saw it. I never met a woman or man who could ever do that and reach me. Everything they ever told us, the Christian stuff, was just junk, you know, like everything else. What she said, I don't know where she got it, but it wasn't junk.*" Looking frankly into the monk's eyes. "*It corresponded, you know?*"

"*Corresponded?*"

"*With everything that ever happened to me. The mother who wasn't a mother, just some strange woman acting a part in a soap because she didn't know what else to do with me. The father who wasn't there even when he was. All the stuff people talk about. She said the invisible men control everything on the planet. The misery they make in the West is opposite and equal to what they do in the East: in the West the high standard of living but no heart at all; elsewhere you get the big heart steadily eaten away by the poverty. It was the most convincing theory of everything I ever heard.*"

"*And?*"

"*It's a bust, according to her. A total bust. The biggest mistake of all is to value being alive.*" Looking away at a wall and apparently quotes: "*Once you stop wanting to live, you become free.*" Looking back at the monk. "*It was the best sex I ever had. The price she made me pay was to agree to kill her. I don't have to tell you I was in love with her by morning.*"

"*But you went ahead with it?*"

"*I promised her, didn't I? And after that night, even I could see there was no other way.*"

"*She gave you a little something to help?*"

"Heroin. Never used it before. I thought it would neutralize the
Viagra. It didn't."

There's a pause for so long you wonder if the interview is over.
Then Phra Titanaka says in a soft voice, as sly as a snake:

"You dream about her, don't you?"
"Every night, man."
"Except they are not dreams."
"Don't say that."
"Even you know they're not dreams. She's glowing when she
visits you, isn't she?"
"How d'you know that?"
"And she fucks you. You wake up all wet."

Screams.
The monitor turns blank. I stare at it for ten minutes before I can
rouse myself to leave the darkened room and return to my desk.

I've not yet told you how the Damrong video ends, *farang*. Well, I never
did bring myself to watch it again, and I don't suppose I ever will. I
don't need to—it is etched into my memory for a thousand lifetimes:
He is having her from behind while she supports herself on a trestle, thrusting back eagerly with her loins. His timing apparently is equal
to the challenge of simultaneous orgasms, and she really does seem to
be enjoying it more than he is. In the terrible moment during which he
unwinds the orange cord that is coiled around his left wrist, he loses it.
The hand holding the rope shudders, and it is quite obvious that his
nerve has failed. He does not so much drop it as allow it to fall in a gesture of defeat. She notices immediately and delicately disengages in
order to pick it up. She turns to him and holds his masked mug with
one firm little hand for a moment while she says a few words, then
hands him back the cord. Still he hesitates, so she cleverly makes a feature out of his reluctance and elaborately, with the utmost narcissism,
takes the cord from him. She finds the center and presses it against her
Adam's apple, at the same time throwing the two ends over her shoul-

ders. Now watch while he so reluctantly pulls on the orange cord, high-lighting every sculpted muscle in those massive forearms that gleam under the lights from Johnson's baby oil. Her face fills the screen: the supreme bliss of the last climax morphs into the bloated paroxysm of death.

It is my misfortune that I can hear her shout of triumph long after her heart has stopped beating.

ELEPHANT TRAPS

30

My desk phone rings. It is Vikorn's secretary, Manny, summoning me to his office, pronto. In a whisper she lets me know that something has gone wrong with the Tanakan case. He does not speak when I enter, merely hands me a sheet of paper, which is a printout of a photograph that has been sent by e-mail. In the picture an elephant is about to bring its trunk down on a bamboo ball in which a trussed-up, tattooed man has been imprisoned.

"Where did you get it?"

"Guess."

"Tanakan? Someone sent it to him?"

Turning away from the window. "This is serious stuff, Sonchai. I was working him to the limit of his tolerances. As it was, Tanakan was only a couple centimeters from having me assassinated—I had to calculate the figure pretty precisely."

"Five dragons?"

My Colonel nods gravely. "I was keeping within my rights, but only just. Another million, and he would have felt entitled to take the risk of a hit team." He points at the photocopy I'm holding. "Now this."

"He thinks it comes from you?"

"Of course he does. He thinks I'm inventing a third party to protect him from so I can keep squeezing. He thinks he's going to have to fork out a few million every year. He thinks I'm a low-rent crook who'll just keep sucking his blood forever." I refrain from comment. "That's what happens when the lines start to get blurred. Honor and respect are the first casualties."

"What d'you want to do?"

"It's what I have to do. We're going to see him now. We're going down on our knees. We're acknowledging that the situation has swung in his favor. We are even reducing our fee." Pointing at the photograph: "We have to convince him this isn't us."

In back of the battered old patrol car I watch Vikorn move the assemblage point of his mind to a position of total humility. The receptionist at the bank was charmed enough on our first visit; now she's overwhelmed at the Buddhist quality of this senior cop: so self-effacing yet at the same time firmly professional. We are whisked up to Tanakan's suite at lightning speed by a couple of heavily built guards. As before, we wait in a conference room. This time it is the perfect secretary, not the man himself, who arrives to call us into his office. There is no offer of tea, coffee, or soft drinks, and she doesn't look at me. Tanakan does not bother to stand up when we enter, and the secretary closes the door behind us without a word. Vikorn sinks to his knees on the carpet, at the same time showing a high *wai*, and I have to do the same. This does have the effect of warming the atmosphere, from maybe minus five to zero.

"Khun Tanakan," Vikorn says, "I am aware of what Khun Tanakan must be thinking, but it is not so." Vikorn is careful to keep his hands together at his forehead. "Your humble servant is an honest trader."

Tanakan glowers, somewhat theatrically in my view. "I wish I could believe the Colonel. What began as an honest negotiation between men of honor seems to have—"

"Not at my instigation, Khun Tanakan. Would Khun Tanakan take it as evidence of my sincerity that I am prepared to lower the value of the vase?"

Tanakan stands up and emerges from behind his desk.

"From now on the vase has no value, Vikorn. From now on if I hear anything in relation to the vase, I will press a certain autodial number on my cell phone. A cell phone belonging to the owner of a motorcycle and his armed assistant will ring somewhere in the city. I am sure the Colonel understands. Certainly one always prefers to play the game and avoid loss of life. When someone starts to break the rules, however, one must take one's chances. After all, I have a position to defend, and I thought it was implicit in our discussions that you were my principal defender. You have failed, Colonel. You're not doing your job, man."

Vikorn has turned gray. However, he masters himself, bows his head, stands, and all of a sudden we are on our feet at the door. Tanakan calls us back for a moment, however. He reaches into his drawer to take something out and chuck it across his desk at Vikorn. It is an elephant-hair bracelet. "It came with that abominable picture," he snaps, then turns his back to look out of the window.

In back of the car on the way to the station, Vikorn delivers one of his homilies:

"You see what happens when the work of professionals is screwed up by amateurs? Tanakan knew he'd been caught with his knickers around his ankles and was ready to cough up like a pro so long as the negotiations were courteous, discreet, and professional and the price was reasonable. Now some barbaric clown has poisoned the well. I want you to find him and give me the address. You don't have to be there when the men make the visit, understand?"

He raises haggard eyes. I gulp and nod.

Back at my desk, the cell phone rings.

"You watched the video?"

"Yes."

"So now you know what to do."

"What are you talking about?"

"You can adjust the technique according to the personality of the subject. Kowlovski was very stupid. I think your subjects will be more fun."

I'm not sure I'm really understanding. If I am, I don't want to. "What subjects?"

"The ones I have identified with the bracelets."

My jaw drops. "How can I interrogate them? One is a senior banker, one is an eminent lawyer, the other is a bum, and all of them have perfect alibis."

"No, they don't."

"But they weren't even in the country. *They weren't even in the same country as one another.* One was in the U.S., one was in Angkor Wat, and the other was in Malaysia."

"Isn't that a coincidence?"

"Well, it may look suspect, but it does prove that none of them were directly involved in the"—I grope for the right word—"killing."

"My sister said there were meetings. You know, as in major shareholders."

"How did she know?"

"She was one of them."

The revelation causes quite a jolt. "She attended business meetings at which her body and her death were the proposed profit center? I'm going to need evidence."

"Confessions are always the best evidence. Is that not so?"

"You can't get confessions like that out of free men."

"Free men? I'm working on it." He closes the phone.

With cynical intent to deceive I call Vikorn directly on his cell phone. "I've been looking into it. I'm going to raid Baker and Smith. I think one of them must be behind this elephant crap."

"Why bother with a raid? I'll send a motorbike."

"No, Colonel, I'm not sure it's one of them. I'm just sure I can find out something from them."

"Have it your way. But I want the one who sent that photograph strung up by the balls and presented to Tanakan in a nice neat velvet package."

"I know."

"I think our banker might prefer a living body he can have some fun with."

"Yes, I guess so."

· · ·

I balance my chair on its back legs, put my feet on my desk, and make a cathedral of my hands. It never works, but it does make me feel like Philip Marlowe. I am frowning. The same three suspects: Dan Baker, Tom Smith, Khun Tanakan. But suspected of what, exactly? I am not even sure if Damrong's contract was illegal in Thailand. I am not even sure there was a contract. Perhaps no crime was committed at all, beyond manslaughter by Kowlovski? It was a crime against the heart, though—a crime against humanity, you might say—which led to others: Nok, whose butchered innocence rests heavy on my heart; the otherworldly Pi-Oon and his flamboyant lover. This surely is the monk's message. I agree, but who to scare first, Baker or Smith? Tanakan will have to be left alone for the time being since he's under Vikorn's protection; I'm not at all sure how to finesse that. I guess even Marlowe didn't get himself into these kinds of jams.

On the face of it, Baker would be the obvious first choice. A weak character, accustomed to doing deals with cops, probably incapable of loyalty. I have more or less decided on him, then change my mind. The trouble with Baker is that he doesn't fit and has started to puzzle me. Instead of Chinese boxes, in this case we have Chinese pyramids, all fitting one inside the other. Tanakan and Tom Smith are part of an elite Great Pyramid of international players. Smith is near the bottom and Tanakan is near the top, but it's the same exclusive global pyramid. Dan Baker, the small-time hustler, belongs to a quite different low-rent pyramid, where he subsists somewhere near the bottom.

Puzzling it through: something about Smith the lawyer attracts me—that modern British hysteria just below the surface, despite his brilliant mind and worldly wisdom. The man who lost his head more than once in a jealous frenzy may lose it again and again. I think about busting him, then decide to go to his office on a fishing expedition instead. Then I suffer from what one of my uncles calls "a touch of the seconds."

The problem is not normally featured in police thrillers, but it goes like this: How exactly does a low-ranking, humble, third-world cop go about browbeating a smarter, more powerful, better-educated, and, most daunting of all, better-connected, senior, respected lawyer? Yes, it's called a sense of inferiority, but just because you feel like a victim doesn't mean you're not about to become one. I would like some concrete facts to confront him with, but when I think about his various cameo appearances, none of them adds up to much more than a mirage. Perhaps his fondness for brothels and prostitutes would count against him in a more hypocritical society, but, thanks to our natural openness, no one would doubt he was in the same boat as most other men who live here. I need something more, something that will at least give me more confdence, even if it isn't a killer point. I sit immobilized by an apparently insurmountable reluctance and only slowly formulate a plan. It's about six in the evening when I finally decide to call Lek over to my desk.

"Lek, do you keep a skirt in the office?"

Covering a smirk: "Of course not. Don't you think I have enough to put up with?"

"So go home and change into your Saturday-night best. Tight T-shirt or sweater to flash the estrogen, very short skirt, rouge, mascara, earrings—the whole works. Be as provocative as you like, but not too vulgar. The Parthenon is up-market, after all."

"What do you want me to do?"

"I want you to go there asking for work again. This time look serious, and make sure they believe you. When you leave the premises, you will pass the doorman. Give him a scrap of paper with my name and cell phone number. Whisper, *Anywhere, anytime, any price.*"

I put my feet up on my desk again and wait.

31

"Chatuchak market, tomorrow, eleven-twenty, stall 398 in the northwest corner." The caller, a young woman, hangs up immediately. I am thinking, *Smart, very smart.* Chatuchak, that vast, unfathomable labyrinth of covered market stalls, amounts to a city of open-air merchandisers, selling anything and everything from tropical fish, brightly colored birds, and exotic orchids—which rarely survive the journey home—to plastic pails, to offers of irresistible real estate opportunities on islands with dubious land titles—just about everything. You can even get your Toyota serviced while you're browsing. Today is Friday, so it will be jam-packed. Hard to say, these days, who are in the majority, vacationing *farang*, trendy urbanites, middle-income Thais looking for genuine bargains, or the browse-only bunch who simply love markets. Anyway, I'm reduced to a shuffle-and-twist technique to get me through the narrow body-packed alleys that lead, finally, to stall 398 of section 57 in the northwest corner.

I don't know why I'm intrigued that the produce on sale consists of orchids and tropical birds; something in the back of my mind links these two, but I cannot remember the scam just at the moment. Two young women, pretty in their aprons with large money-pockets, are calling out to passersby, with particular interest in well-to-do *farang* families with that wide-open look which comes with one's first arrival in the exotic East. Now I remember the scam and smile. When the young women take no notice of me, I go to a cathedral-shaped cage which is the prison of a particularly vivid crimson and yellow parrot, lick an index finger, and start to stroke the crimson crown on its head. That gets their attention real quick. "I am Sonchai," I say, before they have a chance to scold. At the same time I hold up my index finger, the end of which is now slightly crimson. The older of the two whisks me through to the back of the stall, which is shut off from the front by a tarpaulin curtain. The doorman, wearing spectacles, sits at a table in navy surplus shorts and flip-flops, no shirt. The brown bird he is holding firmly in his left hand looks somewhat like a macaw but owns streaming central tail feathers that make it ideal for this kind of exercise. I don't know its name in English, but it's very common, particularly in Isaan, where it is considered a pest. Actually the feathers are delicate shades consisting mostly of dark chocolate on café au lait; their somewhat monochrome beauty has no appeal to the vulgar, though, and like the Acropolis in its day, it needs plenty of help from paint to appeal to popular taste.

The doorman is clearly an expert. He uses a tiny artist's brush and works from some authoritative tome with full-color plates. "It's going to be a red-tailed tropic bird," he says, looking down and reading. " 'Phaethon rubricauda.' " He casts me a glance before continuing with the pink, orange, and black markings he is laying across the eyes and wings. Little by little he adds value with the concentration of a Picasso. "This is what I used to do before I went to work for him." He gives me a quick, shattered look. "Before I lost my innocence, you might say. I do it for free now, just to keep my hand in. This stall belongs to my sister. Those girls out front are her daughters." He manages an ironic smile. "You could call it a family business handed down from one generation to the next. Frankly, it has always been the boys who make the best painters, with a couple of exceptions. My father was brilliant—he could turn a blackbird into a flamingo if he wanted to. I don't even come close." Neither I nor the bird is convinced by his modesty. His masterful makeover has improved the creature's self-esteem immeasurably. When he places it back in its cage, it prances and preens and cannot wait to impress the opposite sex with its irresistible new wardrobe. I say, "What about the orchids?"

"Oh, that's women's business. Boys never have the patience. They're amazing." I check out the dozens of varieties of exotic flowers, heavy-headed and liable to break their stems if not cunningly supported by concealed wiring. "Actually, there's no real deception involved."

"Only the implication that they're going to survive the next few days."

He smiles thinly. "They are the products of intense cultivation—a lot of work. They're grown from hybrids, and it's true, only an expert can produce those kinds of blooms, and then usually only once in the plant's life." He points at a collection of books on a shelf. "The girls have to study the names in English—we get a lot of amateur orchid growers coming to ask complicated questions. It's a headache because their English isn't so good, and there aren't any Thai translations." He takes another brown bird out of a cage, fondles and strokes it, examines it as a portrait painter might examine a subject, and says, "Excuse me. It's so much easier for me to talk to you while I'm concentrating on this. Painting takes me into a better world. What exactly do you want to know?"

"Everything you can tell me."

"About the death of your girlfriend Nok? Not much. I didn't do it. I was put in charge of the clean-up. He uses professionals for his wet work. I'm just a doorman."

"But she got the key from you. You snitched on her."

It is not guilt so much as a profound sadness that turns his flesh gray. "What could I do? I told her to be discreet. I warned her that if she were spotted anywhere near his room, I would have no choice but to tell the boss. And what do you two do? You walk past those girls in the swimming pool like you were returning to a hotel room. I had no choice."

"That's all you have to say? A young woman is snuffed out because of you, and you just shrug?"

He pauses, stares at me, and puts the brush down. He will not release me from his stare.

I say, "Okay, I'm sorry."

"Because of me she died? Or because of your obsession with that witch Damrong? Know what the boss told me? He said no cop in the whole of Krung Thep has any interest in that snuff movie except you. You could stop the investigation tomorrow, and Vikorn would breathe a sigh of relief. So tell me, did she die because of me or you?"

I cough, look at the floor, turn my gaze to the birds and the orchids, try to lose myself in the voluptuousness of color, only to find a monochrome dust has settled on my mind. As a kind of old-fashioned courtesy, he has continued with his painting, as if he has not noticed my distress. I take time out to stand up and examine some of the orchids. "But I think you know a lot about the organization," I mumble.

He shakes his head. "You just can't stop, can you?"

"I think you take the girls to their assignations with the X members."

He concentrates on the tail, somehow producing a convincing crimson tone without compromising the fluffiness of the feathers. "You know that much? Nok told you?" Casting me a glance: "That's why she had to die."

"The video, the Damrong video. It was filmed in Tanakan's suite at the Parthenon Club."

"Was it? D'you think he tells me more than I need to know? I wasn't involved."

"But you know how the deal came about?"

"What deal?"

"It was a contract, probably voluntary. She offered to die that way in return for a lot of money."

He pauses in his painting and looks into some middle distance. "Really? How much? You don't know? A lot, probably, as you say. Personally, I would jump at the chance. If I could get my family out of his clutches forever, I would die a thousand deaths. You don't know what it's like when your blood is mortgaged for life."

I'm still feeling wrong-footed, still mumbling in a pathetic, pleading tone. "The thing is, deals like that don't just happen. Delicate approaches have to be made. It takes exactly the right suggestion at exactly the right time. I don't know where the original plan came from, her or them. I do know the Englishman Tom Smith was involved." He grunts. "You can at least tell me about him."

He considers this for a moment. "Just another deluded prick. In a society like ours, it's best to be either a prince or a peasant. Anything in between is too stressful." He pauses to give me a shrewd glance. "You know, I have no idea what you boys ever saw in Damrong. To me she was a perfectly ordinary-looking Khmer girl, nothing special. You can hire ten for a thousand baht in Phnom Penh. She didn't give me a hard-on at all. Heartless whores are ten-a-penny anywhere in the world."

What can I say? I swallow. "The Englishman—he was a middle-man?"

"Just another lawyer who didn't know his place. Can you believe he still persisted even after I warned him?"

"Warned him what?"

"That the boss wanted his girl. I thought I was being helpful, trying to save a life. He didn't see it that way."

"He knew Tanakan was after Damrong?"

"He had this *farang* notion about equality, honor, democracy, the righteousness of love, all that nonsense. Damrong told Tanakan about him. I had to do some squeezing."

"You mean Damrong was trying to get Smith killed by telling Tanakan he was a rival? Why?"

"I don't think she wanted him killed. From what you've just told me, I think she had her own agenda. I played the good consigliere. First a polite hint. Second a polite warning. Third time you show them the torture instruments. It was strange. It was as if she were deliberately making both men hate her. She taunted Tanakan with Smith and Smith with Tanakan. Even a novice working girl knows better than that." He looks at me and shrugs.

"By the time you'd finished with him, Smith had seen the light? He had to do something to get back into Tanakan's good books? Tanakan would have finished him professionally, even if he let him stay alive?"

"Like I say, it was part of her agenda to make them both love her and hate her. I thought she was just another whore with her head in a mess. Now I wonder. Maybe she knew what she was doing." He puts the newly painted bird back in its cage. "That's all I can tell you. I've risked my life by talking to you because I want at least some tiny part of my soul to survive this incarnation, or I'll be reborn as an insect. I don't want money, but don't contact me again."

32

At Smith's law offices I do not receive quite the same level of attention from our tall handsome lawyer as on my first visit. I have come not as a player in an international porn deal, after all, but as a humble detective and am therefore undeserving of respect. Somebody must have snitched: Vikorn? In this symphony of treachery a mere double-cross would have the simplicity of "Jingle Bells." I'm not sure even Vikorn knows what side he is on.

As soon as Smith has me in his office, he slouches on his executive chair (black leather and chrome, it seems able to swivel and roll at its master's will; Smith has no idea how closely it resembles the one he used in Chicago in the abundant days of Prohibition in a previous life) and stares at me. He doesn't actually say *Well* in a derisive voice; he doesn't need to.

"I'm a little puzzled by your attitude, Mr. Smith."

"Yeah? What attitude?" A little of his Cockney origins emerging here.

"A woman dies, murdered. A woman you were pathologically fond of, shall we say. A woman whose very flesh—"

"Cut out the third-world melodrama, Detective. I have no idea what you're talking about."

"I'm talking murder, Mr. Smith."

"Oh, that. Who's dead?"

"Damrong Tarasorn Baker, among others." He gives no sign of recognition. "Your lover. Your whore. Your plaything. Your tormentor."

I guess it just doesn't work; once a *farang*, especially a lawyer, gets into "A cannot be not-A," all connection with the heart is lost. It is as if a tap has been turned off at the throat chakra, leaving only a talking head. "A woman you were literally crazy about has been slaughtered like a lamb," I suggest in a tentative voice. No reply, but at least I've made him feel just a tad awkward. "A woman whose ex-husband you have taken to visiting lately." He's good—he can do Stone Face and keep it up under pressure; if I'm not mistaken, though, there was just a flick of his left pinkie, followed by a stroking of his nose with his right index. An experienced hunter can read this kind of spoor.

I pace up and down his office, a technique analogous to the mammalian practice of claiming territory by pissing on it. It does seem to irritate him; mildly though. I take a breath. "A woman dies, as I was saying, killed by a fellow human, a woman whose flesh had proven capable of driving you crazy. As it happens, her demise is caught on film." I cut myself short so that I have quality time to focus on the twitches that have appeared around his mouth. "Yes, on film, Mr. Smith. To be more precise, on a DVD disk. So, what sort of words shall we use to set the international community aflame with indignation? Copyright infringement, perhaps? Yes, let's say I'm investigating a particularly egregious form of copyright infringement. No point dwelling on the collateral damage, which you've kept to three so far: one Nok, a worker at the Parthenon; one Pi-Oon, a harmless transsexual who knew too much; and one Khun Kosana, a buddy-slave of your master Khun Tanakan who had the misfortune to get hold of the DVD and share it with his lover. Your trail is quite bloody, Khun Smith."

He leers. "Copyright infringement? That used to be my specialty. What kind of intellectual property are we talking about?"

I cough. "Ah, you are an expert. How easily you have called my bluff. Of course, foolish of me—how could it be a copyright issue when no one would dream of registering this work? Yes, you are right, I shall have to find some other concept. How about conspiracy to produce pornographic material, conspiracy to murder, conspiracy—"

"I think I can shorten this," Smith says, softly now but still with the leer corrupting his handsome mug. "If you're talking about a video product of extremely poor taste that may or may not have been made for an elite international market, which may or may not for all I know feature a common prostitute with whom I admit I once had a liaison— if that's what you're talking about, then I have to tell you, Detective, I have never seen the product in question."

I halt, because he has quite floored me with his openness. Sure, he knows all about it, and he doesn't care if I know he knows. This man has protection from someone big. Curious. I find I have to jump to point two before I intended.

"You've never seen it? But you have heard of it?"

"I told you, I'm networked here and I speak the language. A lot of people have heard of that video. Lots and lots, Detective, thanks to the infantile fuss you've been making about it. Everyone knows you fell for her like a ton of bricks. Same as me. Does the word *hypocrisy* mean anything to you?" He pauses and stares at me with maximum insolence. "She had a snapshot of your dick on her cell phone. Yours and dozens like it. Hard to recognize a dick in isolation, even your own, so she gave them names. Yours was 'Detective.' Funny how the racial extraction comes out in the area of the genitals. Your face is white, but your dick is more tan than pink."

I don't want him to see me swallow hard, but he does. I try to turn a shudder into a shrug. "I'm afraid I have not expressed myself with sufficient clarity for a legally trained mind such as yours," I mumble, struggling. "What I'm talking about is shareholder satisfaction." I pause and put a finger to my temple. "Yes, I can easily imagine that you might not have seen the product. I can easily believe that. Intuitively, I guess your story might go like this. Let me see, how might one start? Perhaps with that wonderful Australian expression *keeps his brains in his dick*?" Smith's eyes have narrowed. "A vulgar phrase disguising a male phenomenon much researched but little understood. How will it be explained in the future when we are all androgenous again, this strange tendency of certain kinds of men, professional men in particular—one is almost inclined to say especially lawyers, doctors, accountants, and dentists, a disease of the overwrought professional class, plus politicians and senior bankers, of course—a tendency, shall we say, to divide themselves in half. How could it be otherwise, when you have great urban testosteronic warriors like yourself pretending to be interested in serving others when what they're really after is rape and pillage? Yes, one can understand why the extracurricular activities of such men might be a little, shall we say, contradictory." I look at him. "I can believe you never saw the video, Mr. Smith. You are not a voyeur."

I let a couple of beats pass. He is way too suave to break the silence. I continue: "You may even possess the kind of finesse that would prevent you from watching such a product. Perhaps, like me, you would find it almost unbearable to look at. Yes, I'm ready to credit you with that."

He jerks his head: *So?*

"So if I were to construct a theory of your involvement in this— let's call it a copyright issue, shall we? You know how we Thais love euphemism—this copyright matter, then, the theory would go something like this. A man, a lawyer, very well connected to the Thai—and indeed an international—financial elite, is, forgive me, exactly one of those alpha male types whose massive sexual appetite is sublimated into socially useful activities only during working hours. I'll call my example Smith, if you don't mind. Smith, then, as we have seen, is quite hopelessly in love with a young woman who appears, by all accounts, to possess the charms of a Circe, a sorceress. Smith, for all his martial and commercial prowess, finds himself in a difficult psychological trap. This girl has studied other alpha male specimens whom she probably finds indistinguishable from him. She knows what animal lurks behind the business suit and also how to manipulate it. Smith, at first, is simply amused; he has been down this road before. But the girl is far more adept than he realized. She isn't acting out some chapter from *Thai Whores' Guide to* Farang. Oh no, this girl really does understand. Best of all, she can convince him that she's very much that way herself: fast-lane passionate, let's call it. A World Class Triple-A Fucker in other words, someone who really does know how to prolong the ecstasy. She also looks like every *farang*'s idea of the perfect Oriental lover. Her skin is as soft as chamois, her face is demonically beautiful, her body is simply perfect, her voice is soft, yielding, with an exotic accent in English which she speaks with surprising sophistication. After each assignation you tell yourself you must stop seeing her or she will ruin you, but you are haunted by the quality of her flesh, her merciless sangfroid—" I stop, pause at his desk, lean on it to go eyeball to eyeball, and do my best female impersonation: *"Tom, you're just amazing. I don't think I can stand the thought of you with another woman. I just can't."*

I think the words are more of a hard-to-identify echo than a sentence written in his heart. I stand back. "Did you know her husband— sorry, *ex*-husband—was standing in the closet making a film star out of you? Of course not. I think you did not make his acquaintance until much later. Not until all administrative chores had fallen to you to deal with, as consigliere to the *jao paw,* or should I say legal adviser to the board?"

He parts his lips but says nothing. Now I'm doing my best to reproduce his complex accent with its Cockney and transatlantic references, complete with lump in the throat, in an octave lower than that in which I am accustomed to express myself: *"Don't worry about that. There wouldn't be any fucking point, would there?"*

He has leaned back a little in his executive chair, contemplatively, and managed to close his mouth. I'm at the end of my rope and quite incapable of Buddhist patience. With astonishing irrelevance I pick up a cube of sugar that lies in the saucer of a coffee cup on his desk. "You do not take sugar? Too fattening, I suppose." I crumple the sugar in my hand, then toss it over him. "Heroin," I say in a loud voice. "I have caught you red-handed." He does not react, confirming my earlier surmise that he is enjoying protection now. He brushes off the sugar with a go-fuck-yourself leer. I walk around his desk to stand above him.

Scratching my head: "So I ask myself, how could Smith be connected to a video he has never seen that records an assassination he could not possibly have participated in because he was in another country at the time? And yet everything in my third-world-cop instinct tells me that this Smith knows something about the case, is involved in some way." I turn my head to one side and smile. "Of course, it took me a while to work it out. After all, corporate law is not exactly my field. Oh yes, for a very long time I wondered how you fit in, Mr. Smith. Until I remembered that your training is indeed in corporate law. How many corporations are you on the board of? In how many land transactions throughout the length and breadth of the country are you a shadow shareholder? How often have you enabled *farang* to get around our protectionist land laws in order to profit by redevelopment? And I saw it, the perfect revenge for a lawyer driven quite insane by his lover: shareholder in the enterprise. That's what I think you are. She had wounded you more than any woman you ever met. Others merely scratch—she stole bone marrow. You were incomplete until the day she died. How smart you must have thought yourself, reaping perhaps a tenfold, even hundredfold profit from the planned, digitally recorded execution of the demon who laughed as she chewed your guts. What an elegant ending."

I am making a question mark with my eyebrows, which he seems to find slightly comic. It is a good moment to kick his chair, which I do with maximum force. He virtually flies across the floor until he reaches the wall. It looks for a moment as if he will be able to keep his balance and his dignity, but the wheels on the thing are so efficient, they fail to provide stability, and he ends up on the floor with his head rammed uncomfortably against the wall. I walk over to stand on his left arm. He is in pain, but not enough. "I have protection," he mutters. "You're such a pure little fuck-up, I had to go higher."

"Who to? Vikorn?"

A leer. "Higher. You don't know who I'm connected to."

I smile. It may not sound like it, but this surely is a confession of guilt of a sort.

He tries to pull his arm free from my foot but is unable to. I add to his difficulties with my other foot, then squat beside him, placing all my weight on his arm. "If that is your answer, Mr. Smith, then I'm afraid you are out of luck. I'm not working for the Royal Thai Police today. I'm moonlighting for the Buddha." He blinks. "You're looking a little yellow around the gills these days, Tom. I hope you haven't been sleeping with ghosts?"

He grunts in astonishment, and the mask falls. It occurs to me that he could easily overpower me; it is the promise of narrative, the carrot of closure that keeps him prone. "Let me tell you how she comes to you—every night, if I'm not wrong. You experience her first as a kind of erotic stirring, but since you are asleep, the stirring is more an overwhelming feeling of lascivious anticipation, a certainty that the final, ultimate coupling is about to free you from the misery of eternal isolation. Then she appears, glowing, wearing whatever garment you find most erotic—in my case it's a low-cut black ballgown with nothing underneath, but then I'm corny like that. What's amazing is her control over your body. She is capable of working your dick by remote, just by the power of transferred thought. You are her slave—she doesn't stop working you until you've climaxed at least twice. Not the normal, restricted, rationed kind of functional orgasm that goes with the mediocrity of civilzed life. No, Tom, you climax as a satyr might, or a tiger, say: total, wild, ruthless, unrepentant. And you wake up in a pool of spent seed, defeated, wanting nothing except to go through it all again. Am I right?" He says nothing, and yet I fancy I have finally softened him.

Afer a pause I say, "How much was she paid, exactly? About a million U.S.?"

He licks his lips and mutters, "About that."

"That's a lot. In a poor country like Thailand, a million crosses a line, from mere wealth to genuine power. It's always dangerous to give power to ignorant, resentful third-world peasants, don't you think?" He stares. "With no culture of positive thinking, you see, and no faith in human nature—frankly, who has, after age twelve in the lower income brackets?—there is little to prevent—how should one put it?—a negative response? Certainly, a woman from another background, say Essex, would have invested in a balanced portfolio of stocks and shares to provide income and growth for her dependents—although a woman who thought like that would have been unlikely to choose such an early exit. To be sure, Damrong had traveled enough and spent enough time with rich men to know how the other half—more accurately, the privileged five percent—live and think. Hard to imagine why any modern young woman would choose death when she could afford a Mercedes, but we are all products of programming, and hers worked in a different way. Culture."

I see that I have at least begun to interest him in the chain of cause and effect responsible for his predicament. "Let me put it in my simple Buddhist way, Smith, and please forgive the naïveté, but the problem was: no one to love. Not really. In the end even her brother seemed on the point of betraying her for the Buddha. Love frustrated is bad enough, but how about love inverted? Turned on its head by a perverse economic system and a brutal childhood? In such circumstances an apocalyptic mentality is almost inevitable. Nothing like death to bust the illusion of inequality. And she had the money to stage a spectacular finale, of which you are a part." I think he half understands. "Smart as you are, she fooled you. What did you think, exactly, when you took a position—is that the phrase?—in the movie she wanted to make?"

He clears his throat, which seems very clogged. "She acted of her own free will. It was her idea. She approached me, and I approached certain business interests who were clients of mine. She designed the whole thing. It was a product of her own mind. Not everybody loves life, and she was approaching thirty. Things happen to whores at that age."

"Exactly my point, Khun Smith, exactly my point. Had your own culture not caused you to discount the possibility that she might have been, in her strange third-world way, as smart as you—smarter—you might have thought to yourself there was more to her project than met the eye." He frowns. "I mean, you might have perceived that what she had in mind was not self-annihilation at all, not in her terms, but rather a statement, a final testament to the world, an act of revenge part symbolic, part literal. You could almost say she was exercising a form of self-respect, after all."

He shrugs. "So what?"

"Ah! You ask that? So what? So everything." An irritated frown. "Didn't you notice it before? Was it not exactly her self-respect that drove you crazy? That way she had of delivering the sexual thrills of a lifetime, as if your lust had achieved that very level of ecstasy a man like you always wants from a woman? Then when you had paid her, you simply ceased to exist for her until next time. Nothing unusual about that, except for the extreme of the polarity in her case. That was her genius. That was her self-respect. Her capacity to wipe you from her heart at will, like a dirty little mess on the floor."

"What are you talking about?"

"I'm talking about the reason you must die, Khun Smith." A perplexed look. "Don't you see? If you had understood her, you would have understood how dangerous it was to accept such a command performance whenever you engaged her services. Even for her, I imagine, it was an affair of unusual intensity—she even seemed to fall in love with you. In her case that was a sign of homicidal intent. Even you must have noticed how close she came to getting you snuffed by Khun Tanakan? You told yourself that she left you no choice, but perhaps you did not realize that she intended for you to get into a losing battle with your rival, *intended* for you to see your survival as dependent upon her demise." His frown has deepened. "*She planned it from the start.*" Now his eyes have opened wide. "It wasn't an idea that came to her toward the end of your affair—it was the reason she chose you in the first place. She read you. She knew you were the one to provoke and tease and torture. She put you in an impossible position of adversary to one of the most powerful men in Thailand—and you fell for it. Within a month she had put your life, your identity, and your career in peril. She knew you would agree to her idea in the end, as an elegant way of getting rid of her." He is staring wildly. "How old are you? Let me tell you. You are forty-six years old. *Exactly the same age as her father when she had him killed.*"

I stand up with a little hop. "It doesn't much matter whether I take you in or not. I guess you would prefer not. That's okay." I take a piece of paper out of my back pocket, unfold it, hold it above him, and let it gently fall onto his head. It is a printout of an e-mail showing an enraged elephant with sociopathic tendencies. "That's how she had her dad bumped off, Mr. Smith. She took the photos herself." I reach down to touch the lacquered elephant-hair bracelet on his left wrist and wink.

At the door I cannot resist turning back for a moment. He is prone, still, and apparently quite bewildered. "Sweet dreams," I say as I leave, gratified by his gasp.

33

I have no idea how or why Baker might have been involved. The only reason I think he must be directly implicated is because the monk has fingered him with an elephant-hair bracelet and because Smith the consigliere has visited him at least twice. Mentally we're back to *Star Wars*, with me flying blind on instructions from some disembodied intelligence. I have not heard from Damrong's brother for three days. I'm trying to brainstorm with Lek in the back of the cab as to how and why a small-time player like Baker might have wound up as a shareholder in a world-class snuff movie, and I don't notice the new boys on the block until we're out of the cab at Baker's apartment.

One locks eyes with me for a moment; I experience the kind of devastating insight into the void that makes you wish people with those kinds of problems would wear sunglasses. None of his features move, and he doesn't bother to shift his gaze. He is in a guard's uniform, with nightstick and cuffs hanging from his belt. I say something quickly in Thai, to establish that he does not understand. Lek is from Surin province and speaks a dialect of Khmer. I tell him to ask the new guard where the old guards went. The psychopath replies with surprising eagerness, apparently pleased to be speaking his native tongue.

"He says a new security company has been appointed."

"How many of them are there?"

"About ten."

As he speaks, I see some of the others. Not all are in uniform, but I'm prepared to bet they all speak Khmer.

"Tell him I've come to see Khun Baker, the English teacher."

I watch carefully but see no reaction to the name. He knows which is Baker's floor, though, and nods us into the lift, where I have to revise my approach to Baker. By the time we're out of the lift, another thought occurs to me, accompanied by a sharp intake of breath. I tell Lek to go to Smith's law offices and check on the guards there. He is to call me back on my cell phone. Lek takes the lift back down to the ground floor while I knock on Baker's door.

The trouble with inspirational detection: it can make you appear scatty. As Baker opens the door, I forget all about my planned assault on his psyche because a truly extraordinary possibility has occurred to me. I fish out my cell to call Lek again. "When you've checked up on Smith's security guards, go to Tanakan's bank. See if there's anything unusual in the security there today." I have spoken in rapid Thai, so I do not know if Baker has understood or not.

Oddly enough, the moment of random-access intuition has freed up my brain, and now I think I know exactly why Baker was involved in the flick. I'm not angry with him, though—on the contrary, I believe the whole of my approach is tinged with pity.

"Khun Baker," I say as I step into his apartment, "so sorry to bother you again." I stop short. What with nattering to Lek and all, I've not yet focused on his face. Now I see he is crumbling with terror. I stare at him and fish out a copy of the same photograph I gave to Smith. "I guess you've seen this already?" He looks at it, gulps, and stares at me.

"Well," I say, "if you talk, I'll see what I can do."

Instead of replying, he directs my attention to the camera he has mounted on a tripod by the window. It is generously endowed with a huge zoom lens, which I suppose is the point. I go to it to look through the viewer. It is directed at the gate to his compound, where two of the new guards are sitting playing checkers with bottle tops. Even at leisure the impression is of bored souls waiting for a little slaughter to cheer them up.

259

"They're ex-KR," he says hoarsely. "They don't speak a word of Thai. Is this anything to do with you?"

"No, but I can understand your fear."

"You've got to help me."

"You've got to talk."

It seems he can hardly master his mind long enough to put a decent confession together. I decide to help.

"The problem, as always in any great criminal endeavor, was how to bind the loyalty of certain minor players who needed to be recruited for specialist services. The stud was easy enough—he owed money to loan sharks all over L.A., he didn't have a future unless he could get hold of a big piece of money, and anyway he stars in the movie and is therefore incriminated. But what of the technical side? The flick is very well produced by someone who understands movie cameras. It seems as if one lens was fixed to the floor, to enable fuckshots in stand-up mode. There is quite a lot of sophisticated editing too: something well within the range of a gifted amateur, of course, but hardly the sort of expertise you can hire easily in Bangkok, not surreptitiously anyway. On the other hand, no smart operator connected to the proposed victim wants to be in the country at the time the movie is shot, and you after all were her ex-husband, with a criminal record and a known penchant for making skin flicks. What to do? Training, I think. They gave you a couple of ex-KR to train. The thing about them, they will obey all instructions to the letter. You didn't need for them to be inspired—you merely needed them to produce the base product for you to edit, perhaps while you were in Angkor Wat. I think they sent you the rushes via e-mail. The Khmer had to be trained, though, and you wanted a cut. Was it a percentage or cash?"

A long pause, during which I think he will not speak, then: "Both. It was her idea. She insisted on using me. She wasn't going to trust anyone else. She'd worked with me before plenty of times. She knew I wasn't about to screw up." Looking at me: "And anyway, she was Thai."

"Superstition?"

"You bet. We'd been mostly lucky in what we did together, Damrong and me. Even when we were busted, we managed to turn a profit."

"Could you identify the men you trained?"

A shrug. "Maybe. They were homicidal puppets, like all the others. You don't necessarily remember ciphers, even when you work with them for a week."

"There were rehearsals?"

"With tailor's dummies, until they got better. Then we used real live actors."

"In Cambodia?"

"Sure."

"Were you aware of any of the other players, apart from your ex-wife?"

"No. I was kept sealed off from everyone. I never met the stud, either. I just edited his performance."

"But what about Tom Smith, the lawyer? He started visiting your apartment after I came to see you."

"Up to then I thought he was just the john in that other clip with Damrong. I didn't know he invested in the snuff movie. I wasn't invited to meetings or anything. I was controlled by Damrong. Obviously, after they killed her, someone else had to deal with me. They were watching you. After you came to question me the first time, Smith needed to debrief me. He's good. His questions were a lot harder to deal with than yours. I had to persuade him I didn't sing, or he would have had me wasted."

"Excuse me," I say, and fish out the cell, which is vibrating in my pocket.

"Khmer in cars outside Smith's law offices," Lek reports. "I'm off to the bank."

I close the phone and try not to stare at Baker as if he were already dead. "But there must have been arrangements for you to receive your share of the royalties. There must have been some kind of enforcement clause. I can't imagine Damrong or you going ahead without guarantees."

Baker stares at me. "But there wasn't."

Now it is my turn to stare. "How can anyone believe that? This is a contract of death in which the deceased is supposed to get paid post-humously. No way that girl was going into that without security."

Baker shrugs. "They gave her more than a million U.S. dollars up front. She told me it would be used by someone for enforcement if necessary. She was very confident—she told me not to worry about the money. She said I could insist on some up-front dough if I wanted it, but there was really no need to worry. When Damrong said that about money, you had to believe she had the whole thing under control."

I nod. "A million dollars buys a lot of enforcement over here, that's true. But the main players, the invisible men, were never based here." I stop and rub my left temple. "But then she was Thai. She would think in personal terms. Symbolic terms too. Magical terms." I look at Baker and try to imagine how she saw his role. The same image that haunts my nights springs into mind: wild-haired, bent over her breasts, madness in her eyes, a grin of total triumph on her face. In the distance a priestess from the forest period arranges a multiple sacrifice to the gods.

It is as if Baker has read my mind. "Yeah," he says. "With hindsight, you can see why she wasn't so worried about enforcement."

There is a knock on the door. It is not particularly heavy; nor is it repeated. One boot busts the flimsy lock, and the guy I first saw in guard's uniform enters with another behind him bearing a Chinese Kalashnikov. They gesture to Baker to come with them. Baker looks frantically at me.

"I forbid you to abduct this man. I am an officer in the Royal Thai Police." They don't understand a word I say. When I fish out my police ID, they can't read it. It doesn't make any difference—Baker goes with them anyway. I go to the camera on the tripod and look through the viewer. A Toyota minivan has appeared, and they bundle Baker into it.

About ten minutes later I'm still in Baker's flat with no one to interrogate. Lek calls. "Nothing unusual about Tanakan's bank," Lek reports, "except that he's not there. He's at some meeting with other bankers, some kind of all-day thing. I asked about the guards at the bank. They're very carefully vetted—no way anyone who didn't speak Thai could join their ranks."

Another ten minutes, and I see it is Vikorn calling. "Someone's abducted Tanakan," he says in a hoarse voice. "It was carefully planned. Some heavies who looked and acted like Khmer blocked his car as he was leaving a meeting and grabbed him. If you know anything about this that you're not telling me, you're dead."

"Colonel—"

"Do you realize how bad this is?"

"It's not your fault."

"Moron, of course it's my fault. Don't you understand? *I was blackmailing him.* That made him my responsibility. My honor died today." He closes the phone.

It is the next call, though, that surprises the most. "Sonchai," Dr. Supatra says, "they've taken the body." I'm too shocked to speak. "Some men came armed with combat rifles. They held us up for ten minutes while they went down to the morgue and grabbed the body. They didn't take anything else, and they didn't seem to be able to speak Thai. Someone said they were Khmer."

When I've assimilated that, I press buttons on the cell phone until I reach the message window and plug in Kimberley's number:

Can your nerds trace me from my cell phone signals?

She messages back in less than five minutes:

We can try. Why?

I text back:

Because I am about to go on a long journey.

I sit on Baker's bed for more than an hour before another Khmer guard appears with the standard-issue Kalashnikov. He points it at me in a desultory way and beckons for me to walk out in front of him. He prods me with the gun all the way down to the car park, where another Toyota four-by-four is waiting. I get in the back with half a dozen Khmer. We drive in an easterly direction for more than five hours before they decide to blindfold me. At the same time they take my cell phone away.

ENDGAME

34

Dearest Brother,

By the time you read this I will have dumped this stupid body.
Dear one, you are the only man I have ever loved. The only
human being. I have taken care of you as our mother never could.
Darling, I didn't seduce you during those terrible nights when we
were young. Your need was the same as mine, we comforted each
other as best we could. I sold my body for you. I gave you a life no
other boy in the village ever had. You are educated, sophisticated,
not a peasant anymore, a free man. Now I call in the debt:
gatdanyu. All these pigs must die as part of my sacrifice. My spirit
will be with you forever. If you do this thing, we will be lovers in
eternity. If you do not, my curses will destroy you. But I know you
will not betray me.

Your loving sister, Damrong.

Gamon, aka Phra Titanaka, finally showed me a printout of his sister's last e-mail to him. Her orders are in the form of an attachment that
is long and amazingly detailed, from instructions on the best way to
intrigue and befriend me to the crude device of the elephant-hair

bracelets. I was stunned to read her point-by-point guide to destroy-ing the masked man, which included anticipation of his suicide and instructions to make a video of his interrogation by Gamon. It was her intention for him to pass it on to me, to bind me still further to him. The whole case seems to be the product of an evil genius such as I have never before encountered. But not everything is going according to plan. Baker is dead before his time.

They blindfolded me when we reached Surin province, and I can-not guarantee that I am still in Thailand. Perhaps they used a jungle route to cross into Cambodia. The elephant farm is quite small but boasts the telltale ten-foot mounting platforms. Most of the buildings are crumbling. Perhaps it was a tourist venture that failed. My status here is unclear to me and to everyone else, perhaps including Gamon. I do not think the original plan calls for my presence at the denoue-ment; some weakness in him, a fondness for me perhaps or a need for companionship, has nibbled at his resolve. The first I saw of him when they removed the blindfold was an elegant monk in saffron with a Kalashnikov slung over one shoulder. Bizarre though it sounds, I think my presence made him self-conscious, and now he has stopped wear-ing the gun.

The Khmer guards watch me warily, but unlike Smith and Tana-kan I am free to walk around. If I go too close to the jungle perimeter, though, they fire warning shots above my head. At night I am locked in a wooden hut from which I could easily escape, but escape to what? My chances are better here than in the jungle. In this heat it takes only a day of desperate wandering in the undergrowth for one to begin to die of thirst.

I have no idea if Gamon bought the elephant farm or rented it; his conversation does not lend itself to such details. It is hot, hotter even than Bangkok, and there is no air-conditioning in any of the buildings. Electricity is intermittent, depending on whether the Khmer can be bothered to start the generator or not. Most of the time there's nothing to do except watch the guards chew betel or shoot at trees. Or watch the elephants. There are three of them, young, irritable, and weighing about three tons each.

Smith and Tanakan are imprisoned in concrete huts that seem to be new and purpose-built and face the compound, so they can see the animals trundling up and down on their giant carpet slippers. They can see the Khmer building the giant bamboo spheres too, out of a great pile of slats. The KR work slowly and often take time out to grunt at one another or shoot off rounds into the air. They are also given to inexplicable bursts of energy that they use not for work but to fire their Kalashnikovs into the jungle because they imagine they see something move. Only Gamon and I know that Baker's death may have changed everything.

He tried to escape, or perhaps he simply preferred to be shot. Somehow he managed to bust the locks on the steel door of his prison. There was a burst of machine-gun fire in the middle of the night, but this was not unusual. No shouts, no audible conversation. I imagine the guard simply shot on reflex, without giving the matter a second thought, then went back to sleep until morning. They called me at dawn because Gamon, who was meditating in his hut, had given orders not to be disturbed, and I followed them to the body lying on the perimeter of the compound. The spray had caught him in the head. He lay as he fell, twisted weirdly, because his brain died instantly and his body folded on itself. He was naked save for a dirty pair of green shorts with a camouflage motif. Already armies of insects were frenziedly feeding (reincarnations of souls that have been falling for a million years, they are drawn irresistibly by the odors of death—hard to believe they once enjoyed the privilege of human consciousness, which only goes to show where a string of poor choices can lead). Twin trails of red ants lead to and from the cornucopia of his mouth; larger monsters with proboscises, also imbued with a ferocious work ethic, lapped at cerebral matter dripping from the wound. Feeling grim, I walked over to Gamon's hut and kicked the door. He was deep in meditation, so I kicked him too. Still, I had to almost drag him to Baker's corpse. In the ten-minute interval a great swarm of flies had enveloped it. At first he seemed tempted to take it as another meditation exercise, another knot of karma to dissolve under the power of absolute truth. The law of cause and effect played on his mind, though, and I watched an unendurable anguish take over. He had turned the highest form of life on earth into a banquet for the lowest; turned Buddhism and evolution on its head. I think he suddenly saw the karmic price he would have to pay. Panic presented itself as an option. I grabbed his arm. "If you run away now, the Khmer will kill the rest of us."

He seemed to wake up from a dream. "Come on," I said, and led him back to his hut. "Meditate now." And I left him. I don't know if he is alive or dead.

Time slows in the jungle without TV. The Khmer are used to it—they can put their bodies in almost any position, then stare at nothing for hours on end. They are conditioned to obeying orders, though, and since Gamon is paying, he is the one they look to. But Gamon meditates sometimes for twelve hours at a stretch. I'm quite impressed. Before they shot Baker, I used to check on Gamon in his hut to see if he really was practicing *vipassana*. I think he was; his body has that combination of suppleness, emptiness, and immobility that is a good clue to what he is doing with his mind. My theory, for what it's worth, is that this man uses meditation as another might use morphine. Something happened to him when he ordained; he realized there was a way out, that the mind was infinite in its possibilities, so why choose constant pain? It didn't do much for his grasp of the here and now, though, a criticism that is often leveled against our form of Buddhism. It was never designed to build caring communities or create social welfare programs; it was brought to us in times quite as desperate as our own, when there seemed nothing left to our species but a downward spiral into barbarism. *Plus ça change.* I ought to visit Smith and Tanakan in their cells, of course, but so far I have not had the courage. Sometimes, despite myself, I spend hours staring at the elephants.

Knowing the business plan gives a sinister aspect to these animals. One cannot help but be morbidly aware of them. In midadolescence they are already many feet taller than the tallest horse, and possess the independent minds of jungle lords. There seems to be only one *mahout*, a Khmer man in his sixties, dressed in filthy rags that in color and texture bear a resemblance to the pachyderms themselves. They are not tethered but wander around the compound at will. Yesterday one came up behind me, for they can be quite silent on those padded feet, and swung its trunk gently across the backs of my knees, bringing me to the ground. For a moment I thought I was done for, but the several tons of pure muscle were simply carrying out an experiment of some kind and trundled off with his conclusion, as if to share it with his three companions.

I know that I have to go see Gamon in his hut again sooner or later, but I have no idea what to do or say. The whole of his sister's careful planning seems to be unraveling. I decide to wait until tomorrow. Finally I summon the strength to see the prisoners. Despite the cultural divide, it is easier to approach Smith than Tanakan, who somehow still towers over me from his great height in the feudal hierarchy. I rouse myself and hitch up my sarong, a frayed, largely gray piece of cloth I found in the washhouse the day I arrived; my shirt and pants were sweaty and already beginning to stink; it was liberating to change into traditional dress.

Smith is in a bad way. It is a shame to see that big, attractive *farang* body in a corner of its cell, curled up in a fetal position. His depression may be terminal, and I wonder if it would not be more humane for me to leave him alone. I press my head against the bars, watching. I see movement in his eyelids and the occasional twitch of a hand or leg. "Khun Smith," I say, "it's me, Detective Jitpleecheep." He blinks and looks up at what must be a single intense shaft of light.

My face disorients him still further. He cannot be sure it is really me, and if it is me, have I come to save or to gloat? We remain like that for perhaps ten minutes, neither of us sure of what kind of communication may be possible. Eventually he shifts his body, like an animal coming out of hibernation, and manages to stand. Like me, he is reduced to wearing an old sarong, which gives him the aspect of White Man Gone Native: an image from tales of the Raj. The bars impose a grid of vertical black shadows, like a giant bar code. "You," he says, as if I am the source of his misfortune. He approaches the window with the curiosity of a man toward the devil that is tormenting him. "You."

"I didn't do this," I say. A jerk of his chin points out that I am free and he is not. "Damrong," I explain. The name triggers a shudder. "It is hard for a *farang* to understand, perhaps impossible." I scratch my head exactly because it has struck me just how difficult it must be for a Westerner to comprehend, even a man who has spent time in the East. "She left instructions." He shakes his head. "She was not afraid of death, in a way had been looking forward to it all her life. Then came the money, you see, Smith, the money."

He glares in a vulnerable kind of way: defiance that expects defeat. What is it about Asians that makes us feel apologetic toward the West, as if we always knew in our heart of hearts the catastrophe toward which it was headed? Perhaps we should have done more to prevent it? I, at least, feel compelled to try to explain. "Death," I say. "Tom, have you ever thought what it might mean? Never mind religion—I'm talking basic observation. Tom, what she knew is what nine-tenths of humanity also knows: *Death trumps money.* I'm not talking machines for killing people—that's just Neolithic butchery. I'm talking about Death as an idea, Death as a weapon of the mind, Death as a reality only adults can confront. You were never going to win, Tom. You lost the war the moment you gave her that first lustful stare. While you were thinking about hiring her body, she had a much bigger plan, more holistic." I pause, trying to find the words. I'm not sure if I really mean what I say next, but it seems inevitable that I say it: "Tom, are there any adults at all where you come from?"

I have failed to get through to him, of course. Now he's certain I'm just an unhinged half-caste, a kind of Oriental gargoyle sent by some barbaric power to torment him. I give up, feeling bad.

Khun Tanakan has heard our conversation and come to his window in the cell next door.

"How much?" he hisses. "Just tell me how much you want." Even in such a short sentence, his exalted level in our culture, his familiarity with the highest echelons, his sophistication, and his innate toughness are implied in every syllable. His Thai is so much more elegant than mine I am almost tempted to speak English.

"It is not up to me," I say.

"Vikorn? Is Vikorn behind this?"

"No," I say. "It's the girl herself."

"What are you talking about? The girl's dead."

"Only in a manner of speaking. You might say her will is very much alive." He glares. "It was mostly your money, wasn't it, that financed the project? You handed over the million-plus for her services, less whatever minor investment Smith made. Of course, you knew you needed an aide-de-camp, a fall guy, a consigliere, for you could not afford to get too close to the scam itself. And of course, there was always going to be a need for enforcement: Khun Kosana, your fatally indiscreet slave-buddy, with his lover Pi-Oon. If not for that, I think you would have had Smith killed just because she used him to make you jealous. He is after all taller, younger, stronger, and Caucasian. Yes, certainly, you would have killed him as a casual reflex of power, so to speak: Nok. How Damrong must have insulted you, how she must have poisoned your days and nights for months on end for you to even think of doing anything so reckless as to invest in that snuff movie. Can you admit that you loved her?"

"What are you talking about?"

"Yes, with you I can use that word. Strange, isn't it? You are so much harder, so much tougher than your accomplice Smith, and yet with you that word comes to mind. She was, after all, your total and complete opposite—dare I suggest your other half? You in the penthouse, she in the gutter. She twisted a knife in your heart by telling you all about Smith, the handsome, phallic *farang* whose cock was so much bigger than yours. She was an expert at injecting acid into your veins just when you thought you were winning. Am I right?"

"Go on."

"Lust is blind to class. What drove you out of your mind was her total and intimate understanding of that reptilian side of you. She knew where your ambition came from. It came from a kind of hatred of life—exactly the same impulse that drove her. You got rich out of revenge on life. So did she, in the end. And then there was always your mother. At the end of the day, only a whore could really turn you on."

His eyes pierce like needles. "Bring on the elephant. Get it over with."

He retreats to a corner of his cell where light does not reach.

"Ah, no one doubts that you are harder than steel, Khun Tanakan. All who know you would agree. But think about this. If she is able to reach you at will, night after night, and rape you dry even while you are in the body, what chance will you have on the other side?" Chinese are even more ferociously superstitious than we are. I observe a twitch in his right hand, then a shudder as he turns to the wall.

Over in a corner of the compound the Khmer have gone back to work on the first of the bamboo spheres. It's taking shape but is still very wobbly. After an hour or so they give up. Too hot. There is no hurry. The show won't begin today, or even tomorrow.

35

The first you see of dawn is blood in the eastern treetops and a universal glowering heralding another unbearable day. Twenty minutes later the sky starts to blind while it boils, and you do everything in your power to get out of the way. The sun itself is usually invisible behind a pulsating screen of humidity, so that the whole sky seems to radiate an unhealthy intensity of light and heat. I awaken early, before first light, wash myself down at a stone trough outside my hut, and wrap my sarong around me.

My body still wet, my sarong soaked, I make up my mind to climb the stairs to Gamon's hut. I decide not to knock but press the door. It opens, and I step over the threshold. I guess he could not be dead and still be in a semilotus position, but the vital signs are few. I step over to him where he meditates with his back against a wall under a window. I think I am about to shake him, but the Buddha directs differently. I caress his beautiful face and kiss him gently on the forehead. "Phra Titanaka, my brother," I whisper.

He opens his eyes in another universe. He smiles with the generosity of one who has dumped ego and accepts eagerly the love in my eyes; then he remembers, and the anguish takes over.

"Gamon," I say, "we're going to have to let them go. Baker is dead because of us, but it was not really our fault. We don't have a lot of bad karma arising from his death. But if we go through with Damrong's plan, what will become of us? We'll be locked in granite for a million years."

Horror in his eyes: "And if I don't obey her? Have you any idea the power she has? She visits me every night. *I still have sex with her.*"

"Because you let her. You're a Buddhist monk—how can you allow yourself to be enslaved?"

My words startle him. He blinks at me then stares at his robes. "Of course, I'm so used to these, I've forgotten I no longer have the right to them."

In his disoriented state his childlike response is to stand and disrobe in front of me. This is not the effect I expected, and I want to tell him to put them on again, but as he stands in a pair of boxer shorts with the heap of saffron cloth at his feet, I watch a fascinating transformation. The monklike comportment quite melts away in less than a minute, together with the personality that went with it. That other side of him emerges: harder, more primitive, more built for survival, more criminal. I see clearly now the young man who once smoked and traded *yaa baa*. His voice is stronger, hoarser. He goes to the single window of his hut to look down on the compound where his elephant assassins graze.

I say, "Gamon."

He sighs. "There is more."

"Tell me. It might save someone's life."

Controlling his tone: "Her last e-mail didn't tell the whole story. It didn't tell the story at all."

I think he wants to turn his face to me but cannot. I have him in profile while light starts to bleach the compound. "Things she didn't want to remember or think about simply ceased to exist in her mind."

He summons the courage to face me. "You saw the reference to incest, but you didn't pick up on the significance."

"Tell me, my friend, while there is still time."

A groan comes from the heart. "It started just like she said, two frightened kids in a wet and stinking two-room hut, Mum and Dad drinking, smoking *yaa baa*, and screwing in the next room—partying, you understand—no food for a day or two because they were too far gone. Then when Mum was unconscious and Dad was out of his head, he would call for her. He liked to mix sex with his voodoo. She would go to him, then come back looking like death. Looking like a seventy-year-old fourteen-year-old. But she stopped him from using me. Even then she was using her body to protect me." A long sigh. "But she had her needs too."

After a pause, he starts again in a stronger voice. "Sure, that's how it started. She showed me what she wanted and how she wanted it done. When I was a little older, she showed me what *I* wanted and did it for me. That was after her first tour. My first experience of sex was world-class, you might say."

He coughs. "Nothing wrong with that, apart from some primitive taboo designed to keep the tribal genome healthy, which hardly applies in an age of contraception. People who worry about such things should worry more about how Damrong and I would have turned out without incest."

A long pause. "But when she came back from her first tour in Singapore, she had changed. She was only eighteen, but she was a woman." Licking his lips: "And a whore. Whores suffer from terminal love starvation—you know that. They screw and they screw and they screw, and not a drop of love comes out of it no matter what they try. A kind of madness takes over them. They must have a real lover, even if he's some ugly, broken-down, old white man—"

"Or a close family relation."

He nods. "After every tour she came home panting for me. Usually she would get to Surin and call for me. I would go see her in a hotel. If she'd done well that month, she would rent a five-star suite. She liked showing me the power of her money. She was so hungry for me, it was almost like being raped. But of course, I wanted love too." A couple of beats pass. "She would always spoil me afterward, buy me motorbikes, whatever I wanted. One time she'd made so much, she bought me a Harley-Davidson Fat Boy—we had to sell it a few months later when times got tough. She would say over and over again that our love was the only way, that she couldn't keep on the Game and support me if she didn't have me to come back to." Looking at me curiously: "How did your mother handle it? Did she keep asking you if you really loved her?"

"We went through that stage." Paris, old Truffaut snoring in his gigantic Belle Epoque bedroom under the silk bedspread, Nong embarrassed in front of me for going with such an old man: *You do love me, Sonchai, don't you? You forgive your mum, darling, don't you?*

"But she never seduced you?"

"Nong? No. Impossible even to imagine."

"From the age of fifteen I heard the same words over and over: *If you ever leave me, I'll kill myself.*"

Light dawns in my skull just as the heat starts to bite, and sweat magically appears all over his brown body. I think: *Of course, foolish of me, she would have needed a real lover just to carry on.* But he would have had to be a cripple, hobbled. Memory flash: once walking with her on Sukhumvit, hand in hand, insanely happy, I tripped on a manhole cover—a stupidity you commit only when you're in love. I had to limp for a couple of days. I expected Damrong to despise me, but her reaction was opposite to that. She took care of me, urged me to lean on her shoulder, massaged my ankle in the middle of the busy street, showed love while I was helpless, used kindness from her palette of seduction. "I see."

"Perhaps you don't. She did a tour in Switzerland that lasted eighteen months. She was making so much money, she didn't want to lose her clientele until she felt she'd cleaned up."

Two beats pass while he brings his heart under control, then: "I was the one who couldn't stand it. I simply couldn't. Without her I was less than half alive. I smoked too much *yaa baa*, started selling it, got caught. She had to rush home to bribe the cops to get me out of jail."

A terrible choking takes hold of him. He coughs hoarsely and shakes his head. He points to that short, thin white scar on his left wrist, which precisely replicates the one on his sister's arm. "Childish, third-world melodramatic—but the blood was real. We vowed our lives away to each other. She said she'd never leave me for so long again, I promised to reform, go to some fancy school in Bangkok that she wanted to send me to, learn to speak English—I would be the saved one. When she was totally burned out by her late twenties, I would be able to look after her. Repay the debt: *gatdanyu*. That's what this case has always been about, Detective. You could call it a Case of Third-World Debt."

"But you ordained," I say.

He rubs his eyes. "She did try to make more regular visits, but then the chance came to work in America, and she was greedy. She used some Mafia connections to get a visa. She was away two years that time. I wasn't a teenager anymore, I was in my early twenties. I'd graduated from university with a degree in sociology, of all things. I don't think she realized how useless that was going to be." He looks frankly into my eyes. "I knew I could never work—too fucked up. But I didn't want to betray her by going back to drugs. I did what any young Thai or Khmer man might do. I took refuge in the Buddha, the Dharma, and the Sangha. But the Thai Sangha wouldn't have me because of my criminal record, so I crossed the border to Poipet, the Cambodian gangster town where our parents came from. No worries about criminal convictions there. When I e-mailed my decision to her, she didn't mind at all. She thought I would stay in the robes for a month or so before boredom forced me out. So did I."

I am staring at him, lost in horror, wonder, and admiration. I say, "Oh."

"Yes, oh."

"You found you were a natural."

"Everyone said so, from the abbot to my meditation master. A *reincarnate for sure*, they said. *This kid has been around for millennia, flirting with Buddhism, never quite taking the final step.* I found *vipassana* so easy, I was able to meditate for a full two hours after only the first week. After a year I could manage a full day and night. I was experiencing freedom and happiness for the first time in my twenty-four years on earth."

"While she was in the States."

"Yes."

"It was easy to believe that the Buddha had intervened and relieved you of all karma, even *gatdanyu*."

"Yes. Exactly."

"But when she came back?"

He turns again to the window. "She'd been busted for prostitution and running a bawdy house in Fort Lauderdale with her American husband. She didn't give a damn about that, but she was in a rage against American men. According to her, they were either pubescent boys in men's bodies, or total animals. She despised her husband. Two years with not a single emotional event in the life of a young woman, even a woman like her, was hard to take. She'd spent the last twelve months craving me."

"She wrote to you?"

"E-mail. In Cambodia the rules are very relaxed. Monks surf the Net all the time—it's not even frowned on."

My sharp intake of breath sounds like a hiss in that hot little hut. "You were living two lives."

He nods. "I couldn't tell her by e-mail that I was the real thing, a genuine monk. I didn't have the strength."

"Then she returned from the U.S."

"Then she returned," he agrees, with a grunt not totally devoid of humor. "She was boiling with rage that I did not make myself available." He coughs. "You know how Cambodia is. She bribed some monks to look the other way, shaved her hair, dressed in white like a *looksit*, and sneaked into the monastery." He challenges me with a sudden ironic smile. "Can you imagine? I hadn't had sex for two years. How erotic, her naked body with her head shaved. Silent and furtive in candlelight. Insane." A pause. "Of course, after that night she had won no matter what I did. I tried counting how many precepts I had broken: sex, harboring a woman under the same roof, deception of the abbot, habitual reoffending. She came to see me every night for two weeks, until her next tour."

"A pattern was established?"

"Certainly."

"You could not adapt—that would have been impossible. You had no choice but to divide yourself in half."

"Whenever she went back to prostitution, I would meditate for twenty-four hours every third day, until my mind had relinquished her. *Vipassana* works whatever you use it for." He flashes me a dark look. "But for a weak monk, even his successes come to haunt him. In the midst of serenity, demons."

I stand up to go to the little window and look over his shoulder. The three elephants are grouped together, sniffing the ground where Baker's blood was spilled. When you have been around these animals for a while, you start to notice clues as to their extraordinary intelligence. I have no doubt that some kind of communication is taking place, as if they too are discussing the case. I've come to feel awe at those gigantic, know-all craniums, those probing trunks. They seem to comprehend everything. I guess the jungle is getting to me.

"But the biggest scar, surely, was the elephant game itself, when the cops killed your father."

He shrugs. "Not a scar, exactly. An initiation. I was in my early teens. Until then adults, my sister, had belonged to the realm of the gods. When they first rolled the bamboo ball out, I thought it was a game. I grew up in the fifteen minutes that followed. The real revelation was her joy, her incredible enthusiasm with the camera—she'd bought an expensive Minolta with a big black zoom lens. When I started meditating, that was the first, persistent image I had to deal with: not him dying but her with the camera, filming his death. Her glee, her insane cries of triumph. She was all I had, and she'd taken me into her world, which I assumed to be reality—what else?"

A cough. "It changed her, though." He challenges me to ask. I nod: *Go on.* "It was a major success, her first. She started to realize how powerful she could be. After all, in one stroke she'd destroyed the monster that tormented our nights. She wasn't a victim anymore." He is shaking now, all pretense of control abandoned: "She was the one who insisted on watching. When she knew what the cops planned, *she persuaded them to let us watch.* They didn't really want us there." I gasp. Nothing to say. It is as if an age passes.

When I turn to him, I see that he too is fixated on the elephants. "Sorcery uses the power of ritual, which is no more or less than the power to refocus the mind on forbidden knowledge, black powers buried deep in every culture until someone like her digs them up. She was not prepared to be a victim ever again, not even of death. She had to turn her death into another victory, an even bigger one, with even more blood to power it. She knew she would lose me sooner or later to the Buddha. She wanted to bow out at the height of her game and control me from the other side, where she would be infinitely more powerful."

He looks down at the saffron pile, then at me. "I'm a second child, Detective. I follow leads. What should I do?"

"Put your robes back on, Phra Titanaka. It's against the rules to disrobe yourself. Only the Sangha can do that."

I leave him, descend the crude wooden stairs, cross the compound to my own hut, and try to prepare my mind for another unbearable day in the oven. From the shade of my hut I gaze on Gamon's closed door, wondering what kind of monster is rebirthing there, its hour come round at last.

36

Yesterday another event occurred to disrupt the terminal boredom. Some of the Khmer decided to liven things up by killing one of the elephants, which, after the death of Baker, was superfluous. It was possible to understand much of what they intended by watching their body language and the smirks on their faces. They spoke to the *mahout*, who remonstrated with them. He seemed to be telling them they were crazy, that this was a very bad thing to do, that no good could come of it. They laughed at him and took out their machine guns. They fired from the safety of a hut, straight across the compound, ripping through the elephant's skull, chopping off its trunk. Its great strength kept it alive for more than an hour after they stopped shooting. They were fascinated by the anguished groans of the other two animals, the way they came to sniff at their dying brother and comfort him with their trunks, all the time making heart-wrenching noises of dumb distress. The KR thought it hilarious.

In late afternoon they were asleep on the balcony of the hut when the animals attacked. One of the Khmer managed to escape. Smith, Tanakan, and I watched while the animals destroyed the hut as well as the remaining human in a fantastic orgy of primal rage, snorting and honking furiously, masters again at last. Within minutes there was no more than splinters, bones, and blood and a pile of firewood where the hut had been. The two giants tossed wooden beams around with their trunks and stabbed at the dead Khmer with their tusks in wild downward thrusts—a quite superfluous expression of vengeance considering they had already stamped on his chest. The remaining Khmer thought this hilarious also. Tanakan and Smith turned gray; I expect I did too.

It's shocking how quickly we all got used to the new reality: a hut in splinters, an elephant carcass in the middle of the compound, human remains among the firewood already starting to stink. Survival on earth is our true god, or we would have migrated to less challenging planets millennia ago. We are all savages now, Smith, Tanakan, and me, by virtue of our acceptance of the barbarism. I'm not so sure about Gamon, who did not emerge from his hut all day today, not even in the midst of the shooting, screaming, yelling, and laughing. We have made even the animals hate us.

When I finally took a look at the hut the elephants had destroyed, I saw a couple of sacks of *yaa baa* in powder form. I had seen the Khmer licking their fingers from time to time but had not paid it any mind. Typical of them, they did not measure the amount of the drug they were using but simply wet their fingers and stuck them into a sack of the stuff whenever they felt their high beginning to wane.

The elephant rebellion did have the effect, however, of concentrating the minds of the remaining Khmer. All of a sudden they went to work manfully on the bamboo balls, and by the end of the day they were ready. I watched, as no doubt Smith and Tanakan watched, while they rolled them out into the open area between the huts, tested them for durability, and checked the hinged hatches they had installed. Two of them went to the window of Smith's hut to check his size against the ball they had built for him, which is quite a bit bigger than Tanakan's. That exercise complete, they returned to their own huts and watched. Little by little, I suppose, the gaze of everyone came to rest on Gamon's closed door.

Hours have passed. I have come to recognize every subtlety of heat. The fierce sudden heat of the morning is quite different in texture from the relentless heat of midday, which is different again from the sullen molten copper of late afternoon. It is, I guess, about four P.M. when I notice a shuddering in the structure of Gamon's flimsy hut, signifying that he is moving around. Finally the door opens slowly, and it remains so for a full five minutes before the human form emerges.

I know I inhale sharply, and I bet everyone else does too, when the figure in a black ballgown and a wig of long black Asian hair begins to walk sedately down the stairs. You would need to be in the grip of some Western superstition to suppose that this new creature is simply a gifted transvestite. I don't think any of us believe that, except maybe the English lawyer Smith. It is Damrong in every movement, every gesture, down to the last nuance. Goose bumps have erupted on both my forearms and the back of my neck is rigid; in the unendurable heat I am frozen to the spot. Appalled and fascinated, I wait for the first words to emerge from those lips that she has enriched with purple lipstick.

She crosses the compound elegantly with a beautifully straight back, not a trace of exaggeration in the seductive swing of her buttocks. "It's time," she calls out in that soft, compelling voice. Astonished and profoundly impressed, the Khmer stand and roll out the giant bamboo balls. "Bring the prisoners," Damrong commands; it is *her* voice. She has spoken in Khmer, but there is no doubt about her meaning.

"No!" I yell in an involuntary outburst, and stand up.

She turns toward me curiously, daring me to meet her gaze. This I am unable to do. No matter how hard I try, I cannot bring myself to look into those eyes. "Hello, Sonchai," she says in a mock-seductive tone. "Have you eaten yet?" Struck dumb, I shake my head. "Look at me, lover. Look into my eyes." Again I shake my head like a village idiot. "Aren't you pleased to see me, darling?"

"Wha, wha, wha," I start to jabber. "What have you done to Gamon?"

She smiles. "Just like you to ask the most difficult question. Do you love him more than you love me? I think you do. Why Sonchai, he's in the hut meditating. Why don't you go and say hello?"

If I was scared before, I'm suffering a paralyzing extreme of terror now. At this moment I think that nothing in the world would induce me to walk over to Gamon's hut—except for one thing. "Go to the hut, Sonchai," she commands, "or look into my eyes." She takes a step toward me, leaning her head to one side, as if to force me to meet her gaze. I turn away and find myself making toward the hut.

I climb the rickety stairs slowly, with more than an inkling of what I might expect. Sure enough, when I enter, he is all dressed up in his robes, sitting in a semilotus position. It is Damrong's corpse, of course, beginning to rot and filling the hut with the stench of formaldehyde, the eyes glazed and wide open. In a strange way, everything suddenly fits. Somehow the logic of sorcery would have required her cadaver; but has she really imprisoned her brother's spirit in that corpse? Outrageous, even for her. But at least the cadaver is immobile. I take the opportunity to rummage around until I find my cell phone, which the Khmer confiscated. I press an autodial number, and Kimberley answers, "Where are you?"

"I have no idea."

"Drama?"

"Plenty."

"Leave this line open as long as you can. I'll see if I can patch you over to Virginia."

I lay the cell phone on the floor with the line to Kimberley still open, hoping the battery holds out.

Now I hear sounds of steel doors opening down in the compound. When I step out onto the balcony, I see the Khmer have tied the hands of Smith and Tanakan behind their backs and are bringing them out. Smith, with his *farang* addiction to logic, is able to maintain his mental balance, terrified though he is. Tanakan, on the other hand, is trembling like a child and appears to have peed into his sarong.

"Hello, lovers," Damrong says. "Are you surprised to see me?" She walks elegantly up to them and caresses Smith's face with one hand.

"Fucking pervert," Smith says.

Damrong responds with that cynical-joyful laugh of hers that I remember so well. "Tom, Tom, you always did miss the point. That's why you're in this mess. If only you'd been born Asian, you would have understood so much better." He turns his head away from her and spits. I have to admire the way he has found his courage again. But he won't have it for long, I fear. "If you're so sure I'm just a screwed-up pervert in drag, why don't you look into my eyes, Tom? Please, do that little thing for me."

I see that he too cannot bear to meet her gaze. The idea is profoundly counterintuitive, like an animal's fear of fire. She reaches out to hold his jaw. "Call me a 'fucking pervert' again, Tom, please."

Something has happened to his identity. He would like to show true British spirit at a time like this, but he cannot. She is destroying his center, that complex, contradictory, illusory, but vitally necessary idea of self, without which we are no more than helpless infants. She nods to the Khmer, who have melted into her slaves. One of them holds Smith's head, while another tries to keep his lids from closing. I cannot help my fascination as she takes one step closer to him and stares directly into his retinas. I am thinking, *No, no, you cannot do that. You cannot bring a virgin soul into contact with the other side without preparation. You will destroy more than his body.*

The effect is electric, as if he has been whipped. Suddenly he is a limp rag, a shadow, all autonomy lost. I turn away as he bursts into tears. He is blubbering something that sounds a little like "Mother," but it is hard to be sure. She has raped him.

She turns away from him in contempt and steps toward Tanakan, who starts to speak rapidly in Thai. I strain to catch his words, which are incomprehensible until I realize he is listing his assets, all of them—mansions, palaces, islands, gold, stocks, shares—offering them to her, begging her to accept them, at the same time painfully aware that he doesn't have anything the dead might need. He is using terms of address normally reserved for royalty and Buddhas. No Caucasian resistance here, he has accepted the new reality without reservation. "I will build a temple to you," he is saying. "Your name and image will be worshiped. I am a billionaire—for me such things are easy to accomplish."

She laughs gaily and says something in Khmer. It is not difficult to understand, because the guards start to take Smith and Tanakan toward the bamboo balls.

I try to think of the most far-fetched, illogical solution, the one thing Aristotle would never have considered in a million years. Revolted though I am, I know I have to go back inside the hut.

It takes only a minute to undress the cadaver. I change quickly into the saffron robes; then, trying not to gag or to fixate on the hideous Y-shaped gash in her torso, I pick her up (she is much lighter without her internal organs) and make for the door, grabbing Gamon's Kalashnikov and at the same time picking up the butane lighter that he used to light his candles.

Unaccustomed to the robes, or to carrying a corpse for that matter, I stumble on the stairs, but no one pays any attention. A primal orgy of sadism is in progress, and everyone is enthralled to watch the Khmer bind Smith's and Tanakan's feet, then force the two men into fetal position and bind them further like hogs. Tanakan is smaller and therefore easier to force through the hatch into one of the balls. His face is closed tightly like a fist when I reach the compound. Still nobody notices me as I set down the cadaver, take out the lighter, and apply the flame to the cadaver's left pinkie.

Damrong now lets out a diabolical oath and turns around, at the same time shaking her left hand exactly as if she has accidentally burned it. She is incredulous to see me, the holy fool, in Phra Titanaka's robes. But I am pointing the gun at the head of the corpse.

Any vestigial notion that there might be a rational explanation, or that "A cannot be not-A," is quite erased by the way she flies through the air toward me (she adopts the diagonal like a banking helicopter, about ten feet from the ground, black hair flying wild, no broomstick), her face distorted with rage. In the circumstances I feel I have no choice but to pull the trigger on the cadaver. In the far distance I believe I can detect the sound of rotor blades.

It is not the approaching helicopter (somehow I knew the FBI would find a black one) that freaks the Khmer, though—it's the sorcery. Even as the chopper circles above the compound, the thugs are fleeing into the jungle, taking the *mahout* and the elephants with them. Somewhat disheveled, I fear, and not managing the robes very well at all, I walk toward the figure in the black ballgown lying facedown a few yards from me. The wig has fallen off. When I turn him over, he is still breathing, but there is a terrible head wound in the region of his left temple, where I shot the cadaver. He opens his eyes, though, and seems to recognize me. I cradle his shaved head in my hands.

"She's gone, I can feel it, she's gone for good," he says with a smile. Then: "Whatever you do, don't save my life."

"Of course not," I reply. "Of course not, Phra Titanaka."

"I was a real monk, Sonchai. If I hadn't been, I wouldn't have felt so much pain, would I?"

"You were born a monk, my friend."

He smiles at that. "I scaled the heights, Detective, I really did. People don't realize how available nirvana is. I experienced total love, the cosmic power of compassion, Buddha mind, but I could never sustain it. Too many previous wasted lifetimes, all of them spent with her. She was too strong for me. I wanted so much to save her. I thought if I became a monk, a serious one, and transformed myself, then she would have to follow. But she had other ideas. She always did things her way."

I think he wants to say more, but he fades away at that moment.

I drag myself over to the bamboo balls. Tanakan is snugly inside his, but the terrified Khmer dropped Smith outside the other one. From within his lattice womb Tanakan has recovered his nerve and starts to demand that I get him out. I stare at him for a moment, frown, then go over to Smith. "I need a cell phone," I tell him, but he is not responsive. I have to climb back up to Gamon's hut to retrieve my own, but the battery has run down. Never mind, Kimberley has jumped out of her chopper and is running toward me, combat style, dressed in black coveralls, carrying a sexy-looking two-tone carbine (café au lait on dark chocolate). "What happened?" she says, coming to an abrupt halt, not sure where to point the gun.

"Damrong's ghost trapped her brother in her own cadaver so she could use his body while supervising the ritual slaying of those two," I explain, pointing at Smith and Tanakan. "But I shot the cadaver in the head, which put an end to her scheme. I believe the technical expression is *sympathetic magic*. It's not due to become available to humanity at large again for another thousand years. Can I borrow your cell phone?"

She hands it to me, and I plug in a familiar number. "Yamahatosan," I say, "I have a job for you."

Epilogue

Vikorn sent a couple of heavies to arrest me as soon as I reached Bangkok. He has thrown me into the cells while he decides what to do with me. He doesn't know everything, but he knows enough to realize I stopped being a cop for a certain period of time, during which his squeeze on Tanakan was ruined and the sweetest scam of his life was taken from him. I know he is deciding whether to bump me off or reduce me to some degrading condition of absolute slavery. I'm not too bothered, though. After all, I have a trump up my sleeve. In the meantime I'm enjoying the solitude, the reliable rhythms of incarceration. I don't even mind the slopping out, although the stench makes me gag; I'm using it as an exercise in Buddhist humility. After forty-eight hours, however, I'm starting to get bored, so I send the Colonel a handwritten note in Thai: มีวีดีโอ: I have a video.

Never one to be coy when a glittering prize offers itself, he writes back within the hour: มีวีดีโอออะไร: What kind of video?

ยอมรับไม่มีเสื้อผ้าคุณธนาคารและคุณสมิท: Naked confessions of Khun Tanakan and Khun Smith.

. . .

My rehabilitation is as precipitous as my fall. Now I'm in Vikorn's office, sitting opposite him.

"Want a cigar?"

"You know I don't smoke tobacco."

"How about some ganja? One of the boys busted a dealer with export-quality stuff. Here." He reaches into his top drawer and tosses a Ziploc bag of dense green vegetation onto his desk. I wasn't about to accept, but the deep shade of the grass, together with the superabundance of buds, weakens my resolve. As I reach for it, however, he clamps it to his desk with a heavy gnarled old hand.

"Where's the video?"

"At a secret location."

"Does it really show them fessing up to everything? Conspiring to make a snuff movie, taking shareholder positions, all that?"

"Yes. Naked, bent over trestles in a compromising position. It's very elegantly done. Yammy's come a long way."

"Yammy? You used Yammy?"

"Is there anyone better?"

"Okay, how much do you want?"

"I want thirty percent for charity, plus twenty-five million dollars in seed money for Yammy's feature film. It sounds like a lot, but you're going to grab half of Tanakan's fortune, so why should you care?"

"Show me the video first."

"Do I look that stupid?"

"Okay, okay, if it's as good as you say, I'll agree."

"Write that down. I want you on your honor."

He frowns, then takes out his pen, writes, and hands me the contract. I fish a disk out of my pocket, walk over to his DVD player, and switch it on.

It was kind of cozy watching Yammy's private masterpiece, which had the Colonel chortling and congratulating me. With the FBI standing next to him wearing her new gun, Yammy used two cameras to somehow make magic of a sorry tale. He made Smith and Tanakan confess slowly, deliberately, as if reciting poetry on a stark stage in front of the hut the elephants had shattered. They speak in solemn, well-modulated voices, as they recount every detail of their contract with Damrong and the morbid passion that led to it. Yammy and I used her extensive notes as a kind of film script.

Sometimes I think things are almost normal again, but of course they are not, because they never were. The illusion of continuity is busted, my concentration shot. Yesterday, hardly aware of what I was doing, I bought a bronze statue of the elephant god Ganesh to use as a paperweight on my desk. Not a minute passes without thoughts of Gamon. I frequently find an excuse to go to the *wat* to meditate. Even then I see him everywhere. Something he said almost inadvertently one day repeats itself over and over in my mind: *When you tear away the last veil, you know with certainty that love is the foundation of human consciousness, that there really is nothing else. It's our constant betrayal of it that makes us crazy.* Hard to live by, but I guess you have to try.

There's one other little thing I ought to mention. Damrong came to me a few nights ago, and I found no strength to resist her; but in the dream (it is comforting to call it that) a figure in saffron robes, with a machine gun slung over his shoulder, held up a Buddha hand of peace, and she disappeared. When I awoke with a jolt, Chanya was sleeping peacefully beside me.

It's Vikorn, of all people, who keeps reminding me that I have a loving pregnant wife waiting for me at home. Who would have guessed that he was capable of worrying about my mental health?

But what of the FBI, whose sudden passion was quite eclipsed by events? Seduced, in my turn, by the sickly temptation of do-goodery, I took her last night to Don Juan's, because I knew Lek was rehearsing there for a *katoey* cabaret they were planning. I sneaked her in surreptitiously and had her sit with me at the back of the bar while Lek and his chums laughed, screamed, ad-libbed, and made wicked jokes about how Pi-Lek would soon go under the knife. I took Kimberley's hand by way of comforting her, but she removed hers very quickly. I thought she was angry because I was showing her just how perfectly Lek fitted into his *katoey* world, and how impenetrable that world was even for me, let alone a female *farang*. Wrong.

Afterward, sipping drinks at a bar in Pat Pong, she said, "That was sweet of you, in a way, Sonchai, but you're behind the curve. A week has passed, and I've grown up. I know that different cultures produce very different human beings. Americans find that hard because the empire that dare not speak its name doesn't like us to know there are alternative cultures on earth—but I'm not stupid. I know he can't love me. Hell, maybe he *is* a spirit in human form. I also know that if I deny love one more time, I'll turn into just another drone with no life outside of work. That's a trap in the States, especially for a single woman over thirty-five. Bizarre it may be, incompatible we may be, but I have to see this through. We've done a deal. There's no way he'll be able to remain a cop after his operation, and I can't stand the thought of him selling his body in a bar on Soi Four. I'm going to be like one of those lovelorn white men—I'm going to send money every month from the States to keep him off the Game, and he's going to come visit me from time to time, except he'll be a *she* then, of course. It finally dawned on me that money is something I have that he needs. And guess what, I made him laugh the other day—so some communication is possible between alien species, right? I think we're going to be good friends. Don't underestimate the glamour of my country—he can't wait to see Hollywood and the Grand Canyon. If you want to be useful, keep an eye on him and send me reports." She smiled.

Well, that's it, *farang*, save for one loose end: I never did find out who sent me the Damrong DVD.

I am yours in Dharma, Sonchai Jitpleecheep.

Appendix

Erotica Inc.—A Special Report:
Technology Sent Wall Street into Market for Pornography

By Timothy Egan (*The New York Times*), 4297 words

Published: October 23, 2000

Correction Appended

The video-store chain that Larry W. Peterman owned in this valley of wide streets and ubiquitous churches carried the kind of rentals found anywhere in the country—from Disney classics to films about the sexual adventures of nurses. Mr. Peterman built a thriving business until he was charged last year with selling obscene material and faced the prospect of bankruptcy and jail.

Just before the trial, Mr. Peterman's lawyer, Randy Spencer, came up with an idea while looking out the window of the courtroom at the Provo Marriott. He sent an investigator to the hotel to record all the sex films that a guest could obtain through the hotel's pay-per-view channels. He then obtained records on how much erotic fare people here were buying from their cable and satellite television providers.

As it turned out, people in Utah County, a place that often boasts of being the most conservative area in the nation, were disproportionately large consumers of the very videos that prosecutors had labeled obscene and illegal. And far more Utah County residents were getting their adult movies from the sky or cable than they were from the stores owned by Larry Peterman.

Why file criminal charges against a lone video retailer, Mr. Spencer argued, when some of the biggest corporations in America, including a hotel chain whose board of directors includes W. Mitt Romney, president of the Salt Lake City Olympics organizing committee, and a satellite broadcaster heavily backed by Rupert Murdoch, chairman of the News Corporation, were selling the same product?

"I despise this stuff—some of it is really raunchy," said Mr. Spencer, a public defender who described himself as a devout Mormon. "But the fact is that an awful lot of people here in Utah County are paying to look at porn. What that says to me is that we're normal."

It took only a few minutes for the jury to find Mr. Peterman not guilty on all charges. His case illustrates what has happened to an industry that used to be confined to the margins of commerce, in the seedy parts of most towns, run by people who never dreamed of taking their companies to Wall Street.

Spurred by changes in technology that make pornography easier to order into the home than pizza, and court decisions that offer broad legal protection, the business of selling sexual desire through images has become a $10 billion annual industry in the United States, according to Forrester Research of Cambridge, Mass., and the industry's own Securities and Exchange Commission filings.

Whatever the phenomenon may say about the nature of American society, the financial rewards are so great that some of the biggest distributors of explicit sex on film and online include the country's most recognizable corporate names.

The General Motors Corporation, the world's largest company, now sells more graphic sex films every year than does Larry Flynt, owner of the Hustler empire. The 8.7 million Americans who subscribe to DirecTV, a General Motors subsidiary, buy nearly $200 million a year in pay-per-view sex films from satellite, according to estimates provided by distributors of the films, estimates the company did not dispute.

EchoStar Communications Corporation, the No. 2 satellite provider, whose chief financial backers include Mr. Murdoch, makes more money selling graphic adult films through its satellite subsidiary than Playboy, the oldest and best-known company in the sex business, does with its magazine, cable and Internet businesses combined, according to public and private revenue accounts by the companies.

AT&T Corporation, the nation's biggest communications company, offers a hard-core sex channel called the Hot Network to subscribers to its broadband cable service. It also owns a company that sells sex videos to nearly a million hotel rooms. Nearly one in five of AT&T's broadband cable customers pays an average of $10 a film to see what the distributor calls "real, live all-American sex—not simulated by actors."

For all the money being made on sex—legally—by mainstream corporations, the topic remains taboo outside the boardroom. The major satellite and cable companies do very little marketing of their X-rated products, and they are not mentioned in annual reports except in the vaguest of euphemisms.

None of the corporate leaders of AT&T, Time Warner, General Motors, EchoStar, Liberty Media, Marriott International, Hilton, On Command, LodgeNet Entertainment or the News Corporation—all companies that have a big financial stake in adult films and that are held by millions of shareholders—were willing to speak publicly about the sex side of their businesses.

"How can we?" said an official at AT&T. "It's the crazy aunt in the attic. Everyone knows she's there, but you can't say anything about it."

For hotels, the sex that can be piped through television generates far more money than the beer, wine and snacks sold from the rooms' mini-bars. Just under 1.5 million hotel rooms, or about 40 percent of all hotel rooms in the nation, are equipped with television boxes that sell the kind of films that used to be seen mostly in adults-only theaters, according to the two leading companies in the business. Based on estimates provided by the hotel industry, at least half of all guests buy these adult movies, which means that pay-per-view sex from television hotel rooms may generate about $190 million a year in sales.

At home, Americans buy or rent more than $4 billion a year worth of graphic sex videos from retail outlets and spend an additional $800 million on less explicit sexual films—all told, about 32 percent of the business for general-interest video retailers that carry adult topics, according to compilations done by two trade organizations that track video rentals. Chains like Tower Records now stock nearly 500 titles in their so-called erotic category, far more than films about history or dinosaurs.

On the Internet, sex is one of the few things that prompts large numbers of people to disclose their credit card numbers. According to two Web ratings services, about one in four regular Internet users, or 21 million Americans, visits one of the more than 60,000 sex sites on the Web at least once a month—more people than go to sports or government sites.

Though estimates have been greatly inflated by some e-commerce sex merchants, analysts from Forrester Research say that sex sites on the Web generate at least $1 billion a year in revenue, providing a windfall for credit card companies, Internet search engines and people who build Web sites, among others in the commercial food chain.

Some of the most popular Web properties—which feature quick links to sites labeled "Virgin Sluts" and "See Teens Have Sex"—are owned by a publicly held company in Boulder, Colo. That company, New Frontier Media, has stock traded like any other, and it expects its video network to be in 25 million homes within a few years. It does business with several major companies, including EchoStar and In Demand, the nation's leading pay-per-view distributor, which is owned in part by AT&T, Time Warner, Advance-Newhouse, Cox Communications and Comcast.

Another company, LodgeNet, whose chairman is Scott C. Petersen, does $180 million in annual business selling sex videos and other forms of room entertainment to hotels. LodgeNet is a major employer in Sioux Falls, S.D., its home base. It is a client of the accounting giant Arthur Andersen, and nearly a fifth of the company's public shares are held by a Park Avenue investment firm, Red Coat Capital Management of New York.

"We feel good about what we do," said Ann Parker, a spokeswoman for LodgeNet, which trades on the Nasdaq market. "We're good corporate citizens. We contribute to local charities."

The biggest provider of hard-core sex videos and adult Web content, Vivid Entertainment Group of Van Nuys, Calif., whose founders and principal owners are Steven Hirsch and David James, has been making the rounds of investment bankers of late, preparing for an initial public stock offering next year that could ultimately lead to the first porn billionaire.

"The adult entertainment business is just exploding," said Bill Asher, the president of Vivid, whose offices are in a new granite and glass building that houses investment and venture capital firms. "Right now there are a lot of people making a lot of money. Somebody's got to take control of it, and we figure it might as well be us. We see ourselves as the designated driver of this business."

To the astonishment of Mr. Flynt, who began in the pornography business by selling poor-quality pictures of naked girls as a way to build interest in his strip clubs, his competitors in the $10 billion annual adult market are mainstream corporations whose board members are among the American business elite.

"We're in the small leagues compared to some of those companies like General Motors or AT&T," Mr. Flynt said. "But it doesn't surprise me that they got into it. I've always said that other than the desire for survival, the strongest desire we have is sex."

The Technology Factor
Look, Ma, No Staples!

Thirty years ago, a federal study put the total retail value of hard-core pornography in the United States between $5 million and $10 million—or about the same amount that a single successful sex-related Web site brings in today. It seemed likely that the industry would remain where it had always been—largely out of sight, but profitable, and faced with consistent legal problems.

What kept the market relatively small, in the view of people in the industry, were the barriers between consumer and product. Typically, a person would have to go to a run-down part of town, among people considered less than savory, to find hard-core adult films or bookstores. These retail outlets frequently were raided by law enforcement authorities, further adding to the risk for a consumer—a risk of shame, or arrest.

In 1975, the Sony Corporation released the videocassette recorder to the broad market, and within 10 years, about 75 percent of all American households owned a VCR. Once the venue had moved from theater to the privacy of the home, the adult entertainment industry was never the same. For example, a single film, "Deep Throat," generated more than $100 million in sales, thanks in large part to the popularity of VCRs, Frederick S. Lane III writes in his book "Obscene Profits: The Entrepreneurs of Pornography in the Cyber Age" (Routledge, 2000).

But even with most Americans owning VCRs, people still had to take a trip to the video store, risking some embarrassment. Pay-per-view television and the Internet removed the final barriers.

Cable and satellite programmers allow people to buy a variety of sex-based programming, from Playboy, on the lighter side, to the Hot Network, owned by Vivid, and the Erotic Television Network, distributed by New Frontier, on the more explicit end of the spectrum. Consumers could watch movies of people having sex without ever leaving home.

What investors and bigger corporations soon discovered was the vast audience for pornography—once the privacy barrier was eliminated. Twenty percent of all American households with a VCR or cable access will pay to watch an explicit adult video—and 10 percent will pay frequently, according to the distributors New Frontier and Vivid. That interest explains, in part, why the production of pornographic films has grown tenfold in the last decade. There are now nearly 10,000 adult movies made every year, according to an annual survey of the films produced in the Los Angeles area.

Last year, there were 711 million rentals of hard-core sex films, according to Adult Video News, an industry magazine that is to pornographic films what the trade publication Billboard is to records. It even has its own film awards—modeled after the Oscars.

But video rentals have reached a plateau over the last two years. The future is pay-per-view at home—driven by the easy access and good technical quality of digital television—and pay-per-view from the Internet, driven by the technological innovations of new cable and phone lines that carry far more images, more quickly, to a computer screen.

"Videos changed the way people could view porn because they were able to watch in the privacy of their homes," said Barry Parr, an electronic commerce analyst with International Data Corporation. "Internet pornography takes that a step further—they can do it with absolute privacy."

The number of people visiting sex sites on the Web doubled over the last year, outpacing the number of new Internet users. Some of the more popular sex Web sites attract in excess of 50 million hits, or visits, a month, according to the ratings services Nielsen/Net and Media Metrix. About one in a thousand people who visit a site will subscribe, for fees averaging $20 a month, according to some of the leading Web pornography providers and Flying Crocodile Inc., a company based in Seattle that tracks and services the sexual-content market.

At the same time that technology was making it easier for people to view pornography, legal obstacles were falling. The 1973 Supreme Court case Miller v. California established a threshold for defining illegal pornography; a major test was that it had to be considered obscene to the "average person, applying contemporary community standards."

Initially, the case helped prosecutors clamp down on publications and movies. But that proved to be short-lived. If "Deep Throat" could sell $100 million worth of copies, then what was the community standard?

"The court may have handed off the determination of obscenity to the local community, but the standards of local communities had fundamentally changed," writes Mr. Lane in "Obscene Profits."

When Mr. Peterman was prosecuted for distributing obscene material in Utah last year, he became one of the few video retailers in the nation charged with such a crime in recent years. In a state long regarded as a bastion of family-values morality, more than 4,000 people signed petitions supporting his prosecution.

But Mr. Peterman showed that he had 4,000 regular customers for sex videos. His lawyer argued that Mr. Peterman was not violating community standards, because people in Utah County bought 20,000 adult sex videos from one satellite programmer alone in the period that Mr. Peterman was said to have broken the law; it was double the volume in most cities the size of Provo. And in the Provo Marriott, guests were paying for nearly 3,000 explicit adult videos every year, according to court testimony. After the Peterman trial, that hotel dropped its adult movies.

"My client was just a little guy," Mr. Spencer said, "a mom-and-pop dealer in a very big business."

The Corporate Factor
It's the Demand, Companies Say

At a time when political campaigns from the presidential level down to that of the local school board have made an issue of sexual excess in broadcasting, the corporate entanglements in the pornography business have blurred the lines of the debate.

In Missouri this year, Senator John Ashcroft, a Republican, ran ads denouncing "Hollywood's decaying influence" on society, singling out his Democratic opponent, Gov. Mel Carnahan, for accepting donations from Christie Hefner, the Playboy executive.

Mr. Carnahan, who died last week in a plane crash, had countered by pointing to donations to Mr. Ashcroft from Charles W. Ergen, chief executive of EchoStar, which sells adult pay-per-view through its fast-growing DishNetwork satellite division.

"If he's going to start that, he's in greater trouble than I am," Mr. Carnahan had said.

Mr. Ashcroft's supporters had replied that there was still a distinction between the two companies: EchoStar did not produce pornography—it merely sold it, while Playboy created its own videos and pictures, they said.

"We added adult at the request of our customers," said Judiann Atencio, a spokeswoman for EchoStar. "We have something for everybody, from Irish hurling to cricket. Adult is there if you want it."

When AT&T announced that it would start offering the hard-core Hot Network to its 2.2 million digital cable subscribers beginning in August, they were castigated by critics and pressured by religious and civic groups that hold stock in the company.

A group of mutual-fund investors, which included the Sisters of

Charity of New York, the Evangelical Lutheran Church of America and the Mennonite Church, told AT&T its members did not want their three million shares invested in a company that sold pornography.

"At the heart of our concern is the concept of mainstream companies getting into hard-core pornography," said Mark Regier, who manages a mutual fund for 800,000 members of the Mennonite faith. "For a company with AT&T's tradition and its charitable work to be involved with pornography at this level is unbelievable. And I don't think many people understand what it means to take away the barriers to this kind of material, such as AT&T is doing."

For AT&T, there are sound business reasons to start carrying the highly profitable Hot Network. Unlike distributors of mainstream Hollywood pictures, sex-film distributors typically offer the programmers a split of 80 percent of the revenue, compared with 50 percent or less for routine features.

Impulse buys, in which customers tap a code into a remote and a movie follows, have also spurred in-home sales of pornographic films.

"Impulse technology—that's been just incredible," said Mr. Asher of Vivid Entertainment, which makes hundreds of adult films and claims that it sells a million copies a month to cable, satellite, home video and hotel retailers. "You have about 35 million homes with this kind of technology now," Mr. Asher said, "and it's growing enormously. It's easy and it's private—that's the key."

Although the companies that program explicit sex films will not give out their revenue figures for this category, a report by the Showtime Event Television company found that adult pay-per-view took in $367 million last year—a more than sixfold increase from the $54 million of 1993, easily outpacing the growth of pay-per-view "events" like boxing and wrestling.

Time Warner, EchoStar, General Motors and AT&T all say they are simply responding to a growing American market that wants pornography in the home. At the same time, the companies say new technology makes it possible for parents to keep such programming away from children.

"We call it choice and control," said Tracy Hollingsworth, a spokeswoman for AT&T Broadband, the company's cable division. "Basically, you use your remote to block out any programming you don't want. But if you want it, we offer a wide range of programming that is available in the market we're in."

Hotel chains have made similar decisions when, this year, several groups urged them to get rid of the adult pay-per-view programs that are in nearly 60 percent of all middle- to high-end hotels. Only one chain, the relatively small Omni Hotels, chose to remove the sex films.

"What we noticed was that early on, the content was R-rated, but then it migrated rather quickly to really raunchy stuff—just hard-core porn," said Jim Caldwell, the president of Omni. "I thought: What are we doing? We don't have topless waitresses in the restaurant."

Mr. Caldwell said more than 50 percent of all guests were buying the sex films. "The anonymity is the big thing," he said.

Omni's decision to remove pay-per-view sex videos from the company's 15,000 rooms will cost the company more than $1.8 million a year, Mr. Caldwell said. But he said he had received phone calls and letters of thanks from 50,000 people—more than for any other corporate decision.

Much larger hotel chains, like Marriott, which calls itself the world's largest hotel management firm, with nearly 300,000 rooms in the United States, and Hilton, with 290,000 rooms under its control, have not made changes.

Some critics said Marriott, run by several prominent members of the Mormon Church, though not affiliated in any way with the church itself, should drop its adult movies, given the stand against explicit sexual materials that Mormons have long taken. But company officials said they were mostly franchisers, and could not make unilateral decisions for the hotel owners who paid to be a part of the Marriott chain.

The two companies that provide hotels with pornographic films are both traded on Wall Street and have enjoyed big run-ups in their stock prices over the last few years. The leader, On Command, based in Denver, is worth more than $400 million, and its principal owner is Liberty Media, controlled by John C. Malone, the cable and telecommunications magnate who sits on the board of AT&T and recently agreed to buy up to 15 percent of the shares of Mr. Murdoch's News Corporation.

The chairman and chief executive of On Command is Jerome H.

Kern, a former New York corporate lawyer active in civic and volunteer causes, serving on the board of New York University and as a director of Volunteers of America in Colorado.

On Command would not discuss how much money it is making on adult films. But in its annual report, the company said it was generating $23 a room each month for the 835,000 hotel rooms it reaches. The company goal is to get into an additional one million hotel rooms. Analysts say at least half the revenue comes from adult films. The company recently began offering all-day erotic television to hotel customers, for a single price of $15.99.

"Talk about your captive audience," said Mr. Asher of Vivid. "I've heard that in some hotels, 85 to 90 percent of all profits from in-room spending comes from adult channels."

The Money Factor
Big Profits Now, Bigger Ones on Way

While the big companies that deliver sex films to homes and hotels will not talk about how popular explicit sexual materials are, the makers and distributors say the volume is enormous. And court testimony and documents that were made public in the Peterman case also offered some insight into the profit potential.

"Despite the fact that this material isn't marketed, revenue-wise, it's one of our biggest moneymakers," said Peggy Simons of TCI Cable, in court testimony in Mr. Peterman's case. TCI, controlled by Mr. Malone, has since been bought by AT&T.

"When we talk to the companies one-on-one, they tell us we're great, that we're a huge moneymaker for them," said Mr. Asher, whose company owns the Hot Network, which is available in 16 million homes. "And by the way, I tell my biggest customers—don't say you ever met me."

In trying to take public his company, which now does about $80 million a year in sales, Mr. Asher said, "The biggest problem I have is the image of the adult business. People think it's run by the mob, or a bunch of guys with gold chains. I grew up in Paris, Illinois. I have a master's of business administration degree."

The Hot Network portrays people having sex in a variety of methods—what the company calls "widely accepted sexual activity"—and prohibits scenes of violence, nonconsensual sex, drug use, forced bondage and sex with minors.

Analysts of electronic commerce and telecommunications say the mainstream sex market might be leveling off, but new technology is likely to bring in even more consumers.

"The novelty of it has not worn off yet, and I don't believe it will wear off," said Sean Calder, a vice president for e-commerce at Nielsen/Net Ratings, which gauges the popularity of Web sites. "The numbers point to a huge personal need. We see lots of people logging on at 3 in the morning."

The $30 billion project to rewire the cable industry with lines capable of bringing more material, and allowing people to buy on impulse, will play a big part in the emerging home pornography market.

"These companies like AT&T, they're thinking ahead to a time, perhaps in 10 years, when 50 million Americans will have broadband capability and all their television and Internet will be interactive through one big box," said Bryn Pryor, technology editor for Adult Video News, the trade magazine.

"But it's not just technology that made the big boys get into it," Mr. Pryor said. "This just happens to be a business where you can't lose money."

Correction: Wednesday, October 25, 2000: An article on Monday about investments by large companies in sexually explicit entertainment referred incompletely to the relationship between the News Corporation and the EchoStar Communications Corporation, which provides explicit films by satellite to subscribers. The article quoted a lawyer for a video store owner in Provo, Utah, as saying that his client's prosecution was unfair because many companies that provided "adult" entertainment were heavily backed by large corporations, including the News Corporation.

At the time of the trial, which ended on March 31, 1999, the News Corporation owned about 37 percent of EchoStar, but by the next reporting period, in June 1999, the holding was reported as 14 percent.

The News Corporation's last federal filing shows an 11 percent stake, but a spokesman said the corporation's share in EchoStar was now down to 6 percent. The spokesman also said the News Corporation had no direct control over EchoStar and no direct financial investment in "adult" films.

ACKNOWLEDGMENTS

I first learned of the infamous "elephant game" in *The Damage Done* by Warren Fellows, published by Asia Books.

Other sources of inspiration include:

The Bangkok Post.

Corruption & Democracy in Thailand by Pasuk Phongpaichit and Sungsidh Piriyarangsan, published by Silkworm Books.

The Dhammapada, edited by Narada Thera, published by the Buddhist Cultural Centre, Thailand.

The Funeral Casino by Alan Klima, published by Princeton University Press.

Guns, Girls, Gambling and Ganja by Sungsidh Piriyarangsan and Nualonoi Treerat, published by Silkworm Books.

Kum Chat Luk, a Thai daily newspaper.

The Sandhinirmochana Sutra, under the title *Buddhist Yoga*, translated by Thomas Cleary, published by Shambala South Asia Editions.

Very Thai by Philip Cornwel-Smith, published by River Books.

Welcome to Hell by Colin Martin, published by Asia Books.

Welcome to the Bangkok Slaughterhouse by Father Joe Maier, published by Asia Books.

A NOTE ABOUT THE AUTHOR

John Burdett is the author of A *Personal History of Thirst*, *The Last Six Million Seconds*, *Bangkok 8*, and *Bangkok Tattoo*.

A NOTE ON THE TYPE

The text of this book was set in Electra, a typeface designed by W. A. Dwiggins (1880–1956). This face cannot be classified as either modern or old style. It is not based on any historical model, nor does it echo any particular period or style. It avoids the extreme contrasts between thick and thin elements that mark most modern faces, and it attempts to give a feeling of fluidity, power, and speed.

Composed by Creative Graphics, Inc.,
Allentown, Pennsylvania
Printed and bound by Berryville Graphics,
Berryville, Virginia
Designed by Virginia Tan